GUARDIAN OF TIME

An Eastfall Novel

J.R. LESPERANCE

This is a work of fiction. Names, characters, organizations, places, events, and incidents are either products of the author's imagination or are used fictitiously. Any resemblance to actual events, locales, or persons, living or dead, or actual events is entirely coincidental.

Copyright © 2023 by J.R. Lesperance

All rights reserved.

No part of this book may be reproduced in any form or by any electronic or mechanical means, including information storage and retrieval systems, without written permission from the author, except for the use of brief quotations in a book review.

ISBN-13: 978-1-7349012-2-1

Cover design by Caroline Teagle Johnson

Cover images © AdobeStock

Map of England by S.E. Davidson

For my mom, who supports me in all things, and loves me unconditionally. I wouldn't be where I am now without you.

This one's for you, mom. It's no Outlander, but I hope you enjoy it all the same.

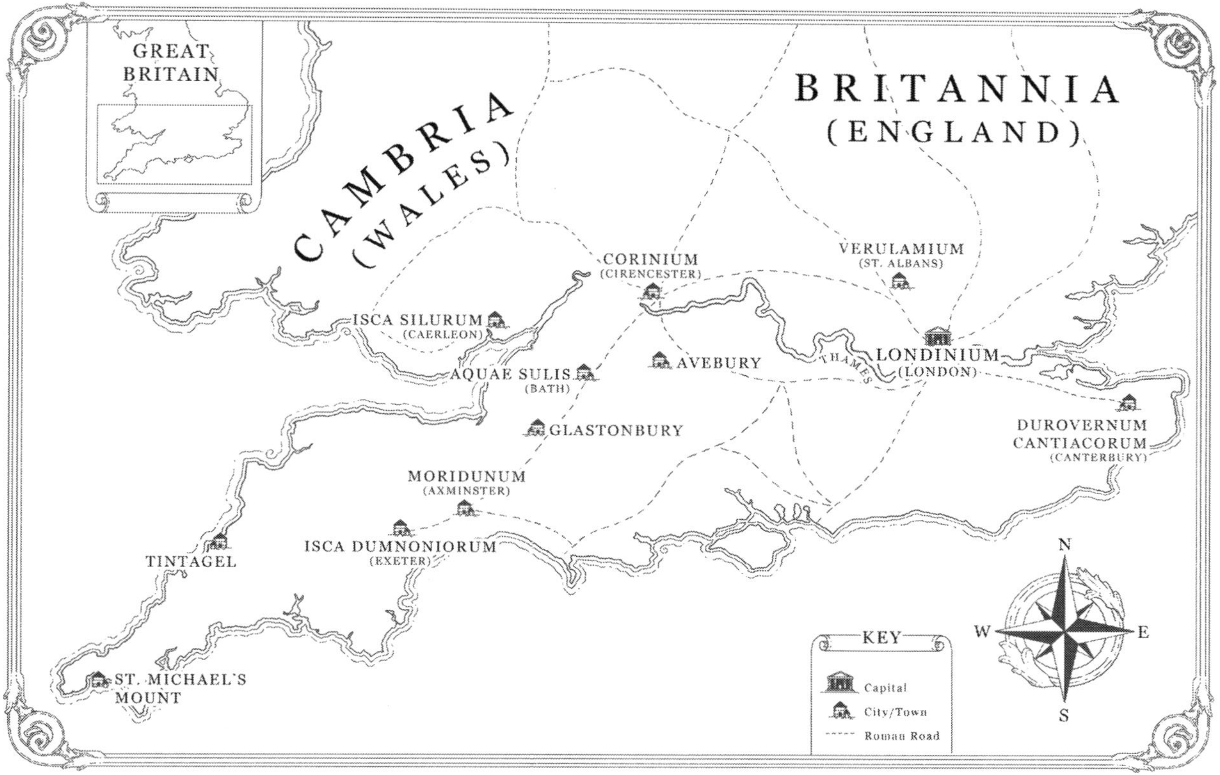
GREAT BRITAIN
CAMBRIA
(WALES)
BRITANNIA
(ENGLAND)
CORINIUM
(CIRENCESTER)
VERULAMIUM
(ST. ALBANS)
ISCA SILURUM
(CAERLEON)
AQUAE SULIS
(BATH)
AVEBURY
THAMES
LONDINIUM
(LONDON)
GLASTONBURY
DUROVERNUM
CANTIACORUM
(CANTERBURY)
MORIDUNUM
(AXMINSTER)
ISCA DUMNONIORUM
(EXETER)
TINTAGEL
ST. MICHAEL'S
MOUNT
KEY
Capital
City/Town
Roman Road
N
W
E
S

THE PROPHECY OF
DELIVERANCE HOWE

The last words of Deliverance Howe uttered January 22, 1693, as recorded by Josiah Wainwright, clerk of the court. Once finished, her execution by hanging commenced.

Oh seekers of truth, gather near.
Listen to this oracle's voice, crystal clear.
In shadows' dance, four fates entwined,
A cryptic path, destiny defined.

A witch with magic deep in her core,
Shall rise to fight, her heart a fervent roar.

Through temporal currents, a traveler shall traverse,
Unveiling truths, the world's fate to reverse.

A goddess radiant, with healing touch shall mend,
The light of hope she will lend.

A villainess turned, her past she shall defy,
Embrace the light, her old ways she'll belie.

An ancient order, veiled and sly,
Conspires in silence, their aims to try.
Fire and brimstone, creatures so vile,
Seek to destroy, bones all in a pile.

The four shall unite, a force untamed,
Against the tide of evil, they're named.
Each sacrifice to bring the dark to heel,
Agonies untold, but their spines as steel.

Seek the signs, heed the call,
For destiny's script shall enthrall.
Through trials endured, united they'll be,
To save the world, and set it free.

PROLOGUE

The funeral was beautiful.
At the front of the church, Lynn Rickerson's picture stood on an easel by the oak coffin. Lynn's mother sat in the front pew, silently sobbing. There were teachers, students, custodians, and many others packed into the space.

Everyone had loved Lynn.

Of those at Eastfall High School, perhaps none would miss Lynn more than Jennifer Cassidy. They had been the closest of friends, bonding over school and life. The news of Lynn's death had gutted Jennifer. And even now, she couldn't shake the spiraling sadness. The sadness of a life extinguished too soon.

God, and in such a horrible way.

Jennifer hadn't heard the details. She wasn't sure she wanted to know. But the murder had been gruesome, and Lynn's body mutilated to the point that the funeral was closed casket.

"And I will raise you up..." Jennifer intoned under her breath, singing the old hymn that was all too familiar. It was her mother's favorite, and she'd always sobbed whenever it played during Mass.

Growing up Catholic.

That had been something Jennifer and Lynn had bonded over.

They'd shared the view that organized religion was a scam and hadn't set foot in a church in years. Jennifer could only imagine what Lynn must be thinking now, wherever she was.

Jennifer tipped her head back, craning her neck as she gazed up to the rafters of the vaulted ceiling of Saint Michael's. Maybe if she squinted hard enough, she could see Lynn looking down, shaking her head with that wry smile of hers.

Tears welled, spilling over. Jennifer quickly swiped at the rivulets, batting them away.

The hymn ended, the final note echoing into silence, like the life that had been snuffed out.

What is death if not a reminder of life?

The funeral Mass came to a close, and the pallbearers processed up the aisle with Lynn's coffin. As they passed Jennifer, she couldn't help but think Lynn would have hated the rich, light-brown wood.

As the processional hymn played, the churchgoers filed out, gathering at the bottom of the steps outside. Everyone watched the casket being loaded into the back of the hearse where they'd haul Lynn's body to the funeral home to be cremated, and then bury her ashes in the cemetery.

Once safely secured, the hearse took off. The crowd remained silent until the vehicle turned out of sight, and then they dispersed.

That was that.

A young life cut short, an hour-long funeral of remembrance, and that was that. Everyone would go back to their lives, their quaint New England houses, complain over Patriots' football, and Lynn would simply be rotting in the earth forever.

The fucking injustice of it all...

A shock of jet-black hair in the crowd caught Jennifer's eye.

Oh, he had the damn nerve to be here...

Jennifer stormed over, as fast as her black pumps could carry her.

"You have some balls on you, Braddock," Jennifer hissed, putting herself in Zachariah Braddock's path.

The handsome police sergeant looked stricken, as though she'd led with a slap to the face rather than biting words. "Jennifer, hi."

"What are you doing here?"

"The same thing you're doing here."

"No, you don't get to be here."

"Why not? I loved her too. For years, if you remember."

"Oh, I remember," *Jennifer huffed, her hands balling into fists at her side.* "I remember you breaking her heart."

Zach shook his head, shoving his hands in the pockets of his black wool jacket. "You don't know as much as you think you do."

"I know you being here is an insult. You're being investigated for her murder, Braddock."

"You know damn well I didn't kill her, Jennifer," *Zach replied vehemently.*

"Do I?" *she asked snidely.*

Zach sighed. "You know we didn't end well, Lynn and I. And you also know I would've never harmed a hair on her head."

Dammit. Of course he was right.

Of course Jennifer didn't actually believe he'd be that evil, that cruel. She'd watched Zach and Lynn together for years, and though it hadn't ended happily, she'd not seen two people more respecting of each other.

The anger deflated, taking the wind out of her sails. Jennifer's shoulders sank. "I know. I know you wouldn't."

"Do you have any idea who would?" *Zach asked, damn near pleaded.*

"She was talking to someone. I never met him, but she seemed happy. I told the investigating lieutenant."

"Yeah, Nadeau. I think...I think she'll find this guy."

"I hope so," *Jennifer said softly, brushing an errant tear from her cheek.*

Zach reached out, hauling Jennifer against his chest. His strong arms wrapped around her as she collapsed into him. Though it had been a minute since Zach and Lynn had been an item, the three of them had made a good trio. Jennifer had never felt like the third wheel, had never felt slighted when Lynn wanted to spend an evening with Zach. They'd been good together, until they hadn't. Jennifer had believed they would marry, but sometimes, even people that seemed meant for each other drifted apart for no other reason than they were people, *and therefore ever changing.*

"If you need anything," Zach murmured against the crown of her head, rustling the auburn tendrils where he'd rested his chin. "If you need anything at all, just call, okay?"

Jennifer nodded.

"I mean it. Anything."

She pulled away, stepping back from his warm and comforting presence. Jennifer nodded again. "I will. Just do me a favor, Zach."

"Name it," he replied.

"Catch this bastard and make him pay."

CHAPTER 1

EASTFALL, MASSACHUSETTS - A WEEK BEFORE THE END OF THE SCHOOL YEAR

The remainder of the school year after Lynn's funeral passed in a chaotic blur.

Every morning, Jennifer passed Lynn's old classroom, now occupied by a long-term substitute. And every morning, the wound ripped open just a little, so much so the rest of the day would be shaded with grief and loss.

They always speak about the dearly departed, but they never talk about those left behind.

The school events Jennifer and Lynn would have attended together in the past just seemed like a chore. Football games, basketball games, baseball games, and the odd hockey game or two. Not to mention the winter play and the spring musical. Chaperoning the dances, bitching about the workload...

When would it get better?

When the news broke the lieutenant in charge of Lynn's case had uncovered the murderer, Jennifer thought that would be that. She would feel a million times better, the pain would lessen, and she could go back to some normalcy.

But grief did funny, incomprehensible things.

There was now a week left of school, and the students had already switched to summer mode. Hell, so had the teachers, and Jennifer would be lying if she said she hadn't been ready for summer back in the winter.

With the imminent end of the school year came the annual cleansing of her classroom. Jennifer would go through all paper materials and decide whether to salvage or recycle. Most of it ended up in the recycle bin, but there were a few student projects she wanted to keep for posterity. Case in point, she'd just pulled one such project from her filing cabinet.

As the sounds of *Zootopia* played in the background—either enthralling her sophomore history class or sending them into dreamland—Jennifer flipped through the exemplary project from one of her favorite students. She remembered being impressed by the level of research and originality of the content and writing. She'd expect nothing less from the son of the curator of Eastfall's tiny museum. The paper, perfectly formatted in Chicago style, was about a series of witch trials that had taken place around the same time as Salem's. The trials were by no means as notorious as Salem's, but Eastfall did have a sordid history of hanging alleged witches.

She flipped to the next page, coming upon the infamous prophecy allegedly given by a witch facing the gallows. Legend said that when asked for her last words, she seemed to go into a trance-like state, and in a dramatic voice recited some vague rhyming poetry. There was an entire section of the Eastfall Museum dedicated to this, and no doubt that's where the student had pulled most of his information.

Deciding she'd keep it to use next year as an example, Jennifer shoved the paper back into a hanging file and closed the drawer.

The bell signaling the end of the day clanged, startling her for a moment. She'd lost track of time in her cleaning haze.

"Have a good day, everyone!" she called out to the exiting students.

Once all had cleared from the room, Jennifer sat heavily in her desk chair and began sifting through the contents of the two drawers of her desk. Nearly buried at the very bottom of the last drawer, Jennifer found a familiar folder.

Emblazoned across the front was the logo of a local travel agency and their tagline—*We take the WORK out of VACATION.*

Jennifer chuckled. God, how could she have forgotten about this?

Opening the folder, she leafed through the papers, reading the carefully scripted notes written in Lynn's precise handwriting and her own messier scrawl.

The two friends had started planning a summer European vacation at the end of the previous school year.

Of course I don't plan on going! Lynn had scoffed. *There's no way I'd be able to afford it.*

Me neither, Jennifer had admitted.

See, the fun comes in the planning. Maybe in about fifteen years I'll be able to go. If I make a dent in my student loans, anyway.

That had always been their problem. They were both too practical, and never saw an international trip, or really any trip outside of Massachusetts, to be worth the spending of precious money. Not when there were bills to pay and credit card debt to chip away at.

It'll be the trip of a lifetime! one of Lynn's notes proclaimed.

Jennifer thumbed back through the literature a little closer, taking notice of the destinations Lynn had circled. They aligned with one particular tour group, an excursion around the southwest of England.

It's Arthur country, Jennifer had pointed out.

I know. Lynn had shrugged. *It's why I picked it out. I knew you'd be invested in planning a trip to see real-life places Arthur allegedly made his stomping ground.*

You know me so well. Jennifer had chuckled, excited at the prospect to explore the Britain the legendary King Arthur might've known.

Maybe one day we'll venture away from this place, Lynn had said after a week of planning the vacation they would never actually take. *There's a whole world to see and fun to be had. The kind of fun that won't happen here. We've gotta get out there! And live!*

How loaded those words seemed now.

Lynn had been right, of course.

Over the past decade, Jennifer had dug herself into the cushiest of ruts. Since day one of her teaching career, she'd taught the same subject, cracked the same jokes, and carried out the same chores day in and day out.

While she didn't mind this particular rut—hell, it could be worse—she'd been thinking more and more lately about the brevity of life. About Lynn's unfailing optimism that life would always be worth living. And now that Lynn would never be able to do so herself, it seemed only appropriate Jennifer do it for her.

Taking in a deep, shaky breath, Jennifer closed the folder and shoved it into her computer bag. Glancing at the clock, she saw she was now past contract hours and therefore free to go home. Or anywhere that wasn't this place.

She gathered all of her things and packed her bag, then

when she was sure she had everything, she clicked off the lights and locked the door to her classroom.

The halls were empty, no children or teachers in sight. After-school activities had ended the week prior, so there were no loud and boisterous noises echoing down the corridor. As Jennifer neared the science department's office and copy room, the emptiness of the school allowed her to overhear a conversation happening inside.

"Did you see her? Always eating in her room now. She's been a wreck ever since..."

"Right? Like, girl, everyone's had to deal with that kind of pain. Get a grip."

Jennifer stopped short, breath catching. It was one of the biology teachers chatting with a PE teacher. They all shared a lunch period, which sometimes turned into a group meet-up to commiserate. Lately, Jennifer hadn't felt the energy to be around many people, so she'd taken to eating lunch in her room, alone.

"To be honest with you, I'm not completely surprised," the biology teacher started again. "She's always been a bit antisocial, hasn't she?"

"Could you believe that icebreaker at the second semester Professional Development? Her response was tragic." This time, the PE teacher.

"Seriously, like, buck up, buttercup, and get a life."

The two teachers tittered and giggled like they'd made the funniest of jokes.

Jennifer didn't want to hear any more. She scurried past the door, hoping to be missed, and rushed to her car, a beat-up Honda Accord. Once settled behind the wheel, the dam broke, and she started sobbing.

God, she was tired of crying. Tired of big emotions.

Losing Lynn had hit her more than she ever imagined. Death hadn't touched Jennifer Cassidy's life to this point, except for the death of a grandmother when she was ten. Lynn had been a special person, one of the best friends she'd ever had. The way she'd been ripped from the world? It was nothing short of tragic and gut-wrenching.

Snuffling, Jennifer swiped at her tears.

No, she'd never been a particularly social person. And no, she'd never been a particularly adventurous person either. But that's part of what made her friendship with Lynn so special. Lynn was adventurous enough to get Jennifer out of her apartment on a Saturday, making day trips into Boston and heading out west toward the Berkshires. Now, Jennifer had no one she wanted to venture out with, no one to tag along with her to see the latest Marvel movie.

She rested back against the headrest, eyes slipping shut. The hollowness in her chest was a chasm, and suddenly she felt rather lost, as though adrift at sea with no oar.

Her thoughts flitted across her ten years of teaching, the stagnation she felt, rudderless, with no direction but linear. She thought of the jokes again—the ones she delivered every year with fervor, that every year were met with lukewarm chuckles. She thought of her apartment—one bedroom, nothing spectacular, and no one to greet her when she got home. Not even a goldfish.

She thought of the travel folder she'd found, the one nearly forgotten. She thought of Lynn's steady handwriting, the loops and whirls of *It'll be the trip of a lifetime!*

Taking a steady breath, Jennifer stuck the key into the ignition and trundled out of the parking lot.

It was on her all too familiar drive home, at the end of an all too familiar school year, in her all too familiar car wearing her all too familiar clothing, that Jennifer made a stop at an unfamiliar place.

When she left, a trip of a lifetime booked, airfare and all, she thought maybe...maybe things would be okay.

CHAPTER 2

OVER THE ATLANTIC - PRESENT

In hindsight, Jennifer should have expected the beginning of her grand adventure to go much the way it did, rather than the ideal version she'd envisioned.

The moment she arrived at Boston's Logan Airport, she'd come close to not getting her luggage checked—something about weight concerns, *yeah, right*—and then Jennifer almost missed her flight due to heightened traffic in the security line. She'd nearly bowled over a completely unamused TSA agent as the public intercom paged the final boarding call for her flight into Heathrow Airport.

Thankfully, Jennifer hadn't been the dead last one to board the plane, but the gate attendant had damn near closed the door on her.

Next came the walk of shame up the airplane aisle.

Jennifer stalwartly trekked to the back of the plane, eyes

facing forward. Despite her best efforts, she didn't miss the narrowed eyes of annoyance from her fellow passengers as she journeyed into the bowels of the plane.

She couldn't blame them. She'd be annoyed at her too.

Hell, she *was* annoyed at herself.

Once she reached her designated row, she took note of which seat was hers and sighed.

Jennifer tried for her best sheepish smile, excusing herself to the gentleman sitting in the aisle seat. He harrumphed and stood, allowing for Jennifer to wedge herself into the middle seat.

Yes, another win.

Figures she'd get stuck with the middle seat. Taking note of that fact on her boarding ticket beforehand should have been clue number one of how this trip would unfold.

Once settled, she shot off a quick text message to her mom and dad, powered down her phone, then shoved her backpack under the seat in front of her and collapsed against the chair.

Flying made her nervous.

Every metallic sound of the engines revving, every whirring flap of wing components as the pilot continued through his preflight check made her heart thump all the more. She probably should've taken her mother's advice and taken something to knock her out. Since she was traveling alone, Jennifer didn't trust being unconscious around strangers.

Not with the way this trip had started.

"Ma'am, can you please put on your seat belt?" the flight attendant said, startling Jennifer from her thoughts. Glancing down, she realized in her rush to get seated, she'd forgotten about safety.

"Yes, sorry," she mumbled, while fumbling for the two straps. One had gotten stuck beneath Mr. Aisle Seat, and she didn't realize until she tugged hard enough to dislodge it. Jennifer shot him another apologetic smile, then made quick work of uniting the buckles and tightening the strap.

The copilot's voice filtered into the cabin, welcoming everyone aboard and giving an estimated time of arrival to London. As he spoke, the pilot began to reverse the plane and taxi toward the runway.

With her hands folded in her lap, Jennifer allowed her fingers to lock together, holding tightly to herself. A few minutes later, the plane zoomed forward. As it took off, her hands shot out and gripped her knees tightly, because, of course, both of her arm rests had been commandeered by the passengers on either side.

Once the early evening city lights began to fade away on their ascent, Jennifer allowed herself to let out a deep breath and relax. She attempted a pep talk, trying to convince herself that this trip may not have started off with a bang, but it could only go up from there.

"First time to the UK?" the middle-aged woman in the window seat asked about an hour into the flight. Her accent was thick enough that Jennifer was able to pinpoint that Window Lady was from Northern England. That harsher lilt was characteristic of old industrial areas. Identifying accents had been a useless skill she'd picked up from watching way too many movies and television shows.

"Uh, no. Went on a school trip in high school. It's been a long time though," Jennifer replied, clutching the latest paperback of her favorite romance series. She'd pulled it out in an effort to distract herself from the fact that she was thousands of feet above the Atlantic Ocean and therefore a potentially horrible, watery death. The contemporary romance afforded the diversion she needed though, and she'd found herself sucked into the storyline before Window Lady had spoken.

"Oh, how lovely. Be a bit of a different experience as an adult, eh?" Window Lady asked.

That was putting it mildly. This was the first vacation Jennifer had been on in over a decade. In fact, it may be the first vacation she'd had since that trip in high school.

"Yeah, sure hope so," Jennifer sighed, and thankfully, Window Lady didn't engage in further conversation.

The relative quiet of the plane lulled Jennifer to sleep for about thirty minutes, but when the gentleman sitting in the aisle seat slumped over, head resting on her shoulder, there was no falling back asleep. She'd just have to face the fact jet lag would rule her world for the next few days.

A few hours later, after a full-length movie and a few more attempts at sleeping, pressure and popping in her ears caused a wave of relief.

The plane had begun its descent.

It'd been a long damn plane ride, and she was ready to get out of this seat and stretch her legs. She'd opted to forgo using the restroom in an effort to not bother Mr. Aisle Seat any more than she had already. It didn't matter her right leg had cramped on and off for the better part of an hour. Or that her bladder would soon burst.

She just hated to inconvenience people.

The copilot came over the intercom again, informing passengers of their imminent arrival, and tacked on the usual reminders about customs and duty-free opportunities. Anticipation mounted in Jennifer's chest, nerves and excitement clashing together as second thoughts and doubt began to encroach.

Maybe she hadn't thought this whole spontaneity thing all the way through. Guilt for leaving Eastfall gnawed at her, though why she felt so tied to her hometown, she didn't know. It wasn't as if the place held her hostage. She could come and go as she pleased. Not even college had permanently taken her from Eastfall. After she graduated with her bachelor's in history and master's in education from the College of William and Mary, she immediately jumped on the job opportunity at her old high school.

Now, ten years later, Jennifer was happy. Or at least she'd thought she was. With Lynn gone, something was missing. Hell, even before Lynn had died, something had been missing. On the last day of school, Jennifer had had the dawning realization the overheard conversation hadn't been far off—she *was* in a rut.

The trip had not only been a means of honoring Lynn, but also her brilliant idea to kickstart her joy for life again.

That remained to be seen.

Her mother's usual nagging had shaken the confidence and resolve of her decision to go. The only reason her mother hadn't gone full hog on her was because she was going with a tour group. It had appeased her mother and alleviated a little extra stress for Jennifer, though she knew the sixty-eight-year-old woman was three thousand miles away, worrying her head off over her only daughter. Never mind that said daughter was in her thirties and perfectly capable of taking care of herself.

But hey, she was with a *group*. Maybe she'll make some friends. Maybe there'd be a supremely attractive, rich man that'd sweep her off her feet, take her back to his expensive penthouse in New York City, and she wouldn't have to teach anymore.

Or she'd spend the trip mostly to herself, only tagging along with the group because she had to, thinking about all the things she and Lynn would have commented on or joked about.

The plane jolted as it hit a pocket of air. Jennifer's hands shot down, grasping the armrests, and ultimately, the hands of her neighbors, like a lifeline. Her knuckles turned white from the grip, and her jaw began to ache from clenching.

This had definitely been a bad idea. She was going to go down in a fiery plane crash, and the only way they'd ever be able to identify her remains was dental records. Or not find her remains at all, and instead be eaten by carnivorous fish.

Thankfully, neither of her fellow row mates said a word when the plane leveled out, and her heart rate slowed. Jennifer unfurled her vise grip from Mr. Aisle Seat and Window Lady, and gave them a genuine grin this time.

Chancing a glance out the window, Jennifer watched the slightly hazy skyline of London appear, lit by the early morning rays of sunlight. Then, the plane dipped behind a cloud, and she saw nothing more.

A few moments later, the plane gave another jerk as the landing gear touched down on the tarmac. Jennifer let out a long breath through pursed lips, a breath she hadn't realized she'd been holding.

She'd finally arrived.

London was not how she remembered it. Then again, to a sixteen-year-old, the thriving, ancient metropolis would beguile and captivate anyone.

But not thirty-something Jennifer.

The airline had "misplaced" thirty-something Jennifer's luggage, and despite the strangled desperation in her voice, the angel at the baggage claim counter spoke to her in nothing but a soothing tone, reassuring Jennifer over and over that the airport would recover her bag and get it to her wherever she was.

Armed with only her carry-on backpack that held a single set of clothing and a few travel-sized toiletries for just this eventuality, Jennifer set out for the exit, searching for the tour company's representative who was meant to retrieve her.

No luck.

After waiting a half hour, a middle-aged man, clothes haphazard, rushed into the baggage area holding a sign with the tour company's name on it.

Excalibur Tours.

"Ms. Cassidy?" the man huffed when Jennifer approached.

"Yes, that's me," Jennifer replied, holding out her passport to verify her identity. He didn't seem to care, only giving the identification a cursory glance and nod.

"I believe a few more of your tour fellows will be arriving soon, then I'll take you to the hotel." The man's accent was thick. Maybe East London?

Jennifer sat with the man in silence, watching the world go by. Men and women arriving back from business trips, families huddled together in reunion. Harold—"Call me Harry, like Harry Potter"—shifted from foot to foot as they waited, until an elderly couple approached and verified their names. The couple glanced at Jennifer, shooting her a small smile, before turning back to each other to converse. A few minutes later, another elderly couple appeared, and after giving their names to Harry, he escorted them from the terminal to the large, white van he'd double parked, hazard lights blinking. Harry unceremoniously tossed the luggage into the back of the van and rushed around to the right side to climb into the driver's seat. Jennifer and the two couples took that as their cue to hurry on.

Jennifer should've climbed up first.

Instead, she waited, debating whether or not to help the elderly people into the van. She stood back awkwardly as the husbands, in turn, assisted their wives into seats. If she wasn't so damn tired and worn out from Murphy's Law having a field day, Jennifer might've chuckled.

Finally, it was her turn. She nimbly hiked herself into the van and slammed the door closed. Harry took off immediately, before Jennifer had even gotten a chance to climb all the way into the back seat. Letting out a sigh, she watched the city pass as Harry navigated the busy motorway and streets farther into London proper.

The drive afforded Jennifer, once more, too much time to lose herself in her thoughts.

Her first thought? She needed to never use the travel agent in Eastfall again. When Jennifer had begged the woman to find the cheapest trip she could—with most, if not all, expenses included—she hadn't imagined it would be with the Blue Hair Society.

She should've just stayed home for the summer. Is this what her life amounted to now? Not only traveling solo, but doing so with a tour group meant for retired married couples?

Harry zipped through London too quickly, but it seemed Jennifer was the only one that noticed. The couples had introduced themselves and chatted amiably, as if they'd known each other for years. They were too busy to notice the poor pedestrian Harry nearly ran over while turning a corner.

Jennifer braced her hand on the roof of the van and couldn't fight the wave of exhaustion creeping in at the edges. Jet lag was a bitch, and she knew it'd take a couple of nights to catch up. It'd be an early one tonight. The itinerary, despite it being for the AARP crowd, was jam-packed with places to visit. She'd need all the sleep she could get.

"And what's your name, dear?" one of the old ladies asked, turning in her seat. The poor woman wasn't wearing a seat belt, and with the way Harry drove, it'd be a miracle if any of them made it out of this van alive.

"Oh, uh...Jennifer. Jennifer Cassidy. I'm from Massachusetts."

"Oh how lovely! We're from Ohio," the woman replied. "I'm Nancy, and this is my husband, John."

"Nice to meet you." Jennifer forced a smile, nearly sliding across the bench seat as Harry took a sharp left turn.

"And I'm Diane. This is my better half, Roger," the other elderly woman greeted. Jennifer nodded and forced another smile she hoped looked friendly.

For the rest of the ride, the couples tried to loop her into their conversation, but she found there wasn't much in common between them. They were retired nurses or lawyers or doctors, living up their golden years while they still had all their faculties. Direct quote from Roger.

Harry came to a screeching halt in front of the Continental—their hotel for their first and last nights. A decent hotel with a fantastic breakfast spread and comfortable beds, according to the Yelp reviews she'd scoured before leaving Eastfall.

Jennifer hopped out of the van and shut the door behind her. The two couples had already made their way into the lobby, and Harry was just taking out her backpack.

"Tough luck, eh?" Harry said. "How'd you end up with this lot?"

"I trusted my travel agent," Jennifer deadpanned, slipping Harry a few pounds for his troubles, and then made her way inside to check in.

When the bright sunlight of the English morning subsided from her bleary eyes, Jennifer noticed the couples had already found more members of their group.

It hadn't been a fluke.

More steel-haired retirees.

"Oh, there she is!" Nancy beckoned Jennifer over vehemently. Jennifer sighed, hiking her backpack up her shoulder, and crossed the shiny, marble floor. "This is Jennifer! She's traveling with us!"

The new couples gave her the once-over, clearly noting she was of a certain age that was...well, not theirs. But they greeted her graciously and genuinely, and despite it all, Jennifer felt herself relax for the first time since she'd boarded the plane back in Boston.

After check-in, Jennifer rode the elevator to her room, scoping it out. It wasn't the Four Seasons, but it was clean and the bed was soft and cloud-like. So much so that as soon as she lay back on it, her eyes closed and she napped.

Banging at the door jerked Jennifer from her slumber. Using the side of her hand, she swiped the drool from her mouth and swayed to her feet. One glance at the alarm clock on the nightstand told her she'd been asleep for quite a few hours. Groggily, Jennifer padded to the door and peeked through the peephole.

It was Nancy and John.

"Hello, darling, we were on our way down to the welcome dinner and... Oh, I'm so sorry, we woke you up?" Nancy had taken one look at Jennifer and trailed off in her enthusiasm. Jennifer had never felt so bare, Nancy's gaze taking pity on her bedraggled appearance.

"Y-Yeah, no, that's fine, I...thank you. I just fell asleep." Jennifer glanced behind her, noticing the faint light of day dimming the room. She'd been so tired she slept through an uncharacteristically sunny England afternoon.

"Dinner doesn't start for another fifteen minutes," John supplied. "Take your time, and we'll see you down there." Then the man ushered his wife away quickly.

Jennifer groaned and let the door click shut behind her as she went to freshen up.

A private room toward the back of the Continental's in-house restaurant had been commandeered for their group's welcome dinner. A middle-aged woman, presumably the tour guide, greeted Jennifer as she came through the door.

"Oh, hello, I think you may have the wrong room," the woman said, not unkindly.

Jennifer, having expected this, held up her Excalibur Tours paperwork.

"Ah," the woman said, mouth parted slightly, nodding. "Believe it or not, this isn't the first time this has happened."

Jennifer chuckled. "I do believe it."

"Between you and me," the woman—Grace, according to her Excalibur Tours official name badge—leaned in, her tone hushed, almost conspiratorial. "I'm happy to have you here. I know I'm a bit closer to their age than yours, but it's refreshing to have some young blood."

That got a real laugh from Jennifer. She found she rather liked Grace's soft British accent, almost like a sympathetic, motherly voice. A far cry from her mother's usually manic one.

"I'm at the head of the table. Why don't you take the open seat next to me?" Grace suggested, pointing down the great table cobbled together with smaller tables. As Jennifer walked along, she did a quick count of people already seated. She smiled and nodded at them all as she passed, everyone looking curiously at her. There were twenty of them.

Jennifer pulled out her assigned chair, sat, and scooted herself forward.

"Hi there," the woman next to her greeted with a warm smile that reminded Jennifer of her Grandmother Cassidy. "I'm Vicki. From Toronto."

"Jennifer. From Massachusetts," Jennifer replied.

"Oh, lovely state," Vicki commented. "Absolutely gorgeous in autumn."

Jennifer lapsed into easy conversation with Vicki until Grace took her place at the head of the table. She introduced herself and ran over a quick overview of the tour. She then bid them all to go around the table, taking turns introducing themselves. Funny how Jennifer was old hat at icebreakers with her students, but when the shoe was on the other foot, she couldn't stand it.

When it was her turn, she did her best to keep things succinct, despite the fact that everyone still couldn't stop staring at her like she had two heads.

The restaurant staff soon entered the room to take their drink and food orders from a set menu of preselected items. Jennifer opted to tack on an alcoholic drink, thinking it would help her sleep easier that evening, and because she damn well deserved it.

It'd been a long friggin' day.

Surprisingly, Jennifer rather enjoyed conversation with Grace and Vicki. Grace was indeed a mother, with two grown children. Being a tour guide was her way of coping with an empty nest. Vicki, on the other hand, had no children and had never been married. Instead, she spent her money on travel, seeing all corners of the globe.

"Stick with me on this trip, and you'll be right as rain." Vicki winked and grinned at Jennifer, which immediately put her at ease. It wasn't that she had a hard time connecting with older people—in fact, she often got along better with the older crowd. It was just that she'd hoped to have some kind of life-altering experience with people her own age, and gain perspective on her place in the grand scheme of the universe.

Apparently not this trip.

For a brief moment, she considered calling the tour company's all-hours hotline to see if she could get her money back. There had to be a flight back to the States that left in the morning?

But a familiar face floated into her mind, a stark reminder of what life could deal you.

Lynn.

Emotion churned in her gut, souring the gin and tonic she'd ordered with dinner.

Lynn would've laughed hysterically at this entire situation, and she'd also tell Jennifer to suck it up. There were worse things than trouncing around a foreign country with a bunch of senior citizens.

No. She couldn't leave. Not with the memory of Lynn hanging over her head. Living for Lynn. Living for herself. That was the whole purpose of this trip.

She just had to keep reminding herself.

"What a beautiful ring you have," Vicki commented over dessert.

Jennifer glanced down at her right hand where the opal ring sat on her ring finger.

"Oh, thank you," she replied. "It was my dad's mother's. She's almost ninety and living well in an assisted living place back home. She gave it to me on my eighteenth birthday, and I haven't stopped wearing it since."

And that was not hyperbole. Jennifer adored her Grandma Cassidy and had felt honored when the older woman gifted her the ring that'd been hers, and her mother's, and her mother's mother's, and so on back generations from Ireland. It was a beautiful gem, set into a silver band. The days in which Jennifer didn't wear the ring were rare. Fiona Cassidy had never taken it off either, except the day she gave it to Jennifer.

"My mother passed on something precious as well..." Vicki began, launching into a story from her childhood.

And Jennifer found she didn't mind.

After dinner, Jennifer bid everyone good night and headed to her room. The group looked as though they were nowhere near turning in for the night. How in God's name could they do it? Were they not exhausted? Wasn't going to bed early something old people did?

Shit, she needed to call her mother.

"Ms. Cassidy!"

Jennifer paused at the sound of her name, noticing the front desk person that checked her in earlier waving her over.

"I was just about to call your room. This gentleman is from the airport," the young woman said.

Jennifer then took notice of the man at the counter, but a brief glance was as far as she got. Her eyes caught sight of her suitcase, and she felt as though she might weep for real this time.

Okay, maybe things were looking up. Lynn was with her, looking out for her.

Once she was safe and ensconced in her hotel room with her suitcase always in her sights, Jennifer pulled out her phone.

After toggling the setting on her iPhone that would allow her to make the transatlantic call, she pulled up her mother's contact information and clicked send.

Karen Cassidy answered after the first ring, her frantic voice immediately flooding the line.

"Oh, thank God. I was wondering when you were going to call me. You hadn't texted to say you landed!"

"My bad, Ma. I got to the hotel and passed out," Jennifer replied, trying to keep a heavy sigh at bay.

"Dear God, you had me worried! I thought all sorts of horrible things! What if you'd been taken aside at Customs and some official blackmailed you into becoming a drug mule?"

Jennifer's face screwed up. "Ma...what the fuck?"

Before her mother could answer, there was a muffled exchange between Karen and a deeper voice. There was some rustling, then George Cassidy came over the line. "Hey, honey, how's it going?"

"Hey, Dad," Jennifer greeted, feeling the nervousness uncoiling from her gut just a little. Her dad always had that soothing effect on her. Someone in that house had to be the voice of calm and reason.

For the next fifteen minutes, she caught her dad up on her situation, and declined his offer to help her find a flight home.

"Thanks, Dad. I appreciate it. But I'm going to stick this out. See what happens."

"Good," George replied. "I'm proud of you, kiddo."

There was a pause as George said something to her mother, but it was too muffled to hear.

"Your mother says she loves you. I love you. Please get a good night's sleep and have as much fun as you can. Send us a text or email when you get a chance."

"You got it, Dad. I'll send something daily to put Mom at ease."

"Probably for the best." George let out a fond but long-suffering sigh.

Jennifer hung up the phone and lay back on the bed.

"I've got this," she declared to the ceiling.

The wakeup call came rudely early the next day.

Jennifer rolled out of bed and got to freshening up. She hit herself with a splash of cold water, piled her auburn curls on top of her head, dressed, and made her way down to the lobby where she was to meet her group.

Amazingly, she was the first to arrive, so Jennifer took

advantage of the Wi-Fi to check email and socials from her phone.

Her mother had sent her several messages with updates on what she'd missed since leaving home.

Literally less than a day away and she had five emails about their neighbor, a stray cat, something her older brother, Patrick, had done, and so on.

Jennifer typed out a reply to the latest email about the newest gadget her mother had bought from the Home Shopping Network. Jennifer knew if she didn't there'd be some kind of hell to pay. She made sure to reference the other emails, acknowledging them, lest her mother think she wasn't reading everything.

After sending a lengthy reply, Jennifer noticed a few of the other couples from last night had arrived. They milled about, sipping on coffee from cheap foam cups and munching on a simple Danish.

No Grace yet.

Jennifer scanned through the emails not from her mother, went on Facebook, and shot a few iMessages to her other good friend, Nikki Webb. The more people that knew her whereabouts the better, just in case.

She *had* seen *An American Werewolf in London* after all.

Grace soon appeared and called for the group to gather. She once more gave an introductory spiel of their trip itinerary.

They'd hit Stonehenge first.

Jennifer wished they could spend more time in London on the front end of the journey, but that time was scheduled for the return. That way it would allow people to linger as long as they wanted, depending on when they chose to depart from Heathrow to head home. She hadn't opted to linger too long in London at the end, but enough to make a visit to the British Museum and a few other stops.

Grace let out a rousing cry to rally the troops, then led everyone outside to where the motor coach waited for them at the curb. Jennifer hung back to take the rear, making sure no one fell behind or went astray. This wasn't lost on Vicki, her newest friend, apparently.

"You know, we're all still fully capable of sticking with everyone, despite our advanced age," she teased.

Jennifer, caught, blushed in embarrassment. "Sorry, it's just—"

"An instinct. It's sweet. You protect your teenage students, and now you want to protect your geriatric tour buddies."

Jennifer laughed. Stepping up to the side of the coach, she handed the driver her suitcase. His name tag proclaimed him as "Stu." He had to be about Grace's age, and did not have a hair out of place. Stu wore a tie, perfectly knotted, with a sweater layered over his button-down shirt. He had some wrinkles, but they only heightened his congeniality. Reaching out for Jennifer's bag, he flashed a toothy grin at her, brown eyes twinkling.

"Bit young for this lot, aren't you?"

Ah, is this what the rest of her trip would be like?

"You could say that. Or maybe I just look really good for my age," Jennifer joked.

Apparently, Stu found that lame attempt at humor hilarious, nearly doubling over from wheezing in delight.

"Oh, you're a witty one. M'glad you're around. You'll keep things interestin'."

Jennifer wasn't sure she liked the implications behind that, but thanked him all the same for placing her luggage in the compartment safely.

Being the last one on the coach besides Stu, Jennifer had little pick of where to sit. It didn't seem to matter, as she caught Vicki's hand waving at her to sit in the unoccupied seat beside her. Relieved, Jennifer headed down the aisle. About halfway there, she jumped when Stu brought the motor coach roaring to life and wasted no time in pulling out into traffic. She lurched to the side, and nearly took one of her tour mate's toupee off in her attempt to hold on to something.

Thoroughly embarrassed, Jennifer hurried to the back of the bus and used her momentum, coupled with the bus taking a turn, to slip right into the seat.

"Have you seen Stonehenge in person before?" Vicki made conversation as Jennifer settled in. It'd be about a two-hour drive to Stonehenge. Maybe Jennifer would try and nap.

"I have," Jennifer replied. "It's been a long time though. I seem to remember being underwhelmed."

"Bit smaller than you imagined, huh?"

Jennifer nodded, as did Vicki.

"Avebury is the true beauty," Vicki said. "At least that's what I've heard. Stonehenge I've seen. Not as exciting as I thought it would be. But Avebury? That'll be a magical place."

They chatted idly for a bit, before Jennifer attempted to catch a few z's.

It was a miracle she did, but it felt like as soon as she shut her eyes, she was being jarred awake by Vicki, informing her they'd arrived.

Jennifer filed out at the back of the crowd, and they all mingled while Grace went ahead to present their tour information for admittance.

Salisbury Plain was a sea of green. A wide open field with high mounds in the distance and Stonehenge at the center of it. Even from far away, the sight of the megalith gave Jennifer a shiver.

Perhaps she'd misremembered Stonehenge.

Yes, indeed, in person it seemed a lot smaller than how it was perceived on television or in movies, but the size did not diminish the ambiance. Despite the very modern trappings that surrounded Stonehenge, it seemed frozen in some ancient time, waiting to reveal its secrets.

Too bad no one *knew* its secrets.

Oh, sure, there were plenty of educated and convincing guesses—an astronomical calendar, a temple. And then, the more outlandish—aliens, Merlin, the theories were endless.

One thing was for certain, the Neolithic peoples that began construction on this monument were ahead of their time.

They walked through the museum and then back out onto the plain. Jennifer followed along behind Vicki as they wound their way through the gravel pathways.

Jennifer pulled out her iPhone and began snapping pictures.

"It's not about what it looks like, am I right?" Vicki whispered, taken by the spell of Stonehenge as well, in complete awe of such an ancient marvel.

"It's the feeling." Jennifer nodded.

CHAPTER 3

AVEBURY, UNITED KINGDOM - PRESENT

"Jennifer, could you be a dear and hold this for me?" Eloise Kennedy asked, handing off a bag of stuff she'd just purchased in a gift shop, no doubt full of souvenirs for the grandchildren. Eloise was one half of a darling Canadian couple that had been married for over fifty years. Earl Kennedy, the husband, was somewhere nearby, probably collecting rocks. Every location they visited, Earl searched for the most perfect rock specimen he could find. It was important, he claimed, to find a rock in each place they visited to commemorate the trip. Jennifer couldn't imagine what their house back in Ontario looked like.

Besides, the man had been an insurance salesman, not a geologist.

So far, in the first day of travel, not only had Jennifer

become the designated pack mule, but had witnessed the removal of dentures, made a quick run into a convenience store for antidiarrheal medicine, and a whole host of other memories she would never shake.

Despite these unfortunate circumstances, the trip may have turned out to be a happy accident. As embarrassing as it was to have been put with a group of senior citizens, the experience only reminded her of why she was on this trip in the first place. To see people in the twilight of their lives, living it up like they were Jennifer's age, gave her the motivation to keep pushing forward—to find the thing that would scoop her from the hole she'd found herself in and the depression of losing a great friend.

After Stonehenge, the tour moved on to Avebury, a quaint little town in the southwest of England. It was home to the largest stone circle in the world, bigger than Stonehenge. The henge surrounded nearly the entirety of the town, with two stones at the entryway, standing as sentinels to what lay beyond them. They looked old, weatherworn, and covered in lichen. The stones reminded Jennifer of the not quite so ancient stone walls of New England, old boundaries farmers had erected as far back as the seventeenth century.

As Jennifer stood in the middle of the town square, holding on to the items she'd been entrusted with, she recalled the information Grace had regaled them with on the drive there.

"The Avebury megalithic complex is made of ditches, stones, and embankments, constructed around 2800 BCE. It's theorized Neolithic Britons used Avebury for their religious ceremonies. Not much of the landscape has changed, other than the buildings that make up the village. About five hundred fifty people live in this quaint little hamlet," Grace had said, voice sounding tinny over the tour bus's intercom.

The group had until four o'clock to spend time exploring, and then needed to rendezvous with the bus to journey to Wells where they were staying for the night. Jennifer had yet to pull herself away from the group to explore on her own, and they had about forty minutes left. She remembered studying this place in Early England History, an undergraduate class she'd taken, and wanted to wander.

It had been a relief to get off the coach, as the ever-lingering perfume of Bengay, musk, and mothballs had started to cloy and overwhelm her olfactory sense. Jennifer had been taken hostage right off, reluctantly tagging along with the few seniors that apparently wanted to adopt her for the trip.

"You're such a gem," Eloise said, reappearing at Jennifer's side. The woman only came up to Jennifer's shoulder—petite and trim for her years.

"Sure thing, Eloise," Jennifer replied with a genuine smile. That brought a grin to the older woman's face.

"Let me leave you alone now, dear. Go explore. I think there are a couple more shops I'd like to check out."

Before Jennifer could protest, the woman took her bags back and hobbled away. So, she did as instructed and started wandering around the town square until she found a shop that looked interesting.

A bell tinkled above the door as Jennifer pushed her way in. The lighting was surprisingly dim for a bookstore, but floor lamps stood tall, peppered throughout the ground floor. The musty smell of books accosted her senses, but instead of gagging, Jennifer basked in the aroma. It reminded her of the library stacks of William and Mary. It smelled like home.

Shelves upon shelves of books were situated in tight aisles, giving the floor plan a cramped feel. Yet another facet that thrilled her. While she loved Lola's, the independently owned bookshop back in Eastfall, nothing quite compared to a bookshop in a building older than even her town.

"Hello, welcome!" a wizened old man greeted with a friendly wave from behind a makeshift front counter. An ancient cash register sat in front of him, and there were piles of books stacked around him. He'd been making notes and evaluating the state of the volumes. "If there is anything I can help you with, please let me know. Otherwise, happy browsing."

"Thanks!" Jennifer replied, picking the space to her right as a starting point.

This was the type of store she could spend hours in, staring in awe at the spines of so many classic books, some that were even first editions in mint condition. Teaching, books, and historical research brought her true joy, much to her mother's chagrin. While her mother supported her in all things, she felt Jennifer might be distracted from having more of a social life. Jennifer knew Karen Cassidy wished she was married with at least two children by now. Jennifer had already given up the idea of a PhD because it didn't seem practical. Or at least, according to her mother it wasn't practical.

Ever since childhood, Jennifer had wanted to be a teacher and a historian. History had been the only subject in school she connected with. There was something about times past, lives lived, that fascinated her. Jennifer lived in the past often, preferring to study and learn of people long dead than face the present. The present lacked everything the past could offer her—adventure, intrigue, romance, subterfuge, thrills... her best work friend.

The singular focus she held for her job and her own historical interests might alarm an observant outsider. When not at school, Jennifer sat in front of her computer at home, combing the archives of JSTOR, a digital online library of academic writing, for that one article on that one subject she had yet to read.

The glint of faded gold leafing caught Jennifer's eye, pulling her attention from thoughts of the mundane.

Le Morte D'Arthur.

The Death of Arthur.

It was a copy of the pivotal work of Sir Thomas Malory, printed in the eighteenth century. Why this was not behind a glass case or in a better climate-controlled room, Jennifer had no idea.

Her hand reached out, but froze.

No, she couldn't possibly touch it. The thing looked frayed, like it would disintegrate on contact. The only thing keeping it together was sheer will and probably a little magic.

Jennifer wrenched her feet onward, forcing herself to move away.

Continuing on, Jennifer skipped quickly past the self-help section, as there was no hope for her there, and stopped to skim over the romance section, which was flanked by two large windows that looked out onto the fields beyond. Jennifer could see part of the stone circle from here. What an amazing place it must be to live, to see those ancient stones every day as you sipped your morning coffee.

Jennifer found her mind wandering, pondering what it would be like to have seen the Avebury henge back when it'd first been built. As she thought, gazing out the window at the old stones, she swore that for a split second her vision blurred, then it was as though she could almost see *just* the henge, the buildings of the town completely gone, with only sheep grazing in the fields close by, with thatched-roof huts and enclosures instead of modern structures.

Blinking rapidly, the scene in front of her returned to focus. Jennifer rubbed her eyes, wishing she'd gotten over the jet lag. Moving away from the window, Jennifer sped through the rest of the shop, wishing she had more time. No doubt the blue-hairs would be ready to mount up and head out to the next destination very soon.

"Have a nice day," Jennifer called out and waved back to the proprietor of the shop. The old man waved his pencil at her in farewell, then continued appraising his new haul of books.

The heat of the day caused distant mirages to dance, and Jennifer figured that must've been what she saw. There were no thatched-roof huts anywhere, but there were definitely sheep.

"Hot one today, ain't it?" a man's voice asked.

Jennifer turned, coming face-to-face with yet another over-sixty type. He was short, about Jennifer's height, and pudgy, with eyebrows as bushy white as his beard. He wore slacks, scuffed boots, and a cardigan. With the heat of the day ramping up over the past few hours, it was odd to see someone wearing a sweater and newsboy cap nestled on his head.

"Not so bad as back home," she replied, trying to make polite conversation. She didn't recognize the man as being part of her group.

"Ah, American, then?" he asked. His accent placed him as English, but it was odd, unlike any English accent Jennifer had heard before.

"Yes, from Massachusetts."

"What's brought you here?"

At this point, Jennifer assumed the man must be a local, and probably lonely. She was doomed to be the companion to all the geriatrics in the world. Ironic, considering she spent most of the year with adolescents.

"Vacation. I'm on a tour. The highlights of southwestern England."

"A trip around Arthur country, eh?" he asked.

"Yep, apparently," Jennifer replied.

"Not many people know the settings of the legends anymore," the man replied, rather forlornly. "Ah well, you have a great rest of your trip. Watch out for those questing beasts."

With a brief touch of his finger to the side of his nose, the man gave a little bow and disappeared up the street, as quickly as he'd appeared.

Looking around, Jennifer tried to spot her group members. There were none in sight. Not even Vicki. She walked the town square for a few minutes, and when nothing else caught her interest, she headed toward the stones.

Jennifer ambled along the road, making her way to the outskirts where a gaggle of other tourists admired the stones.

Henges had always fascinated her. No one would ever know for certain their purpose. Were they an astronomical calendar or a religious site? Archaeologists and historians alike could only make the best of educated guesses. But the knowledge that earlier peoples, well before the beginning of civilization, were building such magnificent structures? This, and many other reasons, had drawn her to history, and subsequently to teaching it.

But these mysteries weren't contained to just England. Such was the case all around the world. Evidence of ancient peoples building structures most modern people did not think possible for them to build. But they did. From the Mayan pyramids to the Great Wall of China, humankind has continuously marveled its future generations.

Jennifer wished she could say the same about her own life history.

Her childhood had been normal, perhaps even a little boring. She'd been a fantastic student, part of extracurriculars and community service. She went to college, up to a master's degree, and decided to teach. Why she'd engaged in an underappreciated and underpaid job, she could not say for sure.

She didn't regret her decision.

Jennifer did regret she'd not pursued a PhD in History, hadn't traveled the world more, hadn't made more friends, hadn't invested more in romantic relationships...

Shoulda, coulda, woulda.

The late spring sun was beginning to dip farther from its zenith. It was unseasonably warm for England, and even after piling her auburn curls up into a loose knot, sweat dripped down the back of her neck and spine.

Once face-to-face with a large standing stone, the heat didn't seem so unbearable. The large rock radiated a cool breeze, its ancient wisdom nearly palpable. Reaching out, Jennifer pressed her fingertips to the rock face, as though she might absorb the knowledge the rock had collected over thousands of years. For a brief moment, she thought she felt a little tingle creep up her arm.

Continuing along the henge, the ring came to an abrupt end, broken by removal of some of the stones. They'd been carried away long ago, needed for other reasons. To her left was a small copse of trees, and to her right the inner field of the henge. Turning toward the tree line, the light filtering in through the canopy entranced her for a moment, so much so that a little tug behind her belly button had her trudging forward, step by step, until she entered.

It was cooler in the shade of the small thicket of trees. Jennifer welcomed the relief from the blazing sun. She continued forward, compelled by an unseen hand. She couldn't describe the sensation—it was an urge, a need to move. If she moved in a direction that wasn't forward, the sensation ramped up, an uncomfortable pressure, urging her back on the right path. How bizarre. Her mind felt cloudy, muddled, like she was in a daze.

The trees disappeared and she entered a clearing. It was empty of life—no other humans or animals scampered through the underbrush. The quiet gave the place an ethereal, relaxing atmosphere.

A sound echoed through the trees behind her, coalescing in the clearing, filling the space, surrounding her.

Jennifer, it said, voice human, but not male or female.

Sluggishly, Jennifer turned, expecting to see someone behind her.

The space was empty.

Blinking slowly, she turned back and moved farther into the clearing.

Her name echoed around her again, whispering through the trees. It displaced the leaves on the branches, like a cool breeze. The soft sound through the canopy only served to make her head fuzzier. It was as though something hypnotized her, though she'd never experienced hypnosis and wouldn't have known the sensation.

Her gut told her the voice wasn't something she needed to be afraid of. In fact, it made her feel pleasantly warm, whole, loved. Strange prickles shot down her right arm, gathering at the spot where her grandmother's ring sat against her flesh.

Jennifer.

Her feet moved forward of their own accord, stopping in the middle of the clearing.

Giving in to the sudden inclination to sit, Jennifer eased herself to the ground. Once she felt the hard earth beneath her knees, she tipped over and lay down, head positioned toward the center of the clearing. A faint hum began, a low vibration, enveloping her, like a melody or a tone. Jennifer thought it an odd sound, so out of place for the location. Shouldn't there be birds chirping and the rustle of animals on the forest floor?

The hum continued, and as it did, her eyelids grew heavy, as if the sound was a lullaby coaxing her to sleep.

Darkness enveloped her, accompanied by a strange weightlessness, as if floating right off the ground, heading for the sky.

And then she remembered nothing.

CHAPTER 4

※

AVEBURY - ?

Consciousness came rushing back, crashing against Jennifer's skull like a rogue wave. Eyelids flew open, and the sun above blinded her momentarily. Curling onto her side, Jennifer groaned before getting to all fours. After a quick assessment that involved patting down her entire torso, a long breath passed her lips. Her pack was still with her along with everything she needed, from passport to money. At least no one had taken advantage of her weird, impromptu nap.

Getting shakily to her feet, eyes squinted, still reeling from the shock of light, Jennifer gazed around, seeking answers.

What the hell happened? Why had she fallen asleep? She was still hungover from jet lag, but not enough to risk public shut-eye.

GUARDIAN OF TIME

It took a few moments to steady herself, legs like noodles. Jennifer waited until she was certain she could move and set off in the direction she'd come. It'd been a straight shot from where she entered the trees to the clearing, so she hoped it wouldn't be difficult to find her way out.

It wasn't long before the trees began to thin, and Jennifer stepped from the underbrush, relieved to break free and find the path again.

Relief quickly fled from her lungs like a gut punch.

There was something very wrong about the landscape. Glancing around, she immediately noticed the familiar henge, but that wasn't the alarming part. The alarming part was the lack of modern housing, road signs, and the motor coach. Instead, thatched-roof huts stood in the interior of the henge, with sheep grazing in an open pasture. The scene looked quite familiar. Like she'd seen it before...

After rubbing her eyes yet again, as if she could wipe away the unfamiliar, Jennifer reevaluated her surroundings. A barely there path stretched a few steps in front of her, leading around the embankments of the henge, following the tree line. Jennifer took a chance and began to follow it. It wasn't lost on her that the tree line was a lot longer than it'd been what felt like only moments before.

Anxiousness and dread surged, burning her insides with every step she took. Her breaths came sharper and quicker, hands shaking at her sides. Something wasn't right. Was she lost? *Severely* lost?

She halted abruptly when two figures stepped out of the woods. The men cut strong figures, well over six feet tall and peculiarly dressed. They wore wool tunics, trousers, supple leather boots and...was that *chainmail?*

Were they part of a reenactment group?

Jennifer approached, and in her hurry and desperation,

she missed the way they both tensed and the looks on their faces, expressions incredulous.

"Hi, um, is there any way you can help me?" Jennifer called out. The men's bearing turned into confusion, brows furrowed.

They spoke, but not in English. Their language did seem familiar, like she'd heard it in passing. Perhaps German? Or something Germanic, but less guttural?

"I'm sorry, I don't—" she began, taking one step back, and then another. The two men, bearded, rugged and dirty, like they'd spent too much time camping, advanced. The one on the left wrapped his hand around her bicep, squeezing. His grip was calloused and not at all gentle. "P-Please...don't..." Jennifer jerked, trying to pull free of his hold, but the man only squeezed tighter.

The other spoke again. This time, his voice sounded off, almost like a radio being tuned—scratchy at first, unintelligible, but then the white noise cleared, and inexplicably she was able to understand.

"... this must be her. We will bring her back to camp."

What?

"Let me go, please!" she shouted, straining against their steel grips, shoving her body weight around. They were a lot stronger than they looked, or she was just a lot weaker than she thought. When Jennifer tried to lash out with her foot, to try and connect to sensitive bits, one of them huffed and unceremoniously threw her over his shoulder.

Jennifer most certainly wasn't adept at self-defense. Fear clamped around her throat, freezing whatever effort she might've given to wriggle herself free. The voice in her head suddenly sounded like her mother, going on and on about young women alone in foreign countries being kidnapped into a sex-trafficking ring. Jennifer swallowed, managing to get her body to move, to respond. She balled her hands up tight, reared back, and brought them down like hammers against the small of the guy's back.

Nothing. He didn't even flinch.

The leather he wore was thick enough to soften the blows, much to Jennifer's chagrin.

She beat her hands down again, and for good measure attempted to kick and flail her legs, but she might as well have been a fly on the back of an elephant.

The men cut into the trees a ways down the road, picking their way around roots and branches. The man holding her paid no regard to whether she got scratched by a passing tree branch, and in fact seemed to seek them out just so they would nip at her arms.

"Please let me go," Jennifer croaked.

When he didn't respond, Jennifer began to thrash her arms and her legs as wildly and as hard as she could, trying desperately to get free. She finally connected with the man's gut, effectively knocking the wind out of him. His hold loosened, and Jennifer collapsed to the ground in a rumpled heap. Stunned, the man didn't react at first, and neither did his companion.

Jennifer scrambled up, chose a direction, and ran for it.

Except she didn't make it very far. The man that'd been carrying her recovered quickly and caught her around her waist.

A minute later, she was slung back over his shoulder.

Jennifer had some time to consider her situation as they moved deeper and deeper into the woods. She thought back to the moment she'd deemed this trip not a colossally bad idea. Despite the fact she almost missed her plane, despite the misplaced luggage, despite being put with a bunch of senior citizens and being their gopher.

The more she thought about what it might mean, being a captive of these men, the more fear began to truly set in.

How would she get back to her group? Were they even still around? On this plane of existence? Would the old people miss her? Would these men kill her, or do something far worse?

Jennifer shook her head, trying to push such thoughts from her mind. It was her mother's catastrophizing manifesting. She needed to get a grip. Hysteria wouldn't get her away from these men. Only careful planning and a golden opportunity to escape.

Once it presented itself.

If it ever presented itself.

The men looked more like hardened warriors than reenactors, though. Then there was the strange period clothing...

Reenactors taking their craft too far, perhaps?

They were fit, as though they'd trained their whole life to wield an axe. They picked their way through the forest like they knew where they were going. Like they'd done so a hundred times and had never gotten lost. Jennifer had already lost her own bearings, despite her efforts to try to remember.

When her captor came to a stop, Jennifer swiveled her head to take in her surroundings. The two men had come into a clearing where a fire crackled, and six other men sat around it. In total, from what Jennifer could see, there were eight of them.

Any hope of escape she might've had died.

With no thought to her, the man unceremoniously dropped her in front of a gnarled tree, then proceeded to tie her to the trunk with a bit of rope he had with him.

When he was satisfied with the bindings, he stood and walked away.

Jennifer thrashed and tugged at the ropes to no avail. They were tight, just this side of uncomfortable. They wound around her shoulders and chest, pinching. She tried to wiggle down, to slip out from under them. No luck. Too tight.

With her upper arms immobile at her sides, range of motion was very limited. Jennifer tried moving her arms around, shimmying, but no luck with that either.

After another few attempts, Jennifer settled, realizing she wasn't going anywhere.

Panic flared in her gut again, along with that genuine fear she'd never felt before. The stark reality of her situation settled deeper. The fact this seemed like reality, *period*, rather than a dream, caused nausea to roil.

What was happening?
Where was she?
Who were these guys?
And dare she think it... *When* was she?
Oh God, was this real?
Okay, breathe. Rationalize.

Jennifer could only process what she saw, what she heard, felt, smelled...but she didn't want to acknowledge what her senses told her. The men were filthy, to say the least. And the guy that'd carried her reeked of sweat and leather and campfire. For a split second back on the road, before the strange radio effect, they'd spoken in a language she didn't know. Then all of a sudden they spoke English—with an accent!—and she could understand them?

Should she call it like it seems?

Could she admit to herself she wasn't in Avebury anymore?

Or, at least, not the Avebury from an hour ago?

There were a couple of things Jennifer knew for certain. One, she'd never had a dream this vivid and this intense, engulfing her senses, right down to the scratchy rope tying her to the tree, and two, she was sure there was no immediate family history of mental illness and psychosis, and she'd not been so in her grief that she was headed for a mental breakdown.

There was a Sherlock Holmes quote to recite here. Something about the improbable being the truth...

Jennifer was *not* in the twenty-first century, and that was the part she was struggling to accept the most.

Something had overtaken her back in that clearing. *Something* had made her jet lag and world weariness get the better of her. Like Dorothy in the poppy field, Jennifer, unable to help herself against a sort of siren call, had gotten on the ground to take a nap...and woke up here.

Technically, still in Avebury.

But *definitely not* in the twenty-first century.

As the men conversed and sat around the fire, Jennifer watched them.

They didn't move like modern people. Their word choice wasn't quite the same as modern people. But they joked, and laughed, and every so often they'd look over at her, mostly with annoyance and not lusty hunger, thankfully.

So, not in twenty-first-century Avebury anymore. Okay, maybe she could tentatively come to terms with this predicament.

But again, she couldn't help but wonder what they would do with her? Would they take her back to their village? Would they put her to work as...something? Is this how she would live out the rest of her days? Trapped in not-twenty-first-century Avebury?

No, she *had* to get home. But how could she get out of this? If possible, maybe she could make her way back to that clearing, take a nap, and wake up back where she'd come from.

Would anyone realize she was missing and look for her? Would anyone in Eastfall, besides her parents and brother, miss her? Would Eastfall High School hold yet another memorial service, except this time for the teacher that went missing in Southwestern England?

Did it matter? Would her death mean anything in the grand scheme of life in Eastfall? It isn't like the district wouldn't have a replacement in her classroom long before she was cold in her grave anyway. She was expendable.

Whew, where were these thoughts coming from? Had she always been so doom and gloom? Had she always thought the worst? About herself? About how people saw her?

Did Jennifer Cassidy really dislike herself and her life *that much* she believed people wouldn't miss her when she was gone?

Apparently she did.

One of the men around the fire stood up and walked to her. He crouched at her side, well out of kicking range.

"Food?" he asked, holding out some cooked *thing*. They'd been preparing it over the fire for the last half hour, but from this distance, Jennifer hadn't been able to identify what it was.

Jennifer shook her head, her stomach revolting at the idea of putting anything in it.

The man shrugged and stood.

"What are you going to do with me?" Jennifer blurted.

The man crouched down again, meeting her gaze. "Someone has been looking for you, girl. Tomorrow, we will take you to them."

Jennifer's throat burned. How could someone *here* be looking for her?

"Who?"

The man's lips curled into a rather frightening smile. "You will soon find out. And then I imagine you'll be brought home with us."

"A-And...where is home for you?" Jennifer asked.

The man's lips moved, forming words, but they seemed to fizzle out in the air before reaching her ears. Instead, there was a crackle, like candy wrappers, and a short delay before it all processed in her brain.

"Right now, Kent. But I am sure you will be needed in Saxony."

Saxony?

What?

Were these men...*Saxons?*

But that would mean...

Judging by the fact she was still in England, that these men looked road-weary, as though they didn't quite belong in this landscape, and the mention of *Saxony?*

Never had Jennifer thought that Early England class would ever be helpful for more than just trivia night.

Because somehow, some way, she'd woken up in the fifth or sixth century.

She couldn't even fathom the idea of the year 400 or 500.

The world blurred and spun for a moment, lightheaded, the rope the only thing keeping her from succumbing completely to dizziness.

How in the hell had she gotten to early medieval England?

CHAPTER 5

AVEBURY - CIRCA 500 BCE

Okay, Cassidy, breathe. Panicking will not get you home.
Jesus Christ, what will get me home?
No, no panicking...

Resting her reeling head against the gnarled trunk of the tree, Jennifer took a couple of deep breaths. She focused on the shaky sounds, tuning out everything else, attempting to regain some semblance of control.

She liked – even thrived on – control. She hated messy emotions, and she hated messy situations. It's partially why she'd never ventured far from the East Coast. Now, here she was, in a foreign country, in a foreign *time*...

Once she felt like she might be able to open her eyes and not want to vomit, Jennifer allowed her gaze to focus, to see all of the men—Saxons—gathered around the fire, her bag at the feet of the one that'd carried her earlier.

She watched as he began sifting through the contents, while the others chatted and laughed and shared whatever had been cooking over the fire. Every so often, their eyes would slide toward her, one would mutter something too low for her to hear, and then they'd laugh.

The man had discovered her passport and was leafing through the pages, looking at the stamp from Heathrow, and her picture, in utter awe. The writing might as well be an alien language to him. He glanced her way warily, and Jennifer was certain he'd utter the word "witch" really soon. It always seemed to be the answer for "strange" women throughout history.

A Chapstick tube went flying next, as did a couple of tampons, tissues, and any positive thoughts Jennifer clung to. The items from her bag were passed around, and once more, the men laughed and jeered at them and her. Jennifer was thankful they'd either not paid her grandmother's ring any mind or they hadn't seen it. The familiar weight on her finger was perhaps the only thing keeping her grounded.

"She's just as strange as the she-wolf," one man commented.

"At least she does not look as though she could hold any of us by the balls," another jeered, causing a roar of laughter to erupt around the circle.

"Which makes me wonder what the she-wolf wants with that one," a third pondered, tipping his head in her direction as if there could've been anyone else they currently held hostage.

This hadn't been the first time one of them had alluded to someone looking for her. If indeed this was true, could they be the reason she was here in the first place? Whoever it was, they were not the most pressing problem on the heap of problems she currently faced.

"That is for her to decide," the man that had carried her

piped up, glaring at his companions. He clearly didn't mind whomever the she-wolf was. "Torvulf trusts her. He's *wed* to her. That is enough for me."

"It will not matter in a few weeks," another Saxon said. "The rest will have arrived from Kent, and soon this island will be ours."

Jennifer wasn't sure how much time passed after that conversation, but the sun dipped lower and lower in the sky until twilight appeared. One by one, stars began to twinkle in the inky expanse, and if it wasn't for her current situation, she would've appreciated the view.

God, she was hungry. Her stomach ached, and her bladder burned. But she might as well not exist with the amount of attention they paid to her after rooting through her bag.

"Any chance I could go to the bathroom?" she called out to the remaining few around the fire. Half of them had reclined on the ground, taking the opportunity to rest. Jennifer wished *she* could sleep, but she didn't dare close her eyes.

One man looked over at her, and in the firelight, she could just make out his craggy, dirty face.

"Hold it or soil yourself."

Jennifer received no further reply. He and the others simply turned back to the fire and continued conversing.

Squirming her hips at the discomfort, Jennifer collapsed back against the tree again with a sigh.

She was so very tired, hungry, thirsty, not to mention scared shitless.

But mostly, what she wouldn't give to just be able to curl up and let whatever happen happen. The helplessness won out far sooner than she hoped, but for that moment, Jennifer had no idea what to do.

As the night shadows began to lengthen, and the men quieted as a couple others lay down, Jennifer could feel herself drifting. Unfortunately, it wasn't the kind of tired that had struck her back in the clearing. It felt natural this time.

Jennifer tried to fight it, but her eyelids drooped of their own accord.

A guttural cry roused her from slumber.

Jennifer opened her eyes just in time to see a figure, shrouded in darkness, standing behind a Saxon still seated at the fire, slitting his throat with a short blade. A scream stuck in her throat as she watched in horror as red blood sprayed from the wound along with a hideous gurgling sound, and then the body slumped forward. The rest of the Saxons, roused by this, scrambled to their feet, drawing swords along with whatever other weapons that were within reach.

It seemed it wasn't to be for her captors, as more shadowy figures detached themselves from the trees, descending upon the Saxons like wraiths. In the skirmish, one of the newly arrived figures approached her, sword drawn and raised, dripping with blood. A scream finally ripped through her throat, but the figure brought the blade down on the ropes, slicing them into pieces.

Jennifer didn't sit in shock for very long, before immediately jumping to her feet. In the light of the fire, she took in the figure that had freed her—a man, dark-haired and light-eyed. He opened his mouth to speak to her, and much like with the Saxons, she was unable to understand the words he said, at first. The language was different from what her abductors had spoken.

That weird radio effect kicked in, tuning, finding the right frequency, before dialing in to something comprehensible.

"... cover over there. We will come back for you. Bloody Saxons trying to take our women now," the man hissed before turning back to help his comrades finish off the rest.

Rescuers or not, Jennifer sure as hell wasn't going to wait for this new group to kidnap her too. She turned and dashed for the trees. Not the smartest plan, as she had no idea where she was going and could barely see. It seemed her luck had limits. As she nearly disappeared into the darkness of the forest, a solid object collided with her, sending Jennifer to the ground.

She cursed, the wind knocked right out of her. Jennifer rolled over in an instant, just in time to see a massive, shadowed figure rising up as though straight from hell. Her heart jumped into her throat, believing this was the end for certain.

Instead of a death blow, a vise-like grip clamped around her wrists, yanking her up from the ground. It was so dark she couldn't make out the man's face. The sounds of a skirmish echoed around them, metal clanging against metal, distracting her for a moment. Her captors were vastly outnumbered by the newcomers and easily came to heel as a result. The part of her not overcome with fear was satisfied.

"Did they hurt you?" came the gruff question from the man that had knocked into her. Turning her attention back to him, she found only half his face highlighted by the fire. Jennifer caught flashes of a linear jaw, covered in hair so fair for a moment she thought it was one of her original kidnappers. The one eye she could make out was a luminescent blue, and even in the half-light she could tell his nose, slightly crooked, must have ended up that way from being broken before.

There was something in the visible eye that made Jennifer want to trust the man, but her fight-or-flight senses were strung too tight. She tried to wriggle from his hold on her wrists, but he held fast.

"Let go of me!" she exclaimed.

"Trying to help you here!" the man replied, exasperated.

"Don't need your help!" Jennifer all but growled in the same clipped tone.

"Of course. You seemed to be handling things just fine," the man replied sarcastically.

"I was, until you knocked into me!"

"Ungrateful, aren't you?"

"Asshole!"

In the firelight, Jennifer saw the man smirk. Before he could come back with another witty remark, a cry for help came from one of his companions. The man's attention immediately turned from her, and he was off, relinquishing his grasp on her. Jennifer took this opportunity to immediately reset her course and fled, scrambling into the trees.

The moon above was only a half-moon, and therefore didn't afford much light. Out here in the country there were millions of stars visible in the sky, but they were no help either. Jennifer had never been much of a runner, so she knew she wouldn't get far. However, if she could just get far enough away...

Tree branches reached out toward her, scratching at her face, arms, and legs. Not letting that deter her, Jennifer didn't stop until she couldn't breathe, lungs constricting in her chest, tight and unbearable. She slowed to a stop, still surrounded by trees and more trees. Jennifer fell to her knees, ignoring the damage done to them and her shins, skin tearing, oozing blood, thanks to the rough underbrush. Flopping forward, she lay splayed, chest rising and falling rapidly as she tried to catch her breath, heart hammering wildly.

Exhaustion, both mental and physical, overtook her.

She thought about her mom and dad again, wondering

what they were doing in that moment. She wondered, ridiculously, who would continue paying her student loans. She hated she'd been wanting to buy a house and now would probably never get the chance to do so.

Despite the darkness already surrounding her, something even darker began to set in at the edges of her vision. She tried so desperately to stay alert, to stay awake, to figure out some sort of solution to her crazy predicament. But her limbs felt like lead. God, she was so tired. She didn't think she could go any farther even if she tried.

She found herself wondering, again, what her newfound friends on the tour were doing. If they were having drinks at their hotel in Wells. How Jennifer wished and wished she could be there.

Unconsciousness took her.

CHAPTER 6

The smell of burning wood and leaves jolted Jennifer back to awareness. For a time, she didn't move a muscle, unsure whether the forest was burning around her or if someone else had found her and brought her to their camp. Slowly, she opened an eyelid just enough to see it was now daylight. A fire crackled cheerfully not a couple of feet away from her, and there was a gray figure moving about the fire, stoking it, as something hovered over the flames.

"You can stop pretending. I know you're awake," came a vaguely familiar, masculine voice. Jennifer's eyes fluttered open fully, momentarily blinded by the sunlight above, as she pushed herself to a sitting position.

When her vision returned, she noticed a small animal of some sort roasting over the fire, fat dripping off its hind legs and sizzling as it hit the logs below. Jennifer had never been much for advocating the consumption of woodland creatures; however, her stomach was empty and aching enough that the smell was heavenly.

"Hot one today, ain't it?" the person said. Shock splashed

across Jennifer's face as soon as she registered the words. And it dawned on her where she'd heard the voice before.

Her vision finally came into focus, and sure enough, there stood the old, friendly man she'd met earlier in Avebury village.

"Oh, thank God," Jennifer groaned, nearly collapsing back to the ground in relief. It *had* all been a dream. Truly. "I think I got lost in the woods. Any chance you might be able to point me in the direction of my bus?"

The man just snorted and continued twisting the spit cradling the cooking game.

Jennifer realized, though this may be the same stranger she'd met earlier in the village, he certainly wasn't dressed in his worn cardigan, and gone was the newsboy hat. In place of the clothes she'd first seen him in, the man wore wool robes in a drab gray color, with a bit of cord tied around his waist. He resembled a cloistered medieval monk.

That horrible sinking feeling returned. Lost, unmoored, and floating away from the known world.

"Quite an adventure you've had so far, eh?" The man spoke again, seemingly trying to do his best not to look her in the eye.

"Wh-what the fuck happened? How are you here?" Jennifer stumbled over her words, despair and panic welling in her chest for the second time in less than twenty-four hours.

"Such horrible language for a lady," was all the man replied.

"No, screw that, tell me what's going on. I've been kidnapped, tied up, carried around like a sack of potatoes, I haven't eaten, God knows I haven't peed, and I just want some damn answers!" Hysteria mounted in Jennifer's voice. She grappled to her feet, swaying as soon as she stood fully upright. Her brain felt foggy, but every moment she was conscious burned away the mist like the rising sun. "I have a right to know!"

"Alright, alright, calm down," the man cajoled, motioning for her to sit nearer to the fire. "No need to get your hackles up, young lady. Sit, eat, and I will explain."

Jennifer really had no other choice but to comply. The fact she might get an explanation, no matter how outlandish, was enough. She stepped closer to him and the fire, and plopped back down on the ground. The man pulled the spit from atop the flames, produced a knife from within the sleeve of his robes, and hacked the little animal into two larger pieces. He held out a chunk, and Jennifer hesitated for a moment before accepting the offering. He waved it at her when she didn't accept it fast enough, but seemed relieved when she did.

The man tucked right in, gnawing at the poor rodent with his teeth, ripping off huge chunks of flesh. Jennifer, still a bit hesitant, delicately pulled off a chunk and chewed slowly. She was surprised to find it wasn't awful, but it certainly wasn't a honey barbecue chicken wing. Regardless, the two unexpected companions ate in silence for a time, the only sounds around them being animals in the trees and underbrush and the crackling fire. At one point, Jennifer popped off into the trees while the man continued to eat, and finally, blessedly, emptied her bladder. Lack of any toilet paper was a problem, but it was hardly the worst thing to happen to her.

"You're wondering where you are..." the man said when she returned to the fire.

"Among other things," Jennifer replied.

"You're a smart woman, Ms. Cassidy. I think you have some idea of where you are," the man said, continuing to be frustratingly enigmatic.

"How do you know my name?"

"I know a lot of things," the man replied wryly. "You have an idea where you are. Tell me," he repeated.

"I have an idea, but I can't wrap my head around the possibility."

"You've fallen victim to ancient magic, Ms. Cassidy. The how and why of it, *I* do not even know. But you *are* in the past. A very distant past from your own. The men you encountered in the woods were a band of Saxons. The group that attacked them are natives. Native Britons, Britons of Roman descent...blokes simply trying to defend their home."

"So...the 500s CE then?" Jennifer hedged a guess.

"You would be correct."

"Putting that aside for a minute, because—*holy shit*—how is it *you're* here, but you were *there* before?" Jennifer asked, motioning with a wide arcing arm movement.

"It's quite simple, really," the guy replied, as though she were a bit slow. "I traveled here. Not unlike you did, but differently."

"Okay, great, get me back to my time, and we'll be all set."

"Unfortunately...it isn't *that* simple," the man said, looking quite sheepish.

"But you just said it was!" Jennifer replied incredulously.

"Simple for me, but not for you," he said, condescension returning.

Jennifer rubbed fingertips at her temples and attempted to take a few deep breaths to calm herself. It wasn't working.

"Look, man, can you please just explain and be less confusing about it?"

"I'm not *man*," he huffed. "My name is Emrys."

"Can you please stop talking to me like I'm five, *Emrys*. You know my name, but you never had the common courtesy to introduce yourself."

Emrys held his hands up, palms out, in capitulation.

"My apologies, my apologies," he said in a tone that said he wasn't sorry at all.

"Emrys, I'm waiting..."

"Right, right. It is simple for me because I possess the ability to travel in my own corporeal form to another location and time at will. You traveled here by a rather different method. Magic is all around you. There are many different kinds of magic. Some 'magic' has been explained by modern science. Some magic is inherent in the environment, not controlled by a conscious mind, per se. Other magic is wielded by certain special individuals. I am one of those individuals. I have a different kind of magic. Different from the magic that brought you here. I cannot undo the magic that was done to you. But I can tell you where to go to get back to your time."

Jennifer's thoughts spun, trying to make sense of what it was Emrys was saying. The more she thought about it, however, the more realization bloomed. She'd stepped into the forest, guided by some unseen hand, been pulled in and rendered unconscious, until she awoke in a familiar yet strange place.

"Back into the forest?" she asked, hopeful.

Emrys shook his head. "No, I do not believe that will work again. You see, though there is magic inherent in environments—certain places and such—it triggers for a specific reason. My thought is the magic in the forest, made more potent and powerful by the henge in Avebury, brought you here for a particular reason. It won't bring you back until you have fulfilled that reason."

How convenient.

"Okay, but, you said you might have an idea?" Jennifer replied, grasping at thin strands of hope.

"There's a tidal island off the coast farther south and west of here. It is called, in your time anyway, Saint Michael's

Mount. It isn't just significant for Christians. There are far more ancient works going on there. Go, and I have a feeling whatever magic is there might help you."

"Yeah, or send me to when dinosaurs roamed," Jennifer muttered.

"Look, your negativity is not going to get you anywhere," Emrys scolded, standing up in a huff and beginning to douse the flames of the fire. "Stop feeling sorry for yourself and accept your situation. The moment you are able to do this, the moment you will be better off, and you can move forward and get yourself home. Oh and, uh..." At least here, Emrys had the decency to look sheepish. "You need to get there and back to Avebury before the summer solstice."

Jennifer, caught somewhere between confusion and anger, scrambled to her feet. "That's on the twenty-first, isn't it? That gives me less than a month to get there and back. Can you just snap your fingers and get me to Saint Michael's Mount? You want to help me, but so far you haven't been entirely helpful. You keep giving me obstacles."

Emrys sighed. "I cannot do *everything* for you. By the gods, you millennials... I have made enough educated guesses as to whatever the plan is for you. Besides, I have business I must attend to. Head in that direction,"—he pointed a finger to his right, toward some invisible path through the trees— "straight, until you leave the forest. You will hit an old Roman road. Go left on that road, follow the distance markers, and you will eventually make it to a town called Corinium. You'd know it as Cirencester. It'll take you about eight hours of walking. If you start now and take few rests, you'll make it by nightfall."

Reaching down, Emrys picked up one of two packs he'd been keeping close. He held out one to her. Which reminded her...

"Shit, what about my passport, and money..."

Emrys waved his free hand. "If all goes well, you'll wake back up where you left, and your pack will be there. For now, in this pack I put an animal skin with fresh water, a pouch with some nuts, berries, and dried meats, two sets of suitable garments, and some coinage if you meet any business that will accept them as payment. The food should last you at least until you get to Corinium."

Jennifer reached out, accepting the bag. She slung the strap across her torso. She'd ask how it was he'd known to prepare this pack for her, but she was afraid of his answer.

"Oh!" Emrys exclaimed, reaching into the folds of his robe. "I nearly forgot." Out of some hidden pocket, he extracted a piece of leather string. He held it out to her, and Jennifer noticed hanging from it was a wooden charm shaped like a six-spoked wheel.

"What's this?"

"A very essential talisman," he replied. "You will need it to help you get back to your time. *Do not* lose it. *Do not* let anyone else touch it. It is meant *only* for you."

Jennifer slipped the leather string over her head and tucked the necklace into her shirt. If it would help her get home, the thing would never leave her person for any reason.

"So...uh, what am I supposed to do when I get to Corinium?"

Emrys groaned in annoyance. "I don't know! Figure it out. Good gods..."

Without another word, he turned on his heel and began walking in the opposite direction of the way he'd indicated for her to travel. Jennifer watched, appalled and very much nervous, as he disappeared. Literally, he disappeared into the foliage of the forest like the baseball players walking into the cornfield in *Field of Dreams*.

"God dammit," Jennifer muttered, looking first at the space where he'd disappeared, and then to the indicated direction she should travel. She really had no other choice but to do as he suggested. He was the only one, other than the natives that had fought off the Saxons, that had helped her since her arrival.

Letting out a forlorn sigh, not seeing any other options, Jennifer picked up one foot, then the other, heading along the invisible path dictated to her by Emrys.

On the road to Corinium.

Jennifer didn't know exactly how long she'd been walking. It could've been eight hours or it could've been two minutes. Regardless, she was glad when eventually she was free of that infernal forest and able to move along the road, wide open spaces all around.

Before she'd completely left the forest, she had sheltered herself behind a couple of closely packed trees and pulled out the clothing Emrys had packed for her. One set included a pair of trousers with a tunic, something that, if Jennifer wasn't mistaken, would normally be worn by men in this time. Regardless, she was happy for the pants, considering the other set of clothing was a deep wine-colored wool dress. It was a basic design and had a leather strap to cinch at the waist. Digging into the pack, Jennifer also found a pair of simple leather shoes, which were surprisingly supple and giving. Quickly, she dressed, carefully shoving her normal clothes deep into the pack. She opted to keep her modern undergarments on, and found the trousers were actually very comfortable, along with the tunic. The material didn't itch like she assumed it would. The shoes, while comfortable, she didn't particularly care for. They felt odd, entirely foreign to her trusty Converse. However, as they say, when in Rome... And if it came down to it, she could switch to her burgundy pair of Chucks stowed in the pack.

Along the way to Corinium, Jennifer passed the time singing about the *yellow brick road*, switching from the *Wizard of Oz* tune to the Elton John song, and then back. She thought again about Lynn and what she would've said about this entire shitshow.

A couple of times, she happened past other travelers, but for the most part, no one greeted her or interacted with her in any way, for which she was grateful. Jennifer did stop a few times just to have a sit. She wouldn't say she was a slouch, as she was on her feet most of the day at school, but she definitely wasn't fit enough to walk this distance without a few breaks, including bathroom breaks, which were something else to become accustomed to.

After a few hours, her legs and feet began to ache, and she knew if she didn't get to Corinium soon, she'd either collapse from exhaustion and pain or succumb to the coming nighttime. God only knew what lurked in the darkness if she opted to camp on the side of the road.

Thankfully, Jennifer didn't need to worry about any of those things. She passed a distance marker pointing toward Corinium, and soon after, the blessed walls of the ancient Roman city appeared just as the sun dipped low in the sky.

She supposed that "ancient" wasn't the right word to use in this circumstance. At this point in time, Corinium was simply *old*.

If it hadn't been obvious before, the appearance of the walls and interior of Corinium made it more so—*this* was Sub-Roman Britain. A time period mired in little to no primary source documents or archaeological evidence, these were the years succeeding Rome's abandonment of the Britannia province, ultimately leaving its inhabitants to fend for themselves against invaders from Ireland and the Continent, as well as the Picts from the north—what is today Scotland. The walls had crumbled in certain areas, signs of ill upkeep and pilfering natives.

Once Jennifer entered the city proper, the open space where the forum would've been, she could tell the town was a mere shadow of what it once was. It might've been a thriving town, but now it was sparsely populated. People still milled around, but nowhere near the grandeur it would've been as the provincial capital of the local native tribe.

Corinium Dobunnorum, as was the full name, at its zenith would've looked much like any other Roman town in the empire. Surrounded by fortified walls that afforded protection, there would've also been a central forum for market days and other general administrative purposes.

Shops would have spiraled outward from the center. The shopkeepers would've lived above or behind their shops in order to be near their livelihoods. The rest of the town would've been housing—apartments and grander homes.

If Jennifer remembered the information she'd read in a guidebook on Roman Britain, the section about Corinium said the only thing in modern day that gave testament to the fact a teeming Roman town once stood in this place was the presence of the wall ruins, the overgrown bowl of an amphitheater, and a museum housing tons of valuable artifacts excavated through the years.

Corinium, in this particular moment, was somewhere between what it'd once been and what it was to become.

Now that she had reached her destination, Jennifer wished Emrys was there to tell her what to do next. Standing nearly dead center in the old forum, Jennifer received a few curious looks. It was concerning, as she definitely didn't need to bring attention to herself. Scuttling off to the side, trying to stay out of people's way and therefore their line of sight, Jennifer trudged up and down the street, trying to find a tavern of some sort, or, to a Roman, a *taberna*.

It took a few tries, but after walking what felt like the equivalent of three city blocks, Jennifer found a tavern still very much in use. It had an open front with the counter close to the street for ease of access. She couldn't imagine it turned much of a profit anymore, not without the aid of Roman soldiers. Still, it was pleasant to find there were a few customers sitting around, drinking and eating and carrying on. In a dimly lit back corner sat two people—one playing a wooden flute and another playing some sort of stringed instrument. The patrons of the tavern were so enraptured by the music, clapping along to the tune, they didn't notice Jennifer sidle up to the counter.

Leaning against the stone countertop, Jennifer waited to be noticed by the man behind the bar. He was preoccupied with listening to the music as well and had yet to notice her. Jennifer's appearance, however, didn't go unnoticed completely. A woman that had come from the back of the establishment spotted her. Her eyes immediately locked on Jennifer, dropping to her shoes and then back up to where she'd piled her auburn curls. The slant to the woman's eyebrows said she did not approve of Jennifer's presence.

"Evening," Jennifer greeted with what she hoped was a kind, nonthreatening smile.

The woman opened her mouth, and instead of words, Jennifer heard that strange radio-tuning sound. Once the white noise cleared, she understood the woman.

"... get for you?"

With a bowl of stew and a mug of some sort of alcoholic liquid, Jennifer settled at a roughly hewn table toward one end of the bar. She silently thanked Emrys for including the pouch with metal coins. Jennifer had been a little surprised the woman accepted the form of payment, since Jennifer assumed formal currency had fallen by the wayside.

Regardless, it was truly astounding to know that whether modern or ancient, public drinking establishments were still very much the same. The musicians had ceased playing, probably on a break, and the regular, familiar bar din returned to the tavern.

The stew was...well, Jennifer didn't want to know exactly what was in the stew. She was so hungry it didn't matter; what did matter was how fast she could shovel the stuff into her mouth. A gulp from the mug confirmed the unknown liquid was some kind of beer. Relief washed over her for a moment as her hunger abated, however the look the tavern owner's wife gave her was scathing. The woman didn't want Jennifer here for some reason. Probably assumed she was a prostitute or some other woman of ill repute. Perhaps women didn't generally travel unaccompanied in this time.

After imbibing a bit more of the ale, Jennifer sighed and pondered.

What was she to do next?

Emrys hadn't told her what to do once she reached Corinium. What little he had told her seemed preposterous. There was a *reason* she was here, in post-Roman Britain? If Emrys had no idea, Jennifer sure as hell didn't know.

"'Ello, darling..." came a slurred voice from behind her. Jennifer tensed.

Bars were seriously no different in ancient times than in modern.

Turning, she was met with a scraggly looking man. He was tall and entirely too thin, with closely cropped hair and an unkempt beard. Dark eyes leered beneath equally bushy eyebrows.

"Can I help you?" Jennifer asked.

"I was jus' wonderin' why it was that a girl like you was all alone," the guy replied.

It would take Jennifer time to get used to her brain and hearing magically tuning to whatever language these people spoke, as if all sound around her came from a radio.

"Traveling," she replied, turning back to her cup of beer.

The man didn't take that as a dismissal. In fact, he sat down in the vacant chair next to her.

Jennifer sighed again.

"I thought you might like some comp'ny," the man said.

"You would assume incorrectly," Jennifer replied.

"Aw, don' be like that, a spoilsport."

Clearly, *no* didn't mean *no* to this guy. Jennifer stood and made to leave, beer mug and Emrys's pack in hand. However, the man's grubby hand shot out, latching on with a steel-like grip to her forearm.

"Where do you thin' you're goin'? Was it somethin' I said?"

"No, it's definitely your breath," Jennifer replied without missing a beat.

The drunk's glazed-over look instantly disappeared, replaced with fiery anger. It caused her stomach to churn. He shakily got to his feet, towering over her, leaning in.

"I've been nothin' but nice to ye, and this is how you treat me in kind?"

"Look, dude, I don't know who in the hell you are—"

Jennifer's words were cut off by the tight squeeze of his hand. Pain bloomed up her arm, and she knew she'd have finger-shaped bruises there later.

"You need to learn to shut your mouth," the man gritted through clenched teeth.

"And you need to learn that no means no."

"You little bitch," the man hissed, raising his free hand.

Jennifer tensed and clenched her eyes shut in preparation for the hit, but none came.

"Did your mother not teach you any manners?" a new voice asked.

Slowly peeking, she saw a hand firmly clasped around the drunk man's wrist, ceasing his action in midswing.

"This is none of your business, friend," the drunk man said. "I'd like for you to see yourself away."

"Now, I think you and I know I can't do that," the newcomer replied. His voice was deep, rather calm for the present situation. Facing off against a belligerent drunk person could never be an easy task.

In an instant, the drunk man shoved Jennifer away and swung wide at the newcomer. Jennifer, losing her balance momentarily, landed heavily against the wood of the bar, the edge of it jamming painfully into her back. It kept her from falling to the floor though, and she didn't spill a drop of beer. Small victories.

Whirling around, she gasped at the scene before her. The drunk man threw sloppy punches at a fair-haired man, the newcomer, who in turn easily dodged them all. He moved so quickly, Jennifer didn't instantly get a look at his face. Regardless, he appeared skilled in hand-to-hand combat, and it didn't take the drunk very long to figure this out. His eyes became wider the harder he tried to land a blow, while the newcomer just smiled.

It wasn't long before the drunk tired himself out, arms hanging heavy at his sides as he panted.

"She ain't worth it anyway," he spat, looking evilly back over his shoulder at Jennifer before moving away.

Jennifer glanced around the rest of the tavern. No one seemed at all disturbed by what had just occurred. In fact, they all appeared bored, as if this sort of thing happened all the time.

Turning to her savior, Jennifer was prepared to thank the man graciously, but he was already gone, back across the room from where he'd apparently come from. She was shocked, to say the least. Abandoning her beer mug, Jennifer hiked her pack over her shoulder and crossed the large open space to where the blond man had settled back in to finish his own ale.

"You didn't let me get a chance to thank you," Jennifer started right in.

The man didn't immediately look up at her. In fact, he appeared to be ignoring her.

"Uh...sorry, did you hear what I said?" she pressed on.

"Certainly did. And don't mention it," the man replied, the word "it" flourished with a hint of finality.

The brush-off was rather annoying, and for a moment Jennifer didn't know how to proceed.

"You won't let me get in a proper thank you?" she asked.

The blond man finally looked up at her, and for a moment, Jennifer was stunned. Looking back at her were the most stunning blue eyes she'd ever seen. His hair was light in color, as had been her previous assessment, but upon closer inspection it was streaked with slightly darker strands. Despite her assumptions of the time and seeing other men in the town, his hair was closely cut around the sides of his head and longer on the top, which had come loose in the scuffle. His face was stubbled with darker blond hair, though still rather fair. His chin was rounded, and his jawline perfectly angular.

Those eyes, which she'd just been admiring, glanced down to her leather shoes, and then quickly raked their way up her body. It wasn't an appreciatory look, but more clinical and businesslike.

"No, thank you, I'm not really interested in the kind of 'thank you' you're offering."

What the hell?

Jennifer's mouth gaped open. "I... I am not..." she stuttered, babbling like an idiot, aghast at such an insinuation.

"Look, darling, there is no need to thank me. That man needed a lesson in how to treat a lady." One shoulder lifted and lowered in a shrug that was almost mechanical. Like this was something he did every day. "I taught it, and now I'll be on my way." The blond man lifted his mug, taking a couple of deep pulls.

A closer look at the man's jawline and the fair hair that covered it prompted a memory from the previous night, in the woods, when she'd been held captive. There was a recollection of a half-shadowed face, a crystalline blue eye...

"*You,*" she whispered.

"Me?" he asked, glancing at her, one eyebrow arched.

"It was you in the woods."

"I spend a lot of time in the woods. You must be more specific."

"Last night, with the...the Saxons."

The man's eyes widened slightly, but otherwise gave away no emotion.

"Ah yes. The ungrateful lady."

Jennifer's fists balled at her sides. "What do you think I've been trying to do?"

"I find it strange you would thank me for saving you from a drunkard, but would not thank me for saving you from a band of bloodthirsty invaders."

Jennifer couldn't help it then; her eyes rolled toward the ceiling. With a heavy sigh, she pulled out the nearest chair and sank down.

"Did I say you could sit here?" the man asked.

"No, but I'm sitting anyway," Jennifer replied.

For a time, the man didn't speak. Perhaps he refused in an effort to get her to leave. It didn't have the desired effect.

"Cool sword," Jennifer commented, tipping her chin at the sheathed sword lying across the table.

He didn't reply.

After another few beats of silence, he finally broke. "What were you doing in the woods anyway?"

"I was trying to find my way back to—to the group I was traveling with. We've been separated."

"And where were you heading?"

"Saint Michael's Mount," Jennifer replied, after a moment's hesitation.

This time, he couldn't hide his sudden surprise.

"What?" she pressed.

"Nothing," he grumbled, lifting his mug and draining the rest of the ale. He set it down with a thunk and made to get up, grabbing his belongings. Jennifer didn't move, didn't try to stop him. It'd be no use anyway.

The man turned but only made a few steps toward the exit before he stopped. The line of his shoulders was tense, until they sagged, resigned. He turned on his heel and sat back down.

"Okay, here's the thing. We just so happen to be headed to the same place. Seeing as you are alone, and we don't need you getting yourself taken by Saxons again, you can...you can travel with me."

Jennifer was shocked at the offer. Up to this moment, she believed she'd have to find her own way to Saint Michael's Mount. Here was a capable fighter and protector, offering to bring her along with him. Perhaps this is why Emrys had told her to go to Corinium. The answer to her traveling woes was here.

"Lucky me," Jennifer mused, referencing the fact he was conveniently going to the same place she was. She couldn't imagine many people made the journey to Saint Michael's Mount.

"Do you want to come with or not?" he asked, exasperated.

Could he be trusted? Was he truly safe to travel with?

He'd already played her savior twice now. What had she to lose? Besides, it wasn't like other opportunities were making themselves known.

"I'll come with you," she replied, resigned. "Thank you for the offer...?"

The man nodded. "My name is Lucius Artorius Aurelianus. You may call me Lucius."

Why did it feel as though she'd heard that name before?

"I'm Jennifer," she replied.

"I'm sorry, you want me to sleep where?"

"As I said, you have two options. You can sleep on the floor of the room I have for the night, or you can sleep in the stable with my horse."

Jennifer found herself rethinking her luck. She'd quickly come to learn Lucius was taciturn, at best, and completely unhelpful. Ungentlemanly, even. Not that she expected anyone knew what that meant in this century.

After Lucius reluctantly offered her a way to St Michael's Mount and their lukewarm formal introduction, he'd informed her of the plan. They would rest at the inn for the evening, then at daybreak begin their journey.

Jennifer couldn't argue, as she was simply elated she'd found someone to take her where she needed to go. Seriously, her luck was never this good, and she had her suspicions that Emrys may be behind this sheer happanstance.

She'd been so happy at this good fortune it hadn't occurred to her she'd be required to stick close to this man, this stranger. She couldn't go without sleep for very long or she'd be useless. This trip would require her, no doubt, to camp out on the road with him. The stark reality of this hit her when he gave her the options for the evening.

"I...I can't have the bed?" she asked.

Lucius didn't look at all accommodating. "Not unless you wish to share it with me. And seeing as we just met, I am sure you are not inclined to that scenario."

Jennifer furiously shook her head.

"I didn't think so. So, once more, your options are to sleep on the floor or to sleep outside in the stables with Llamrei."

Llamrei being the horse, most likely.

"Um...I'll take the floor."

Lucius didn't say anything, but he had that sort of smug look that said *that's what I thought*.

Jennifer wasn't able to sleep more than a couple of hours. Despite Lucius giving her a few blankets, the wooden flooring was unsurprisingly uncomfortable. Not to mention it was entirely uncomfortable to be in a room, alone, with a stranger. Something Jennifer had never thought to add to her bucket list, that's for sure. But desperate times and all that.

It seemed she had nothing to worry about, though, as Lucius fell asleep as soon as he'd settled in the bed and stayed that way for the entire night, lightly snoring. Jennifer wondered what he must've thought about being in the room with a strange woman. It seemed he wasn't at all afraid Jennifer could've been an unsavory character, because he slept like the dead.

Lucky for him.

As Jennifer tossed and turned on the awful floor, she constructed a skeleton of a plan. Considering she didn't know what lay ahead of her, there wasn't much to add to the mental plan, but it made her feel better to have one all the same.

She also spent a great deal of the night thinking on why Lucius had offered her a place with him on his journey. Would he expect anything in return? Dear God, Jennifer hoped he didn't think she would...

He did offer her a degree of protection she knew she wouldn't have on her own.

And she offered him... well, not *that*, that was for sure. Travel companionship? Jennifer didn't exactly have much to offer in the way of practical skills. She didn't know how to fight, didn't know how to start a fire, didn't know how to hunt...the list went on.

What she did know was history. Lord knew that wouldn't help her here, not when the best primary source documents about this period had been written at least a hundred years later.

There were some things she could surmise, though. The people themselves were definitely somewhere between Romanized and native British.

Most historians believed business went on as usual after the Romans left. Or as usual as it could've been with external invaders to worry over. Some archaeological evidence showed people had either moved away from the larger Roman cities or remained. Those that left were thought to have returned to the ancient hill forts of their ancestors. They didn't have to worry so much about Romans anymore as they did about the invading migratory groups from the continent. The Angles and Saxons were only a couple of the Germanic tribes that had moved from their homelands, eventually settling in England.

The Anglo-Saxons, over the course of a few hundred years, made England their home, establishing seven kingdoms and living that way, until eventually England became one unified monarchy.

And thus, the basis for English culture in the present.

There were Viking invasions, of course, as well as rough

relations with the Picts to the north in what would become Scotland.

Early medieval England had been a favorite subject for Jennifer in college, but she found herself wishing, as the sun rose the next morning, sunlight trickling in, she'd read more about it. And she wished she'd gotten more than an hour or two of sleep.

It wasn't long until Lucius woke. He didn't speak a word to her as he got out of bed and began to gather his things. Turning, he glanced down at her at the foot of the bed.

"Oh, good, you're awake. I'll be downstairs. We leave in five minutes."

And indeed, it wasn't but ten minutes later Jennifer found herself walking next to the infamous Llamrei, a beautiful brown mare, on their way out the west gate of the city.

And so, the journey to St Michael's Mount began.

CHAPTER 7

ON THE ROMAN ROAD - CIRCA 500 BCE

Looking over at her companion, she couldn't help but notice how few words he'd spoken to her since they began their journey.

"You're a quiet one, aren't you?"

Lucius shot her a sideways glance, but said nothing.

"So we're going to be quiet all the way to St Michael's?" Jennifer asked.

Remaining defiant, Lucius once more said nothing.

"Lovely..." she murmured under her breath.

And thus it was for the first half a day of traveling. By noon, judging by the height of the sun in the sky, Jennifer's feet were killing her. Soft, supple leather shoes or not, she surely had blisters on the soles and heels of her feet.

Thankfully, Lucius halted for an all too brief break, where Jennifer was glad to find an uprooted tree to take a seat. The day was warming a bit, and the sun glared down upon them. A fine sheen of sweat had formed on her forehead and upper lip and down her spine, causing the tunic shirt to stick awkwardly to her skin.

Jennifer drank greedily from the animal skin pouch Emrys had included in the pack. She then munched on some of the cured meat as well. It wasn't a gourmet meal by any stretch, but it was something.

"How long to St Michael's Mount?" Jennifer asked.

Lucius heaved a long-suffering sigh from where he sat, as though she'd been asking this question every hour since they'd begun.

"About a week and a half's worth of traveling," he replied shortly.

Jennifer choked, as a piece of dried meat stuck momentarily in her throat. She didn't respond right away, trying to hack up the food morsel and quell the cold despair and panic that settled in her belly.

"It's going to be one hell of a long week if you're going to pass it in silence," Jennifer snapped, sucking in air.

Lucius didn't reply.

"So, I'm going to get the silent treatment, is that it?"

More silence.

"What fuckin' luck," Jennifer muttered.

A few minutes later, Lucius stood and stepped back onto the road. Jennifer took that as her cue to follow, which she scrambled to do.

Another hour into their travels, and the pack Emrys gave her began to weigh heavily across her body, but Jennifer refused to whine.

"Where are we headed first?" she asked.

For a brief moment, she thought Lucius wouldn't answer her.

"Bath."

Jennifer winced, pressing her fingers to her temple.

The word "Bath" hadn't been the first sound from Lucius's mouth. Instead, it was more of a screeching sound, like feedback from a microphone, that sounded very much like *Aquae Sulis*. The manner in which it happened was akin to the tuning radio sound she normally heard when she met someone new. Only after the jarring sound had dissipated did she hear the word Bath.

Why did that keep happening to her? Was there some magic at work translating things for her?

"What's in Bath?" Jennifer asked. She did remember from her readings on Roman Britain that the Romans had called the town Aquae Sulis for the natural warm springs that occurred there. They built a lavish building to house the famous baths, a building which was on her itinerary back in the present, oddly enough.

"A good place to stop on our way to the Mount," Lucius replied, as though it were the most obvious thing in the world.

"Where else are you planning to stop?" Jennifer asked, trying very hard not to sound annoyed. She just wanted to get to St Michael's Mount, figure out how to get the hell out of this place, and return to her old people. But she didn't know the island, not like Lucius did, no doubt, and would easily get lost.

Lucius sighed *yet again*, and muttered something under his breath she didn't quite catch. She might have heard the word "regret," but she couldn't be sure.

"We will stop in Bath, Glastonbury, Axminster, Exeter, Tintagel, and then St Michael's Mount."

Jennifer regretted asking the question, as the microphone screech seared across her eardrums with every new location Lucius listed. She welcomed the last place, as she'd heard it before and therefore that dreadful sound didn't manifest. She realized it hadn't happened with Bath either, only the four locations in between.

"Are you okay?"

It took Jennifer a beat to realize Lucius had spoken to her.

Blinking, she looked around to see she'd stopped, hunched forward, her right hand gripping her head.

Jennifer righted herself and squared her shoulders. "Um, yeah, I'm fine."

Lucius didn't look convinced but continued walking. Jennifer followed after him.

It was interesting to hear amongst the shrieking noise the Latin names for some of the places Lucius listed. It wasn't as though Jennifer hadn't heard Latin before. In fact, she'd studied it in high school and college.

Axminster was a place she'd never heard of, but had once been called Moridunum, apparently. The Romans had called Exeter, Isca Dumnoniorum. And she didn't quite catch Latin names for the other places, if there were any.

Jennifer let the silence be for a while and tried shifting her mindset, this time to attempt to enjoy the situation for what it was worth. The trees were vibrantly verdant, lining the impeccable Roman road, shading them from the sun. It was a bit of a relief, though the temperature in the past was not as hot as her present.

At least the weather was nice.

Thirty minutes later, she regretted thinking that.

Out of nowhere, dark clouds appeared. Nature held its collective breath, then let loose a deluge. The rain poured for at least an hour, soaking Jennifer to the bone. Lucius pulled on a cloak and placed the hood over his head, looking unperturbed by the turn of events.

Even Llamrei wasn't bothered. She plodded along next to her master as if there was nowhere else she wanted to be.

GUARDIAN OF TIME

At one point, Lucius looked back at her, a half smirk pulling at his lips. Jennifer glared, hair plastered to her head.

Any other time, she might've gladly basked in this spring rain shower. It was warm, pleasant, and the kind of rainstorm you might dance around in, arms outstretched. This hardly seemed the time to have fun, not to mention her shoes were soaked through. Every step she took squished, a very unpleasant feeling. At least they weren't slogging through mud. Jennifer didn't think she'd ever feel so grateful for the Romans and the meticulous way they cared for their roads.

The rain disappeared almost as quickly as it had appeared.

Lucius shed his cloak, laying it across Llamrei's back like she was his portable clothesline.

Jennifer, on the other hand, felt like a drowned rat.

"Lucius, are we going to stop anytime soon?"

The man didn't acknowledge her, which only stoked her ire.

"Lucius," she said again, with no response. Was the man *that* lost in his thoughts? "Lucius!"

The man's shoulders jolted, and he turned around, confused for a moment before he schooled his expression.

Odd.

"Yes?"

"Are we going to stop anytime soon?" she repeated.

Lucius looked forward, up the road, for a moment. "We will stop in a few more hours. We are almost to Bath."

The next leg of travel was absolutely miserable.

The sun showed its face as quickly as it had disappeared behind the rain clouds, and thankfully helped dry her a bit. Her clothes remained damp enough to stick to her skin, the trousers caught around her legs, and God, the shoe situation.

"Lucius," Jennifer sighed.

Once more, he either ignored her or didn't hear her.

"Lucius!" she shouted.

The man turned around, irritation scrunching at his brow. "*What?*"

"Look, I know I'm not exactly part of your travel plans, but the least you could do is not ignore me."

Lucius had the decency to look sheepish. "Sorry, I..." He trailed off, stopping himself. Whatever it was, he didn't want to tell her. Lucius glanced down to the tip of his boots, thinking, and then lifted his gaze to look at her, evaluating. "It's just, no one calls me Lucius. Not anymore."

"And you wanted me to call you that *why?*" Jennifer huffed.

Lucius—or Not Lucius—shrugged. "I dunno. It popped out."

Jennifer snorted. "What do you prefer to be called then?"

"Arthur."

It was as though the entire world fell silent at the proclamation. Jennifer stopped dead in her tracks with mouth dropped open. The world shook and tilted on its axis, or perhaps it was her, falling to the ground in a faint.

When she came to, Lucius's—no, *Arthur's*—concerned face hovered over her. The bright light of the fading sun blinded her for a moment, and she groaned, rolling onto her side.

"Are you alright?" Lucius—*Arthur*—asked. "You just...swooned."

If Jennifer hadn't just had an intimate and quick meeting with the ground, she would've thrown a few choice, harsh words his way.

Arthur reached for her, but she swept her arm out, and he froze.

Jennifer continued to roll onto her hands and knees, not

even really bothered she was hunched over in the dirt, then took a few deep gulps of air.

No wonder his full Roman name had sounded familiar.

Lucius Artorius Aurelianus.

Several writers in the sixth century and beyond had alluded to a figure, Ambrosius Aurelianus, a war chief of both Roman and British descent, that led the Britons in a decisive battle against the invading Saxons. Even slightly earlier, some sources made mention of a man named Lucius Artorius Castus, a Roman military commander in Britain.

What made these names so memorable was the fact they were names spoken often on the side of academia that believed there was a historical basis for the King Arthur of legendary fame. Ambrosius Aurelianus and Lucius Artorius Castus were two contenders for the mantle of *The Once and Future King*.

How fascinating that the man standing in front of her had an amalgamation of both names.

Lucius Artorius Aurelianus.

Arthur.

"Can I—?" Arthur began, but Jennifer interrupted him again with an outstretched arm.

"No. Just...give me a second..."

Written sources of post-Roman Britain were hardly reliable, which made constructing the history so difficult. Authors such as Gildas and Geoffrey of Monmouth penned their tales hundreds of years after "Arthur" most likely had lived and died. Some historians believe some of the inspiration for Arthurian legend came from Welsh tales and Celtic myths. Archaeological evidence existed, but the material culture was hardly enough to really prove anything.

Since Jennifer had arrived here, it was just one thing after another after another. But all of the ingredients were there... the name, the time period, the Saxons...

Somehow, of all the time periods she could've found herself in, Jennifer had made it here, had crossed paths with *him*.

Out of all the things that had happened to her so far, this was the one thing that didn't seem even an ounce believable.

Yet there he was...standing over her, no doubt annoyed for having taken on a "swooning" woman holding up his journey's progress.

Jennifer sucked in another steadying breath and slowly got to her feet. She was exhausted, wet, uncomfortable as hell covered in mud, and now her traveling companion was fucking King Arthur.

"Are you—" Arthur tried again, but Jennifer held up a finger, shaking her head.

"I'm fine. Let's go." And she continued walking in the direction they'd been moving.

She could feel Arthur's eyes on the back of her head, but she didn't stop, didn't look back.

Ever since watching Disney's *Sword in the Stone* when she was a kid, Jennifer had been a bit of an Arthurian nut. She'd always loved the dashing stories of knights, fair maidens, courtly love, and questing beasts. She'd loved the idea that a sword could divine a person most worthy of leading. Someone fair and just and capable of caring deeply for the people they ruled. History was full of lascivious Roman emperors and fascist dictators, all exploiters of the common folk, all who put their own best interests in front of those they were supposed to be leading, nurturing.

And though the Arthur of myth was hardly without his own faults, he'd still done what no one in history had really been able to do. He'd ushered in true peace and prosperity.

Shit, had Emrys not mentioned questing beasts back in Avebury?

Jennifer nearly halted midstride.

That asshole had *known*.

He knew way more than he let on, and she had no idea why she was so surprised by this. In all of those stories of gallant quests, did the hero not run into half-truths and manipulations?

"Are you going to be okay?" Arthur asked, falling into step beside her.

"Y-yeah," Jennifer breathed, despite the fact her face, knees, and palms ached with how familiar they'd become with the Roman road beneath her feet.

Arthur didn't say anything after that. In fact, neither of them did for a long while.

"You said you prefer to be called Arthur?" Jennifer asked, breaking the silence.

"Yes. It was something my mother called me since I could remember. It stuck."

The coolness of the shaded trees over the road made Jennifer shiver, but the dimness was a pleasant relief from the hot sun.

"It's a…it's a good name," Jennifer replied lamely, trying to act nonchalant, as though the sound of his name had not just sent her into fits.

For the next hour or so, she found her thoughts spiraling, most of them centered around the silent man next to her. She wanted to ask him if the sword he wielded had a name. It seemed like an unassuming sword, but he'd wielded it expertly against her Saxon captors. God, she really wanted to ask him if that was Excalibur…

The sun began to dip lower and lower, and just when Jennifer thought they weren't actually going to make it to Bath before night fell, they came upon the city's walls.

It seemed fitting the first major town they reached on their journey to St Michael's Mount was Bath.

Jennifer had been to Bath once before, back on the high

school trip she'd mentioned to Mrs. Window Seat. She remembered Bath Abbey, but mostly she remembered the baths themselves.

The baths, a popular retreat for the Romans and later peoples, were built on top of a natural spring that, according to legend and lore, were natural healing waters. The baths themselves had been well-preserved, despite the more modern building that had been built around them.

The two companions passed through the walls and into the city proper. It was more populated than Corinium had been. In fact, the way people moved around the streets, it seemed business as usual, despite the absence of the Romans. Someone was lighting torches, a sort of primitive streetlamp. Merchants were packing up their wares for the night, and others were returning to their homes either inside or outside the city walls.

Arthur led the way down several streets, taking turns confidently, like he'd been here before. Eventually, he brought them to a tavern off the main thoroughfare.

"Here," he spoke, handing Jennifer the leather straps of Llamrei's reins. "Hold on to her." Arthur didn't hesitate before stepping in through the open doorway, disappearing into the dimly lit establishment.

Jennifer stood uncomfortably in the street, holding the reins at arm's length like Llamrei would bite her or something.

The mare just shifted her feet, stepping close enough to Jennifer to nudge the hand holding the reins. Swallowing, she tentatively reached out her free hand, and when Llamrei didn't make a move, Jennifer brushed her palm gingerly up the horse's snout. Llamrei quietly snorted like she rather liked that, and Jennifer relaxed a little, getting a bit closer.

It's not like she didn't like animals; she loved them. But horses were...well, *large* animals and she'd never liked riding even the ponies at Eastfall's Harvest Festival when she was a kid.

Arthur reemerged from the tavern not too much later and took back Llamrei's leads. "I secured Llamrei a stall in the tavern's stables. I'm going to take her around back and get her settled. The innkeeper said there are several buckets of fresh water there as well. It is not a proper bath, but you can at least wash your hands and face of the, uh, mud."

That may have been the most thoughtful thing the man had done for her thus far.

"Lead the way," Jennifer bid.

Arthur moved a little farther up the street and then around into an alley. They soon reached the tavern's stables where a couple of horses stood silently in their stalls. When they saw new arrivals, however, they fidgeted and shuffled to see who was there.

While Arthur led Llamrei into her room for the night, Jennifer took some time to rinse her hands in the buckets. She wondered if the water had come from the spring or if it was rainwater. It didn't matter to her in that moment— bacteria be damned. Once she'd rid her hands and face of mud, she ducked into an empty stall, braving the hay and horse smells, and changed into the simple dress Emrys had provided in the pack. She almost switched out the shoes for her Chucks, but thought better of it. At least for now.

Once in a set of fresh clothes, she returned to the bucket of water she'd been using and dunked the muddy trousers and tunic shirt into the cool depths. It wasn't a washing machine, but it would do in a pinch. After getting as much of the mud from the clothing as she could, she wrung out the material and decided she'd find a spot near a fire where she might set them to dry at least a little bit.

When Arthur emerged from situating Llamrei, he looked her over for a moment.

"What?"

"Nothing," Arthur replied, clearing his throat. "I just... didn't expect the gown."

Jennifer snorted, following him back into the alley and then onto the street. "Well, my swooning landed me in the mud, so..."

"Is there another word for what happened to you?" Arthur asked, and Jennifer was almost surprised to hear a teasing tone to his words.

"Um...well," she stammered, trying to decide on how she would respond. "No, I suppose not. Swooning just sounds so...I don't know. 'Fainting' is better."

Arthur snorted. "If you say so."

Jennifer bristled. "I do!"

He seemed to know then not to respond, but that didn't keep him from displaying a borderline smug smile.

The interior of the tavern was blessedly warm and slightly hazy from the fires in the grates on either side of the open space.

"Ah, you have your horse settled then?" a thin, middle-aged man asked upon emerging from a back room. "Please, have a seat. I'll get you and your wife some supper."

Jennifer's head snapped toward Arthur, and her eyebrows lifted. He looked resolutely forward at the presumed innkeeper, thanking the man, as he made for a vacant table in a corner. Jennifer trailed behind and sat in a rickety chair across from him.

"Wife?"

"About that..." Arthur began, but the innkeeper returned, carrying two mugs of some sort of brown ale, and behind him a young girl, probably his daughter, followed with two bowls filled with meat and bread.

"Thank you," Jennifer said to the girl, who smiled, revealing two little dimples, one in each cheek. Both innkeeper and daughter returned to seeing to their other patrons.

Jennifer looked back toward Arthur and leveled her best glare at him.

"Er, yeah, sorry. I thought it might be received better if people believed us to be married."

She did see the merits of that, of course, though she wasn't sure of the moral code of this time period. For all the ways the Romans could be so self-righteous, they could also act heathenish. Quite the paradox.

As for the native Britons, Jennifer couldn't speak much to their moral code. Did they accept unmarried women at her age accompanying an unmarried man?

They ate in silence, and as time passed, the room darkened along with the disappearance of the sun outside. The space filled more and more, hard workers coming to de-stress from the day. Once again, Jennifer was struck by how similar humanity of the past was to the humanity of the present. There was a bar back home called Bucky's, and every so often she and Lynn would get a drink after school, staying well into the night, laughing and complaining and drinking.

The human condition, in this respect, had not changed over the past millennia.

"So, tomorrow, where will we head to next?" Jennifer asked after the pair had finished their meal. She now sat back in her chair, cradling the mug of ale and nursing it. The meat and bread were surprisingly good, and she did have the presence of mind not to question what kind of meat it was. She wasn't sure she would've eaten it otherwise.

"We will make for Glastonbury in the morning," Arthur replied, taking a long pull from his own mug.

Jennifer nodded. She'd only ever seen pictures of Glastonbury. It hadn't been a stop on her high school trip, unfortunately.

"Look, Arthur..." she began, setting her cup down and leaning in toward him. Jennifer watched as a muscle in his sharp jaw clenched and unclenched. She sighed. "I don't know why you're so...so surly...but this is going to be a long journey, and we're going to be around each other a lot. If you didn't want to help me get to St Michael's Mount, I don't know why you offered."

"I don't know either," he muttered to himself, but Jennifer had heard him, clear as day.

"You can just leave me here. It's fine."

Arthur sighed. "I'm not going to leave you here."

"Then you could at least stop acting like I'm an inconvenience."

He didn't reply. He took another sip of his ale, gaze caught somewhere over Jennifer's shoulder, until finally he set down the mug and nodded.

"Okay, fine. You're right. I apologize. I have...I have no idea why I offered to take you to the Mount, but I did, and I shouldn't...I shouldn't be rude. My mother would be highly disappointed in me."

Jennifer chuckled, until she realized he wasn't joking. He actually looked bothered at the thought that his mom would be annoyed at him.

"It's okay, really," Jennifer replied. "I'm just... I really need to get to St Michael's Mount, and you have no idea how grateful I am you're willing to let me tag along with you. I wouldn't know how to get there myself otherwise."

Arthur seemed a little startled by her honesty, but he seemed to appreciate it either way. "I am happy that I am able to help."

They lapsed into quiet again, simply taking in the scene of the tavern before them—all of the patrons and the raucous laughter and the free-flowing ale.

A strange sensation crackled in her spine. A feeling like

she was being watched. With a quick sweep of the room with her eyes, she wasn't able to find anyone looking at her. The feeling didn't go away. But after a while, when she still couldn't seem to figure out the source of the discomfort, she let it go, chalking it up to anxiety of where she was and her situation.

"Are you from this area?" Jennifer asked, leaning in to their newfound understanding and a way to distract herself from the feeling.

"No," Arthur replied. "I traveled from Caerleon."

Jennifer's face scrunched in thought and pain as the microphone screech reverberated against her eardrums at the mention of a new place name.

Caerleon?

Wasn't that a place in Wales? Why did the name sound so familiar?

"Is that somewhere...uh"—she had to think for a second, pulling up a mental map of England—"to the north of where we are now?"

Arthur nodded. "Indeed it is."

"Were you born there?" she asked.

"No, I was actually born in Tintagel, which will be our last main stop before St Michael's Mount."

Of *course* he was born in Tintagel.

He's *Arthur*.

The legendary birthplace of Arthur had long been associated with Tintagel. It was on the itinerary with Excalibur Tours, and she'd been looking forward to that stop. Looks like she'd get to experience it in a different way.

"What brought you to Caerleon?"

Arthur heaved a sigh. "Is there a reason you are asking *this* many questions?"

Jennifer shrugged. "Just trying to make conversation, getting to know my travel companion a little better."

"Alright then. Where did you come from?"

Shit, he would have to ask.

"Uh...the continent. A little, um, town in Francia."

"You've come a long way."

Jennifer nodded. *You don't know the half of it, dude.* "That I have. But I, um, I have some family here on the island."

Arthur nodded slowly, and Jennifer had the impression he didn't quite believe her story fully. But he also didn't push, and for that she was grateful. How else would she explain where she was from? Tell him the truth? That would go over well...

He didn't ask any more questions, thankfully, and Jennifer went back to watching the crowd. That strange feeling from before had abated a little, but it still nagged at the back of her mind.

All around, conversations swirled. And not for the first time that night did Jennifer hear mentions of Saxons in the crowd of people. She turned back toward Arthur.

"What is going on with the Saxons?"

Arthur scowled into his cup. "There have been reports for months of them amassing an army to attack west. I have happened across more and more war bands than I would like, that is for sure."

"How long have they been a problem?"

"A long, long while now. Well before my time, and even my father's father's time. For the past many years, they have lived rather peacefully in Kent, but it was always a matter of time before they made another move to expand west."

Jennifer hated knowing that eventually they would succeed. Such was the curse of knowing history. But she knew she couldn't risk telling Arthur that.

"*I said, let go of me!*"

At the cry of distress, Jennifer's head whipped around for the source. It'd been loud, but not loud enough for everyone in the room to have heard over the din. One glance back at Arthur said he'd heard it as well.

"No, please, stop!"

Arthur got to his feet first, with Jennifer close beside him, their mugs of ale forgotten on the table. There was a disturbance in the crowd, toward one of the other corners of the tavern, where some looked over toward the feminine cries of objection. Arthur charged through, bowling over a couple of people in his haste, Jennifer close on his heels.

And once the crowd had parted, that's when she saw what was happening.

A man had clearly been getting handsy with a young woman, dark-haired and slim. And much like the guy in the tavern back in Corinium, he had not understood the meaning of no.

Jennifer gasped as she watched the man rear his hand back and slap the woman across the face, right before Arthur could get to the man. Arthur hauled him off her, reared back his hand, and clocked the man across the face with a sickening crack. Blood gushed from the offender's nose, and once the rest of the crowd had caught up with what was going on, they all surged forward to grab the creep and haul his struggling ass out the door and into the street.

The tavern had fallen silent for a time, but didn't stay so when they noticed the perpetrator had been taken out. Conversation picked back up as though it had never stopped, and Jennifer took the opportunity of the clear space to rush forward to get to the young woman.

"Are you okay?" Jennifer asked, clutching one of the woman's elbows to steady her after that hit.

The woman was stunned, and Jennifer opened her mouth to ask her question again, when the woman finally nodded.

"Y-yeah, I'll be okay, thank you." She glanced from

Jennifer to Arthur. "Thank you both. I...I don't know why that happened."

Jennifer shook her head. "What happened was that guy didn't know how to leave well enough alone."

The woman sighed and nodded, the palm of a hand still clutching at her cheek which would probably be bruised in the morning.

Despite the situation and the horror of the violence against her, the young woman was stunningly beautiful. The bruise wouldn't do much to put a damper on that, that was for sure. She had dark, almost-black hair with electric-blue eyes, fair skin, and a lovely figure. She was almost too beautiful to be real.

"It'll be okay. You're safe now." Jennifer put her arm around the slightly taller woman's shoulders. "I'm Jennifer, and this is Arthur. You're safe."

The woman nodded vehemently, failing at biting back tears.

"I-I'm...I'm Morgan."

Jennifer paused, frozen.

Morgan?

Shit.

CHAPTER 8

AQUAE SULIS (BATH) - CIRCA 500 BCE

To Jennifer's credit, she didn't completely lose it.

Instead, she ushered Morgan to where she and Arthur had been sitting, settling her in a chair and plying the dark-haired woman with ale. Her hands shook, but to her credit, she recovered more and more each passing second.

"Th-thank you," she murmured to Jennifer, accepting a fresh cup of ale from the innkeeper's young daughter.

"Of course," Jennifer replied. "Are you here by yourself? Is there someone we can find for you?"

The woman shook her head. "No, I'm by myself. On my way to see family."

"Where's your family?"

"They live near Tintagel. I was in London, visiting a cousin, and now I'm on my way home."

Jennifer shot Arthur a pointed glance. He caught it, his eyebrows raised in question. Judging by the annoyance in his eye, Arthur understood what she was attempting to broadcast. His eyebrows scrunched, clearly not happy. Arthur shook his head curtly, quickly, so Morgan wouldn't see it. Jennifer tilted her head slightly, narrowing her eyes at him. Arthur shook his head again, this time more noticeably. Jennifer didn't move, simply stared at him. Arthur held her gaze, and eventually his shoulders sagged and he sighed.

"If you will feel safer, we are traveling toward Tintagel. You can accompany us."

Jennifer smiled, pleased. Arthur, on the other hand, was not.

"Oh, no, I could not impose—"

"Of course you're not imposing. You can come with us! It will be better. Safety in numbers."

"I can keep pace!" Morgan replied. "And I can cook well enough if the need arises."

Jennifer smiled softly. "That will be a needed skill, I'm sure."

Out of the corner of her eye, she saw Arthur clenching and unclenching his fists. He did not look happy.

"Jennifer...could I speak to you a moment, over there?" Arthur bid through gritted teeth, pointing somewhere away from where they were now.

"I'll be right back. Keep drinking the ale, okay?" Jennifer pressed a comforting palm on Morgan's shoulder before stepping to the side.

"What the hell do you think you're doing?" Arthur hissed.

"Helping," Jennifer replied, as though the most obvious thing in the world.

"We cannot pick up every single stray that needs help, Jennifer. We will never make it to the Mount at this rate."

"Stop being so dramatic. She's going the same way we are.

Why couldn't we bring her along? She's by herself, like I was. Surely you can't be *that* much of an ass."

Arthur breathed heavily through his nose, clearly seething with annoyance. Instead of fear, Jennifer felt rather, well... smug. She felt she knew him to an extent now. Knew the sort of person he was even after a short while together. He wouldn't say no to helping someone. No more than Jennifer could say no.

"Fine," he gritted through clenched teeth. "But if she slows us down..."

"I'm sure she won't. No more than I'm slowing you down."

His crystalline eyes locked and held with Jennifer's green, conversing as though telepathically. Something passed behind his eyes, and Arthur's shoulders fell.

"Take the room. If you need me...I'll be with Llamrei."

And that was how Jennifer found herself with another travel companion.

The next morning found Jennifer enjoying the last bit of coolness of the night that was rapidly burning away by the climbing sun. The three strangers were about an hour away from Bath, keeping pace with each other.

Jennifer and Morgan hadn't slept much the previous night, having instead remained awake, just talking. Morgan had been born near Tintagel, and had been visiting a close cousin in London who'd been due to have a baby. After the successful birth of a baby girl, Morgan began her journey back home.

In return, Jennifer told Morgan what she could, feeding her the same story she'd given Arthur, about being from Francia, about visiting family herself.

It was easy to converse with her. They were similar ages, from similar family upbringings. Morgan had a brother herself, along with sisters, and both parents still lived.

Jennifer couldn't help but feel like if they'd met in the present, they'd be good friends. Morgan was conversational, but rather unassuming. She didn't take up space, something Jennifer had also subconsciously been doing her whole life. Always reserved, and not one to readily share her opinion. Jennifer couldn't tell, from the previous evening to now, whether Morgan was simply her name or if Morgan was *Morgan*.

Morgan le Fay, generally a villain in Arthur's story. A sorceress almost as powerful as Merlin, Arthur's half sister in some stories, mother to Mordred in others. So far, what Jennifer would have expected from Morgan le Fay, she wasn't feeling with *this* Morgan.

As they walked along the Roman road, chatting, Arthur silently leading Llamrei—no doubt thrilled there was someone else for Jennifer to talk to—she couldn't help but feel there was something about Morgan that made it easy to converse with her.

Jennifer found herself laughing at some antic Morgan's brother had apparently gotten into as a child. It was the first time Jennifer had laughed since she'd gotten here.

The majority of the day passed easily enough.

In the early afternoon, they paused for a quick meal and a rest.

"Are you okay?" Jennifer asked, stepping up to Arthur who was adjusting the packs on Llamrei's back. "You haven't said much all day."

Arthur slid his eyes to her.

"Alright, alright, geez."

Arthur went back to adjusting a pack. As he did, an object about the length of her forearm fell from the depths, landing with a metallic thud on the ground. Jennifer bent down, picking up...a knife.

"Wow, this is cool," she couldn't help but blurt out as she looked the sheath over and the hilt of the knife. Detailing in the leather near the hilt caught her eye, a familiar symbol.

She'd definitely seen it somewhere before. In her own time.

It was an eight tipped on its side, an infinity symbol, but instead of plain lines, the symbol was formed by feathery wings.

Where had she seen this?

Jennifer stared and stared, watching the light of the sun bounce off the brown leather, to the point it almost hypnotized her. She racked her brain again and again, searching.

It was right there, on the tip of her tongue.

"Can I have that back now?"

Jennifer jumped, forgetting Arthur stood beside her.

"Um, yeah," Jennifer replied. "I just... I've seen the symbol before."

"Maybe from one of your Saxon friends," Arthur shrugged. "That's where I got it."

Ah, of course. He'd pilfered it off a Saxon.

"That's not it..." Jennifer mused quietly.

She knew for a fact she'd not seen it from her Saxon captors. She'd seen this *way* before.

And now it rankled that she couldn't remember where.

Dammit. Oh well.

Jennifer held out the knife to Arthur, who looked down at it and then back to her.

"You know what? You should keep that. Just in case."

She nearly dropped the knife at the mere idea, but she nodded regardless. He was right. There was a very real possibility she might have need of it.

The trio continued on not long after that, walking in silence for a time.

Even for Jennifer, a natural introvert, the quiet was daunting.

Normally, she didn't feel compelled to fill gaps in conversation, but with Arthur, it felt different. Like she should be asking him anything and everything, despite the fact he didn't seem to want to share.

She was still ninety-nine percent sure he was indeed the man, myth, and legend himself. The Arthur that would persist into the future, more divine status than mortal.

He seemed pretty mortal to Jennifer.

Mortal failings. Mortal hubris. Mortal attitude.

Neither did Morgan seem like an evil witch.

"So, Caerleon..." Jennifer hedged, stepping closer to Arthur.

"What about it?" Arthur asked, voice even, not breaking stride, simply continuing on as though a pesky fly had buzzed close to his ear.

"What's Caerleon like?"

Arthur shrugged. "It's green. Bit hilly. There's an old Roman fort where a garrison used to be stationed. It's where my father's family has lived since they came to Britain."

"Your father is Roman?" Jennifer asked.

If indeed it was the 500s CE, the Romans had been gone a couple hundred years. But their influence and presence couldn't have disappeared *that* quickly. Knowing Arthur's father's family was Roman told her that some Romans had indeed stayed. No doubt because they'd set down roots. To a native of the Mediterranean, that couldn't have been an easy transition to make. The weather in England could be relentless. But if you, say, met someone you loved, perhaps you'd do anything you could to stay with them.

"My father was Roman, yes. And his father. And his father... back several generations." Arthur responded.

"And your father married a Roman woman?"

Arthur didn't reply immediately. In fact, he seemed to be weighing whether he wanted to answer at all.

"My mother was a native Briton."

Jennifer wondered if his mother's name was in some way a derivative of Igraine. It would be appropriate, considering in the legends his mother was pretty much always named Igraine.

She didn't follow up further, and neither did he offer more.

At one point, Jennifer started singing a song under her breath. She made up a tune first, but then morphed into "Bohemian Rhapsody."

"Do you mind?" Arthur grunted when she'd gotten to the high and low parts which she sang both herself.

Jennifer stopped midnote. She glanced over at Morgan, meeting a sympathetic look. Jennifer stepped back over to match pace with the dark-haired woman, who at least seemed to appreciate her company.

The companions entered a bend in the road, following the curve, and when they came out the other end, Jennifer stopped dead in her tracks.

Coming toward them, in the middle of the road, was a tall, lithe, *stark naked* man.

He walked like nothing was amiss, his skin dirt-smeared, with dark purple bruising mottling the skin around his left eye. Other than that, he looked none the worse for wear. Jennifer couldn't imagine how his bare feet had held up with the concrete of the Roman road beneath them. The man's hair stuck up every which way as though he'd been tugging at the strands.

Arthur looked stunned, as did Morgan, so Jennifer

concluded that happening upon naked men on the road was *not* a common occurrence in this century.

As the man drew near, he shot them a soft smile, then walked right past them.

Arthur glanced to Jennifer, seeing his shock mirrored on her face. She shrugged.

But there was something else on Arthur's face.

Recognition.

"Oi!" he called out to the man, who froze after being addressed. "Kay...? Is that you?"

The nudist turned cautiously, as though afraid of what might happen to him. But when he actually took closer inspection of Arthur, his eyes widened.

"*Arthur?*"

"Kay, what the...? Are you alright, mate?" Arthur asked.

The man known as Kay walked back toward them. "Oh, I'm just fine, Wort. Beautiful day, isn't it?"

Jennifer tried so hard not to laugh at the man's cavalier tone, but he was buck-ass naked in the middle of the road, as if he did it every day. And then started discussing the weather.

"Yeah," Arthur replied. "Absolutely splendid. Where are your clothes?"

This time, she had to stifle a laugh.

The man bristled, affronted. "Can't imagine what business it is of yours?"

Arthur looked stunned, to say the least. "Kay, have you been hit in the head? You're my cousin, mule. What are you *doing here*? And...*naked*."

When Kay was not forthcoming with answers, Arthur shook his head. "You know what? Forget I asked. Still as stubborn and idiotic as usual. Just thought I'd help *family*. But never mind." Arthur turned, and Jennifer followed suit, continuing in the direction they'd been going.

"Wait!" Kay called out. The trio stopped, turning. Kay scrambled over the pavers of the road, stepping closer, but not too close. "Sorry. I'm not proud of what happened to me."

"*What. Happened?*"

Kay looked at Jennifer, then Morgan, and seemingly just realizing he was in mixed company, promptly cupped his hands around himself. As if he hadn't been hanging out there for the world to see the past five minutes.

"Uh, I..." Now that Kay was closer, Jennifer could see his eyes were a shade or two darker blue than Arthur's. His hair was copper-colored, not unlike her own. He was taller than even Arthur, and thin to boot, though one could tell his thinness was a bit of a deception. There was underlying muscle there. "I stole from the wrong person."

Arthur didn't bat an eye. He wasn't surprised at all.

Instead of asking more questions, though Jennifer was sure he had more he'd ask his cousin and very soon, he reached into a pack on Llamrei's back and pulled out a cloak. He handed it over to Kay who promptly slung it over his shoulders, holding the sides closed tightly in front of him.

"Who are your lovely traveling companions, Wort? Quite rude you haven't introduced us."

"This is Jennifer, and that is Morgan. Ladies, this is my cousin Kay."

The man executed a jerky bow toward her and Morgan. "It is a pleasure to make your acquaintances."

"Nice to meet you," Jennifer murmured. At this point, she wished she had a BINGO card or a list of Arthurian characters to keep track of how many she'd meet.

This man...was *Kay*. In legend, Kay was Arthur's foster brother, son of Ector, who raised Arthur as a boy.

"Pleasure to meet you," Morgan greeted with a nod.

Kay turned back to Arthur. "Where're you headed?"

"Glastonbury."

"Oh, lovely, just came from there. Great town."

Arthur rolled his eyes. "Kay...are you going to tell me what happened?"

"I told you," Kay said, almost defensively. "I stole from the wrong person in a game of chance, and...well...he stole from me in return."

"And this happened in Glastonbury?"

Kay nodded, humming in the affirmative.

"What were you going to do? Keep walking like that through the night?" Arthur asked.

"Well, yes. What other choice did I have?"

"Right now, you've got plenty. We're going to Glastonbury, and when we get there, you're going to tell me who took your things, so we can get them back."

"And how do you propose to do that?"

"Maybe if we find the man, you could apologize real nicely, and he'll give you your things back?" Arthur suggested with a wry smile.

A slow smile spread across Kay's face, like there was a hidden meaning behind Arthur's words only he understood. "And if he doesn't give it up nicely?"

"If he doesn't give it up nicely, then we'll fight him for it."

Kay laughed and laughed. "Oh, cousin, how I've missed you."

Arthur laughed. It was the first time Jennifer heard the sound coming from the stoic man and, well, she didn't hate that look on him.

About a half hour from Glastonbury, Jennifer found herself catching up to Arthur finally, who'd been bantering back and forth with his cousin.

"What was it you said about picking up strays?" she whispered to him.

Arthur glared.

CHAPTER 9

GLASTONBURY - CIRCA 500 BCE

The traveling band reached Glastonbury just before the sun disappeared for the day.

From what she could see in the semi dark, Jennifer noticed it wasn't the city Bath had been, but wasn't small by any means. There were people still milling about, heading home for the day. A little ways off was the dark shadow of the tor, the high hill that overlooked the town.

If Jennifer remembered correctly, the Romans didn't have much of a presence, if at all, in Glastonbury. It had been settled by Neolithic peoples and didn't become much of anything for another hundred or so years when the Anglo-Saxons dominated. As far as Arthurian lore, though, Glastonbury was believed to be the front for the magical island of Avalon and possibly the site of Arthur's last resting place.

They pressed on through what was most likely a marketplace during light hours, and following Kay's lead, they found a tavern.

"This is the place. The man's a local. The local drunk no doubt, so he should be here," Kay explained. Jennifer felt for the poor guy, especially his feet. They were dirty and blistered and bloody, but it didn't seem to bother him much.

"I'll go in first to secure Llamrei a place to rest for the evening," Arthur spoke. "Ladies, feel free to find yourself a nice place by the fire, have a drink, and we'll be with you shortly."

Morgan and Jennifer exchanged a look, shrugged, and did as suggested. There was no use for either of them to get in the middle of whatever it was the men would get themselves into. Kay remained with Llamrei while Arthur spoke to the tavern owner, and the ladies found a nice cozy place by one of two fires heating the space. There were a handful of people in the tavern—not as many as one might expect, but it was still early yet.

"How much trouble do you suppose they'll find?" Morgan asked, amused.

"I'm not sure I want to know," Jennifer replied.

A young woman brought them drinks Arthur must have ordered for them. The two women sat in companionable silence, drinking their ale, waiting for Arthur and Kay to appear.

"I have been meaning to ask you," Morgan began, "about your necklace. It is quite beautiful in its simplicity. Did you make it yourself?"

Jennifer looked down, having nearly forgotten she'd been wearing the necklace Emrys had given to her.

"Oh, uh...a friend made it and gave it to me as a gift." She picked up part of the leather strand and tucked it under the neckline of the gown.

A strange look overtook Morgan's face. Almost like she

was annoyed or angry that Jennifer had hidden it. But as soon as it was there, the expression was gone.

"Ah, well, as I said, it is a beautiful piece." Morgan took a sip of her ale.

Before Jennifer could ask about Morgan's reaction to the necklace, Arthur and Kay appeared at the doorway. Kay was dressed, weapons at his waist. She found herself letting out a relieved sigh.

"Well, that must not have taken much," Jennifer murmured, watching the men make their way over.

"Ladies," Kay greeted with a grin, settling himself next to Morgan.

"You're dressed," Jennifer teased. "I almost didn't recognize you."

"Hah, hah..." Kay replied drily. "The man gave up my things without much of a fuss."

Jennifer glanced at Arthur who nodded to verify. "Indeed. He was already sleeping off his drink in the stables. We were rather fortunate to have run into him."

"Amazing," Jennifer chuckled.

The four companions chatted for the rest of the early evening. Jennifer had to admit while this may not be the vacation she'd planned, it was turning out rather well regardless. She'd made friends—her own age this time—and they were making decent time to St Michael's Mount.

"Have any of you seen the view from the top of Glastonbury Tor?" Morgan asked at one point. She was met with head shakes. "I have, once, when I was younger. The view is indescribable. On our way out of town tomorrow, we should climb it. Just for a few minutes."

"Sounds like a wonderful idea!" Kay declared, thumping the table.

Jennifer looked at Arthur expectantly. Arthur, in turn, shrugged.

"Sure. We can climb up to the top of the tor in the morning, but only for a few moments. Then we must be on our way."

Morgan clapped her hands excitedly. "What fun! In that case, I think I should like to call it a night."

It had been decided earlier that the two women would share the room while Kay and Arthur bunked with Llamrei. It surprised Jennifer, just a little, that Arthur kept sacrificing his comfort in their favor. He hadn't had a problem that first night they'd met, which Jennifer found rather amusing.

A few minutes later, Morgan and Jennifer let themselves into their designated room. It wasn't much, but it served its purpose. The room was small, with nothing but a bed, a small one at that.

"You have the bed, Morgan," Jennifer bid, already using blankets from Llamrei's pack to set up a little spot on the floor. There was no way the both of them would fit on the bed.

"Oh, no, I couldn't. You take it, please."

Jennifer shook her head, pointedly settling down on her little makeshift bed.

If Morgan offered any other arguments after that, Jennifer didn't hear them, as sleep took her quickly.

The forest grew thick. The dense treetops blotted out much of the sunlight. It was difficult to pick through the underbrush, as her foot caught multiple times on tree roots and fallen, leaf-covered tree limbs. The air was heavy, and an unseen presence hung around her like warm, wet velvet. Her eyes were open, her hands free to reach out in front of her, but connected to nothing.

Odd.

A noise in front of her made her freeze. She held her breath to make out what it could be. She heard nothing more, and so continued on, this time more cautiously.

A breeze picked up around her, starting low at her feet and swirling upward like a tiny maelstrom. It caught in her hair, whipping the strands around her face, blinding her for a moment.

It dissipated as quickly as it appeared, and then silence.

She took another couple of steps forward, and that's when the whispers began.

The voices sounded like children, or perhaps women. Their words were unintelligible. The hair on the back of her neck stood up. A frozen finger crawled down her spine, and she whirled around to and fro, trying to find the source.

When she turned again, she startled at the sudden appearance of Arthur, standing about ten feet away. He looked worried. His lips moved, but she couldn't make out what he was saying over the whispers. As though someone continued to turn the volume dial toward maximum, the whispers grew so loud, she clamped her palms over her ears.

It helped to muffle them only just.

She sank to her knees, curling in on her body as if that would stop the incessant chattering. She looked to Arthur again, trying in vain to call out to him, to make it stop. The worry on his face had grown to terror, but his eyes weren't on her anymore.

They were focused on something behind her.

The heaviness of the air was oppressive now, weighing down on her shoulders and her chest, stealing the breath right from her lungs. It took every ounce of strength to turn, to face whatever was behind her.

Before she could lay eyes on it, the whispers turned into one, unified noise, and screamed.

Jennifer's eyes shot open, her chest heaving from exertion. She pressed her palm flat to her sternum, willing her racing heart to calm. She couldn't remember the last time she'd had a nightmare. Especially not one that scary.

The stress of the journey and the fact she was currently hundreds of years from her own timeline probably would make the body respond in just about any way, nightmares and all.

Yeah. That had to be it.

"Oh, you are awake. I thought I might have to rouse you," Morgan said, appearing from around the other side of the bed. She saw Jennifer's face, and the small smile she'd been sporting fell. "Are you okay?"

Jennifer forced a nod. "Fine."

Morgan didn't seem to want to accept that answer, but nodded anyway.

Jennifer climbed to her feet and got to work gathering the blankets. She hurried from the room before Morgan could leave and headed outside to find Arthur and Kay.

The two men stood just outside the tavern. Llamrei looked rested and ready to go. Jennifer nodded briefly to both of them as she made for the horse, putting the folded blankets in the pack on the mare's back. She took a moment to run her palm along Llamrei's snout, and the horse pushed into the touch. Feeling the softness of the horse's hair and strength in her neck calmed Jennifer's still-racing heart. The warmth from the beast transferred to her, chasing off the icy residue along her spine.

As soon as Morgan appeared, they took off toward the tor.

Soon, they'd reach the end of the Roman road, and Jennifer was curious to see what, if anything, would take its place.

The tor, or hill, was shaped like a cone, and in the present had the ruins of a tower at the summit. It was deceptively steep and a bit hard to climb. Jennifer huffed and puffed as the group crested the top of the hill, the morning sun fully visible on the horizon. She had to hand it to Morgan for her suggestion. The view truly was unmatched. Rolling green hills spanned outward from where they stood, stretching as far as the eye could see. There was something rich about the hues of green in England. Or perhaps it was just the time period. Either way, Jennifer hadn't seen a sight this breathtaking since…well, since she could remember.

"Magnificent," Arthur's smooth voice said as he came up beside her.

Jennifer turned, only to find him half looking at the view and half looking at her. When he realized he'd been caught, he turned his gaze fully to the view.

A small stab of annoyance gripped Jennifer, yet her heart did an odd little flip.

"It's very beautiful," she agreed with a nod.

"I have never actually been up here. Sure, I have passed through Glastonbury a time or two, but I have never made it up here."

Behind them, Kay rambled on and on to Morgan about something or other, and one quick glance over her shoulder told Jennifer the dark-haired woman didn't look thrilled. Jennifer tried not to chuckle.

"What is the most beautiful place you've ever seen?" Jennifer asked, turning her attention back toward Arthur.

Arthur stood in thought for a moment. "Tintagel."

He sounded surprised to have given that answer. She wondered why Tintagel, the place of his birth, would be such a shock.

When Arthur didn't elaborate, Jennifer nodded. "What about Tintagel makes it so beautiful?"

He shrugged loosely. "It's where I was born. It's right on the coast, and the sea is stunning. I suppose calling it 'home' has something to do with it."

"There's nothing wrong with that."

"I know. I just... my mother's family is from there. She... she died there. It is a beautiful place, yet also full of much sorrow."

Jennifer nodded. "That must be hard to reconcile."

Arthur hummed his agreement.

She wanted to press for more information. This was the most he'd willingly volunteered about himself without her prying. But she didn't want to miss out on an opportunity.

"What's at St Michael's Mount for you?"

He looked thoughtful, his hand immediately resting on the pommel of the sword he kept around his waist.

"Hopefully righting a wrong." Arthur sighed.

"What sort of wrong?"

His eyes remained on the horizon, and Jennifer was convinced, based on the tension in his face, that he would turn on his heel and walk away without saying more. She wouldn't blame him. Whatever this was sounded personal. Deeply personal.

Just as Jennifer was about to turn and leave him be, Arthur spoke.

"Many, many years ago, before Rome abandoned the island, an ancestor of mine was sent to defend what we now call St Michael's Mount. According to family lore, he had been a newly arrived Roman military officer sent to prove his worth by defending the west coast against attacks from the Irish. The island had been sacred to the native Britons for many, many years prior, because of a natural well that was believed to be a door to somewhere else. In this well, many offerings were made to the gods to curry favor.

"My ancestor was besieged, outnumbered, and about to lose the island. The story goes he lost his sword, disarmed, and was beaten down by the well. As he lay there on the verge of his demise, he saw the glint of metal in the water of the well. He reached inside, grabbed the hilt, and yanked it from its watery confines. It is said the sword was—is—miraculous because it had no rust or sign of wear, despite the fact it was clear the sword had been in the well for a long time.

"So, with sword in hand, my ancestor was able to rally his cohort and beat back the Irish, all with this special sword. He was greatly rewarded for his valor and victory, and returned to his legion with high honors. He never put the sword back."

"So...is it cursed?" Jennifer asked.

Arthur laughed heartily, a deep roll that made Jennifer's stomach clench.

"You sound like my grandfather. There are those in my family that would believe it is cursed. That because my ancestor took the sword from the well, its wielder has only ever known great victory in battle but also profound personal sorrow."

"And I am guessing you don't believe that?"

Arthur pondered this for a moment, then shook his head. "No, I really don't think so. I believe it is merely a sword, and that its power is only in the minds of the men in my family."

Jennifer felt there was more about it he wasn't saying, but she didn't push.

"But just in case, you're returning the sword to the well and therefore negating the curse?"

The light of humor left Arthur's face. "It was my father's wish it be returned."

Before she could think better of it, Jennifer reached out and settled a comforting palm on his shoulder. "I'm sorry, Arthur. Has he...?"

Arthur nodded. "Just a couple of weeks ago. I left Caerleon so I might do as he wished."

"Jesus, it's not been very long. You should have mourned him longer."

Arthur shrugged, but not to shake her hand from his

shoulder. Indeed, it felt as though he leaned in to the touch. "I did my duty as his son and left. There's...there's nothing left for me at Caerleon now. My uncle Ector, maybe, but no one else. My mother is gone, and now so is my father."

"I am sure your father is happy you are taking the sword back."

Arthur nodded once, his blue gaze looking from the grass-covered hill to her. "My mother's people are the Cornovii. She would tell me stories of how they showed devotion to their gods. Many offerings have been given to a watery depth all over this island, never meant to be touched again. She would never go near the sword while my father wielded it. And she never wanted me to have it. The men in my family that have carried this sword...they were great war heroes, but they suffered many personal losses—wives, children, parents. She used to say there was a price that needed to be paid, and it would reap the payment until it was put back."

"Were your father and grandfather war heroes?" Jennifer asked.

"I suppose they were in their own way. My father's family were from a small population of Romans that remained after the legions left. My father was the first to marry a non-Roman woman, oddly enough. My grandfather was born about twenty years after the last official Roman left these shores. What glory he and my father were able to obtain came from fighting the ancestors of the Saxons currently occupying Kent."

"What happened to your grandfather and father that made them believe in the curse?"

Arthur shook his head. "My grandfather only had one child that reached adulthood—my father. All of the others died before they reached their seventeenth year. As for my father, well, he and my mother were deeply, deeply in love. And she died when I was fifteen. A sickness overtook her.

She never stood a chance. My father blamed the sword, but could never be compelled to rid himself of it. Until he lay dying and made me promise I would bring it back."

Jennifer shook her head, taking a few steps closer. "I'm... I'm so sorry. For the loss of your mother and your father."

He shrugged again. "Sooner or later, we must all say goodbye to loved ones, do we not?"

"Well, yeah, but still...it doesn't mean you can't grieve for them."

"I know," he said softly.

Jennifer finally let her hand drop from his shoulder and looked to his hip where the sword sat. It seemed like any other sword—pommel, hilt, and blade. Hardly a cursed object. "Is this the first time you've used the sword yourself?"

"No, I learned to fight with this sword. I have had need of it only a handful of times since."

"And has it brought you glory in battle?" Jennifer teased.

"No, it has not," Arthur replied, almost ruefully. "But then I have not had the misfortune of being in a large-scale battle. Perhaps that is for the best."

The two stood, looking out from the tor at the rolling green land below for several moments. Jennifer thought of her own parents and legacies she might inherit from them. Would she inherit her mother's compassionate healing from her time as a nurse? Or would she simply inherit her father's construction tools? Jennifer couldn't fathom the depth of importance legacy meant to people of this time. She imagined it had to be of grave consequence, and to an extent, the same could be said of those seeking legacy in her present.

Kay's boisterous laugh and Morgan's trilling giggle shook her from her thoughts. After glancing over at where they stood huddled close together, Jennifer turned to Arthur. "I hope it didn't hurt you."

"What?" he asked, facing her with eyebrows scrunched low.

"Telling me personal things about yourself."

Arthur snorted and shook his head. "Come on, ungrateful wench. We must be on our way."

Any other time, Jennifer might have actually taken offense to being called a wench, but she knew he only meant it in jest. "If you're gonna give me a nickname, at least give me something good."

Arthur stopped midstride, heading for the edge of the hill to begin his descent. Turning slightly, he looked her over, and Jennifer felt her cheeks heating. When he'd done this before, it had been with thinly veiled annoyance and contempt. This time, he was actually *looking* at her. His blue gaze landed somewhere around the crown of her head.

"Red," he said, matter-of-factly. "Does that suit you better?" he teased.

Jennifer reached up, twirling a lock of her auburn curls around her forefinger. No one had ever called her anything else than her name her entire life. Almost as though her parents hadn't believed in silly nicknames or something. But she found she rather liked it. *Red.*

"'Red' is acceptable," she replied haughtily.

"Good. Now, *Red*, get a move on. We must not lose any more daylight."

Jennifer stood in place, watching his height disappear as he climbed back down the hill, thinking on all they'd talked about in the quiet escape of Glastonbury Tor. She took one last glance over her shoulder at the rising sun, and then scurried off to follow Arthur and the rest of their party.

CHAPTER 10

EASTFALL, MASSACHUSETTS - PRESENT

"Has there been any word?" the CEO asked, addressing his question to Dr. Robert Gibbons, Assistant Director of Research and Development, as the pair conducted their daily walk-through of Angylion's various labs, both secret and non-secret. This particular lab currently housed five of the best biochemists in the world, all bent over high-powered microscopes, pens and pencils scribbling notes as they worked.

"None," Dr. Gibbons sighed.

"This month is when she said the book would resurface, is it not?"

"Indeed, sir," Dr. Gibbons replied. "Or so she has claimed."

The two men stopped at one of the workstations, where a Swedish scientist had just sat back and released a heavy sigh.

"Dr. Lindstrom," the CEO greeted.

"Oh, sir, pleasure to see you." Lindstrom smiled slightly.

"Make any breakthroughs?" the CEO asked, his tone nearly joking.

"I believe we are close to clinical trials," the Swede replied, snapping off his latex gloves and tossing them in the nearby trash can. *"The prior trials were...unfortunate. But I believe I am close to perfecting the formula."*

Finally, some good news.

"Don't let us keep you, Dr. Lindstrom," the CEO said, his mouth twitching upward in as close as he got to a genuine smile. The man reached out and clapped Dr. Lindstrom on the shoulder, then moved on. They did not stop at another station, opting only to glance over the scientists' shoulders as they passed. Once they had reached the opposite side of the lab, they stepped out into the brightly lit, sterile hallway.

"Tell me, Dr. Gibbons," the CEO began, scratching at his chin. *"Do you fear our lovely little ally?"*

Dr. Gibbons's mouth dropped open, reading his superior's meaning quite clearly.

"N-no, sir," the man replied.

The CEO arched a dark brow.

"How does she not terrify you?" Dr. Gibbons let out a breath, as though his fear had been a long held secret he could finally get off his chest.

"Because she is a woman, *Gibbons,"* the CEO replied. *"They are all the same, no matter how long they have been alive."*

The assistant director's mouth dropped open again, wider, almost comical.

"Y-you kn-know what she can do, sir," Dr. Gibbons sputtered. *"She is a* very powerful *woman."*

"And I am a very powerful man," the CEO shrugged, waving his hand as though swatting at a pesky fly.

Dr. Gibbons, though agreeing with his boss about his power, was not so sure. Gibbons had been the one acting as a go-between for Angylion and her, dreading every time he had to make that call or arrange a rendezvous. The woman was ancient, though she didn't *look it. And her very presence exuded a heaviness that came after jolting awake from a particularly terrifying nightmare. Every time Gibbons hung up the phone or drove away, he couldn't shake the terror of the sickly sweet sound of her voice fast enough.*

"I-I will reach out to her again, sir. And inquire about the book."

"Good," the CEO replied with a nod. He looked down to glance at his watch and startled slightly.

"Shit, is that the time?"

His face became strained, like his next appointment was something he was dreading. "I must go back to my office. I have to prepare for a meeting with our benefactors."

Dr. Gibbons swallowed thickly, once again thanking his lucky stars he did not have to deal directly with them. "Of course, sir, we will finish our walk-through later."

The CEO nodded, spun on his heel, and walked up the hallway to the nearest exit. The line of his shoulders was taut, already bracing himself for what would come soon.

At least Dr. Gibbons had the slightly better task of liaising with the woman, rather than going through hell to speak to their patrons. He did not envy his boss that endeavor.

With the hairs on the back of his neck standing on end, the assistant director palmed the cell phone in his pocket, taking a few deep breaths before lifting it out and dialing the now familiar number that made him gag in fright anytime it appeared on his caller ID.

CHAPTER 11

MORIDUNUM (AXMINSTER) - CIRCA 500 C.E.

The day passed uneventfully, and when there looked to be no town or settlement in sight as the sun began to set, Jennifer inquired if they would be sleeping on the road that night.

"If we must," Arthur replied, glancing back at her where she walked with Morgan. He and Kay had been up front, waxing poetic about their childhood. She'd heard some rather amusing stories about their exploits. It certainly put this stranger, Arthur, in a new light. "But I do believe we are close enough to Moridunum that if we push on a little farther, we may have something over our heads while we sleep tonight."

Luckily, they were able to do just that.

Jennifer was unfamiliar with Moridunum, but according to Arthur there had once been a Roman fort and settlement there before being abandoned. Now, the native Britons had returned to the land, reclaiming what had once been theirs.

Moridunum was no Bath, not even a Glastonbury. It was a small town with residential structures, and they met not a soul as they came off the road and into the village limits. There were a couple of people out, tending to the livestock, bedding them down for the night. Arthur and Kay briefly stopped to speak to one such person, who pointed toward the town center where a larger building loomed in the near dark, the peaked roof issuing smoke from within.

"What is it?" Jennifer asked.

As they drew closer, more details emerged from the gloom of the coming night. It was as tall as a three-story house, with a thatched roof and a lumber frame. The outside looked almost wattle and daub, and a large entryway stood open, welcoming them.

"It is a temple," Arthur replied quietly, almost reverently.

"Oh," Jennifer breathed. "People are...not Christian?"

Arthur shook his head. "Perhaps they are on the continent where you're from, Red. Rome was, of course, Christian. At the end. But the old gods never left, and in the rural spaces, their presence is as strong as they ever were."

Jennifer nodded, eyes wide and curious as they got ever closer. On her other side, she could feel Morgan tense and then stop. Jennifer looked over her shoulder, and in the light of the fire within the temple, she could see Morgan's face turn ashen.

"Hey, are you okay?" she asked.

"Y-yes... fine..." Morgan stuttered.

Jennifer stepped to her side, looping her arm with Morgan's, and helped guide her forward.

Morgan's gait was jerky, hesitant. She was clearly uncomfortable.

As the group stopped at the threshold of the entryway,

Jennifer peered inside. There were three fires forming a triangle on the edges of the temple. In the middle of the space was a stone statue, tall and skinny. She couldn't make out the features of the roughly hewn surface, but she figured it was humanoid.

Now that they were in the shadow of the temple and in the presence of this statue, Jennifer could feel a familiar energy swirling around her. It was a light caress against her skin, but applied more pressure than a breeze. Her arm dropped from where it clung to Morgan's, and she took several steps forward, as though compelled. Her feet moved on their own, stepping across the threshold of the entry and deeper into the temple. There were stone benches situated around the large, open space, pilfered from Roman fortifications, no doubt. In front of each were smaller statues, some of stone and some of wood. But she couldn't help but move closer and closer to the larger stone figure in the middle.

Jennifer had been so focused on the compulsion, she didn't notice a stooped figure emerging from a darkened corner.

"Welcome, seekers. Please, warm yourselves by the fires."

The soft but strong sound of the woman's voice snapped Jennifer from her trance-like state. She blinked, regaining her bearings.

"Good evening," Arthur spoke, his voice quieter than usual. That hint of reverence had remained. Jennifer recalled what he'd said about his mother, and she wondered if perhaps his mother had instilled in him some level of devotion. "We are traveling to Tintagel and seek shelter for the night. We would be grateful for the chance to stay, and in return, we will make offerings."

"Good lad," the old woman said.

Jennifer searched, and eventually the outline of the woman took shape, slightly hidden by the smoke from the fires and the dim light. What she could see was an older petite woman, clad in well-kept, gray robes, with steel-gray hair pulled back from a thin, yet sagging face. Her hands were folded and rested in front of her.

"My name is Nim. I am the priestess in the care of this temple. The gods are always welcoming of weary travelers, so please, stay the evening."

Arthur bowed his head in thanks. "This is much appreciated."

"Child, please, come in. There is no need to stay in the doorway."

It took a moment for Jennifer to notice that Nim had spoken to Morgan. She'd been stopped in the entry, looking almost stricken at the idea of entering into the confines of this space. Holding her breath, Morgan looked down and watched as she directed, or forced, her foot to step forward. When her body had physically entered the space, Morgan let out a breath in relief, having calmed a little.

"And you are?"

Jennifer startled at the voice so close to her ear. She hadn't noticed Nim coming closer. Now that she had, though, the older woman had emerged fully within the light of the fires, her face clearly visible.

"Vicki?" Jennifer gasped.

Right in front of her stood the near exact copy of her newfound friend back in the present. This woman, however, was older, judging by the presence of deeper and more prevalent wrinkles. It's as if Nim was Vicki's mother or aunt, the resemblance so uncanny.

"No, dear. Nim. As I said," the old woman replied with a curious expression.

"My apologies," Jennifer rushed to reply, taking a conscious step back. "You...you look like someone I know."

The curiosity in the woman's glassy eyes disappeared, and

for a brief moment, Jennifer felt as if the woman were reading her thoughts. Some other emotion passed across her face, akin to recognition. But how could it be recognition?

Nim repeated her question. "Your name?"

"Oh, uh...J-Jennifer."

"Welcome, Jennifer, to the house of the gods. I saw you were curious of Lord Taranis."

Turning, Jennifer finally took in the statue that had drawn her to the center of the temple. The details of the carving were clearer now, that of a bearded man with curly hair. At his feet, as though propped against him, was a round object. Jennifer squinted, leaning closer to get a better look.

It was a wheel. With six spokes.

She pressed her palm to her sternum where the talisman sat against her breastbone. The one that looked exactly like the wheel carved into the stone.

"Taranis?" Jennifer asked.

The woman hummed. "Indeed, lord of the sky, our thunder god. The Romans called him Jupiter."

"What is the purpose of the wheel?"

Nim glanced at the object in question. "It is meant to represent the great wheel in the sky, the sun. How the sun rolls across the heavens, marking the passage of time."

"Interesting..." Jennifer murmured, fingers still pressed to her sternum.

"Come, the hour is growing later and later. Rest by the fire with your companions."

Arthur had settled by one of the three fires with Kay and Morgan. They were passing around some of the bread they'd procured from the tavern before leaving Glastonbury. Nim followed Jennifer, and Arthur shot up, holding out a hunk of the bread to Nim.

"No, no, child. That is yours. But I thank you for the offer. It is I that should be showing hospitality." There was a glimmer of cheekiness in Nim's eyes as she half smiled at Arthur. "What other nourishment might I get for you?"

"I think we have enough of our own stores, Nim, but thank you. I would not wish to unnecessarily take from your own supply."

Nim made a dismissive sound, waving her hand. "Not a problem. But if there is nothing I can get for you, I will be closing the doors for the night and retiring to my own living space."

"Good night," they chorused. Nim hobbled over to the main doorway, shutting it off for the night, and then disappeared back into the corner she'd emerged from, presumably to her rooms.

The four companions settled in for the night, building little sleeping spots around the fires. Arthur and Kay spoke quietly, agreeing to take turns remaining awake for the night. Jennifer turned to Morgan to check in, finding she had calmed.

"You okay?" Jennifer asked softly.

Morgan nodded her head. "Yes, I'm just—"

"It's okay, you don't have to explain."

Morgan sighed, smiling gratefully.

Jennifer dozed to the crackling sounds of the three fires, which seemed to run on their own brand of magic, never dying out, always going.

Always going...

The inky blackness startled her, the light of the fire long since snuffed. The quiet was so eerie, it caused the hair on Jennifer's arms to rise. She couldn't see her hand in front of her face, it was so dark. Rolling over onto her hands and knees, Jennifer stumbled to her feet. There were no sounds, not even of crickets or owls or other nighttime crea-

tures. She couldn't make out the forms of her travel mates, hesitant to move because she didn't want to step on them. It was disarming, to say the least.

The air inside the temple was stagnant, so still that Jennifer startled when she felt the whisper of a breeze on her face.

Then the voices began.

Just like before, a tangle of unintelligible whispers of high-pitched voices, like children whispering behind their hands to each other.

The sound began to grow louder, swirling around her body and burrowing deeper into her head.

Out of the din, Jennifer heard her name.

It was a familiar voice, suspiciously akin to her Grandmother Cassidy. Only she had ever said "Jennifer" in such a Bostonian way.

"Grandma?" *Jennifer called out, unable to hear her own voice over the growing volume of the whispers.*

Jennifer!

Her grandmother's voice came again, this time more urgent, worried.

"Grandma?" *Jennifer cried out, louder this time. How she and the whispers hadn't roused her companions, she had no idea.*

Jennifer, listen to me!

She whirled around, sure her grandmother was behind her.

"I'm listening!" *Jennifer screamed into the maelstrom, the previous breeze now a gale, whipping her hair around her head.* "Grandma, I'm here! Where are you?"

You must return home!

"I'm trying, Grandma, I'm trying!" *Tears streamed down Jennifer's face, her heart beating faster and faster.*

The book! Protect!

Grandmother Cassidy's voice sounded farther away now, as though the whispers were carrying her away. Jennifer stumbled forward, blindly trying to follow.

"What book? Protect what?"

Get the book and go! Danger! Trust! Don't!

"GRANDMA!"

Jennifer's eyes snapped open, her heart pounding an intense beat within her rib cage.

What the hell was that?

Sitting up, she clutched her hand to her chest, willing her heart to slow, to still itself back to calm.

"Are you alright?"

Jennifer jumped, craning to see who'd spoken to her.

It was Arthur, sitting close to the nearest fire. He'd kept it going, while the other two had finally died out.

Taking a steadying breath, Jennifer climbed from her makeshift bed and ambled over, taking a seat across the fire from him. She pressed her fingertips to her eyes, trying to shake the fog of sleep.

"Just a bad dream," she replied.

"Ah. I am sorry."

Jennifer shrugged. "They can't be helped. They just happen. But thank you."

Arthur nodded, tossing a twig into the fire.

"You've asked me about my home, but have not told me of yours," Arthur said after a moment of quiet.

"Not much to tell," Jennifer replied, carefully picking her words. "It's a small...village. I've lived there my entire life. My mother and father are there, as is my brother. It's a good place. Woodsy, quiet."

All true aspects of Eastfall, there was no doubt.

"It sounds lovely," Arthur said genuinely. "Do you...have a husband waiting for you back home?"

Jennifer couldn't help it—she laughed, then promptly clamped her hand over her mouth to silence herself.

Arthur looked stricken.

"Did I—?"

"No, no!" Jennifer waved her hand, giggling into her palm. "No, I'm sorry. I just... you sound like my mother." She gasped a breath, then asked coyly, "Are you asking for a reason, Arthur?"

His eyes widened again.

"What? Oh, uh, no, I was just—"

"It's okay. I'm teasing you."

If it weren't for the warm glow the fire gave off, Jennifer would've sworn Arthur was blushing.

"I did not mean to pry, I just..." He trailed off, as though realizing it'd be better for him to just stop.

Jennifer laughed again, then stood. "I'm going to let you get a handle on yourself while I go answer nature's call."

She made her way across to the door and slipped out into the cool night. Everyone in the village was abed, the quiet reminiscent of the dream she'd just had. Still reeling from it, Jennifer wondered if it had truly been just a dream or something more. A week ago, she would've thought it was just random firing of the neurons in her brain. But now, she wasn't sure.

Jennifer chose the copse of trees near the temple to do her business. At this point, she didn't even bat an eye at peeing in the open.

Finished, Jennifer began to walk back toward the hut, but before she could reach the door, a gritty hand clamped over her mouth, and a strong arm banded around her waist, immobilizing her.

Her scream was muffled by the hand, gripping so tightly her jaw ached. Jennifer kicked out her legs, struggling against the iron hold.

"Stop struggling," came a rough voice at her ear. The breath sent a shiver of fear down Jennifer's spine. It wasn't a voice she recognized, and had a similar tonal cadence as the

Saxons that had held her hostage in Avebury. She wasn't going to let that happen again. So she threw her weight around as furiously as she could, kicking out her legs, trying to scream round the muzzle of the accuser's hand.

The cracked entry of the temple was mere feet from where she fought against the man. Teasing her, taunting her with the promise of safety. She knew if Arthur heard her, he'd come running immediately.

The man began to haul her backward, and Jennifer saw her window closing rapidly. If she didn't do *something*, she'd never make it to St Michael's Mount. The memory of her dream came back in a flash, her grandmother's frantic voice warning her.

Suddenly, the hold on her tensed, and for a long, heart-wrenching moment, Jennifer thought he might be preparing to snap her neck. But then, the arms fell away, her would-be captor's body falling slack to the ground. Jennifer wheeled around to see Morgan, looking a little green around the gills, holding a thick branch aloft.

"Gods," Morgan breathed, dropping the branch like it was a slippery snake.

Jennifer looked down to see the man stiffen and stay motionless on the ground. Out of an abundance of caution, Jennifer lurched forward and grabbed Morgan's arm, towing her back to the temple's open door. They both burst inside to find Arthur still sitting by the fire, this time with Kay. The two men looked up, concern falling across their faces as soon as they saw them. In a moment, they were on their feet, knives drawn and already halfway out the door.

Following behind them, Jennifer gasped when they reached the spot the man had occupied, but was now empty with no trace of him in sight.

"What happened?" Arthur asked, as he looked around corners of the closest shelters.

"I was just trying to pee, and this guy grabbed me. I tried to get free, but thankfully Morgan hit him on the head."

After a few more minutes of searching, the two men circled back around to where Jennifer and Morgan stood.

"Sorry, he is probably far from here now," Kay said to Jennifer. "Did he say anything to you?"

Jennifer shook her head, her heart finally coming down from the fright. Between nearly being nabbed again and the dream, she was surprised she hadn't had a heart attack. "No, he just told me to stop struggling. That's it."

"This is the second time this sort of thing has happened to you, Red. What aren't you telling me?" Arthur asked, looking at her with suspicion. Jennifer didn't much like it, or what he might be implying.

"Nothing!" she yelled, before remembering she didn't want to wake anyone. "This is as much of a shock to me as it is to you. I have no idea what they want with me."

Kay looked as though he wanted to say something but thought better of it. Arthur continued to look at her skeptically, and for some reason, his skepticism made her feel as though she'd disappointed him in some way. It was odd to think she didn't want to disappoint him.

"Let us get back inside." Arthur motioned toward the open door of the temple. "We should rest a little more. It will be dawn soon, and we will continue." He brushed past Jennifer to get back inside, as though dismissing her. Jennifer's chest clenched, hoping she hadn't lost the only ally she felt she'd found since arriving here.

CHAPTER 12

ISCA DUMNONIORUM (EXETER) - CIRCA 500 C.E.

Jennifer hadn't been able to sleep much more, instead tossing and turning on the little pallet she'd made for herself. At dawn, the foursome set off, thanking Nim profusely for her hospitality.

"It was a pleasure," Nim had said, touching the hand of each of them as they filed out of the temple. Jennifer had been the last to leave, and when Nim didn't let go of her hand, she was forced to stop.

The older woman seemed different in the stark light of day, but the resemblance she had to Vicki was still so uncanny.

"I dreamt of you last night, child," Nim had said softly, so only Jennifer would hear. "Of an older woman too, a grandmother perhaps? She was adamant I warn you not to trust someone. She couldn't tell me who. Be mindful of who you trust. Do so, and you will make it back home in one piece."

Jennifer had been too stunned to do anything but nod. What were the odds she would dream of her grandmother, and so would Nim? Jennifer had given the gnarled old hand in hers one last squeeze, then scurried to catch up to her travel mates.

A little more than an hour into their travels, the group came upon a small village. The buildings visible from the road were empty, devoid of life. It was as if it was a ghost town, abandoned. Jennifer looked to Arthur.

"Perhaps they are in their fields," Arthur pondered.

"I think we should keep going," Morgan said, worried.

The quiet of the village certainly was disarming.

Perhaps it was because they'd only been in bustling towns, or only ever arrived in the evening when it was time to tuck in for the night. There hadn't been an in-between thus far. But Jennifer felt they should have seen at least one person, perhaps a woman hard at work weaving, sitting outside of her home.

But there was no one.

Arthur looked to Jennifer and then to Kay. The two men exchanged an unspoken word, nodded, and diverted from the path to walk amongst the thatched-roof huts.

Jennifer made to move forward, but Morgan clasped her shoulder in a surprisingly strong grip.

"I do not have a good feeling about this," the woman said, worriedly.

"I'm sure it'll be okay," Jennifer replied, and set off after the men with Morgan on her heels.

As they ventured farther from the road, the quiet continued.

Until it didn't.

The villagers, or so Jennifer assumed, had gathered in a

clearing in the woods bordering the village. Large oak trees created a half-moon boundary, and the space was at least fifty feet wide. The crowd was packed in, watching something Jennifer couldn't see. At times, they hollered in agreement or opposition. She found Arthur in the crowd and pushed through to get to his side. Arthur looked over his shoulder, saw her, and beckoned her nearer.

What the villagers were observing finally became clear.

An older man stood in the center of the half-moon of oak trees, his arms crossed over his chest. His long hair was a shock of bright white, and his beard matched. Another man, probably in his early middle years, shouted, passionate, with his arms waving, pointing toward a little boy. His hair was a chestnut brown, not unlike the boy's he gestured toward.

The child sat on the ground, hunched in on himself, eyes filled to the brim with tears. Not a drop fell, and Jennifer's heart ached. He looked betrayed. His full mop of brown curls fell onto his forehead.

"What is happening?" Arthur turned to one of the villagers. The man glanced Arthur's way but didn't seem surprised to see a stranger. Perhaps being this close to a road afforded them many visitors.

"Counsel has been called. The chieftain will pass judgment," the villager replied. Morgan had slipped to Jennifer's side, having found her and Kay, who stood on Morgan's other side.

"What has the man done?" Arthur asked, because it did seem as though the middle-aged man was defending himself.

"Not him. His son," the villager replied. "Poor Galahad. His mother died last winter. She was our green woman. Our healer. Galahad hasn't been the same since. His father has accused him of putting a curse on their crop."

After momentary shock that the boy's name was *Galahad*, Jennifer scoffed. "That's ridiculous."

The villager shook his head. "No, not entirely so. The boy is...strange, to say the least. His mother must have taught him...things."

The father's ranting and raving continued for another ten minutes, citing all of the instances where things had gone awry in his household, all due to his son's enchantments. After he had finished, the chieftain, the older white-haired man, gave Galahad, the young boy, a chance to defend himself. But the boy couldn't have been more than twelve or thirteen. What could he say in defense of himself from his father? That boy could easily be one of her students in a couple more years, and he reminded her of the days before she started teaching, when she substituted in a middle school.

Galahad could have been any of those children.

No matter how many times he tried, Galahad could not manage words for his defense. Perhaps he felt it to be not worth his efforts? Based on the reactions of the people in the crowd, Jennifer could tell most supported the father.

"Come on," Jennifer murmured under her breath. "Say something."

But Galahad didn't speak, finally allowing the tears to flow.

"Very well," the chieftain declared, backing away from father and son. He stepped off to the side where he spoke to an older woman and two other older men. They deliberated only for a few minutes, before the chieftain nodded and walked back into the clearing.

"Judgment has been reached. The boy will be executed and face final judgment in the Otherworld."

The crowd erupted into jeers, all directed at that poor boy.

Jennifer's heart sank.

She couldn't let that happen. He was just a *boy*. It was

ridiculous to think he'd cursed his father's lands, or believe his lack of defense was an admission of guilt.

She turned to Arthur, finding him looking on, his brow furrowed. Jennifer could practically see the wheels turning.

"Arthur, we can't let them kill him," she said, soft enough for him to hear, but not loud enough for the villager next to them to hear.

"I know," he said, but looked torn. Jennifer imagined he'd seen this kind of justice meted before and respected it was the custom and tradition of the people. But she could tell he'd also seen *in*justice meted this way and had never been able to act on it.

The throng of villagers parted, and an imposing figure strode through the path. He appeared around the same age as the boy's father, but a lot harsher in appearance. A makeshift cloth had been wound around his head, covering his left eye. He clutched a wicked looking axe in his right hand, and she watched as Galahad took notice, finally realizing his fate. His chestnut curls bounced as he shot to his feet, but another villager had already anticipated this and clamped down on his shoulders to halt his escape. The villager spun Galahad around, and she knew to the day she died, Jennifer would never forget the utter terror on that boy's face. The crowd screamed and shouted, suddenly ravenous to see an execution. To see Galahad's all too young blood paint the lush green grass of the clearing.

"Jennifer," Arthur spoke. He hadn't ever really used her name before, and only recently dubbed her with a nickname. This was serious. She turned to him, his expression vacant but set. He'd caught Kay's eye, and after glancing at Kay, Jennifer noticed whatever was passing between them was agreed upon. "Take Morgan. Start walking back to Llamrei; go as quickly as you can."

Her heart thudded in her chest, and of their own accord,

her hands reached out to grasp his sleeve. "Wait, no, what're you going to do?"

"I need you to do as I say," he said, his tone emotionless, the legendary war chief emerging. "Hurry back to Llamrei with Morgan, then lead her down the road. I will meet you farther south. Do you understand?"

Jennifer's mind whirled as the crowd began to close in, the execution nearly approaching. Her heart beat so quickly in her chest she thought she might be going into cardiac arrest.

"Do you understand?" Arthur hissed.

Nodding her head, Jennifer took one last look at Arthur. His eyes pleaded with her, but the rest of his face looked entirely impassive. He had a plan, but he needed her to be with him on this plan. She could do that. Couldn't she?

"I understand," she breathed, then turned to grab Morgan. Both women fled toward Llamrei just as the executioner brandished his axe in the air to the roar of the crowd.

The sun traveled with her, Morgan, and Llamrei, though perpendicular to their course. The rush back to the horse hadn't taken long, and then they'd set off down the road as instructed. It was easy to follow the path, as it was well-worn and a perfectly good road, despite not being a Roman one. They must've walked for hours, and she vacillated between confidence Arthur and Kay would find them and pure fear they wouldn't.

"We should take a break, huh, girl?" Jennifer murmured to Llamrei, who seemed as agitated as she felt. The horse could tell something was up, and was wary at the absence of her master. "Break?" she asked Morgan, who nodded. Jennifer led the horse off the road a handful of yards, until she found a fallen tree to sit on and rest.

Just as she'd seen Arthur do, she tied Llamrei's reins around a tree, but left enough give for the horse to graze, which she happily did. A good distraction for her.

Jennifer pulled a water skin from one of the bags draped across Llamrei's back and sat, taking small sips.

What would she do if Arthur didn't find them, or...or make it? What would she do to keep them alive?

Jennifer *had* to continue on. It was necessary if she ever wanted to get home.

Luckily, Arthur had discussed the route to St Michael's Mount a little with her previously, and if need be, she could find someone in Tintagel to help take her the rest of the way. She'd make it to the Mount on her own. But she hadn't set out to the Mount alone. Arthur had a purpose for going there, just as she did, and he should be with her when she arrived.

For the first time since she'd found herself there, hot tears pricked at the corners of her eyes. She hated the helpless feeling crammed in her gut, holding tightly like a vise.

She could do this. She had Llamrei with her, and with Llamrei, Jennifer felt she could make anything happen.

Swiping at her cheeks, she rid herself of tears. She'd made it before Arthur, and she could make it after.

A far-off snapping of branches plucked her from her thoughts. Jennifer's head shot up, but she couldn't see the cause of the sound. She sat still, palming the handle of the knife Arthur had given her. Her heart stuttered when another snap came, the steady *thud thud* of steps. Could it be an animal? Or a person? Perhaps a villager from that awful place that deemed it necessary to murder children.

Jennifer stood, slowly stepping her way to Llamrei. Morgan shot her a quizzical look. In response, Jennifer put a finger to her lips. The sounds of leaves crunching and the snapping of twigs grew closer and closer, and if she squinted,

Jennifer could see a dark, hulking shape in the forest. It seemed misshapen, at least eight feet tall. What kind of creature existed here looking like that? Llamrei didn't seem spooked by the noises. She'd paused in her eating, sniffed the air, but then went back to her task. Whatever it was didn't alarm her.

The thing grew closer and closer, and Jennifer's heart thudded in her ears. It was within easier eyesight now, and would be revealed by the waning sun any second...

Out of the trees stepped Arthur with the boy, Galahad, clinging to his back and Kay following right behind them.

Jennifer pressed a palm to her chest, willing calm for her racing heart. She let out a thankful, relieved sigh.

A couple of weeping cuts slashed across his forehead and cheek, but other than that, Arthur looked none the worse for wear. In fact, he seemed to already be on friendly terms with the boy, who smiled as his arms wrapped tightly around Arthur's neck. Kay, too, appeared to only have surface injuries, and must have just finished telling Galahad a hilarious joke, because the boy roared with laughter.

"*Jesus*, what the hell happened?" Jennifer breathed as she came out from around Llamrei. Arthur caught her gaze, and he smiled widely, brightly. It was disarming, and for a moment she wished she could slap it right off his face.

"Worried about me, were you?" he teased with a wink.
Cocky bastard.
Yep, definitely a slap.

"Oi, no concern for me?" Kay asked, feelings hurt.

"Of course I was worried about you, Kay," Jennifer soothed, stepping up to him to pat his cheek. Kay grinned widely, then stepped closer to Morgan.

"Were you worried about me, Morgan?"

Morgan rolled her eyes. "Hardly."

Arthur and Jennifer laughed at Kay's dejected, sad face.

"Galahad," Arthur began, calling Jennifer's attention back to the boy. "This is Red, er...Jennifer. Jennifer, this is Galahad."

Jennifer's demeanor changed immediately, lips forming a kind smile. "Hi, Galahad," she greeted, stepping closer to help Arthur remove the boy from his back.

"Hi," Galahad said shyly.

"Don't be scared, lad. She's harmless." Arthur grinned.

Jennifer glared but couldn't much argue.

"Are you hungry?" she asked the boy.

The curls flew as he nodded furiously, and Jennifer led him over to meet Llamrei. After they'd settled on the tree trunk, with Galahad happily munching on a hunk of bread, Jennifer asked Arthur again about what had happened.

"Not much to say." Arthur shrugged, then winced as she tried to dab at his cuts with a clean, wet cloth. They were shallow, thankfully. No way could Jennifer act a surgeon. "The minute you and Morgan disappeared, Kay and I charged the executioner. There was a bit of a scuffle, but nothing we couldn't handle. Then I just grabbed the lad and we ran as fast as our legs could carry us."

"Did they chase after you?" Jennifer asked, satisfied with what she could do for the wounds.

"For a ways," Arthur said. "But they gave up after a while. Probably didn't think it was worth it. They just let the boy go. Suppose they figured that as long as he was out of their village, then all the better."

Jennifer glanced behind her at Galahad, who had heard every word but didn't react.

"That's okay," Jennifer said. "You don't need to be where you're not wanted. But you're wanted right here, Galahad."

The boy's gaze turned from the bread to Jennifer, and that was when she noticed his dark blue eyes. They were wide and searching—searching for lies. But he would find none.

"Aye, Galahad," Arthur agreed. "We'll keep you with us until we can find a good place for you."

Those beautiful eyes filled with tears, but this time they weren't born of fear, but of gratitude.

"Thank you," Galahad said, so softly Jennifer had to strain to hear.

"Of course." She grinned, reaching out to ruffle her hand through his hair. The locks were soft and suited his boyish face.

With what little sun they had left, their group, now five, continued farther down the makeshift road toward Tintagel. Arthur had already warned her they would have to make camp on the road that night. At this point, the idea of it didn't seem to bother her.

As they walked, Jennifer fell into step with her usual partner, Morgan. The woman had been unusually quiet the past hour or so. Jennifer had noticed the side glances Morgan shot toward Galahad. The looks were borderline contemptuous, though Jennifer had no idea why.

Galahad had taken quite the shine to Arthur and Kay. His shorter frame was flanked by the older men, and they talked about whatever it was men of this age talked about. Jennifer couldn't help but smile, and got more and more confused as to why Morgan would look at Galahad in such a way. Jennifer got the impression any older male that took notice of Galahad would be received well by the boy—no doubt a modicum of respect and gentleness was all he had ever wanted. Jennifer continued to watch Galahad closely, noticing him smile more and more as Kay joked with him, playfully shoved him, much like an older brother.

"The road is no place for a child," Morgan murmured, walking in step with Jennifer.

"Are you saying we should have left him in that village to die?" Jennifer asked, looking at Morgan incredulously.

"Yes." She paused, as though realizing how callous it sounded. "No, but he is not our responsibility. The ways of justice here are sacred. A decision was reached, and now we may be in danger. It is quite possible they may come looking for him. It's an unnecessary risk taking him on."

Jennifer's eyebrows furrowed. "Well, the alternative is worse by allowing an innocent child to die when we could have prevented it. We did the right thing, Morgan."

Morgan didn't reply, but muttered something under her breath Jennifer couldn't make out.

"Do you know something we don't?" Jennifer pressed, reaching out to grasp Morgan's shoulder. She tensed under the touch and shrugged off Jennifer's hand.

"No, I am just stating the possibilities," Morgan grumbled, then lengthened her stride to get away from Jennifer. This time, she caught pace with Arthur, and they fell into conversation. Jennifer thought back to the moment when Morgan had been spooked to enter that temple. Perhaps Morgan was just someone who respected tradition. Jennifer, in turn, could almost respect that, but not at the expense of a child's needless death.

She watched as Morgan walked and talked with Arthur. At one point, Morgan tossed her dark hair over her shoulder, laughing at something Arthur had said, then playfully slapped him on the shoulder.

Jennifer gritted her teeth, the blatant flirtation grating. Arthur laughed along with her, which only made Jennifer more annoyed.

Get a fucking hold of yourself, she chided, recognizing the emotion for what it truly was—jealousy—which made her want to kick dirt and throw rocks. She did *not* get jealous.

It was then Jennifer noticed Galahad glancing surreptitiously toward Morgan, and the look that danced across his face was one of wariness, like he could see something beneath the surface no one else could.

Jennifer filed this observation away for later.

They stopped another hour later when the light of the sun had half faded into evening. It didn't take long to set up camp a ways off the road and hidden amongst overgrown trees. Jennifer volunteered herself and Galahad to gather wood for a fire. The boy was happy to have a useful task to complete.

As they picked their way through the undergrowth, Jennifer watched Galahad in his singular aim to find sticks and logs for fuel. From what she'd seen so far, he was a handsome boy and so very sweet. He clearly had a good heart, and why his father hadn't seen that, Jennifer would never know.

"I'm glad we have you with us, Galahad," Jennifer said, arms full of the sticks Galahad had found. The light of day was dimming more and more by the minute.

"I am glad to be with you," Galahad replied.

"Galahad," Jennifer prompted, touching him lightly on the shoulder. He tensed slightly, almost cringing away. She'd noticed he did that whenever someone else initiated touch. She removed her hand quickly, shooting him an apologetic smile. "I'm sorry you had to go through what you did. I hope you know that no matter what those people believed, there is nothing wrong with you."

Galahad's eyes were glued to the tips of his shoes, toes scuffing the leaves that peppered the forest floor.

"Galahad..." Jennifer said softly.

The boy lifted his head, finally looking at her but not looking her in the eye. His gaze was glued to a spot on her shoulder.

"I know, Jennifer," Galahad said, and suddenly he sounded older than his preteen years. "My mother always told me I was worthy. No matter what anyone said about how different I was, that I was a special person."

Jennifer smiled. "Your mother is a smart woman."

"Was."

Jennifer's smile fell. "I'm sorry to hear that."

Galahad shrugged loosely, like it wasn't a big deal, losing a parent.

"I can hardly remember much about her," he explained. "I just recall the sound of her voice."

"Still, it's never easy to lose someone close to you."

Galahad nodded and remained silent, resuming his duty of finding kindling for the fire.

It was interesting to know that, though she taught high school, she knew middle schoolers. Galahad was so like the middle schoolers in her time. Yet, entirely different. There was a wisdom about him you didn't find often, even in adults in her time. He'd seen things. One could tell just by watching him ponder his thoughts and then articulate them.

When they had a sufficient amount of wood, they returned to their camp, and soon a fire blazed. While they were away, Kay had procured a couple of small rodents for fresh meat. When he offered Jennifer a skewer, she tried so very hard not to grimace, but politely refused. Instead, she made a meal out of the cured meats she still had in her pack from Emrys, along with the supply of berries and nuts.

As they sat around the fire and chatted, Jennifer watched Morgan closely.

There was more to this woman, she was coming to realize. After her reaction to Galahad's rescue, there was something there Jennifer didn't quite understand, and wasn't sure it was something she liked.

CHAPTER 13

ON THE ROAD - CIRCA 500 BCE

When Jennifer's eyes snapped open that night, after only a few hours' sleep, she wasn't even surprised. There hadn't been a dream this time around, and judging by the stillness around her of their little camp, there wasn't something externally that might have roused her. Regardless, this now common occurrence was leaving coincidence territory and charging full steam into deliberate territory.

Sighing, she sat up, her eyes immediately going for Galahad first. He was right where he'd been when he fell asleep last night, two feet from where she'd rested her head. Turning, she saw Arthur sleeping three feet away, lightly snoring.

Who she didn't see were Kay and Morgan.

Jennifer sat up straighter, looking around within the circle of light the subdued fire emanated.

There was no sign of either of them.

She quickly got to her feet, and then paused, listening.

First, there were the night sounds, insects and the rustling of small creatures. And just when she was about to turn to rouse Arthur, Jennifer heard it. The distinct sound of larger creatures bustling around in the undergrowth. No doubt the wayward members of the party.

Jennifer began walking in the direction the sounds came from, wanting to make sure everything was all right.

The sounds she'd heard became more distinct the closer she got.

Soft, whimpering moans.

Jennifer stopped in her tracks.

She heard the moans again, but couldn't quite tell if they were moans of pain or moans of something else.

Heart beating wildly in her chest and echoing in her ears, Jennifer continued to creep forward. Oddly, there was a light up ahead, and when she thought she was close enough, Jennifer rested her back against a tree, then cautiously peered around it.

What she saw nearly made her gasp in shock.

Kay's back was to her, his trousers down around his ankles. Morgan was wrapped around him, arms clinging to his shoulders and legs gripping him like a vise around his waist. The rhythmic thrusting was a giveaway, and once she'd processed what was happening, Jennifer clamped her hand over her mouth to stop any sounds from coming out and quickly pressed her back to the tree once more.

The moans continued, feminine and masculine wrapped around each other, filling the space between them and Jennifer.

She shouldn't be surprised, truly. The level of flirtation Kay had been laying down had been thick. Jennifer was not a prude, nor did she begrudge others of their pleasure, but this act of intimacy seemed so out of place for this moment. Then again, Jennifer's situation had certainly put sex far from her mind. She just couldn't imagine anyone wanting it *out here*. It was just...odd.

Jennifer was not a voyeur at all, but something compelled her to peer around the tree again. There was something off about Morgan. Like her face had become harsher somehow, or her eyes darker, perhaps. Her lips were right by Kay's left ear, and they were moving, whispering. But it didn't sound like normal whispering between lovers. It sounded like the whispering Jennifer had heard in her dream. Indeed, she reached down to pinch herself to make sure she wasn't dreaming.

She wasn't.

The whispering continued, but unlike in her dreamscape, they didn't grow louder and more intense. However, the closer Kay got to reaching his release, the faster Morgan whispered in his ear. And the faster she whispered in his ear, the faster he jerked his hips forward, driving into her until he tipped over that edge, crying out in ecstasy.

And in that moment, a smile spread across Morgan's face, unlike any Jennifer had seen on the woman. It was almost feral. Primeval. It made the hairs on the back of Jennifer's neck stand up. The smile unnerved her so much, she crept away as quickly as she could, back to the camp and back under the blankets she'd been sleeping under.

Jennifer lay there, as still as she could, waiting, straining to hear.

A few minutes later, Kay and Morgan returned.

They giggled and murmured to each other, before quieting down. Kay remained awake, as it was his watch, and Morgan settled back in beside Jennifer.

It took a few tries, but Jennifer willed herself to sleep, though her thoughts spun with what she'd witnessed.

According to Arthur, the journey to Tintagel was one of the longest legs.

Which meant she had too much time to think about what she'd seen the previous evening.

Every interaction between Morgan and Kay was cataloged and analyzed. Every glance, every brush of their persons, every word spoken between the two. Nothing seemed different or off. They were a little friendlier to each other, maybe, but other than that, Kay was his normal boisterous self, and Morgan continued to be slightly shy but talkative.

Throughout the day, Jennifer quizzed Galahad on his life thus far, to distract herself. His mother died when he was younger, and had protected him fiercely from his father. It seemed since the day he was born, Galahad's father scorned him. Galahad had been born early, weak, and the village midwife didn't believe he'd last the night. But he did, then the next night, and then the night after that, and continued to slowly thrive through his early years.

"I do not have friends," Galahad responded in answer to Jennifer's latest question.

Unfortunately, this did not surprise her. Knowing adolescents as she did, how they could be so cruel to each other, it didn't shock her to know Galahad had no friends. But surely someone other than the boy's mother had cared for him? How could they not? In the short time she'd known him, Galahad proved to be surprisingly insightful for his age, intelligent, and direct with a very kind heart.

Jennifer also noticed Galahad never met her gaze, nor did he meet Arthur's or Kay's, and definitely not Morgan's, despite the fact he seemed to have grown comfortable with them through the course of the previous afternoon and current day.

Galahad fidgeted often, zigzagging along the entire width of the pathway, sometimes bumping unintentionally into Jennifer, Arthur, Kay, and poor Llamrei. Morgan, though, he seemed to intuitively avoid.

They camped on the side of the road again that night, then continued the next morning as soon as the sun had risen. Jennifer didn't witness anything odd, thankfully, and she could almost pretend as though it hadn't happened.

"Galahad?" Jennifer called out to the boy, now well into their second day traveling away from his village.

Galahad had been in front, swinging a branch like a sword, fighting an unknown enemy. Jennifer didn't know much about technique when it came to using a sword, but he looked like he knew proper moves.

At the unexpected sound of his name, Galahad jolted and swung around, nearly knocking Kay in the stomach with the stick. Kay didn't seem perturbed, just sidestepped the kid and continued up the road, deep in conversation with Morgan.

"Whoa, it's okay. I was just saying your name." Jennifer grinned, hands raised, nonthreatening.

Galahad looked embarrassed, having jumped so dramatically. He stopped in the road, allowing for Jennifer to catch up, and then fell into step next to her.

"Sorry," he mumbled, low enough she didn't process right away that he'd spoken.

"It's okay, Galahad," she reassured him. "I just had a question for you."

Galahad brightened, a little grin on his face, and nodded.

"In your village, did you have a lot of gatherings?"

His face screwed up in a scowl for a second. "Yes. For holidays. But I did not attend many. Which only made me stranger to the others. I do not like being around a lot of people."

Jennifer nodded silently. "I'm not one for crowds either."

As an educator, she'd learned some of the signs in children of disabilities that might impact their learning. Galahad exhibited some pretty indicative signs of a sensory processing disorder or something else.

It was no wonder the people in his village shunned him and believed him to be inhuman, different. He didn't act as they did or follow the norms of their society as they did. His mother had been the only one to understand him, as mothers do. His father had never given Galahad the chance.

Jennifer knew in that moment she wouldn't be able to leave this time until she knew Galahad lived with someone that would keep him safe and take the time to *know* him.

"Hey Galahad," she said, after a long period of walking in silence.

The boy looked to her again.

"You interested in learning how to use a real sword? Something tells me if you ask him real nicely, Arthur here might teach you some things."

Arthur glanced back from where he walked next to Llamrei, looking stunned for a moment, not expecting Jennifer to volunteer him for such a task.

"Sure," he murmured. When she shot him a fierce glare, Arthur's eyes widened. He cleared his throat, and this time sounded more enthusiastic. "Yes! Why not? We should stop for a bit anyway, take a rest!"

Jennifer almost choked on laughter, but they tugged Llamrei off the rugged pathway. For the past few miles, all that had surrounded them were dense woods and the distant sound of the coastline. Now, they pulled off into a nice grassy spot, where Jennifer laid out a blanket from the pack on Llamrei's back, tied the horse's reins around a nearby tree, and sat. Morgan took a section of blanket next to her.

"Must we stop for this?" she asked with a sigh.

Jennifer glanced sideways at the dark-haired woman, that odd feeling returning, causing the hairs on her neck and arms to stand up as if in warning.

"Why not? We've been walking for a long time. We all could use a break," Jennifer supplied.

Morgan huffed, her dark gaze landing on Arthur, as he rooted around for a stick to match against Galahad's. Jennifer didn't like the way Morgan eyed him, as though he were her next conquest or target.

Llamrei continued to graze on the lush green grass, and Kay stood near them, casually propped against a tree, looking all too amused at the idea of Galahad learning a few tricks of the trade.

The temperature felt comfortable for a late spring day, even in the blazing sun. Jennifer noticed she'd not once felt overheated, even after so much walking. The English springs, at least, were similar across centuries.

For the next hour, Arthur taught Galahad basic forms. Then he moved on to defense techniques, all with Kay interjecting his own wisdom. Jennifer watched, charmed by how gentle Arthur was with Galahad, and how patient. Arthur made a great teacher, though she figured he would rather eat his own boot than show this gentler side of himself. Morgan, on the other hand, appeared bored, sulking beside Jennifer and picking at her nails.

Arthur moved on to some offensive techniques, and suddenly, he was yanking off his tunic shirt and letting it fall to the ground beside him.

Of course Jennifer had seen half-naked men before.

She was a red-blooded cis-woman with two functioning eyes.

Dear God, how did a man look *that* good?

His shoulders were wide, and the entire expanse of his chest and back was lightly tanned skin, littered with paper-thin scars of cuts long past. Muscles rippled in his arms as he swung the stick to demonstrate proper form.

"You are catching flies," Morgan muttered, nudging Jennifer with her elbow.

Jennifer blinked, realizing her mouth had actually fallen open. As stealthily as she could, she swiped her hand across the corners of her mouth.

Just in case.

"You are quite good at this," Arthur said to Galahad. "Have you learned much before?"

"Sort of," the boy replied. "I watched my father training with others in my village. I was never invited to learn."

Jennifer wanted to go back to that village and burn it to the ground. The look of sadness and loneliness in Galahad's eyes gutted her.

"You mean to tell me you have only *watched* others?" Arthur asked.

Galahad nodded. "I would watch, and then practice in the woods on my own."

"Well, regardless, you have the makings of a fine warrior."

Galahad beamed, and Jennifer felt pride in the boy swell. Arthur sounded genuine with his praise, something he only ever was, it seemed.

"Jennifer, you should learn!" Galahad declared.

She shook her head furiously, waving her hands back and forth. "Oh no. No, no. No way. I don't need to learn how to use a sword. I'd end up chopping something important off."

"You have that knife," Kay piped up. "You should at least learn how to hold it properly."

Jennifer shook her head again. "No, thank you."

Arthur snorted. "Galahad...I think Red might be scared."

Jennifer straightened.

"Oh, come on, darling," Kay tacked on. "I think you could really use a lesson. Or two."

Galahad, clearly picking up what Arthur was trying to put down, and spurred by Kay's declaration, stood at attention. "I think you might be right, Arthur. She's *afraid*!"

Jennifer scowled, an expression that could rival one of Galahad's finest. "I'm not afraid!"

"Then get up," Arthur goaded, motioning to the space in front of him.

"Yeah, come on, Red. Show Arthur how it's done!" Kay hollered.

She grumbled as she got to her feet, unable to back down from this challenge.

Jennifer had never been one for athletics or really any sort of sport, having preferred tabletop role-play games and other more academic and intellectual pursuits. It wasn't that she couldn't play sports, but rather...well, she lacked the coordination and grace for such things. Sports had always been fun to *watch*, not *do*.

Galahad handed her the stick he'd been using as a sparring sword, then went over to take her place on the blanket next to Morgan, as far as he could get from her. In turn, the woman shied away from the boy, tensing.

Jennifer, palms sweating and preoccupied, looked up to see Arthur smirking. She didn't much like that expression. He stepped over to her, gingerly grabbing the wrist of her hand that held the stick.

"The sword is meant to be a part of you," he said softly. "Like an extension of your arm. As if you were born with the sword in your hand. Your grip should be firm, but flexible."

Arthur wedged his own stick between his arm and side, then used both free hands to position Jennifer's grip. She ignored the heat that flared in her gut and across her skin at his touch, and stalwartly did not acknowledge the way each swipe of his fingers sent little jolts up her arm.

When Arthur seemed satisfied that she demonstrated the proper grip, he stepped to the side and held his stick aloft to demonstrate.

Bless him, but Arthur's patience quickly ran out with her, much to the spectators' glee.

Multiple times, Jennifer whacked herself on the leg or nearly hit her head, and Arthur sported a sore thumb from a particularly masterful hit on her part. Meanwhile, Galahad almost fell backward from laughing so hard, and even Morgan cracked a small smile.

"I just...I'm not good at this," Jennifer huffed in frustration after she dropped her stick trying to execute a couple of forms.

"This is not hard!" Arthur griped, like he'd never met someone he couldn't teach to accomplish at least one form combination.

"Yeah, well, it is, so...tough luck for you," Jennifer sneered.

"I have never in my life met anyone so spectacularly bad at this—"

"Gee, thanks for your confidence, sensei," Jennifer grunted sarcastically.

"Sen what?"

"Never mind," she grumbled. "Next thing you'll say is I'm living proof women shouldn't be fighters."

"No, actually. I would not say that. I have known several women who were better fighters than you, for sure."

Jennifer clenched her teeth, grinding them in irritation, as behind her, Kay howled in laughter.

"And I'm sure they found your charm irresistible."

"Actually, they did," Arthur preened.

"That was not meant to sound sincere!"

"Well, I cannot help it if women find me charming!"

"You're so infuriating!" Jennifer exclaimed.

"And you are a nag!"

Jennifer bristled, her fingers tightening around the stick. "You are an arrogant, emotionally stunted prick who wouldn't know how to treat a woman properly even if she told you how!" She threw the stick to the ground for emphasis and stalked over to Llamrei, who was the only other female close by that had any sense. The mare turned her head to Jennifer, sniffing her distress, and butted her muzzle against her arm. Jennifer reached for her, brushing her palm slowly and gently down Llamrei's head and back up to her ears.

Silence reigned in the clearing except for the sounds of the insects and the soft breeze through the treetops. Kay, looking very uncomfortable, urged Galahad into the woods to search for some safe things to eat. Morgan followed after them.

Jennifer couldn't remember the last time she'd been so annoyed that she snapped. Not even with her students, not even with her mother who worried her to death. Something about Arthur got under her skin at times. Just crawled underneath and would not leave.

Tears of frustration threatened to spill. She turned her head, blinking rapidly to rid herself of them.

A throat cleared behind her, grabbing her attention. It was a deep sound, and judging from the perceived height of origin, it was Arthur. Jennifer jerked her head away, trying like hell to keep her emotions from being seen.

"What?" she grunted.

"Can we talk, please?" Arthur asked.

"Why? What more do you have to say?"

"I want to apologize."

Jennifer stiffened in shock, but she didn't look at him.

"Well, that's surprising," she said, sarcasm lacing her words.

"Can you please look at me?" he begged, his words soft and not demanding.

Jennifer didn't want to look, out of spite. She didn't want to give him the satisfaction. Sighing, she turned to face him, but didn't have to like it.

"I am...sorry," Arthur spoke again, the words forced. He didn't apologize often. "My behavior toward you has been less than...well, good."

It was right on the tip of Jennifer's tongue. *Ya think!* But she held it back. Truth be told, she hadn't exactly treated him in a stellar fashion. Jennifer's gaze softened, and for the first time, perhaps, she saw *him*.

Arthur.

The man.

Perhaps she'd put an unfair layer of high expectations over him. Since discovering he could be the historical Arthur—the one historians and literary folk had sought for so long—Jennifer had put him on a pedestal based only on her ideal image of Arthur. That image was tainted a little by her own interpretations of the man that embodied the perfect ruler, warrior, and noble man.

Jennifer had dwelled so much on this that she became disappointed when he turned out to be just like any other man. But how unfair was it of her to cast such a judgment? He *was* just a *man*, and the legendary Arthur was too close to perfection to be reality.

"I haven't exactly been cooperative," Jennifer grumbled.

Thankfully, he held back the laughter she saw swimming in his azure eyes. He could live a little longer.

"You asked for my help," Arthur said. "You asked for it, and I did not want to give it to you. My father's passing... It was the last ill event in a long line of ill events that comprise my life. I did not want to be so bitter, but despite my best efforts, it seems I have failed. You asked for my help, and I just wanted to be left alone to complete this final task my father gave me and perhaps find some closure at the end. I did not need a complication."

Jennifer could understand that. After Lynn's horrible murder, she was forced to recognize her own mortality. What had happened to Lynn Rickerson might have happened to anyone. She missed her friend terribly, and also couldn't imagine the pain Arthur felt. He'd lost his mother so young, and then his father, and whatever else he hadn't mentioned.

"Thank you."

Arthur, having taken to toeing at a rock on the ground, jerked his gaze up, not expecting to hear such a sentiment from her. Before he could say anything else, Jennifer plowed on.

"I don't think I've ever said it. Thank you for allowing me to come with you. Thank you for your help. Thank you for saving me from those Saxons. I have... There are very important answers I need at St Michael's Mount. Traveling with you and having your protection has kept me alive. So...thank you."

Saying the words "thank you" was not the difficult part for Jennifer. In fact, she often *overly* thanked people. The hard part had been admitting she needed the help badly, or she would not have survived this long.

Arthur looked thoughtful for a moment, then nodded. "My mother and my father both taught me it was the proper thing to do to help someone in need. I have forgotten this, it seems. I needed to be reminded. So, thank *you*."

It was Jennifer's turn to nod her acknowledgment.

"Happy to help. Now, could you put your damn shirt back on?"

In their intense discussion, Arthur had grown closer, so close Jennifer could feel the warmth radiating from him and smell the light scent of sweat and something that was purely him.

All she had to do was reach out a few inches, and she'd touch bare skin. Jennifer couldn't help but wonder if it was as soft as it looked. She swallowed thickly, shifting her gaze to meet his. There was something unreadable in his eyes. His pupils were dilated, and there was an intensity there she hadn't seen in them before. Her breath caught as Arthur leaned in, and God help her, but she couldn't stop herself from leaning to meet him.

Galahad took that moment to pop up between them, exclaiming, "We found food! Are you hungry? I'm hungry!"

Jennifer and Arthur startled apart, the spell effectively broken.

She scrubbed her palm down her face, trying her best to shake off whatever *that* had been.

The man was dangerous without his shirt on. Hell, he was dangerous with it on, that was for sure.

CHAPTER 14

After traveling a little farther up the road toward Tintagel, the group decided to make camp for the night and begin again at first light. Much like other nights since arriving here, Jennifer found she couldn't sleep. She lay on her makeshift bed next to a dozing Morgan, staring up at the stars while listening to the pop and sizzle of their small campfire. Galahad lay close to Kay, both sleeping like the dead, which meant that those restless movements were Arthur keeping the first watch.

After a while longer of staring at the sky and willing it to lull her to sleep, Jennifer rolled to her side and stood, tired of the hard, lumpy ground digging into her back. She made for the fire, and sat on the opposite side of where Arthur sat.

She loved a good open fire. How she longed to have a bag of marshmallows to roast, but unfortunately, there were no s'more makings in sight.

"You should sleep," Arthur said softly.

"Can't," Jennifer replied.

They grew quiet, only joined by the hoot of a distant owl

and the call of a nighthawk. Even the insects had gone to bed, it seemed.

"Let's play a game," Jennifer blurted after too much silence.

Arthur looked across the fire at her curiously.

"What sort of game?"

"Well, I guess it's not really a game... We should take turns asking each other questions."

Arthur stiffened. "I think I would rather throw myself across this fire than answer any more of your questions."

Jennifer rolled her eyes. "You are so damn dramatic. You afraid to come clean about something?"

"No," Arthur shifted. "I just have never seen myself as anyone interesting."

Oh, my dear Arthur, if only you knew, Jennifer thought.

"Come on. They can be really easy questions."

"You are not going to let this go, are you?"

"No. I'm bored and I can't sleep. Why not be entertained?" She shrugged.

"Okay," Arthur capitulated.

Jennifer rubbed her hands together with glee. "I'll start out easy on you... What was your mother's name?"

"Ygraine," Arthur replied.

That odd white-noise sensation preceded Arthur's answer, and Jennifer wondered for a moment what the translation would have been. Sometimes, even with someone she'd been around for a while, like Arthur, her brain still had to auto-tune to pick up the same frequency. Annoying, but she had gotten quite used to it.

"That's a beautiful name," Jennifer commented.

Arthur nodded. "She was a beautiful woman, inside and out."

When he didn't offer any more about her, Jennifer figured it was time to push along. "Your turn. Ask me a question."

Arthur thought for a moment. "If you could be an animal, which would you be?"

"Oooo, good one." Jennifer grinned. "I would have to say... a turtle."

Arthur snorted. Before he could ask, Jennifer continued, "Because I can just pull myself into my shell and avoid danger. Or, you know, people in general. What about you? What animal would you want to be?"

"Is that your next question for me?"

Jennifer nodded.

"A bear. I would want to be a bear. Fierce, and I would also love to be able to sleep through the winter months."

It was Jennifer's turn to laugh. She clamped her hand over her mouth to muffle the sound.

"Alright then. What do you want to ask me next?"

"Do you like having a sibling?"

"I take it you don't have a sibling, but yes, I suppose it's kind of nice to have a sibling." Jennifer shrugged.

"My mother nearly died giving birth to me. My father was not keen on risking it again."

Jennifer nodded.

Sure, there were times when she would love to be able to trade her brother in for a better model, but you get what you get, so you have to deal with the hand you're dealt.

"What was your father's name?" she asked.

Arthur pulled a face. "Why are you fascinated with my mother and father's names?"

"You just asked me a question. It's not your turn."

Arthur huffed, crossing his arms over his chest, and sat back against his pack. "My father's name was Uther." Again with the tuning white noise.

"*Now* it's your turn."

Arthur sat in thought. "Do you really have *no one* at home waiting for you?"

Jennifer recalled this same question, back in that temple in Moridunum.

"No, I don't have anyone. Just my parents."

Normally, admitting that out loud would almost be a point of pride for Jennifer, but in the moment, it kind of hurt. The loneliness. That sense of connection she'd been missing for so long.

She shook her head to clear her mind of such thoughts. Now was not the time to wallow in that level of pity. "Tell me a little more about what Caerleon is like?"

He shrugged. "It's home. My father's family has lived there for many, many years. A family of Romans. After my mother gave birth to me in Tintagel, we moved to Caerleon. But now, other than my father's brother Ector, there's nothing there for me. So, I suppose, after I get rid of this sword"—here, he patted the pommel where the sword rested next to him—"I will pick somewhere else to call home. Maybe Bath, or London."

Jennifer couldn't imagine that sense of listlessness. Not having a place to always come back to, to call home. Since finding herself hundreds of years in the past, she'd been evaluating a little more every day what "home" meant to her. She'd felt Eastfall to be a prison at times, a place that kept dragging her back.

Time traveling to an unknown and rather frightening place certainly put things into fresh perspective.

"Are you scared? Being so far from your home?" Arthur asked.

Jennifer nodded. "I am." *Scared shitless*. "But, at the same time, I'm not."

Oddly enough, that was the honest truth.

Jennifer woke up in fear every day, wondering what would happen to her as she drew nearer to St Michael's Mount. And every morning, she would roll over, get to her feet, and see

Arthur feeding Llamrei, Galahad and Kay play wrestling together, and suddenly, she didn't feel as scared.

For a while, Jennifer and Arthur went back and forth with their questions, covering everything from their childhoods to their future aspirations. Because Arthur didn't want to return to Caerleon, his journey to St Michael's Mount had a twofold purpose—return the sword and scout for a new place to call home. Bath was on the list, of course, but he'd also heard about Cadbury and a hill fort there that may be in need of warriors.

They conversed well into the morning, until the first rays of the sun peeked through the treetops.

By the time the party struck out on their continuing journey to Tintagel, Jennifer felt she and Arthur had reached a level of comfort neither had expected. Indeed, it felt more than that. Perhaps they'd cultivated a friendship of a sort.

Finally, after days on the dusty makeshift road, the traveling band arrived in Tintagel.

It'd been included on the Excalibur Tours travel itinerary, toward the end of the trip. To see it now, before civilization could taint it, was truly a magnificent sight.

It was incredibly lush and verdant...everything was just so green. Buildings scattered the headland, and the Atlantic Ocean crashed against the craggy cliffs below.

"*This* is where you were born?" Jennifer asked Arthur, in awe, as they stood at the town center. It was a bustling trade town, with native Britons and continental natives alike selling their wares and creating a living.

"I was. Tintagel has been a place for trade with the rest of the continent for a few generations now. My mother was the daughter of a Cornovii chieftain..." Arthur replied, his voice far away, reminiscing. "Her family has been here for as long as there have been people here."

Jennifer placed a comforting palm on Arthur's shoulder. There were many things he was not saying, but he had no need to. She could feel what this place meant to him, both good and bad. This place was his mother. And with his mother gone, it was painful to be here.

"Do you have no family left here? You talked about your father's family in Caerleon. What of your mother's?"

Arthur shrugged. "I do not know. As far as I have been told, all close family had died."

"Well, we just have to make the most of our time here. Only fun things!" Jennifer said, attempting to lift his spirits. She glanced over her shoulder to try and get the rest of the party on board. Kay and Morgan had their heads bent close to each other, chatting, and Galahad was swinging his stick about.

"'Ey!" she exclaimed, causing Kay, Morgan, Galahad, and a few people nearby to jump in response. "Look alive, people! We're having *fun* while we're here!"

She looked back to Arthur once the troops appeared mustered. He gave her a small smile, but in that little gesture, he was grateful.

"Come," he said, straightening his spine. "Let us pick up some supplies before the market closes for the day."

The town center teemed with local residents going about their usual daily acquiring of essentials. It was one thing to study history in school, but it was another to experience it. Jennifer always told her students that people in history weren't as isolated as some would assume. Even after the Romans had left Britain, and well before they'd arrived, native Britons had been trading with merchants from as far away as the Mediterranean. In fact, some believed the Phoenicians had made it all the way up coastal Europe to the British Isles.

If Arthur hadn't informed her of the presence of such exotic wares, it was evident in the types of traders Jennifer saw as they wandered the stalls, and in the products they sold. Textiles, metal goods, olive oil... It was quite extraordinary to see.

"Amazing," she breathed, as they passed a stall with pungent-smelling spices. Galahad stuck close to her side, his head swiveling everywhere, trying to take in what he could.

For the next hour, Jennifer and Galahad watched Arthur and Kay haggle with a few of the merchants for food and other essentials needed for the rest of the journey to St Michael's Mount. Morgan had wandered off on her own, promising to meet up with them later at the local tavern.

There were a few occasions where merchants recognized Arthur, despite the fact he hadn't been in Tintagel for years. She watched as they would look at him as though they knew him from somewhere, and then they would glance to Arthur's waist, seeing the hilt of his sword. Recognition would dawn, and they realized who they were talking to. Arthur, his father's son, wielder of a legendary blade. And Arthur, his mother's son, princess of the local tribe.

Jennifer tried and tried not to be charmed and endeared by the way Arthur spoke to old family friends, but she found herself smiling anyway.

"I'll give you a fantastic deal on this gown. Perfect for your wife!"

Jennifer felt her face heat, and Arthur floundered.

"Oh, no...she's—"

"And I have the perfect thing for your son as well! A lovely tunic for special occasions!"

A strangled laugh punched from Jennifer's chest, and Kay guffawed. Arthur scratched at the back of his neck in embarrassment, and Galahad just grinned widely.

Arthur begged off the merchant, giving his undying thanks, then ushered his "wife" and "son" up the street.

It was when Arthur suggested heading to the nearest tavern that a voice called out behind them.

"If it isn't the odorous, Roman slag!"

Arthur froze, tensing. She could feel him vibrating in mounting ire. Kay's hand immediately went to the hilt of his sword, as he muttered to Arthur, "Just say the word."

Jennifer's heart rate kicked up, wondering if her constant worries of a fight with scoundrels had finally come to pass. Galahad looked just as worried, glancing from her to Arthur and back again.

"You must have big balls showing your face around here."

Then, inexplicably, the anger bled from Arthur's body, and Jennifer would swear she heard him...chuckle?

"Better big balls than a tiny brain," Arthur called over his shoulder.

"Better a big cock than a tiny brain!" the rough voice behind them called back, laughing.

Arthur whirled around, and a grin erupted. "You swine! I was certain I was going to have to kill someone today." He lurched forward, enveloping the newcomer in a strong-armed hug. Jennifer, Galahad, and Kay turned, confused.

A man, as dark as Arthur was light, returned the embrace, an equally large smile on his ridiculously handsome face. The stranger pulled back, clapping Arthur's shoulders. If the day had not been so sunny, his smile would have lit the darkest of spaces. A mop of curly, black hair cascaded around his ears, and a scrutinizing, but not unkind, pair of dark eyes gave Arthur a once-over. His nose looked as though it had been broken at some point in his life, but hadn't healed unattractively. A strong jaw rounded out his features, as well as his impressive height and bulk. As soon as Jennifer had finished her assessment, those dark eyes leveled on her, then Kay, and then down to Galahad.

"Oh, and who do we have here?" the man asked, his focus on her. His voice came out in a smooth intonation, having been distorted for a moment as her FM radio tuned into his dialect.

"These are...uh...my travel companions, Jennifer and Galahad, and this is my cousin, Kay," Arthur replied.

"A *travel* companion, you say?" the man asked, words laced with innuendo, looking pointedly toward her.

Arthur ignored his friend's implications. "Everyone, this is Gawain, an old friend of mine."

Jennifer faltered only a moment in her steps as she approached, taken off guard at the declaration that this was *Gawain*. Truly, she shouldn't be so shocked anymore.

Gawain was perhaps one of the oldest figures in Arthurian lore besides Arthur himself.

Galahad stuck close to her side, out of fear for himself or protection of her. Knowing what she knew about the boy now, it was likely the latter. Which was, of course, incredibly sweet. She'd quickly come to learn that Galahad had a fierce protective streak of those he knew and cared about.

"It's a pleasure to meet you, Gawain," Jennifer greeted as magnanimously as she could manage, feathers still ruffled at the implied nature of her company to Arthur. Funny how it wasn't insulting with the merchant, but it felt like a lascivious insult from Gawain.

"Oh, the pleasure is all mine, Jennifer." Gawain smiled again, though this time, the gesture was vastly different, dripping with charm. And while she did have to admit it worked only just, she brushed off his efforts. "And you too, lad." At least he was genuine with Galahad, offering a more friendly smile to the boy. Jennifer felt Galahad relax a little.

Gawain and Kay had a tense moment, staring, which must

have ended positively because the two fearsome men nodded at each other in silent respect.

"What brings you back to Tintagel?" Gawain asked Arthur.

"I am on the road," Arthur said. "For St Michael's Mount."

Understanding dawned in Gawain's eyes. "You mean to return it?"

Arthur nodded. "My father passed not a few weeks past. It was his last wish."

Gawain reached out, placing a comforting palm on Arthur's shoulder. "I am sorry to hear it, my friend."

"Thank you," Arthur said softly. "He has longed to find my mother again in the next life. He is with her now."

Gawain gave a curt nod.

"And what of you?" Arthur pressed on. "I did not know you had remained in Tintagel? You had always talked of going to the continent to make a name for yourself."

Gawain shook his head, his arm dropping to the side. "I was there for a while. Made it to Spain, if you can believe that. But I usually return around this time of year to check on my brothers and their brood and the rest of my family. Even the most wayward of traveling souls finds time to return to their origins." He looked pointedly at Arthur.

"I know." Arthur hung his head slightly. "I have been tending to my father for so long, but I am glad to have returned even for a moment."

Jennifer felt as though she should back away with Galahad, leave the two childhood friends to catch up without them listening in. But before she could, Gawain turned his attention to her, Kay, Galahad, and then back to Arthur.

"Come! We shall toast your father!"

A few minutes later, the five were gathered around a small table in the local tavern, nursing ales, except for Galahad who had brought a water skin. Though the alcohol was vastly different from its modern iteration, Jennifer had gotten used to the bitter taste. At least the streams, lakes, and rivers they'd encountered along the way were potable.

Arthur and Gawain chatted while they drank. Jennifer half listened, mainly examining their surroundings. There were few patrons for this hour in the day, but no less good for people watching. A surly-looking man sat in a dingy corner, hunkered over his own mug of ale, while another man openly flirted with the tavern girl. Jennifer stifled her laughter in her beer as the tavern owner came out to shoo the man off from his daughter with a few harsh words.

"I should like to come with you."

Jennifer turned back to Gawain and Arthur's conversation just in time. Her head snapped around, finding a determined expression on Gawain's face.

It appeared Arthur was just as surprised by the offer. He glanced at Jennifer. With a teasing glint in her eye, she raised an eyebrow.

More strays, Arthur?

"Well, I—" he began.

"Oh come on, it'll be like old times! Plus, it would do you well to have an extra sword with you on the road. They're becoming more and more dangerous these days," Gawain reasoned.

He could only mean Saxons. Or even the Irish, since they currently sat on the western coastline. But the Saxons had been a looming threat, and everyone was talking about rumblings in the east.

God, she hoped she made it back to Avebury without being caught in the middle of what was brewing.

"Surely you have better things to do," Arthur argued.

Gawain shook his head, curls bouncing to and fro. "Of

course not. I am here visiting my brothers. I have nothing but time."

Arthur looked to Jennifer, the question there in his eyes. It surprised her he would even consult her. He'd not done so before, and she figured he never would. She was his tagalong, after all. He was doing *her* a favor, not the other way around.

Jennifer nodded. He then looked to Kay.

"Why not?" Arthur shrugged, lifting the mug to his lips to take a swig.

Gawain clapped his hand on the table loudly, causing Jennifer to jump in alarm along with Galahad. He at least had the decency to look sheepish. "Ta! It will be as though we never parted!"

Arthur laughed.

And their party grew by *yet another*.

Seriously, it'd be the Fellowship of the Ring before Jennifer knew it.

CHAPTER 15

TINTAGEL - CIRCA 500 C.E.

Later that evening, Morgan rejoined them in the tavern, much to Kay's pleasure and, upon introduction, Gawain's. Jennifer thought she'd die laughing at how much Gawain fell all over himself when she arrived, scooting over to make room for her at the table.

Not unhelpful, however, as he had promised them all space to sleep for the night in his brother's barn.

"Gawain seems interesting," Jennifer commented to Arthur as they sat at a different table for the evening meal. Gawain and Kay, who had become fast friends as well, had taken Galahad close to the musicians set up in a corner. Morgan stood at the bar, chatting with a handsome young man.

The tavern owner's daughter came close to where Gawain sat with Galahad and Kay, and Gawain yanked her into his lap, much to the girl's delight. Galahad looked absolutely shocked at the display, and Kay laughed raucously. Jennifer went to stand, but Arthur's hand shot out to grasp her wrist.

"He's harmless," Arthur said in amusement, then laughed as the tavern girl slapped Gawain across the face and walked away. Galahad looked absolutely chuffed, hiding his laughter behind his hand, while Kay nearly fell out of his chair. Gawain, to his credit, didn't look insulted. In fact, those dark eyes started scanning the room for another conquest.

"Harmless, huh?" Jennifer asked wryly. "Galahad's too young for—" But she stopped herself.

Jennifer nearly forgot she was no longer in the twenty-first century. Things were different here, especially average lifespans. No doubt children Galahad's age would be soon married off, starting lives of their own away from their families. Gawain *would* be shameless with women, showing Galahad just how to woo them.

... and failing.

"I've known him since I was a boy. Before I could even pick up a training sword. It may not seem like it, but he and his brothers are some of the best men I've ever known," Arthur said, wistfully, seemingly thinking of his childhood.

Jennifer wondered if Gawain's brothers were named Agravaine, Gaheris, Gareth, or any combination of the three. She supposed they would find out soon enough.

"It's good to have friends like that. Someone who will be on your side," Jennifer mused. She thought about Lynn, how she'd been that kind of friend for her.

"It is," Arthur agreed. "I would not mind having you on my side."

Jennifer shivered. Though the words weren't particularly seductive in any way, they were endearing, and entirely the truth. She shifted in her seat to look at him, making out his features in the dim light of the tavern. She was struck, once more, by how handsome he was. How wise he was for such a young man. How kind... She hadn't even needed to convince him to rescue Galahad. He'd already been planning. And now, the boy and Arthur could barely be parted, even after a mere few days on the road.

Arthur returned her gaze, the crystal-blue hue of his eyes unnerving her, but yet she found comfort in them. They'd never meant her harm, not once, though perhaps a bit of antagonism at first. She felt as though they could laugh about that now, if they wished.

Slowly, to give her ample opportunity to move it, Arthur reached for her hand, laying his palm atop where it rested on the table. The reaction was instant, heat igniting in her hand and creeping up her arm. She twisted her wrist, allowing her palm to press against his. Arthur threaded his fingers through hers, and she couldn't fight back the blush creeping into her cheeks.

"I am on your side," Jennifer said, so softly, but loud enough for him to hear. It didn't matter though; it was as if their surroundings had disappeared, quiet falling around them despite the busyness of the tavern.

"As I am on yours," Arthur breathed. "Wherever I need to go, or whatever I need to do, I shall get you to the Mount. That is a promise."

Jennifer's chest ached at his declaration.

"Thank you, Arthur," Jennifer whispered, squeezing his hand. "I would not have made it here without you."

"Nonsense," Arthur teased with a sly smile. "You would have. And God help anyone who got in your way. You would've nagged them so much, they'd let you go."

Jennifer shook her head and heaved a mighty sigh. "You had to cheapen the moment."

Arthur's smile this time turned more genuine, full of warmth. "Apologies."

Their eyes locked, and Jennifer nearly gasped at the storminess of Arthur's gaze. They had turned darker, a heat simmering behind them. Swallowing thickly, she didn't know who had moved first, but it didn't matter. Slowly, as if afraid the other would disappear with sudden movements, their heads inched closer and closer, Arthur's gaze staring intently at Jennifer's lips. Any other time, she might've slapped him for such boldness. But not now. God help her, but she wanted it. The man was incorrigible, but he seemed to understand her regardless. He didn't cut her down, didn't diminish her strengths.

And yet he lived in the fog of time. In the liminal space history couldn't reach, a space she'd never be able to reach again when she went home. Jennifer would never see him again. She couldn't stay. She couldn't bring him with her. He'd remain here, and she'd return to the present. And if she wasn't careful, she'd end up leaving a piece of herself here with him.

Arthur was so close she could feel his soft fan of breath on her skin. Her heart thudded so loudly, she was sure he could hear it.

Just as their lips nearly met, a shout and the shattering of a table broke through the spell around them, jerking them back to their reality.

Gawain had another tavern patron in a headlock, and Kay held the headlocked patron's friend at bay. Galahad cheered on from his seat next to the musicians. Jennifer felt her eyes widen from the spectacle.

"Get him out of here!" bellowed the tavern owner, in reference to the man Gawain had in a chokehold.

"Gladly!" Gawain called back, yanking the man around to head for the entrance. Kay gleefully escorted the friend out as well.

Arthur sighed heavily, squeezed her hand once, then stood. "I'd better help him."

Jennifer watched Arthur jog after Gawain. Galahad sidled back up to the table and sat in his abandoned seat, clutching his stomach.

"What happened?" Jennifer asked as Galahad calmed down from his wheezing laughter.

"The arse felt it was a good idea to put his hands on Willow. Gawain dealt with him."

Jennifer rolled her eyes. "What about Willow and Gawain?"

"They know each other." Galahad shrugged. "It's a game they play. The cad thought he could have a go at Willow. She didn't take to it none. Gawain took care of him."

But of course Gawain did. At least the guy was defending Willow.

"Gawain said I could live with one of his brothers," Galahad blurted after a few minutes of silence.

The thought of not having Galahad along for the rest of the journey to St Michael's Mount struck something inside of her.

"Oh? Are you going?"

Galahad shrugged. "Haven't decided. Gawain said I could think on it the rest of the trip. The brother he has in mind has a child near my age."

Jennifer let out a breath. "Good. You should really think on it."

Galahad nodded, though his eyes were guarded. "I will, Jennifer. Promise."

Another hour later, and the group followed Gawain from the tavern and toward the outskirts of the main part of the town.

GUARDIAN OF TIME

Galahad was draped across Kay's back, dead to the world asleep. Morgan walked with Gawain, and Jennifer and Arthur lagged toward the back.

With one hand, Arthur led Llamrei, while the other idly brushed against Jennifer's hand as they walked. Sometimes, he would catch her finger with his and they'd share a smile.

Eventually, the group came to a cottage on the edge of a large field. In the doorway stood a woman, with a baby on her hip, and a man.

"Gods above...is that Arthur?" came the voice of the male, a slightly higher-pitched version of Gawain's voice.

"Best believe it is, Gareth!" Arthur shouted back, the outburst causing Galahad to stir on Kay's back.

Jennifer couldn't make out the man's features, but he walked out to meet them, pulling Arthur into a bear hug. Gareth was slightly shorter than Gawain and thinner. Once in the light of the open doorway, Jennifer saw the same dark hair and dark eyes that looked nearly identical to Gawain.

Gawain and Arthur helped make quick work of introductions, acquainting their group with Gareth, younger brother to Gawain, and Gareth's wife, Lynette. The baby on Lynette's hip was a little girl, one of four, named Orla.

Jennifer guessed this might be the brother Gawain had offered to Galahad as a place to stay.

The young couple led the group to show them their sleeping arrangements for the evening. After only a few minutes, Jennifer couldn't help but like them both a lot. Lynette was extremely maternal, and both she and her husband were so kind.

The barn wasn't a barn in the traditional sense. It was more of an oversized stable, with two stalls for horses and an open space for woodworking. The open space was where they made their makeshift beds for the night, and indeed there already was one set up, presumably Gawain's. The space was cozier than where they'd been sleeping for the past couple of nights. They settled Galahad first, who didn't wake even after being jostled around.

Gareth offered them a chance to come into the main house to sit for a spell, but Arthur politely declined on the basis of needing to be up with the sun in order to continue on to St Michael's Mount. Arthur promised to catch up with Gareth another time, and the young couple bid the traveling group a good night and headed inside.

Jennifer found herself walking through a familiar hallway, walls lined with baby pictures and ancient black-and-white photos of the old country.

It was her Grandma Cassidy's house.

In the distance, a record played, something old-timey, invoking the time of Victory Gardens and war bonds and maintaining the home front for those off to war. Jennifer followed the sound, stepping cautiously, though she could navigate the house blindfolded.

"I'm in here, dear!"

Jennifer froze.

"Stop fartin' around and get in here!"

Jennifer took a cautious step forward, and then another, following the sound of the voice to the back porch.

After Grandpa Cassidy died, Grandma had screened in the porch, making a quasi-greenhouse out of the back deck. Her grandmother had always loved plants, talked to them, nurtured them, pruned them...like they were her children. Jennifer hadn't inherited her grandmother's green thumb. She couldn't even keep a cactus alive.

It'd been devastating for her grandma to move from the home she'd been in for over thirty years, even more so that she had to leave behind a bunch of her beloved plants. Now, in her facility back home, she only had maybe five or six.

"Ah, there you are!"

Jennifer peered around a bushy fern and found the familiar site of her grandmother with a spray bottle and some pruning clippers nearby. She wore an apron with dirt stains, and her steel-gray, curly hair was up in a bun. It was odd. She didn't look as she did now in the present, but instead looked as she had when Jennifer was in high school.

"Grandma?"

"I finally got through, Jesus, Mary, and Joseph. I never thought I'd get to talk with you."

Jennifer blinked. "I'm sorry?"

"Mother Mary, look at you. All grown up," Fiona Cassidy gushed.

This was so far beyond any dream Jennifer had experienced yet. It felt too real. Like it was happening, yet the hazy quality at the edges of her vision said otherwise.

"What's happening?"

"There's been a barrier around you for days, my dear. I've been trying to get to you, to warn you..."

Jennifer stepped fully around the fern and approached her grandmother. Fiona had been grooming a plant with small, white flowers. Jennifer remembered some of the plants' names, and judging by the trumpet-like shape of the star flower, these were stephanotis.

"You're at the nursing home, though...back in Eastfall," Jennifer replied dumbly.

"Well, I suppose I am," Fiona sighed, shaking her head. "Could've sworn I told your father to smother me before he did that..."

Jennifer snorted. "Grandma, you're still as sharp as a tack. You're pretty independent still."

Fiona crossed herself. "Thank God."

The old woman shook her head. "Goodness me, here I am lollygagging over something so stupid. Jennifer, you need to—"

And as though someone pulled the plug, all sound fell away. Fiona's lips moved, but Jennifer couldn't hear a word. Realization dawned on Fiona's face, and she glared around her as though to some unseen entity.

Reaching for the stephanotis, Fiona plucked a couple of the blooms from the greenery and shoved them into Jennifer's palm. Then, she tried to mouth something, slowly, yet Jennifer still couldn't make out what she was saying. She shook her head, only frustrating her grandmother more.

As though resigned to the circumstances, Fiona leaned in, stood on her tiptoes, and pressed a loving kiss to Jennifer's forehead. The last thing she remembered was Fiona's sad smile.

And then she was awake, yet again, in the dead of night. The pitch dark curled around her like a thick blanket, and all Jennifer could do was sigh.

Because of the relative safety of where they were, Arthur, Kay, and Gawain had opted against watches throughout the night. When Jennifer sat up, no one else was awake.

As quietly as she could, she tossed the blanket aside and stood, stretching her arms up over her head.

It was only then that she realized her hand was clenched around something. Judging by the lightness of the object and the softness, Jennifer had one guess as to what it was. Pulse hammering in her ear, she practically ran outside where the moon lit the sky just enough for her to make out the shape of the stephanotis flowers in her hand.

"What the fuck?" she whispered beneath her breath.

"Everything okay?"

Jennifer jumped, nearly out of her skin. She whirled around to find Morgan looking at her with a worried and curious expression on her face.

"Oh, uh...yeah, just...needed to get some air."

Morgan nodded, skeptical. "Okay, if you say so..."

The dark-haired woman began to turn back toward the barn, but before she could take a step, Jennifer blurted, "What were you doing out in the forest with Kay? The other night?"

That scene had been playing in her mind for days. Something about it had needled and needled at her.

"So you were watching?" Morgan asked, giving away no emotion.

"I woke up and saw you were gone. I got worried and went looking for you."

"You do not seem like the type to fault a girl for her desires," Morgan said, again not giving anything away.

"Normally, I'm not. Hey, you want to sleep with someone, do it safely and responsibly. But whatever I saw...it didn't seem that way."

As if lifting a mask, Morgan's entire face and demeanor changed. She didn't seem the somewhat shy, reserved woman anymore. She stood taller, chin held high, a confidence and power in her shoulders and eyes that Jennifer hadn't seen before.

"I suppose I am not as discreet as I thought." She sighed, shaking her head.

"What did you do?" Jennifer asked, taking a step back.

"Oh, a quite lovely thing. Would you like to see a demonstration?" Morgan grinned, then spoke again, but this time in a language Jennifer didn't know and, for some reason, her internal translator couldn't translate it. That odd whispering cadence began, along with a slight wind as though the voices were carried on it, a harbinger of what was to come. Morgan spoke a few sentences, then waited.

But they didn't have to wait long.

At the entryway to the open barn, a shape appeared. Despite the scant lighting, the tall, thin figure could only be one person.

Kay.

The whispers grew louder, then suddenly stopped, as did the breeze.

"Isn't he lovely?" Morgan spoke, an awful smile spreading across her mouth.

Jennifer took a step back, ready to bolt.

However, as soon as she did, Kay took a lurching step forward. It was as though a part of him was fighting whatever hold Morgan had on him.

"I would not try to go anywhere, if I were you," Morgan warned.

"Who the hell are you?" Jennifer breathed.

"I am me, Jennifer," Morgan replied, as though trying to soothe a spooked puppy. "You have nothing to fear from me."

"I don't believe that for one second..."

"You truly do not have to be afraid of me, Jennifer. As long as you give me the talisman you wear around your neck." Morgan pointed at Jennifer's sternum. Jennifer's fingers flew up to worry at the wheel. She recalled Emrys's warnings.

You will need it to help you get back to your time. Do not lose it. Do not let anyone else touch it. It is meant only for you.

As far as she could tell based on this warning, the necklace was her ticket back home. And she wasn't about to give up that ticket. Not to anyone.

"I can't," Jennifer replied.

"Oh, darling, of course you can," Morgan said, her words sickeningly sweet. "Either you give it to me voluntarily, or I have Kay take it off your headless corpse."

Jennifer swallowed.

Okay, Jennifer, what to do, what to do...?

She began assessing the situation, how Kay was between her and the rest of the people in the barn. Knowing Kay's skills, Jennifer would be dead before a scream could finish leaving her body.

God, poor Kay...

"Give. Me. The talisman," Morgan gritted out.

Jennifer shook her head. "Not a chance."

Morgan sighed again, then flicked her hand from Kay to Jennifer. Kay began to move, in that jerky, zombie-like gait. He was fighting it as much as he could. Kay was still in there somewhere.

Jennifer turned and bolted, screaming her head off as she went.

"ARTHUR!"

It was a valiant effort. She made it maybe twenty yards before Kay tackled her to the ground. His hands grabbed for her neck, and Jennifer did what she could to slow him down. She slammed her fists into his shoulders, tried fending off his reach, but no matter what she did, she was no match for Kay's strength.

No, this was not *how she was going to die.*

Kay's fingers curled around her neck and began to squeeze, and Jennifer knew it was only a matter of time.

No, no, no, no, no!

As if something had heard her prayers, an odd sensation enveloped her. It felt like she was being smushed into a tube, but the tube was not long, because the pressure began to abate, and suddenly she didn't feel Kay's weight on her.

Jennifer's eyes flew open to see Kay, kneeling on the ground, three feet away.

"What the fuck?" she hissed, looking down at her body to make sure all her parts were there.

Luckily, Arthur was charging forward and rugby tackling Kay to the ground from where he'd been righting himself to come at her again. Kay fought against Arthur, but with one well-placed punch, Arthur knocked his cousin into unconsciousness.

Arthur scrambled to his feet and grabbed for her, framing her head in his hands.

"Gods, are you alright, Red?" She could just make out his frantic eye movements, taking in her face and looking down at her body to make sure she was unharmed.

"I'm fine, Arthur," Jennifer reassured him, but then remembered why they were in this situation in the first place. "Morgan!"

Arthur dropped his hands to spin around, only to watch Gawain and his brother Gareth circling the barn. After a moment, they met back up at the front and shook their heads.

Morgan was gone.

Just like that. *Poof.* Gone.

Arthur turned back to Jennifer, gathering her in his arms and crushing her to his chest. "What in the blazes happened, Red? I nearly lost my mind when I saw Kay on top of you..."

"Morgan, she...you won't believe me..."

"Try me," he breathed against the top of her head. She couldn't help but notice she fit perfectly against him, her head wedged right under his chin. He was warm and solid around her, and he was safe. Jennifer sagged against him, on the verge of absolutely losing it.

"She compelled Kay to attack me. It wasn't his fault."

"What could possibly have been her purpose for such a thing?"

"She wanted to take something from me," Jennifer replied. "Something that I desperately need. And when I wouldn't give it to her, she used Kay..."

Arthur's fingers began carding through Jennifer's hair, and that simple act soothed her more than she thought possible. "She's gone now, Red. I won't ever let her near you again."

Jennifer wished she could believe him, but something told her that wasn't the last she would see of Morgan.

CHAPTER 16

For the rest of the night, Gawain and Arthur took turns on watch. Galahad, bless him, had slept through the whole ordeal and continued to sleep soundly. They had dragged Kay into the barn and slumped his unconscious body up against a wall.

Jennifer couldn't sleep.

All she saw was the harsh smile that had transformed Morgan's face.

Jennifer's thoughts whirled while the men around her took turns with their watch, switching off for a few moments of sleep before they would be off in the morning. She thought back to the first moment she'd met Morgan. A man had been getting fresh with her, and she'd tried to fight him off. After what she'd witnessed, Jennifer knew, just *knew*, that scene in the bar in Bath had been all for show. A way to lure Jennifer in, the long con to gain her trust, only to attempt to take the one thing that would get her back home.

She thought about that moment in the darkened forest, Morgan pinned against the tree by Kay, her mouth near his ear, whispering…that same odd whispering Jennifer had heard on many occasions over the past few days.

There's been a barrier around you for days, my dear. I've been trying to get to you, to warn you…

Her grandmother had tried to warn her about something, but there was a force blocking her from doing so. Jennifer recalled the dream in the temple with the odd whispering, and her grandmother's voice, so far away, trying to communicate with her.

She's just as strange as the she-wolf.

At least she does not look as though she could hold any of us by the balls.

Which makes me wonder what the she-wolf wants with that one.

The Saxons at Avebury. They'd spoken of a woman looking for her, for some purpose. Could Morgan be the same woman?

Morgan had been the one to save her from the attack at the temple in Moridunum. The man had appeared to be another Saxon. Could he have been there at Morgan's bidding?

What was she capable of? What was the extent of…well, whatever it was she could do? She enchanted men to be her lackeys, that was for sure. But what else? Could she control Jennifer?

Dear God, why had Jennifer felt the need to trust that woman? The first sign of odd behavior, the way she balked at entering the temple, probably should have been a red flag. But Jennifer was always wanting to see the good in people, just as she always wanted to see the good in her students and the good they could accomplish once they set their minds to it.

If only she'd admit to herself she was looking for Lynn in this woman. Her friend had been on her mind so much lately, it was as though she wanted to force a round Morgan into the square hole where Lynn had fit. And what had Jennifer gotten as a result?

Nearly killed, to say the least.

Morgan didn't return that night. Nor was there a sign of her in the morning when the sun rose, burning away the fog that covered Gareth's fields.

Gawain had been the last one on watch, spending much of his time walking around the barn. Eventually, Jennifer stopped fighting the fact she wouldn't sleep, and rose, falling into step with the dark-haired man and just talking. Gawain was very forthcoming with stories of his childhood, the times Arthur would venture from Caerleon when his mother wanted to visit her family, how Arthur never seemed to completely fit in because of his parentage.

"He was always straddling two worlds," Gawain had said. "I felt for him."

As though speaking his name had summoned him, Arthur appeared suddenly, barreling around the corner.

"Whoa, are you okay?" Jennifer asked.

Arthur sighed in relief. "I didn't see you in the barn, so I... I was worried."

Jennifer grinned. "I'm fine, as you can see. Gawain here was keeping me company, telling me all these embarrassing stories about you."

Arthur's cheeks reddened slightly as he glared at his friend. "Truly, Gawain?"

Gawain guffawed and shrugged, as if he had no other choice than to share.

"We should go. We'll need to wake Kay," Arthur said.

They went back inside to find Galahad sitting up and stretching, his hair sticking up in odd places. He yawned so widely his jaw cracked. Jennifer couldn't be certain, but the kid might have had drool on his chin.

Must be nice to be able to sleep like the dead.

As Arthur and Gawain worked on rousing Kay, Jennifer made sure all of their belongings had been gathered, then tried to comb her hand through Galahad's hair, much to his chagrin. He jerked his head, only making it worse on himself, but at least Jennifer got a little chuckle out of the act.

"What's wrong with Kay?" Galahad asked, watching as the man in question finally began to regain consciousness with a groan. There was a mottled purple spot on his chin and jaw from where Arthur had punched him.

"He had a bad night," Jennifer said, seeing no reason to go into detail and alarm the child.

With Llamrei packed and ready to go, standing alongside Gawain's horse, a beautiful dapple gray stallion named Gryngolet, the traveling band met Gareth and Lynette outside. They exchanged goodbyes and thank yous, and took off back toward town.

After procuring some extra food stores from the market, they were off. Jennifer had taken Llamrei's reins to lead, yearning for something to do to keep her mind off what had happened. She chuckled when the mare nuzzled at her shoulder, as though Llamrei knew she needed comforting. Gawain sat atop Gryngolet, with Galahad in front of him. The two talked as though they were old friends. Gawain gestured wildly at all of the plants and trees around them, identifying each one to Galahad as they passed them. The boy looked absolutely captivated, and Jennifer couldn't help but smile.

"Gawain has always been good at making friends," Arthur said, quietly, from where he walked beside her.

"He is very personable," Jennifer admitted, turning her head to watch him. Arthur didn't seem angry or annoyed at his friend's presence. In fact, he looked lighter than she'd seen him in a while. His face looked less drawn and tense, as did his shoulders.

"This may come as a shock to you, but I am not as good at making friends as Gawain."

Jennifer snorted, shooting Arthur a sly smile. "Really? *You?* I had no idea."

Arthur chuckled, but his smile slowly faded.

"Are you okay?" he asked softly. Without missing a step, he reached out, brushing his fingertips across her neck. Self-consciously, Jennifer reached up to touch the spot as well, wondering if there were visible marks there. Kay hadn't quite gotten a grip on her neck before...

Well, before she somehow moved from beneath him to a few feet away all within the blink of an eye.

"I'm okay," Jennifer finally answered, glancing back at Kay. The man had kept to the rear of the group the entire morning, unable to look anyone in the eye or talk to anyone. He looked miserable, and Jennifer's chest ached for him.

"Will you take her?" she asked Arthur, holding out Llamrei's reins.

Arthur took them, his fingers brushing against the back of her hand. "We're having a conversation later."

"Oooo, sounds ominous," she teased, before ambling back to where Kay walked. She matched his pace, which was difficult considering his longer legs, but he slowed. For a while, neither of them spoke.

"I'm okay," Jennifer said after a while, eyes trained forward.

"I'm glad," Kay replied, sounding so small, like a sad child.

"Just wanted you to know...still alive..." Jennifer continued.

"Jennifer, I do not know what you want me to say—"

"I don't really want you to say anything," Jennifer interrupted. "What I want is for you to be your usual self. There is no reason for you to be like this."

"Like what?" Kay asked defensively.

"Moping," Jennifer said, waving her arm at him.

"I am not moping!"

"Could've fooled me. You're, like, trudging back here like a sulking child. You're punishing yourself for something you had no control over."

Kay didn't reply, tension radiating from his body.

"Do you know what it is like, Jennifer, to be in your body but not in control of it?"

Jennifer grimaced, but did not respond, remembering the strange sensation leading her into the clearing that then led to her arrival here.

"And to see your body being controlled and used to do a terrible thing?"

She stopped short, then reached out to grab Kay's arm to stop his movements.

"You can't do this to yourself. It wasn't your fault. There's only one person to blame here, and their name is not Kay."

Kay couldn't meet her eyes; he looked everywhere but at her. "I know, I just...I'm *so sorry*."

Jennifer would never consider herself to be much of a hugger, but could recognize when a situation called for one. She leaned into Kay and held on to him tightly. It was awkward, considering he was so much taller than she was, but she held on to that man for all she was worth.

"You don't need to apologize," she murmured. "And I have nothing to forgive because none of it was your fault or mine."

A beat or two of silence passed before either of them said anything.

"I can still feel her in my head," Kay whispered, as though speaking out loud would summon the woman in question. "It was like I was trapped in a cage in my own body, trying so hard to stop myself from hurting anyone, but unable to regain control."

"Jesus, Kay..."

Kay pulled back, but Jennifer held fast to his shoulders, comforting and firm. "Do you think she's still in there?"

God, he sounded so beaten.

"I wish I knew," Jennifer replied. She wasn't going to lie to him. There was a chance Arthur's punch was hard enough to give Kay a cognitive reset, but then there was the chance Morgan was still in there. They wouldn't be able to tell...probably until it was too late.

Kay just nodded, and both turned to notice the rest of their party hadn't stopped and was far ahead of them.

The two started walking again, but this time the silence between them felt less charged, less heavy.

"Why did she want your necklace?" Kay asked.

"I wish I knew that too," Jennifer replied. It wasn't quite a lie. She didn't know what the necklace's purpose was, truly. Other than knowing that Morgan seemed to desperately want it, Jennifer had no idea of its value.

They continued on in more silence.

"I recognize I wasn't in control of myself," Kay said. "But I still want you to know how sorry I am."

Jennifer sighed but smiled slightly. Kay was a *good* man. "I know, Kay. Like I said, there's nothing to forgive, but I appreciate it all the same. Now that we've established this, please go back to being your normal self again."

Kay laughed heartily. "I'm not sure anyone wants that."

"Not true." Jennifer shook her head. "Galahad seems to like your normal self."

Kay chuckled. "He's a good lad."

The party walked at a steady pace down the old, worn road, cutting across the peninsula toward St Michael's Mount. At some point during the early afternoon, she had inquired of Arthur as to what day it was. She was surprised to receive an answer, not because it was Arthur she had asked, but because what she knew to be the calendar would not be the same system used in this period. But after a bit of that radio-tuning white noise, her brain translated—June ninth.

She had almost two weeks to get back to Avebury for the summer solstice. Jennifer realized at some point she'd have to ditch this merry band of men she'd been with for what felt like ages. She would need all the speed she could manage, and she could be faster alone.

The thought of leaving them shouldn't bother her. She barely knew them, and yet... She didn't want to leave Galahad until she knew he was well taken care of. She wanted to make sure Kay would be okay. And even though she'd known Gawain for about a day, she wanted to know he'd be okay when she was gone.

And Arthur.

The man she'd been with since the very beginning.

A big piece of her refused to think about the time when she would have to leave him behind. But then she promptly began questioning herself and her sanity as to why she didn't want to leave him behind.

She had no answers for herself.

As night began to fall, they stopped for their now routine, it seemed, roadside campout.

Gawain got to finding kindling for a fire, and Jennifer had Galahad help her lay out some blankets. When they finished, she plopped down, glad for the blanket barrier between her and the ground, though it did nothing to keep the cold from seeping into her bones. Galahad picked Gawain to sit next to, and though it struck a pang within her, the joy she felt for

Galahad to have connected with someone outweighed the pain.

"Do you mind if I sit with you?"

Jennifer nearly jumped as Arthur's voice whispered across her ear. He'd bent over, so close she could feel the warmth of him.

"Sure," she said, breathlessly, and watched Arthur gracefully sit beside her, with his long legs stretched out in front of him.

Jennifer shivered lightly at his nearness, and Arthur mistook it for a chill.

"Do you need another blanket?" he asked, worry etched across his features.

"N-no, I'm fine. Really. Not cold."

Not anymore. The nearness of his body and the heat radiating from it helped curtail the chill.

"Are you sure?"

Jennifer rolled her eyes. "Seriously, Arthur. Since when have you been so worried about my well-being?" she teased.

Arthur frowned, his blue eyes looking to the ground for a second. She'd upset him.

Right. Last night. Being attacked and all that.

"I am sorry," he said softly, only loud enough for her to hear. Galahad and Gawain had lain back on the blanket, and Galahad was pointing out various patterns in the stars.

"What are you sorry for?" she asked, just as softly, turning back to him.

His face looked much as it had the night he and the others had stormed into the Saxon encampment and set her free. Half in shadow, half in light, the warm red and yellow of the fire gave Arthur an ethereal glow. As though he was an emissary of the gods, or a demigod. Caught between two worlds, as Gawain had said.

"For the way I've treated you in the past."

"We've already talked about this, Arthur," Jennifer said, a corner of her mouth quirking upward. "It's fine."

"No. I shouldn't have been such an arse—"

Jennifer reached up to place her fingers against his mouth, to cease his efforts to apologize for something he didn't need to apologize for.

"In all fairness, I wasn't exactly nice myself..."

Arthur reached up, curling his fingers around Jennifer's wrist gingerly, moving it away from his mouth. He didn't let go, just shifted until their fingers slotted together.

"You had been held hostage by a group of uncivilized Saxons. I should've been more understanding and—"

"Please stop," Jennifer urged, covering their already joined hands with her free one. "It's over. It's in the past. All we do now is move forward."

Arthur looked as though he wanted to argue his point some more, but something in Jennifer's face must have stopped him. Instead, he nodded, giving her hand a squeeze.

They fell silent, the only sounds around them Gawain's low voice telling Galahad and Kay a story, and the crackle and pop of the campfire. Jennifer glanced over at the three, watching for a moment as Gawain gesticulated widely, demonstrating some feat he'd accomplished.

A pair of eyes bore into her, pulling her gaze back to the man beside her.

"Arthur, what—?"

"We never got the chance to finish what we started," he stated plainly.

Jennifer's heart leapt into her throat, choking off words for a moment.

"What do you mean?" she asked, knowing full well what he meant.

"Last evening. In the tavern," Arthur said, his voice dropping an octave lower, sending another shiver racing down

Jennifer's spine. His thumb caressed the back of her hand, stoking the electricity crackling along her skin. She should stop this. No good could come of a kiss. Not with her. Not now. She needed to get home. Had students to get back to eventually. Just too many responsibilities back in Eastfall.

But why did she feel so drawn to him? He'd been an asshole in the beginning, but over time, he'd shown the dents in his armor, so to speak. He'd shown that he truly could care. That he cared deeply about helping others, despite having started off the reluctant tour guide.

Now, days and days later, sitting around this campfire, Jennifer wanted nothing more than to finish what they'd started in the tavern before Gawain had gotten in a brawl.

"Y-you want to—?"

Arthur grinned, using his free hand to caress his fingers along Jennifer's cheek, then jaw. Her eyes fluttered shut and turned into the touch, seeking more of his warmth and comfort.

"Come here, nag," he breathed, before curling his fingers around the back of her neck to close the gap. Their lips pressed together in a closed-mouth kiss and Jennifer spiraled. It was such a chaste touch, but it lit something inside of her she'd not felt in a very long time.

Jennifer leaned forward, parting her lips just a little. Arthur took advantage of that gesture and deepened the kiss. She sighed, sinking more against him, pressing her palm to his chest. The contact was electric, as jolts of energy crackled down her center and outward to her limbs. Warmth rose in her body, and it had nothing to do with the fire mere feet away.

Arthur angled his head, coaxing Jennifer's lips farther apart, and just when she thought she might actually combust, a low whistle caused them to spring apart as though they'd burned each other. Jennifer twirled her head around to see

Gawain sitting up, a shit-eating grin on his face, Galahad asleep next to him, along with Kay on the other side.

"Well, well...travel companion indeed."

Without hesitation, Arthur picked up a nearby stick and lobbed it at Gawain, who ducked it easily. Thankfully, it didn't hit Galahad or Kay.

"Alright, alright, my apologies." Gawain held his hands out in surrender, then promptly lay back, quickly fading off into sleep.

Arthur had volunteered for the first watch, and Jennifer opted to sit with him for the majority of his shift, talking well into the darkest hours of the night. When she couldn't keep her eyes open anymore, Arthur convinced her to sleep, which she did, knowing she'd be protected. She slept on, her lips still tingling from their kiss.

CHAPTER 17

Bare feet pounded along the forest floor, the desperation to get away overcoming the pricks and stabs she felt on the soles of her feet from the underbrush. She could hear her pursuer behind her, lumbering ever closer. And closer. Her heart hammered wildly in her chest, threatening to burst forth and end her flight right then. She didn't know where Arthur had gone. He'd not been there when she awoke, but she'd felt it.

An ancient, malevolent presence. Watching. Always watching. She'd had to get away, so she dashed off into the woods, working her legs until they ached and her lungs felt like they were on fire.

Deep down, she knew she would never get away. Why she wasted her breath to try, she didn't know. Perhaps because she always held out hope, even when it seemed like the slimmest chance imaginable.

Her arms worked back and forth at her sides as she propelled herself through the woods, jumping over tree roots and making a zigzag path. It didn't matter if she ran in a straight line or not; she was already lost, and there would be no easy way to return to Arthur. Or Galahad. Or Kay. Or Gawain.

If something hadn't already happened to them.

With a burst of speed, she ran and ran, until a clearing appeared *in front of her, just through the trees. It reminded her of the clearing where she'd fallen asleep back in Avebury. Maybe if she made it, if she fell asleep...she could return? It was worth a shot, and with one last impossible sprint, she nearly made it to the clearing on her feet.*

Instead, a tree root broke free from the ground, catching her foot. She sailed forward, that feeling of defying gravity worsening her terror, her stomach wrenching up into her throat. She landed in a heap on the ground, her wrists erupting into sparks of pain after trying to catch herself.

Trying to scramble up, she found she couldn't. Her legs were tangled in her gown, and her foot was still caught in the root. How had that thing popped up on its own, anyway?

The sound of her pursuer grew louder and louder as they neared, and she knew she couldn't run anymore.

She'd been caught.

Finally yanking her foot free, but not after incurring a significant cut from a sharp piece of the root, she scurried back, trying again and failing to get to her feet.

The footsteps bore down on her, damn near right on top of her. She peered into the trees, trying to make out a shape, any shape or figure...

Then, into the clearing stepped a blonde woman.

She'd seen this woman before, somewhere. In another life, perhaps? How had she been able to keep up? Why had this woman sounded so...lumbering and creature-like?

"Don't worry..." the woman spoke, and with that, recognition hit.

Charlotte Lothrop.

What was Charlotte Lothrop, the wife of Eastfall's mayor, Sam Lothrop, doing here? *How had she gotten here? Maybe she could help get her back to the present?*

"Wh-what are you doing here?" Jennifer asked, still frozen on the ground, unable to get herself on her feet.

"Don't worry," the blonde repeated, stepping farther and farther into the clearing, slowly stalking her way closer.

"What shouldn't I worry about?" she asked, confusion setting in.

"I'm not going to hurt you," Charlotte said, with a kind smile. For the briefest second, Charlotte's entire appearance changed, almost like a screen glitch on a television. Her hair turned dark, smile becoming sinister, yet oddly familiar...

She didn't know Charlotte Lothrop well. She'd seen the blonde a few times around the city, had spoken to her when she made visits to all of the schools as a show of community, the perfect politician's wife. Charlotte had been a teacher too, once, until she'd moved to Eastfall.

"Why would you hurt me?" she asked.

"I wouldn't," Charlotte replied, as though the most obvious thing in the world. "But you won't find what you seek on the Mount."

"What?"

"You won't find what you seek on the Mount."

Charlotte's mouth opened again, as if to repeat what she'd just said. Her lips began to move, but no sound came. Her visage morphed again, dark hair and sinister smile, flickering back and forth from blonde to brunette.

A great roar filled the air around them, as though a tidal wave was making its way to shore.

"I can't hear you!" she shouted at Charlotte, who seemed oblivious to the sound. "You have to get out of here!"

And just when the static roar crested, as though preparing to break against the bare rocks on a seaside cliff, Jennifer shot upright, gasping.

The early hours of the morning gleamed dully around them. She glanced to Galahad first, happy to see him content and still asleep between Kay and Gawain, as though nothing had happened. Gawain sat next to Galahad, awake, whittling a piece of wood with one of his many knives. Kay snored away, twitching and grunting in his sleep.

And beside her...

Oh, beside her...

Arthur lay, completely out, off in the world of dreams.

He looked beautiful. Especially in the early sun, which gleamed off his golden hair. Arthur seemed at peace in sleep, and she found herself wishing he could have this kind of peace forever.

When she'd sprung up, Gawain's eyes had settled on her, and now concern etched his furrowed brow.

"You okay?" he asked.

"Yes. I'm fine. Just...a weird dream."

Gawain nodded in understanding. "I know how those go, love. Always strange. Sometimes awkward."

Jennifer wrinkled her nose in a grimace. "Please don't keep going. I don't want to know about the awkward. Or the strange really."

Gawain barked out a laugh, before clamping a hand over his own mouth, afraid to wake up sleeping friends.

"You know, I like you," Gawain said, shaving off a decent chunk of the wood in his hand.

"Erm...thanks?" Jennifer didn't know whether to take that as a compliment or not.

Gawain snorted, then fell silent as he whittled a horse out of the wood. It was a simple design, yet beautiful craftsmanship. Before she could get her mouth open to ask him the question, Gawain cut her off, asking if she wanted breakfast. She shook her head, and at his behest, lay back down to snooze just a little longer.

Thankfully, the dream did not recur. Instead, it was darkness and rest.

A while later, Galahad roused Jennifer from sleep, and the group set out once more for St Michael's Mount.

It took one more full day and night, and then a half day to reach their destination. Within that time, the traveling band had grown a little closer, as only a long duration of close proximity can do. Jennifer laughed until she cried, listening to the men sing bawdy tunes. Arthur conducted a couple more sword lessons with Galahad, and tried to teach Jennifer the basics of how to use the knife he'd given her days ago. To be honest, she'd stowed the thing away in the pack Emrys gave her because it freaked her out. But once Arthur showed her proper techniques of holding it and a couple of tricks if she ever found herself in close quarters with someone dangerous, Jennifer felt better about keeping it on her person—where it probably should be in case she needed it.

Violence just wasn't her thing.

Arthur had stolen a few kisses and had remained close to her side as they walked, talking and not talking, just enjoying each other's company.

The rational part of her brain, which she would freely admit ruled her most of the time, would not shut up about how horrible of an idea it was to protect whatever this little flame was between them. She would get what she needed at St Michael's Mount, and then she'd return to Avebury, and home, in the twenty-first century, where she belonged.

And wasn't it just her luck? That she would have to travel thousands of years into the past to find a man that...well, seemed to understand her. That she felt a connection to. What made it worse was getting to know the man underneath the veneer of legend.

Jennifer would be leaving Arthur behind.

To allow this to continue would only be torture for her. And for him.

But she couldn't help it. They'd been in each other's company constantly over the past week and more. She liked him. A lot. There was an age-old wisdom about him that didn't exist in any man she'd dated or even thought about dating back in her time. He was a lot more selfless than he would have her believe. And, she supposed, he could be charming when he wanted to be.

She should put a stop to this. Like, now.

But then he'd turn and flash his smile at her, and she couldn't stop.

The craggy road down the point narrowed little by little as the band trekked along the coast. The wind whipped through Jennifer's hair, giving the illusion of a crackling fire swaying back and forth. Gawain held Galahad tightly to his chest as they trotted along on Gryngolet next to Jennifer, Arthur, and Kay. She'd found herself shifting closer and closer to Arthur's side, finding relief in his warmth from the maelstrom. Llamrei, who had not complained once the entire trip, nickered and snorted her displeasure at the wind. Poor girl.

"Is that it?" Jennifer asked Arthur, as they paused for a moment.

"Indeed," Arthur replied, wrapping an arm around her shoulder to bring her closer.

The island of St Michael's Mount loomed before them, the signifier of the end of their journey.

With any luck, Jennifer would immediately get possession of whatever she needed to get herself back home.

Home. A place she'd craved to return to for days now. But something like regret still gripped her.

She *needed* to return home. Her mother and father would miss her, plus her job... She didn't belong here, an aberration in the space-time continuum. If that was even a thing.

Now, at the end of the natural point, Jennifer peered across the bay at the high hill of St Michael's Mount. She knew a vague history of the place, starting from the Neolithic Era of prehistory up to the Norman Conquest in 1066 CE and beyond. There would one day be a castle on this island, but for now, it appeared there were but a few inhabitants in rudimentary huts.

St Michael's Mount was a tidal island accessible at certain points of the day. One could walk along the bay's floor on a natural causeway in the absence of a watercraft. Luckily, Arthur had inquired back in Tintagel about the time of day it was best to make it to the Mount. The tide had ebbed away, leaving a natural ridge from the point out to the island. They'd dismount and lead the horses across the soft, wet sand.

Legends abound about this place. In the present, it was called St Michael's Mount because the archangel himself had allegedly appeared on a few occasions to unsuspecting people, calling this a haven, a special place. According to Arthur's story of his ancestor, the island also had been inhabited on and off since even before the days of the Romans as a place of special significance to the polytheistic Celts of the island.

Hopefully, it had whatever Jennifer needed to travel home.

Gawain dismounted, then helped his fellow passenger down. Llamrei needed some coaxing, as she was not happy about what they were about to do. Arthur brushed his hand up and down her neck, trying to soothe her, and eventually she settled.

The trek across the bay went better than Jennifer had anticipated. The tide had well and truly receded, allowing them to walk along the natural ridge at the sea floor. The party slogged through the wet sand at a steady pace, traversing the span in a little over a half hour. Seagulls cried above their heads, swooping and circling as they trekked. Galahad seemed delighted by the little creatures.

The island grew larger and larger as they got closer. Jennifer could make out the buildings better. They were indeed simple thatched huts, with smoke billowing from holes in the center. There were a few stone buildings, but no castle or makings of a castle yet. Again, that wouldn't happen for another six hundred years or so.

A man with dark hair and simple gray robes met them at the shoreline where the natural causeway ended. He was on the short side, just a few inches taller than Jennifer, and flanked by two other men in robes. Arthur bade Jennifer to hang back with Galahad as he, Kay, and Gawain approached the men she could only guess were holy men, Christians.

She couldn't hear the words exchanged over the roar of the wind and the distant waves farther out in the bay. The conversation seemed genial though, as the demeanor of all involved was relaxed.

"What do you suppose they're saying?" Galahad asked, looking over at Jennifer. She shrugged.

"Your guess is as good as mine, my guy."

Finally, Arthur turned and beckoned them forward. Jennifer cautiously stepped closer. Knowing what little she did about the early church and its adherents, she didn't know if her gender would be well received on the island. But the man that seemed to be the one in charge just beamed at her, a friendly smile.

"Welcome to the Mount," the head holy man greeted, his voice peculiar in the way all voices were to Jennifer, until the radio tuned itself. "I am Father Lucas. I hear you have traveled far. Come, rest."

Gawain and Kay hung toward the back of the group as they began the ascent to the top of the hill. Arthur stood in front with Father Lucas, conversing back and forth about the happenings on the mainland.

Once at the top of the hill, Jennifer and Galahad both had

to pause to catch their breath. The clerics, Arthur, and Gawain hadn't even broken a sweat.

"Young Marcus here will show you to your lodgings. They are nothing resplendent, that is for certain, but they should be sufficient enough for a peaceful rest. Once you are settled, please find me in the church." Father Lucas bowed, then walked away with the third man whose name they hadn't gotten.

"We're excited to have you here," Marcus said jovially as he ushered them off to the right. He couldn't have been much older than Galahad, if Jennifer had to guess. His cheeks flushed red from his excitement, and his hands fidgeted around as he pointed out the various buildings and their purpose. "We don't receive many visitors to the Mount this time of year. Especially not since the Irish and Saxons began their raids. Luckily, we have remained untouched, and we pray to God it shall stay that way."

The community on the Mount was relatively small. If Jennifer had to guess, she would say no more than thirty to forty men of the cloth called the Mount home. There was a forge and a smith for all their metal needs. There were several men that tended to a farm, though Jennifer couldn't guess how fertile the soil would be on such a craggy island. There were thatchers repairing roofs, stonemasons working on the foundation of some kind of building, and a stable where another had taken their horses.

Life on the Mount had to be mediocre at best, but not one of the men appeared miserable.

"Here are our guest lodgings. We receive a few pilgrims a year. They come to sit upon the western side of the isle in the hopes that Michael himself will appear." Marcus crossed himself and looked as giddy as if he'd seen the archangel himself.

"Thank you, Marcus. We will settle in briefly with our

things and meet with Father Lucas. Will you wait a moment, and take us to where he'll be?" Arthur asked.

Marcus looked positively ecstatic to be asked to complete this task. "Oh yes, it would be an honor." The young man then stepped aside a few paces and sat on a precarious stool, but waited happily.

Their lodgings were a simple, round, thatched-roof hut with a fire pit in the middle for warmth and pelts lining what looked like benches but were places to sleep. It was large enough to fit six or eight people, and Jennifer wondered how many such lodgings they had on the Mount. How many people did they receive in a year for pilgrimage? She couldn't imagine many, though Christianity was on the rise throughout the world at this point. It *was* the official religion of the Roman Empire at its end.

Jennifer set her things on a cozy-looking bear pelt, and the rest of them all picked a spot. Once they had settled, they emerged to find Marcus still sitting where they'd left him, looking anxious. He hopped up when he spotted them and rubbed his hands together.

"Follow me!"

They walked across the community again, receiving acknowledging nods from the denizens as they passed. Jennifer remained pleasantly surprised to be noticed and greeted as well.

Soon, they came to the bottom of a set of stone steps leading up into a stone building that couldn't have been any bigger than a quarter of a football field. It had been built large enough to accommodate the residents of the Mount, with some extra space for visitors. The mere fact it was one of the few buildings built from stone only showed how important the worship space was to these men.

Jennifer glanced down to make sure she had footing on

the bottom step, then climbed to the sturdy wood doors. Marcus heaved one open, and they entered.

It was dark inside, as the windows weren't grand, more like slits. Beeswax candles dotted most surfaces of the room, adding something ethereal to the dimness of the space.

Father Lucas was at the front of the space, knelt in prayer. He had stopped upon hearing the door open and their footsteps. Crossing himself, he got to his feet, still with that same welcoming expression.

"Come, come!" he beckoned, and they ventured forward. Arthur stood at Jennifer's side, his arm brushing hers. The warmth of his presence was a comfort, and she relaxed a little.

"We thank you again for your hospitality, Father," Arthur spoke. "I know our visit must be unexpected, but I promise it is intentional."

"I have no doubt," Father Lucas replied enigmatically, a twinkle in his eye Jennifer hadn't noticed before. To Arthur he continued, "You have come about a sword." He flitted his gaze to Jennifer. "And you have come about a book."

Arthur tensed beside her, and Jennifer felt equally stunned.

How had the priest known the true nature of Arthur's journey to the Mount? What *about* a book? And suddenly, she remembered her dreams, something about protecting a book...

"How do you—?" Jennifer asked, before Father Lucas interrupted.

"How I know does not matter. I must speak with you and Arthur. *Alone.*" He looked pointedly to Kay, Gawain, and Galahad. Kay and Gawain seemed to take offense.

"It's okay," Arthur reassured his friends. "We will be alright. Take Galahad around the Mount. We will be with you again soon."

Gawain looked as though he wouldn't follow Arthur's order, but finally saw something in Arthur's eyes that comforted him. Gawain nodded and put his hand on Galahad's shoulder. Nudging Kay, he steered them both back toward the main entrance. But Galahad put up some resistance, looking worriedly to Jennifer.

"It's okay, Galahad." She smiled wider than she felt possible. "Go on. I'll be back in a flash."

Galahad didn't seem as convinced as Kay and Gawain, but he went anyway, looking back over his shoulder the entire way out of the church. Once they had disappeared outside with Marcus, Father Lucas crooked his finger.

"Follow me."

CHAPTER 18

ST. MICHAEL'S MOUNT - CIRCA 500 BCE

The priest turned toward the altar of the church, rounded the stone setup, and stepped up to a tapestry. He moved it aside to reveal the vague outline of a door, fairly well camouflaged against the stone wall. He pushed in, and the scrape of stone echoed through the church. Arthur and Jennifer glanced at each other, then followed Father Lucas, who had disappeared into the darkness beyond.

Arthur went through the wall first, keeping Jennifer close against his side and slightly behind. Jennifer tried to crane around him, to see what lay in front of them. Up ahead a little ways, Father Lucas had taken a pre-lit torch from the wall and waited for them in the low passageway. Arthur had to hunch forward to pass through, but Jennifer had no issues.

The secret tunnel didn't stretch on for long, but it did

descend rather rapidly. The temperature of the air grew colder as they went, but thankfully the cloak from Emrys's pack kept Jennifer warm.

The way soon opened up into a circular room, no bigger than the size of her classroom back home. There were two stone sarcophagi, a shelf built into the stone that held various tomes, and in the center of the room was a well.

Father Lucas slid the torch into a bracket on the wall and stepped up to the well. Its stone boundary stood about three feet off the ground, and after glancing over the edge, Jennifer saw that it fell deep into the heart of the island, and probably the ocean beyond.

"While many of my brethren would condemn the previous inhabitants of the island for worshiping false gods, I have always been fascinated with our pagan forebears," Father Lucas said, voice soft, as though not wanting to wake whomever lay in the sarcophagi. "Those that worship the old gods still thrive in Britannia, regardless, but a lot of their customs have been forgotten. The Church has destroyed many of their sacred sites. But I managed to preserve this one."

"What was its purpose?" Jennifer asked, though she had a vague idea based on Arthur's story of his ancestor and the sword.

"A popular way to leave an offering to the gods was by sacrificing something to the water."

This was what Arthur had come for.

"I feel as though this is not news to you," Father Lucas said sagely.

Arthur shook his head. "No. My father wanted me to bring his sword here. To return what was stolen."

Father Lucas nodded. "I thought as such. Signs have pointed to your arrival."

"What?" Arthur turned to face the priest, body strung tight. "What do you mean, Father?"

The priest hesitated for a moment, looking between Arthur and Jennifer several times before sighing, then backing up to sit upon a stone bench. He seemed older in that moment, exhausted and world-weary.

"I have been on this island since I was a boy. The Church has cared for me, and for that I am indebted. They put me in charge because of certain gifts I possess."

"What kind of gifts?" Jennifer asked, rounding the wall of the well to see his face up close, to read his meaning.

"God speaks to me in my dreams," the priest said. "I have known when certain things would come to pass before they ever happened. The details aren't always clear but...I have had many dreams leading to your arrival."

Father Lucas looked up to Jennifer, and in that moment, she realized he meant her and not Arthur.

"You mean *my* arrival?" she asked.

The priest nodded. "I knew you would come. And soon. And I knew that you would need my help to return home."

Funny how Emrys had failed to include that detail. That she would be expected.

"How can I get home?" Jennifer asked, breathless, waiting for the solution she'd set out a week and more ago to discover.

The priest stood, and from the shelf grabbed a stack of what seemed to be animal skins, bound by spun wool strings. He held it gingerly, near reverently in his hands, before turning to step toward Jennifer, holding it out to her. "This is what will take you home. They are instructions detailing how to make your journey. However, you will need to return to Avebury before the peak of the summer solstice. The rest of the details are in here."

Jennifer's heart sank.

She hadn't known what to expect when she finally reached St Michael's Mount, but it hadn't been this. What she'd hoped for were more specific instructions. *Easier* instructions. Maybe something involving the well, since it was hidden and guarded as though a powerful portal.

A book.

A book was going to get her home.

Hot, salty tears stung her eyes. Jennifer bit the inside of her cheek to hold them back, not wanting to completely lose it in front of a complete stranger. Or Arthur, for that matter.

Why her? Why now? Why on this vacation that had been about self-discovery and finding joy in the world? Why a *book*?

Jennifer gazed down at the bound set of skins, her hands and the rest of her body feeling not her own. She didn't know how she managed not to drop it, but she did.

What did she even say?

Thanks a lot for nothing, Father?

Thanks for the vague-ass instructions, Emrys. Why can't you just magic me home?

What the hell even was this book anyway?

The top skin was blank, a cover to preserve the writing on the next page.

"So...I have to return to Avebury. Before the summer solstice. And this will tell me what else to do?" Jennifer asked.

Father Lucas nodded. "The book must never leave your possession. There are those that would use it for ill intent."

"What the hell is this book?" she asked, unable to keep the frustration from her tone.

Father Lucas didn't seem fazed. "As I said, it is a guide. Meant for you. What it says...I do not know."

"You can't read?" Jennifer asked, not meaning to be cruel. At times she forgot widespread literacy was a fairly modern phenomenon.

"Oh, I can read," Father Lucas said with a slight smile.

"Latin and Greek. The Church taught me well. I just...I do not recognize the language. It is not written in anything I've ever seen."

Jennifer opened to a random page and nearly dropped the book.

It was written in modern English.

She knew for sure her weird brain translator thing hadn't done anything, because the recognition was instantaneous instead of the usual delay.

"Where did this book come from?" she asked, clamping the cover shut and clutching it to her chest. For the briefest moment, Jennifer would swear the book emanated a comforting warmth.

"I wrote it."

"I'm sorry?"

"As I said before, I have certain gifts. The Holy Spirit came upon me in the throes of sleep a few years ago, and I did not awaken until it was finished. A message from God," Father Lucas said.

Jennifer was stunned. "You wrote this in your sleep, with no recollection, and you don't know the language?"

"That is correct." Father Lucas nodded. He didn't seem at all disturbed or frightened that this had happened to him. If it had happened to Jennifer, she would've lost her mind. Such is the age of religious superstition. It was a wonder they hadn't accused Father Lucas of some sort of pagan devilry and executed him. "And it is meant for you. And only you."

"How do you know that?"

Father Lucas smiled enigmatically, his hands tucked into the opposite sleeves of his robes. "I know, because God told me."

Right. Of course he did.

"I...I don't know what to say."

"There is nothing to be said, child," Father Lucas soothed.

"I am happy to have been the vessel for such an important work. Whatever it may be. My faith has only strengthened. The presence of God is strong on this island, as though it was placed on top of a source of divine energy. Many fates have been decided here, though it does not look like much. I only hope the book contains what you need to find your way home."

Jennifer let out a shaky, false laugh. "Me too, Father. Me too."

Looking at Arthur, she realized her mistake in speaking so freely about returning home. Arthur had no idea what she or the Father were talking about. For all he knew, she'd come from the continent. How would a book help her get back?

Thankfully, before she had to explain herself, Father Lucas turned his attention to Arthur. "And you, my boy. Your father wanted you to bring that sword here, because this is the place where your four times great-grandfather stole it."

Arthur looked stricken. "How did you know that?"

Father Lucas laughed. "I told you. I have dreamt of this very moment. Your ancestor, besieged, had need of a sword, and he found this one"—here he motioned toward Arthur's hip—"and led his men to a great victory. And because of this, he kept it. Know that it was not out of malice, Arthur. He had no way to know the customs of the people here. Your mother's people. He simply saw it as a gift from God. What he did not know was that the sword would cause him great hardship. And everyone in your family that has wielded that sword thereafter knew heartache, despite the victories the sword could bring. Your father believed it to be cursed, because it'd been taken from its rightful place. And because he was a good man with the best of intentions, he bade you to bring the sword back here."

Arthur reached to his waist, unfastening the belt that held his scabbard. He held the weapon reverently in his hands, staring at the hilt, as though staring at a lover he'd already lost.

"What are you doing?" Father Lucas asked, his eyebrows crinkled.

"I am returning the sword to where it belongs," Arthur replied.

"You could, if you truly wish. But there is no reason you need to," the priest said.

"My family has possessed this sword for generations, a stolen relic from its rightful place. I *must* return the sword to the well."

"Have you ever considered the possibility your family—and ultimately you—were meant to have that sword?"

"What do you mean?" Arthur asked.

"Destiny, my son. Think on it. Your ancestor came here at the behest of his commander, to protect the tenuous hold the Romans had upon this island. And it was here that he led a decisive victory that propelled him to glory and many valorous accolades. The priests of the old gods still lived here when he arrived. While they despised the Romans, they were grateful to your ancestor for protecting the island. They could have demanded the sword be returned at any point before your ancestor left. But they did not. Is that not odd?" At that, Father Lucas's gaze dropped to the hilt of Arthur's sword. It, along with the blade, had been cared for meticulously over many years. And despite it being well over a hundred years old, it seemed as new as the day it came from the forge.

"You are saying this sword *belongs* to me?" Arthur sounded so lost, but almost hopeful. Jennifer had seen the way he wielded the blade, even when demonstrating forms to Galahad. The sight was near hypnotic, as though a true extension of his arm.

Father Lucas nodded. "The sword has and will always be meant for you. Just as that book is meant for her." A spindly, wrinkled finger pointed casually at the book clutched in Jennifer's hands.

"But how? Why?"

The priest huffed a laugh. "Everyone always wants an explanation of fate. Fate does not have to answer. It is God's will, and no one may ever know the answer."

Judging by the look on Arthur's face, he didn't appreciate that answer.

"A sword meant for me, stolen by my four times great-grandfather, who would never know I existed, and I am to just...accept that?" Arthur shook his head. "I loathe being a part of anyone's game, human or god."

"I did say that no one may ever know the answer, but...I may have a theory, if that would make you feel better?"

Arthur shrugged, laying the scabbard along the edge of the well. Jennifer thought for a moment he'd push it in and be done with it. To her relief, he didn't.

"Alright, Father, what is your theory?" Now that his hands were free, Arthur crossed them over his chest, waiting expectantly. "Along with what you believe will happen to me the longer I have this sword. I would rather not be cursed."

Father Lucas nodded. "Please, do not ever tell my brothers you have heard me say this...and make no mistake, I faithfully believe in God, the Lord Jesus Christ, and the Holy Spirit. But...perhaps He is not alone. It is possible there are other beings of supreme intelligence and power. They helped form and shape the world as it stands before you now, and influence events in our lives we have no control over. It is my thought that you were chosen a very, very long time ago...chosen by something greater than our minds could ever comprehend. Chosen to be a leader, unlike any that has been seen in the world since its making, or into the time beyond now. That sword is but a mere symbol of this divine destiny of yours. What you are—who you are as a leader—is in here." Father Lucas tapped two fingers against the center of his chest. "As far as the supposed curse... There is none, Arthur. The hardships your family has faced are simply life. The previous wielders have only ever been guardians of the sword. But you? You are its rightful owner. That sword knows when it is in the hands of someone worthy."

Father Lucas was not far off from his theory. What Arthur would become, whether in truth or only in legend, how he would manifest in the minds of those in her present, was not far from the man's grand idea.

Arthur remained as still as stone, his face unreadable. More unreadable than she'd ever seen it. Before, there'd been little tells, things she could glean. This time, there truly was no emotion. What whirled through his head would be anyone's guess.

After a long breath, Arthur shook his head forcefully.

"I do not think I can accept this fate. I am not a leader. I am the son of a Roman descendant and a native Briton. I grew up in Caerleon until both of my parents left this earth. I am merely a warrior. Not a leader. The thought is...it is laughable. Preposterous. I choose my own fate. No one can take that from me. No one can bend me to it."

"No one is trying to bend you to it," Father Lucas pleaded, stepping closer to the well and placing his hands on the rim, gripping the stone. "You have as much choice as anyone. You can choose to leave the sword and walk away. Be the mere warrior you claim to be. But you know, deep within your soul, that it would be the wrong decision. You have always known you were meant for more. Meant for something bigger than yourself. Bigger than you ever imagined. You were meant to be a unifying force for a fractured Brittania. You are meant to do what no one has done before you. You can save so many lives, Arthur. You can help so many people. Is that not what you have yearned for since you were a boy? To help those that needed it?"

"I do not think I can be the man meant for this task," Arthur said softly, his voice a whisper. Jennifer ached at how hurt he sounded, at the pained way in which he said those words. Like he knew exactly what Father Lucas was saying was true, and he wanted to fight against it.

"And because you think thus, means you are the perfect man for the task," Father Lucas replied, and Jennifer could sense the smile in the man's tone. "A prideful and boastful man is never the one for such an undertaking as this. I have a feeling you are none of those things, Lucius Artorius Aurelianus."

Arthur sighed. He stepped away from the well, his hands resting on his hips as he stared at the far stone wall. Jennifer watched the story of his thoughts in the line of his shoulders. Watched it dip and sway as he warred with himself.

Finally, he turned and stepped back up to the well. He didn't look at Jennifer or at Father Lucas. She continued to watch his face, watching his eyes flick from the sword to the well. When his hand reached for the sword, Jennifer held her breath.

Only to let it out in relief as he secured the sword around his waist again.

"I suppose I will take my destiny as it comes," Arthur said, more resigned than she'd ever heard him.

"Good." Father Lucas nodded gravely. "Because we will need you. And soon. The Saxons in the east have amassed an army, and you will lead the resistance."

Arthur didn't seem surprised. In fact, he appeared even more resigned. "When?"

Father Lucas sighed, his face falling into despair. "Soon. *Very* soon. There are darker forces at work here, and I have not been able to see the details. Or the outcome."

Arthur nodded, the line of his shoulders tense.

"If that is all, Father, I need...I need some fresh air."

Father Lucas inclined his head, and Arthur left the room and didn't look back at her.

Clutching the book to her tightly, Jennifer fought with herself whether to go after him or not.

Father Lucas's voice stopped her.

"You are not exempt from your fate either, Jennifer Cassidy."

She stiffened. "How did you know my name?"

The friar smiled enigmatically. "I wrote that book for you, did I not? It seems appropriate that God tell me who I wrote it for."

"What about my fate, Father?"

"Arthur may have a part to play in the here and now, but your part is bigger, and vastly more important for the safety and security of everyone." Father Lucas didn't seem jovial now, his tone deadly serious.

"How do you mean?" Jennifer asked.

"Unfortunately, I cannot say, because I do not know. I was made the vessel for that book for a reason. It was to deliver the knowledge contained therein to you, in order for you to use it against a greater darkness."

Jennifer swallowed thickly, not liking the ominous tone of his words.

Much like Arthur, Jennifer felt her life was insignificant. In what way could she, a school teacher from Massachusetts, play a role in some grand cosmic scheme?

"Your cryptic words are really starting to annoy, Father," Jennifer gritted through clenched teeth. Father Lucas, to his credit, didn't look offended.

"I know, and I am sorry I cannot be of more help. I have not been granted the visions of your future, only this book. Read it. I believe there will be more answers there to questions you have. The one thing that I can say is that you will not be alone in your fight. Others will help."

What a relief, right?

Jennifer turned on her heel, and with her newfound book, she left the well room and stepped back into the church and then outside. She blinked against the blinding light of the sun until her eyes adjusted to the day again.

The world seemed different. Had it always been so green? So blue? So vibrant?

Jennifer stomped down the stairs and made for their hut, all the while looking for Arthur. But she didn't see him. She didn't see Kay or Gawain either.

When she ducked into where they were staying, she saw only Galahad, lying on some furs, napping.

After the events in the bowels of that church, she felt exhausted.

She couldn't sleep though, not yet.

Stepping outside, she sat on the little stool Marcus had occupied not long ago. And in the light of the waning afternoon sun, Jennifer cracked open the book, seeking some answers.

CHAPTER 19

As soon as the cover had been lifted and Jennifer saw what was inside, she nearly dropped it.

There was no writing on this first page.

Only a pressed flower.

A stephanotis flower.

Like the white trumpet-shaped flowers her Grandma Cassidy used to have on her screened-in porch.

But the flowers weren't native to Britain as far as Jennifer knew. They were more inclined to grow in tropical climates. How had it ended up here?

She thought back to the stephanotis flower that had somehow appeared in her hand after the dream of her grandmother. Jennifer had been so shaken by the events with Morgan and Kay's attack that she'd forgotten all about it. Yet here it was. Again.

Hands slightly shaking, Jennifer turned another page.

At the top, in an elegant scrawl were three words:

Agitare Per Tempus

When she had opened the book briefly earlier, she had picked a random page, so hadn't seen the Latin phrase. The words below it, and after a cursory flip through the rest, were all in English.

Jennifer's Latin was rusty, but she thought the title meant something about traveling through time. Or steering through time? Definitely something about time.

So, with nothing else to do, no other members of her party in sight, Jennifer began to read.

The beginning acted as an introduction to the rest of the book. It was pretty straightforward. Almost like reading a *Time Travel for Dummies* book. For indeed, that was what the book was about. Traveling through time. And if Jennifer was reading this correctly, space as well.

The next section detailed the few ways it was possible to Travel, capital *T*, such as through natural portals that could be opened in places of great power. Avebury was one example listed, as was another place in the highlands of Scotland. Another method of travel was unnatural portals. It didn't go into detail, at least in this section, how these were made, but Jennifer got the impression it was bad. Really bad.

The final method the book listed, though it was rare, was for a person to possess an inherent ability to Travel. To bend time, almost turn it upside down, in order to walk through a rift and into another year or another space.

Oh, how convenient it would be to have that ability. With just a snap of the fingers, one could return home in a jiffy.

Then came the rules of time travel. The way Father Lucas had written them in his trance was hardly flowery or elaborate. They were meant to be straightforward, so there were no questions about what lines shouldn't be crossed.

- *Only Travel to observe, and NEVER to change an outcome.*

- *Changing the outcome of an event after it has occurred will result in consequences for the person changing the event and that person alone.*
- *Travel can only work backward, never forward.*
- *The longer one is out of their own timeline, the more likely dire consequences will occur.*
- *Moving across space requires finesse. One wrong move and the Traveler could end up trapped inside a stone wall or scattered across realms.*

Well, these rules weren't startling at all.

She could observe events, but she can't do anything to change them. Had she already unknowingly changed something? Or by virtue of her being here, was she always destined to change something in the timeline, so therefore was not actually changing anything?

Jesus, her head hurt.

The next few sections of the book made her want to laugh. And cry. It became apparent that despite the fact the book had been written in English, a language she knew and understood very well, it still made little sense. She knew nothing but the very basics of physics, yet somehow, some sort of complicated formulae had ended up in the pages of this tome. Calculations and movements of celestial bodies, how that could affect someone during a jump through time. If she had to hazard a guess, some of the information was long sought-after answers to questions on quantum mechanics, string theory, and wormholes and black holes. There was even a good deal of musings on the philosophy of time. From Ancient Egyptians to the Vedic texts of Hinduism to Islamic physicists, no culture was unrepresented here. Their thoughts on the very nature of time, the nature of space, their relationship to each other, and so on.

By the time she got to Einstein, her eyes were crossing.

She closed the book with a thud, needing to take a moment to process. The dark of evening had settled over her, rendering her unable to see the words anyway.

Behind her, she heard Galahad stir. The boy emerged, rubbing at his eye.

"What'd I miss?" he murmured.

Jennifer smiled. "Nothing, actually." Lie. "Was just thinking about waking you up and going to find some food."

Galahad's eyes lit up, and he nodded his head. He realized, though, they were the only two present.

"Where's everyone else?"

"They're around," Jennifer replied, her thoughts returning to Arthur for the first time since she'd opened the book. Where had he gone? Where had Kay and Gawain gone?

Instead of them, however, Marcus appeared with his friendly smile and usual sunny attitude.

"There you are! Come, I will take you to dinner."

Jennifer and Galahad followed, eventually finding themselves in a structure meant for gatherings. There were tables where many men in their gray robes sat, talking, while other holy men hurried about, setting out food.

"Your companions," Marcus pointed.

Kay, Gawain, and Arthur were at one end of a table, heads bowed together, whispering.

"Thanks, Marcus. Enjoy your meal," Jennifer said, then led Galahad the rest of the way to the table.

The men stopped talking as soon as they approached.

"Here, Red," Arthur said, patting the empty bit of bench next to him. Galahad, meanwhile, crammed himself between Kay and Gawain, who immediately began ruffling his hair and giving him playful little shoves.

Jennifer wedged herself in, sitting down. She was somewhat surprised Arthur was speaking to her. She figured he'd have begun questioning her about whatever it was that had happened by the well under the church.

"I'm sorry I disappeared," Arthur murmured, leaning in toward her ear. She shivered slightly at the closeness.

Jennifer shrugged. "It's okay," she said, with a confidence she didn't feel. "I understand. That was a lot to take in."

She didn't look at him, but Jennifer could feel Arthur's eyes on the side of her face.

"May we talk after supper?"

She knew she wouldn't be able to avoid this. Jennifer hadn't thought she'd have to come clean on her circumstances, but she found she didn't want to lie to him. Or omit, rather. She knew she could spin some kind of story, but she didn't think she could sell it.

Besides, she was tired of carrying this secret alone.

She only hoped he wouldn't freak out.

After Father Lucas led a group blessing for the food, they ate and talked with the robed men around them. It was such a strange affair, but something about it was so homey. Almost comforting. Like sitting with the Cassidy clan on Thanksgiving Day, just eating and bantering and enjoying each other's company.

Gawain, who sat across the wooden table from Jennifer, regaled her with more stories from Arthur's childhood and stories of the antics he and his brothers got up to. Kay filled in more blanks about his childhood with Arthur, and by the end of it, Jennifer's stomach ached from laughing so much.

It was almost as if she could forget there was a book about *time travel* waiting back in their hut.

As agreed upon, Arthur and Jennifer hung back from their other three companions as they made their way back to their lodgings. Night on the island was the coldest she'd been since arriving. Despite the month, the wind and proximity to water made this place practically arctic.

Arthur, sensing this, wrapped his arm around her shoulders as he'd done on the point before making the trek out to the island. He yanked her close, eventually stopping behind the walls of the forge to avoid the wind.

"Look, Red, you don't—" Arthur began, but Jennifer interrupted.

"I know I don't. But I'll tell you anyway."

God, who was this man? He wouldn't force the information from her, which only made her want to tell him all the more.

Sucking in a deep breath, she told him. Everything. She told him where she actually came from, how she got to England, and how she got to *his* England. She told him about Emrys, about the dreams she'd been having, about what she saw in the woods between Morgan and Kay...

To Arthur's credit, he didn't interrupt. He listened, only asking questions to clarify.

And when she was done, Jennifer took another deep breath.

"So...that's my story..."

She waited for him to freak out. To get angry. To tell her he didn't believe her. That her story was preposterous.

He did none of those things.

Instead, he nodded. That's it. Just *nodded*.

"Are...are you going to say anything?" Jennifer asked, voice shaking slightly.

"I'm not sure what to say," Arthur admitted. "I know I probably shouldn't, but...I believe you."

Jennifer blinked, absolutely stunned.

"What? You believe me?"

"I do." Arthur nodded. She couldn't see much of his face

in the darkness of the night, but the tone in which he spoke was normal. "Your story certainly explains a lot."

Jennifer swallowed. "How so?"

"Well..." he began. "You could not have been a woman from this time. You are too much of a pain in the ass."

She gasped, then slapped him on the shoulder as hard as she could. Arthur just laughed, trying to dodge her attacks.

They made their way back to the hut, and before she could enter, Arthur stopped her. He pulled her close and dipped his head to press his lips softly to hers.

"I'm glad you believe me," she whispered.

"It's too strange of a story not to believe it," he teased.

Jennifer huffed. "And you? What about you? Are you okay?"

Arthur's smile faltered. "I'll be okay, Red."

She didn't quite believe him, but she wasn't going to push.

"In with ye, Red," he nudged. "We will leave in the morning."

Jennifer ducked inside to find Kay, Gawain, and Galahad huddled around a small fire in the central pit, the smoke wafting up through a hole in the roof. Galahad was wide awake, listening as Kay told some kind of creepy story, from what Jennifer could gather. Even Gawain was hanging on to every word Kay said.

"Here we go..." Arthur grumbled behind her, as though this wasn't the first time Kay had dramatically told a ghost story.

Jennifer settled in where she'd set her things earlier, with Arthur beside her. Together, they sat up and listened to Kay's story. But not long after, exhaustion won out, and Jennifer slept.

More dreamless sleep.

Jennifer awoke the next morning with the sun. No one else was awake. Arthur was fast asleep beside her, and Gawain, Kay, and Galahad had all slumped together, their breathing deep and even.

She took the opportunity of the quiet, grabbed the book, and stepped outside. The chill in the air remained from the previous evening, but the sun that had shown itself at the horizon was already warming the air. Jennifer sat on the stool as she had the previous day, and opened the book again.

Picking up where she left off from yesterday, she struggled through a little more about the philosophy of time. She turned the page, a heading catching her eye.

The Use of Talismans to Travel

Jennifer's fingers once more found themselves reaching for the wheel necklace beneath her gown. Emrys had said she would need this necklace.

The use of talismans in Traveling is not necessary; however, it makes the journey smoother and more precise. Think of a talisman as a wheel, guiding the Traveler onward in the proper direction. It is a way to focus, and centering your thoughts into this object will make the success of Travel that much greater.

Okay, she could do that. Think "There's no place like home" while clutching the wheel, and she'll be zapped home? Sounded like it could be a cakewalk.

If she was that lucky.

Around her, the island began showing signs of life. Clerics were rousing, walking about. Those that passed her nodded their heads in greeting,

She continued to read, and still her companions slept.

Shouts suddenly arose from far off. At first, she didn't

think much of it, but after watching not one but a whole herd of men running past her, she knew something was wrong.

Jennifer shot to her feet, craning her head to try and catch a glimpse of the commotion. It was too far off, closer to the side of the island where they'd arrived. Behind her, Arthur, Kay, Gawain, and Galahad emerged, blinking away the sleep from their eyes. When they looked at her curiously, she shrugged.

A few more men ran hurriedly by. This spurred them all into action, rushing in the same direction as the crowd.

It wasn't hard to find the gathering. It appeared that all of the inhabitants of the island had arrived now. Jennifer nudged her way through the throng of men in gray robes, Arthur right at her heels, until she got near the front.

Jennifer spotted Marcus a few people away. She sidled up to him, and when she didn't see his usual positive smile, she knew something was definitely wrong.

"What's going on?" she asked in a whisper.

"A messenger," he replied, voice soft. "He's inside the church, speaking with Father Lucas. I suspect we shall know the nature of the visit soon."

The crowd shifted to stand at the bottom of the church's steps. Everyone waited, collectively holding their breath. The tension was palpable. Jennifer's mind raced, reeling off the air of anticipation hanging around them. Without thinking, she reached down, grasping for Arthur's hand. He held it tightly, squeezing in an attempt to calm her nerves.

It seemed they didn't have to wait long before the door burst open and out came a young boy, no older than the high schoolers Jennifer taught. He leapt down the stairs like the fire of hell was on his heels, and deftly maneuvered the crowd before disappearing down the hill to where the causeway was accessible.

As soon as the boy had disappeared from view, the crowd

turned as one back toward Father Lucas, who stood at the top of the steps, just outside the church doors. He tried his hardest to school his expression, but the barely discernible twitches betrayed his struggle. His face, at the moment, was impassive, but it couldn't stay that way for long.

"My brothers!" the priest called out, his voice carrying over the din of the crowd, silencing them. "We have received grave news from the mainland. It appears our fears have finally caught up to us. To the east, in Kent, the Saxons have chosen to break our tentative peace. They've gathered an army, and mean to make their way west."

A gasp rippled through those gathered, the concern now turning to fear. Having been in the care of a band of Saxons, Jennifer didn't begrudge them their fear. She knew what they were capable of. She also had the misfortune of knowing her history. England *would* become Anglo-Saxon. There was no stopping that. But she couldn't deny that a small part of her wanted to try.

What of Arthur? Kay? Gawain? Poor Galahad? Were they to be swept up in a tide of Saxon invaders? Was this the moment when their reality became her future myth?

Realization dawned.

In the legends, a decisive victory for Arthur against the Saxons would come at the Battle of Badon Hill.

Historians that believed the battle had truly happened could only guess the location of where it occurred, as there was no modern equivalent to be found in England.

Would she see where the battle took place?

Shit, Jennifer didn't have the time. She needed to get back to Avebury before the summer solstice which was in just over a week. It'd take almost that much time just to get back, perhaps less if she made fewer stops...

"If any of you wish to take up arms for the cause, I will not stop you," Father Lucas continued. "But know, because

Brittania is divided by tribe and by nationality, you will go into battle without a leader."

Murmurs rose up in the crowd.

"My brothers, I have faith God will be with you. Unfortunately, He cannot be the one to lead you. But someone could. Someone whose strength and will are as iron. Someone with the fierce heart and protectiveness of a bear." Jennifer watched as Father Lucas found Arthur in the crowd, eyes falling on the man beside her as though he'd known immediately where he was. "Someone with the determination to unite our fractured peoples. I have prayed to God many a night, my brothers, for such a person. Oh, how I've prayed..."

The whispered conversations grew louder, as the men looked to each other, debating whether it was worth the risk.

Before she knew what was happening, Arthur squeezed her hand again, as though looking for strength. Before she could protest—and truly, would she have done so?—Arthur moved through the crowd, toward where Father Lucas stood at the top of the church steps.

When he reached the priest, they shared a tense gaze, as though communicating without words, and then Arthur turned to face the crowd.

The still-rising sun shone behind him, and Jennifer's breath caught in her chest at the sight. The golden rays of the sun caught his flaxen hair just right, creating a shining aura around his head and upper body, as though it were a halo. Judging from the stirring in the crowd, she wasn't the only one to notice the effect. He looked like a savior, coming in the hour of most need.

Just as the legends said. The once and future king.

"I am Lucius Artorius Aurelianus, son of Gaius Utheris Aurelianus." A hush fell back over the crowd, but then the whispers began around her. The crowd turned to each other, recalling the stories of Uther and his own fights with the

Saxons. The stories came layered with another story of Arthur's grandfather and his glorious victories.

His and his family's reputation truly preceded him, even in a remote place such as the Mount.

"A most dire hour is upon us," he began again. "A menacing foe, who has remained peaceful on our lands for several generations, means to now break that peace. According to the messenger, they have begun marching west. If we cannot stop them, I cannot promise they would spare men of the cloth, for they march to attack us and claim Brittania as their own. But, it will not be so!"

A cheer rose from the crowd, creating a massive roar in response. Jennifer was almost certain that Kay, wherever he may be, had originated it.

"Yes, you are men of the cloth, but most of you are also Britons. This is your island, this is your *home*, and if you feel so inclined you may join me in defending your home from those that would take it. Within the hour, I will leave for the mainland, rallying as many men as I can from here to Bath. And wherever this army may be, we shall meet them on the field of battle. I will not think less of anyone if you decide to stay. But know you will be responsible for the protection of this island."

There were more whispers. Jennifer looked around, seeing several nodding at each other.

"If you wish to join me, you know where to meet me in an hour."

Arthur turned to Father Lucas, who had pride brimming in his eyes. Father Lucas nodded, and Arthur did the same in response. He then hopped down, and the crowd parted for him, making way as he strode with purpose toward the hut. Jennifer, Kay, Gawain, and Galahad scrambled to wend their way through the men, until breaking free and running to catch up.

"Are you sure?" Jennifer asked, grabbing Arthur's arm as soon as he was within reach. "You don't have to do this."

Arthur stopped in his tracks, rounding on her. Jennifer froze, rooted by the intensity of his eyes. They looked more translucent blue than normal, almost otherworldly.

Like a reflection of the water in the well.

"Are you worried for me, Red?" he asked, his tone unreadable.

Jennifer gaped, swallowing thickly. Of course she was fucking worried. Victory in legend, sure, but did that translate to a victory in reality?

"*No.* Why would I worry?" Jennifer scoffed.

Arthur's eyes softened. He reached for her, grasping her face between his large hands.

"When I left the well room yesterday, I went as far west as I could. I sat on the rocks for a very long time. I half expected Saint Michael himself to appear. But the more I thought, the more I knew...this is what I'm meant to do. I have nothing for me in Caerleon. This is my future. I know this is what Father Lucas spoke of. Destiny. This is what I'm meant to do."

Jennifer leaned into his palm. "Have you ever done this before? Led an army?"

Arthur shook his head.

"Are you scared?"

He huffed a nervous laugh. "I'm terrified, Red."

"Roman, you have bigger balls than I ever imagined," Gawain exclaimed, coming around the side of the hut, having finally caught up. Kay was right behind him, Galahad clinging to his back.

Arthur's gaze never wavered from Jennifer's. It made her squirm, like he was reading her mind, looking deep into the recesses of who she was.

"This is what I need to do," he whispered to her.

Jennifer nodded. She believed him. He was so sure, so resigned to his fate. She wished she could be as comfortable.

Besides, one of the rules in the book strictly warned against trying to change events. Would her attempt to get Arthur to give up on this fight be her trying to change events?

Arthur dipped his head to kiss her softly, before pulling away and disappearing into the hut.

"Gawain! Kay!" he shouted, summoning the two. They startled and hopped to, following after. Galahad took a step, as though he meant to go inside as well, but Jennifer grabbed his shoulder to stop him.

Inside, she could hear Arthur's low voice speaking to Kay and Gawain. No doubt offering them their out, the opportunity to go home and not face this. When she heard two griping voices raised, she knew Gawain and Kay were staying. Then, the whispering grew more hurried, this time most likely talking strategy.

Gawain poked his head out of the opening of the hut. "You two, get in here and pack your things. We'll be leaving soon."

Jennifer and Galahad scrambled to do just that.

CHAPTER 20

That morning, it wasn't just the five companions walking back across the causeway to the mainland; it was a full host of holy men at fighting strength. Those too old or too sickly remained behind to tend to the island and to pray.

The mood was somber, silence running the conversation as they braced against the howling winds.

"What happens now?" Jennifer asked Arthur softly, but loud enough to be heard over the sea wind.

"We travel to Bath," Arthur replied. "We try and rally as many men on the way as we can. Tintagel, Glastonbury... wherever we can get the word. I hope to dispatch a few messengers to reach a few other places. We don't have much time, but I am hoping the threat of outsiders will inspire the hearts of all fighting men to heed the call this time."

It didn't seem real. An impending attack from Saxons was not an everyday occurrence for Jennifer, but for warriors like Arthur, Kay, and Gawain...yet more blood to be spilled to save people that, a few days later, may try to attack your lands regardless of what you'd done for them previously. Such was the nature of the warring tribes of Britain, and it had been so when Rome first reached its shores. One wonders what might have happened if the Celtic tribes had been able to form a united front against *them*.

Maybe this time, a united front might stick. Under the right leader...

Hours later, Jennifer began to fall behind the ragtag group.

As soon as they had hit the mainland, Gawain rode off on Gryngolet, at Arthur's behest, to begin spreading the word of the imminent threat.

The caravan pushed themselves; even when night had fallen, they marched. Jennifer had not exerted herself this much before, and exhaustion gripped her legs, slowing her.

Just when she thought she could go no farther, they stopped for the night to camp.

Sleep didn't claim many that night, as there was a tangible restlessness shivering its way through everyone. Jennifer huddled close to Arthur, talking into the night.

She must have fallen asleep because he woke her the next day to carry on.

Another day passed, another night on the road, and then they arrived in Tintagel as night had begun to fall.

Gawain must have already reached the town, spreading the news. The streets were filled with men packing horses and bags. Upon seeing this, Arthur let out a relieved sigh, and walked on ahead.

"Come on. Let's leave him to his work, and we'll get you both settled in the inn," Kay said, grabbing Llamrei's reins to lead her toward the tavern they had patroned a few days before.

Willow, the young barmaid, greeted them when they entered.

The girl ushered them over to a table and began to supply

them with drinks, fretting to and fro, worried for the men that would go off to war.

A little while later, Arthur entered and spoke with the tavern owner for a few moments, nodding and gesturing, then came to their table.

"I've secured a horse," he told Kay, speaking as though midconversation. As if they'd discussed something Jennifer didn't know about. "I'll leave at sunup."

"Wait..." Jennifer blurted, leaning across the table, placing her hand over his. "You're leaving? Alone?"

Arthur nodded, then turned his hand over so their fingers could interlock. "Step outside with me for a moment, Red."

Jennifer stood, and he led her by the hand just outside. He pulled her away from the door and around the corner of the building to afford them some privacy.

"I have instructed Kay to take Llamrei and see you safely to Avebury."

Jennifer paled. "What? No!"

Arthur looked pained. "You have to return home. The solstice will be here before you know it, and I want you as far away from the fighting as possible."

Her mind whirled, too distracted to do the math required to figure out what day it was, let alone how many days she had until the summer solstice. "No, I want to come with you," she found herself saying.

Arthur smiled sadly. "Red, I cannot have you near that battlefield. I will worry too much."

"I can take care of myself!" she blurted.

God help him, but he laughed. And laughed.

Jennifer glared.

"I'm sorry, Red, but have you seen yourself with a sword? It's not pretty."

Her jaw clenched, and her hands balled up. "I proved I was pretty decent with this dagger, didn't I?"

Arthur's smile this time was more fond than mocking. "Aye, Red, you are a fright with that knife."

"Please, Arthur," she begged, entirely unsure where all of this was coming from. Why she felt compelled to stay when she knew she had a fast approaching deadline... "Avebury is not that far from Bath. I can return home *after* you win this fight."

He lifted his hand, tracing his fingers down her cheek. "You're so sure we will win... Do you know something I don't?"

"You know I can't tell you that," she replied, hating rule number one from that damn book.

Stepping away, Arthur began to pace in thought. He paused, and his shoulders sagged.

"Okay...but promise me, whatever happens, you will get yourself to Avebury before the solstice."

Jennifer held up three fingers. "Scout's honor."

His brows furrowed, and Jennifer laughed. "Sorry. Yes, I promise. I will get myself to Avebury before the solstice."

Arthur nodded, his eyes boring into her for a moment as though gauging her truthfulness.

"I will leave tomorrow morning to begin preparations. Kay will see you and Galahad safely to Bath."

"Why Bath?"

"There's an ancient fort there. On a hill just outside the city. It's called Badon. And that's where we will make our stand."

Jennifer felt an icy chill crawl down her neck. Hadn't she been expecting this?

The Battle of Badon Hill.

A legendary victory for Arthur.

And he had to leave her in the morning.

Fear clawed at her throat, and panic began to curl in her gut. For the past couple of weeks, Jennifer had known no one but Arthur. They'd been companions for days, and now he would leave.

Had she become that dependent on the man? That reliant? The thought annoyed her. But she also felt an overwhelming sadness.

"Be careful," Jennifer whispered. The words were so simple, not anywhere near the depth of what she truly wanted to say.

"I will be as careful as I can be," he promised. Arthur leaned forward, their foreheads pressing together. Jennifer's eyes fluttered closed, taking a steadying breath to rein in her worry.

"I must go speak to some of the men," Arthur said. "You should take Galahad up to the room to rest."

Jennifer nodded, but didn't move immediately, nor did Arthur make to leave.

"I must go..."

"Then go..." Jennifer urged him, because she didn't think she could be the one to move away first.

"Go upstairs. I will see you in Bath."

Arthur moved quickly, as though violently forcing himself away from her. Kay had just stepped out of the tavern, looking for him. They conversed quietly, but Jennifer was close enough to see Arthur level an icy gaze at Kay before saying, "Keep them safe."

The fierceness behind his words could not be missed.

Kay, aware that he'd been tasked with a very important mission, stood straighter, then nodded. "On my life, I will."

Arthur, seeing something in Kay's expression that satisfied him, turned and stalked away from the tavern.

Jennifer watched him go, hoping they could share one last glance.

As he walked, long strides carrying him off, he paused to indeed look back at her.

She forced a smile, as did he, and then he disappeared into the night like a specter.

Jennifer didn't sleep a wink that night. She stared at the ceiling of the inn's room, listening to Galahad's soft snores as he slept like only an innocent child can.

Jennifer envied him.

Her thoughts swirled with Arthur, the last fierce look he gave Kay, ordering the man to keep Galahad and her safe.

What did he feel for her? To exhibit such fierce protectiveness?

But her thoughts soon became distracted with the logistics of traveling home. In a matter of days, she would need to travel back to Avebury, and then jump hundreds of years into the future.

And she'd never see the man again.

That hurt.

More than she ever imagined it would.

More than it *should*.

Jennifer wondered if Arthur lay awake, thinking of her in this way.

Galahad grumbled and shifted, turning away from Jennifer, taking his body heat with him. She felt herself relieved, having grown warm from too many blankets and too much of his warmth.

When the first rays of dawn came through the open space of the window, lighting the floorboards, Jennifer climbed from the bed to get a jump start on leaving. She tiptoed around the room, gathering their belongings, then left the room. She'd be back in another hour or so to wake Galahad to leave.

No one occupied the tavern downstairs, but Jennifer

continued as quietly as possible through the open, quiet space. Once outside, she went to the stable to check on Llamrei.

The mare stood in her stall, munching on some hay. Jennifer approached, and Llamrei turned toward her, recognizing her scent.

"Good morning, girl," she said softly, pulling out an apple from her pack, one she'd filched from the tavern the previous evening. The horse seemed pleased, and took the fruit from her proffered hand.

"Ready for more adventure?" Jennifer asked. Llamrei let out a snort of reluctant assent. "Yeah, that's how I'm feeling too."

A couple of hours later, Kay, Galahad, and Jennifer were well on their way to Axminster. The three companions and horse moved at a steady clip, pushing themselves. The trip was tiring, but seemed to pass faster than the original leg.

Arthur had left with the rise of the sun, as he had said he would. He'd be far ahead of them, no doubt.

When they grew close to Galahad's village, they moved as quickly as they could. As they passed, a glance amongst the thatched-roof huts saw mostly females and a few older gentlemen. Perhaps Gawain had gotten there and convinced the men to head for Bath.

Despite what they'd almost done to Galahad, she hoped that was the case. Arthur could use whatever men he could muster.

They stopped for the evening, and Jennifer volunteered to stay up the first part of the night so Kay could get some sleep.

Thankfully, they didn't receive unwanted visitors of any kind, be it animal or human.

The next day they set out again, and reached Axminster a little after midday. The town bustled with the news of the

Saxon army's approach, and many men stood in the street, giving their goodbyes to their women.

More men to join the cause. More men to unite under Arthur and beat back the danger.

Kay let Galahad and Jennifer rest for a bit while he wandered the town, getting a few supplies for Llamrei for the last bit of the road to Bath. They opted to head out again, despite the fact the day waned. Kay wanted to cover as much ground as possible.

Whenever she had a chance, Jennifer studied the book. The more she read it, the more it made sense.

By the time they reached Glastonbury, Jennifer believed she knew how she'd get herself back home using the talisman Emrys gave her and the natural power of the Avebury stones.

It was odd, being on the Roman road. Before, it had been less traveled. Rarely had they met someone else.

But now?

The old Roman road was alive and bustling with travelers. When they camped at night, Kay didn't worry too much about their safety because there were so many other groups also camped along the road. All of their fires lit the way well enough for other travelers to continue on. It was a heartening sight, one that gave Jennifer goose bumps.

To see what generally were uncooperative tribal units banding together just…was unlike anything she'd ever seen in her lifetime.

"Try to sleep," Jennifer bid Galahad that night in Glastonbury. He'd been staring wide-eyed at all the people passing on the road, and all the people in the town. There was no actual room anywhere for the night, but that was fine for Jennifer, who had gotten used to camping outdoors.

A dozen or so feet away from the spot they'd picked sat another group of travelers resting. Around that particular fire sat men *and* women. Jennifer wondered how many women might actually fight in this battle, and if it was common for women warriors to do so.

She supposed she'd find out soon.

Unbidden, her thoughts turned to Morgan for the first time since the incident at Gareth's home in Tintagel. Jennifer couldn't help but wonder what she might be up to.

As if her very thoughts had summoned her, that night Jennifer dreamt of Morgan.

There was no forest this time, nor did Jennifer hear the strangely layered, eerie whispering.

Instead, her dream self was at her desk, in her classroom, back home at Eastfall High.

In front of her, at the closest student desk, Morgan sat, lounged back against the chair, one arm casually braced against the cheap, orange plastic. A smirk curled at her lips, like the cat that got the cream.

Jennifer tried to get to her feet, but no matter how much she tried, her legs wouldn't budge.

"Are you inside my head right now?" Jennifer snarled.

"Indeed." Morgan grinned.

"Get out. Now."

"Oh no, I do not dare. Besides, this won't last long. Connections such as this are fleeting when established."

"What do you want?" Jennifer asked, fingers curling against the beat-up wood of the desk.

"You have secrets, don't you?" Morgan glanced around the room, taking in every detail—every detail that was in Jennifer's head anyway.

"What do you want?" Jennifer repeated.

"Calm, Jennifer, calm."

If she could get up, Jennifer would lunge across the desk at Morgan.

"I simply wish to apologize for the way things ended between us when last we saw each other."

"You mean where you forced Kay to attack me?"

Morgan grimaced. "Yes, highly undignified. I see that now."

"Is he still under your control?"

The dark-haired woman sighed. "Alas, no. When Arthur hit him on the head, it knocked what control I had of him right out."

Jennifer let that sink in, relieved for Kay.

"You purposefully put yourself in my path, didn't you?"

Morgan nodded. "I did. I dreamt of you. I knew you would come and provide the answer to all of my prayers."

"The men in the woods...near Avebury?"

"Yes, they were sent by me to retrieve you. My husband was only too happy to provide a few for the task. But, why send men when all they will do is disappoint you? They could not manage to grab one defenseless woman...so I had to take it upon myself."

"Your husband?"

Morgan nodded again. "Yes, Torvulf. A great chieftain amongst his people. So handsome...and so easily manipulated."

Jennifer leaned forward, palms flat against the desktop. "Who are you and what do you want with me?"

An enigmatic smile appeared, and for a moment, Morgan looked almost...sad. "Who I am matters not. But the book you have in your possession will allow me to do what I need to do."

"The book? I don't know what you're talking about."

Morgan stood, her eyebrows falling into an annoyed V. "Do not play coy with me, Jennifer. I know you received the Agitare Per Tempus *from the bastard priest...and I want it. And that necklace."*

Jennifer watched as Morgan took two menacing steps forward. But for once, she didn't feel fear.

"What do you want with the book?"

"I want to right a wrong," Morgan replied. That strange look of hurt and sadness returned to her light-colored eyes.

"Then you should probably know that's, like, the first rule of time travel. Don't change anything that's already happened, or face consequences."

"I will take whatever consequences it causes. I care not."

There was something old in her eyes, ancient. Like she'd already seen too much despite the fact she didn't look much older than Jennifer.

"You lost someone, didn't you? And you want to prevent them from dying."

A shutter came down behind her gaze, and it might as well be as if staring into stone.

"You will give me the book and the talisman, or you will never see your home again."

Jennifer believed her, but Jennifer also knew she was tasked with taking care of this book.

"No."

Morgan sighed, crossing her arms under her chest. "Me asking was a formality. A kindness. I will take them both off your dead body."

"Then I guess that's what you'll have to do. Why didn't you just go to St Michael's Mount and take it from them? Sounds like something you would take pleasure in doing."

"I could not retrieve the book. Not until it was placed in the hands of its intended owner."

Which meant her. It would have never allowed itself to be in Morgan's possession until Jennifer had been given it first.

It was just a pile of bound parchment. How could it have such power?

The edges of the dream began to blur. Morgan noticed as well, and clenched her jaw in frustration.

"I will be seeing you soon, Jennifer. I won't ask so nicely then."

"I look forward to it."

The sun rose above the trees the next day, and Kay led the rest of the way to Bath.

They arrived at the old Roman city to much the same scene they'd witnessed in Glastonbury. The city had come alive, more so than the first time Arthur and Jennifer had passed through.

Arthur.

She hadn't seen him since that night in Tintagel.

In a matter of an hour or so, she would see him again.

The thought thrilled her.

So what if she had to leave eventually?

She could live a little, couldn't she?

Better to have loved and lost than never to have loved at all, was the saying, right?

Jennifer picked up the pace, picking her way through the streets of Bath, right past the old Roman baths, and back outside the city limits. Kay led the way along the three miles to Badon Hill.

In the present, it was called Solsbury Hill, and as the hill appeared in the distance, Jennifer couldn't help but hum the old Peter Gabriel song. Galahad and Kay looked her way curiously, but she didn't explain.

At the base of the hill, they paused to look up.

"She's a beaut, ain't she?" Kay asked of the hill, a wide grin on his face.

A beaut indeed. Badon Hill, or Solsbury Hill, stood a bit over six hundred feet high and had been the home of an Iron Age hill fort. This meant there would have been stone ramparts and wattle and daub huts on the interior of the fortifications. Which is apparently what was being prepared at the top of the hill. It was smart. Having the high ground did give a tactical advantage.

They began their climb, and poor Llamrei struggled in the soft earth of the hill. Fortunately, they made it without anyone rolling an ankle, but nearly got stabbed by some sentries for their efforts.

"Whoa, whoa! We're with Arthur." Kay held his hands up, palms out to show he didn't mean harm. Two spear tips floated in the air mere inches from his nose. "I'm Kay."

At hearing the man's name, the two guards snapped to attention and parted, allowing them to pass.

The inside of the fort teemed with men, women, and children. Women scrambled around with armfuls of weapons, and some sat in a circle, mending leather armor. Men bustled around, shoring up some of the weak parts of the rampart that encircled the top of the hill. Children ran amongst the legs of those moving about, chasing each other and laughing and giggling. Jennifer found herself envying the innocence again.

A young boy about Galahad's age appeared, offering to take Llamrei. Jennifer felt reluctant to give up the horse, but did so anyway with the promise she'd visit later when she could.

Jennifer turned toward Galahad, only to find him furiously scanning the faces of everyone that passed. He was afraid of finding his father's face, no doubt.

"Hey, stick close," she murmured to the boy. He nodded and grasped her arm. With any luck, Galahad's father was with some of the garrisons at the bottom of the hill.

"Let's find Arthur," Kay said, and headed toward the interior of the hill fort. A great wattle and daub building sat dead center, probably a meeting hall. All around it were smaller buildings that had once been homes. In the present, none of this sat atop Solsbury Hill. It had been dismantled through the years to use the stone for other public works. Only the archaeological vestiges could be found. Perhaps if she ever made it back to the present, on the group's trip to Bath she'd make a side hike to the hill.

The harried atmosphere thickened nearer the center. There were more men in leather armor decked out in all sorts of weaponry here. Other men hauled rocks and timber as well, working on the defenses.

She craned her neck about, searching for Arthur, almost afraid he hadn't made it.

But then...Jennifer heard him before she saw him.

CHAPTER 21

*BADON HILL, OUTSIDE AQUAE SULIS (BATH) -
CIRCA 500 BCE*

Arthur's voice carried over everyone, louder and deeper than she'd ever heard it. It made her heart lurch in her chest, her eyes desperately scanning the crowd. It had only been a few days, but she'd missed him.

They found Arthur surrounded by many warriors. He looked to be giving them a rousing motivational speech. He didn't speak for much longer before he parted from the crowd and stepped off to the side. A smaller group of men, including Gawain, followed. They began to converse and looked to be speaking of strategies. Kay moved faster, not wanting to miss out on talking tactics. Galahad, knowing Arthur was close now, dragged Jennifer forward, leading her by the arm he'd clutched so tightly. With Arthur around, Galahad felt safe. It seemed Arthur had that effect on people.

Jennifer watched as Arthur took in Kay's arrival. Her heart soared this time when she saw him craning his head around, looking for someone. His eyes landed on Jennifer, and his tense shoulders sagged in relief.

Had he been worrying about her?

Probably about as much as she'd worried about him.

He murmured something to the men, then left the circle, striding toward Jennifer with purpose. Her breath caught.

There was no full plate armor in sight—it was too early for that anyway—but he certainly looked like a fierce warlord. He had donned leather armor, complete with bracers around his wrists. None of it would stop a good stab with a sword, but its light weight afforded easy movement and would slow down a slash.

God, he looked *good*. Fiercely handsome, and ready to protect his people.

As he grew closer, Arthur didn't slow. He moved forward swiftly, grasping Jennifer's head between his hands. His lips crashed down on hers, and it was all Jennifer could do to hold on. Her hands reached out to grasp on to something, and ended up curling around part of the leather armor around his waist. It creaked under her grasp, but the give was less stiff than she thought. Arthur kissed her furiously, as though he hadn't seen her in ages. Or as if he were about to lose her.

Arthur pulled away to catch his breath. Jennifer was still too stunned to even realize what had happened. She blinked at him, trying to catch any of his features this close. All she saw was pale blue.

"What was that for?" she asked softly.

"I...I just missed you."

A gagging sound close by had her turning to see Galahad pretending to vomit. Arthur laughed and reached forward to tousle the boy's wild hair. Galahad jerked out from under

Arthur's hand, swatting at it. This only made Arthur laugh harder, and Jennifer chuckled.

"I did miss you," Arthur repeated, turning his attention back to her. "I thought..." he trailed off again, his eyes losing focus for a moment over her shoulder. "Well, I don't know what I thought."

"I wouldn't go anywhere without saying goodbye," Jennifer said quietly, guessing at his thoughts.

His gaze flitted back to hers, startled. She'd guessed it correctly.

"I know, but I would not have blamed you for...for leaving."

She just shook her head, clutching to the leather for all she was worth.

"I'm not afraid of being here when this happens," she said. "I'm tougher than I look."

"You do not have to remind me," he replied wryly.

"Mm-hmm..." Jennifer hummed, a playful smirk pulling at the corner of her mouth. "So, you'll let me take up a sword and go into battle with you?"

Arthur froze. "That is not—"

"I'm teasing," she interrupted with a laugh. "You know I can barely hold a sword anyway."

It was Arthur's turn to smirk. "I know. I have been on the receiving end of your horrible attempts at wielding a sword."

"Hey!" Jennifer pulled back just enough to smack him on the chest. With the leather, he barely felt it, but it still felt cathartic to do. "I wasn't born with a sword in my hand, okay?"

"I am sure I still have the bruise to prove that," Arthur teased, and Jennifer shook her head.

The laughter and levity fell from his face, though, rather quickly, remembering the task at hand. He looked worried.

Afraid. Which wasn't an emotion Jennifer was used to seeing on Arthur's face.

"It'll be okay," Jennifer said, echoing their previous conversation.

Arthur sighed, leveling a firm stare at her.

"I will fight with you," Galahad declared, chin up.

Arthur turned to the boy and shook his head. "No, Galahad. You are too young and too inexperienced with a weapon. I would not have you fight and risk your life."

"But, Arthur—"

"*No*," Arthur said firmly, in the most intense tone Jennifer had ever heard him take with Galahad. Like a father about to chastise his son for bad behavior. When Arthur saw Galahad's stricken face, his own softened. "No, Galahad. You need to stick to Red's side. You will be her protector while I am gone."

Galahad looked as though he would protest, but Jennifer watched as he realized it was a losing battle. Galahad looked to her, then nodded.

"I will keep her safe."

Jennifer's heart swelled. How she would leave Galahad behind after all this, she didn't know. But when she did, she could only hope someone would keep him close and keep him safe. If it was Gawain's family, great. But to her, she wanted it to be Arthur.

Snaking an arm around her shoulders, Arthur led her and Galahad toward the group of men who had been looking curiously on.

Once Arthur had rejoined the group, he spoke for a couple of minutes on general formations and scenarios. Then, he dismissed the men to head back to their respective people to pass along the plan.

Kay and Gawain remained, their little travel party.

"Alright there, Red." Gawain shot her his patented lopsided grin. Jennifer rolled her eyes, but couldn't stop the smile.

"Gawain," she greeted with a nod.

They ambled over to the nearest section of rampart and began to talk more strategy. Gawain would lead one flank, and Kay the other. They discussed splitting the cavalry, what little cavalry they had managed to muster. Arthur looked at her, as if she knew anything about tactics. She had a feeling he would win the battle, but she didn't know *how* he would.

"Yeah, splitting the cavalry is probably your best option. Outflank them," Jennifer commented, completely talking out of her ass. She figured she would go with whatever his plan was, because that was the winning plan as far as she knew.

The men talked for a little longer before dispersing—Gawain and Kay to the meeting hall for some ale and Arthur and Jennifer to walk along the ramparts. Galahad opted to go with Gawain and Kay who didn't seem to mind having an extra. They jostled Galahad around as though he were their little brother and bantered back and forth between them.

The sun began to dip below the horizon, and dusk began to fall.

Arthur clasped Jennifer's hand and held tightly, perhaps more than he meant to. They eventually stopped, and he rested his elbows on the battlement.

For a while, they stood in silence, looking out over the wide open field before them. Flickers of campfires began to pop up like fireflies. It didn't matter; both sides of the battle knew where the other was. Arthur's army was at the foot of the hill fort, and the Saxons were across the field, sheltering half hidden in a tree line.

"Do you know how many there are?" Jennifer asked softly.

"A scout gave us a rough count. No more than a couple

thousand. We have less, but...we have the ferocity of desperation in our favor."

Arthur spoke with a confidence Jennifer knew he didn't actually feel.

"It will be okay," she told him, resting her hand on his forearm. Arthur turned his head to catch her gaze and smiled slightly. His other hand came to rest on top of hers.

"If you keep saying it will be okay, then it will be so."

"You know,"—Jennifer grinned—"that may be the first time you've ever agreed with me."

"How dare you!" Arthur scoffed in mock indignation. Jennifer laughed.

In the light of the fading sun, they stood, looking out at the field that would become many men's graves. They remained silent, as there was no reason to speak really, only to enjoy each other's company.

Jennifer squinted, trying to make out any shapes she could at the far tree line. She *knew* Morgan was there, amongst them, could practically feel the other woman's eyes on her. It sent a shiver through her body.

The uncertainty of the morning and the rest of the day weighed heavily on them as Arthur led her from the rampart. Twilight had fallen, giving the hill fort an ethereal appearance, coupled with the sporadic groups of people around campfires. Arthur stopped to share a few words with every group.

Most of the men had retreated down the hill to bed down amongst their comrades, but a few had remained atop the hill to be with their families. In the early hours of the morning, the women, children, and older men that couldn't fight would be herded into the meeting hall. Jennifer didn't like this idea for herself, but she knew it would give Arthur peace of mind.

Slowly, they made their way across the hilltop, making for the very meeting hall that would be her refuge tomorrow. Or the place she would die. Who was to say? Maybe the legend was just that—a legend. Maybe Arthur actually lost at Badon Hill.

But intuition said she wasn't wrong. That tomorrow would be a win.

His hand gripped tightly around hers, Arthur led Jennifer up the low steps and into the spacious room of the meeting hall. It resembled all of the mead halls Jennifer had seen in any movie about Vikings, but the Britons had their own style. The rafters above were barely visible in the low light of the fire in the center of the room. A hole in the ceiling allowed for ventilation, and afforded a great view of the star-filled sky beyond.

There were many people scattered about the room. A quick scan showed Galahad had found a spot on the wood planks of the floor, and slept as though there'd be no battle tomorrow. Gawain and Kay sat in a corner, drinking something from mugs and chatting with a group of young women.

Typical.

Arthur tugged Jennifer over to where Galahad lay, and sat on a nearby bench, guiding her down next to him. He pulled her against his side and set his chin on her head. Jennifer took in a deep breath, memorizing the scent of him. Leather, campfire, the fresh air outdoors, and something purely him. It was surprisingly soothing, and Jennifer settled against him, basking in his warmth.

She had expected the hall to be filled with raucous laughter and vibrant conversation, anything to take their minds off the impending day. But the mood was somber, subdued, and the conversations were hushed murmurs, until there was a commotion off to the back of the hall, and a group of men pushed a young man and woman forward. They looked embarrassed, like they wanted to make a break for it.

"Sing!" the men cried. "Sing, sing!"

The man and woman wanted to protest, but seeing the hopeful and expectant eyes of the rest of the crowd, they looked at each other and nodded.

The woman began first, her voice low. And as she sang louder, the man joined in. The melody was haunting, but Jennifer became mesmerized by their voices and the lyrics. The song spoke of a man, about to embark on a long journey. But first, he had to bid goodbye to his lady love. Both were certain they'd never see the other again.

Months passed, then a year. The hero was away, searching for something. While gone, his lady love gave birth to a boy. When the boy turned two, the lady love knew she'd never see her hero again. But her love for the hero manifested in her love for her son. The boy grew to manhood, strong and a capable warrior like his father. And then one day, a stranger came to their village. A man cloaked and shadowed. The son, ever protective of his mother and his village, halted the man to ask his business. The stranger claimed he knew the whereabouts of the boy's father. The boy was aghast, only ever knowing that his father was dead. The lady love hurried over, desperate to hear of a word, anything, about her hero. The stranger threw back his cloak to reveal he had been the hero all along. The lady love was beside herself, and the reunited lovers embraced. As it turned out, the hero had been held captive and lost in a distant land. But he never stopped trying to get back to his lady love.

The song ended happily, which Jennifer hadn't expected. But a happy song seemed like the appropriate kind, and when the woman sang the last note, the sound resounding and echoing around them, there was silence for a long beat. And then the room erupted into applause. The young woman blushed and did a little curtsy motion in thanks. Then the men behind them started chanting for another song. This time, the tune they struck up was lighthearted and funny, and the men joined in. Soon, the whole hall sang, and Galahad slept on like the dead.

Arthur stood, holding his hand out to Jennifer. She took it curiously and followed him as Arthur led the way around the perimeter of the room. He brought her to a door that blended well with the back wall, and he pushed through it.

Jennifer took in the space. It was a room about the size of her apartment's living room, perhaps a little smaller. It was devoid of furniture, having long since been taken away by someone. There were two openings on the far side meant to be windows, which allowed for minimal light to trickle in. It was enough for Arthur to see himself over to the far right corner to light a candle.

"Whose room is this?" Jennifer asked.

When Arthur succeeded in lighting the candle, it illuminated the space a little more, enough for her to see where he had set up a pallet of blankets.

"It would have been for the druid of the hill fort," Arthur replied, turning back to her. "They would have been in charge of keeping the hearth fire in the hall lit. I commandeered the room for you."

"For me? Really?"

Arthur shrugged. "Sure. Something a little different."

What a thoughtful gesture. One that Arthur wouldn't have enacted lightly. She had seen several instances where he would never want to take any more than what his soldiers had.

It was endearing, to say the least.

For a long moment, neither of them spoke. They simply stared across the room at the other, the light of the candle sending eerie, flickering shadows against the wall. Jennifer's chest felt tight, panic and fear gripping at the muscles. There was something else hanging between them too. Something charged, sending little sparks against her skin. Whatever it was mounted, heating the air between them.

Before either realized it, they were meeting in the center of the room with a clash, lips hungry and seeking, seeking something. Companionship? Knowing that tomorrow was not guaranteed and deciding to make the most of it?

Jennifer's hands buried in his hair. It was softer than she thought it would be. Arthur's arms banded around her waist, holding tightly.

"Wait..." Arthur wrenched away, forcing himself to unravel his arms from her. He took a step back, and then another.

"What?" Jennifer asked, slightly stunned from the abrupt end to a kiss that had made her toes curl.

"I did not bring you in here for..." he trailed off, and Jennifer was certain there was a pinker tinge to his cheeks.

She couldn't help it; she laughed.

Arthur looked indignant at first, offended. But then he chuckled.

Jennifer closed the space between them, this time to take his face in hand. She framed his cheeks, yanking him forward to press a softer kiss to his mouth.

"I know you didn't bring me in here for *that*," Jennifer teased. "But I'm telling you...I don't mind one bit."

"Is that so?" he asked, voice rougher than she'd ever heard it. His arms came back around her, pulling her close.

"Mm-hmm," Jennifer hummed, in that same teasing tone from earlier near the ramparts. "In fact, I am prepared to be the one to seduce you."

Arthur snorted. "Oh? I am not sure you would be up to the task."

"You've underestimated me before."

"That I have," Arthur said softly. He brushed his thumb across Jennifer's cheek.

Curling her hand around the back of his neck, Jennifer brought Arthur's mouth to hers once more, starting slowly, quickly becoming more heated. They fumbled in the dark, toeing off their shoes and divesting each other of their clothing. Jennifer loved untying the leather straps of his armor and watching it slide across his broad shoulders, down his arms, and then fall to the floor.

Jennifer's gown soon joined it, and she couldn't help but laugh as Arthur struggled with the concept of her bra.

Slowly, they lowered themselves onto the surprisingly comfortable bed Arthur had constructed. The blankets were a little scratchy on her skin, but it only added to the sensation. Arthur's touch was slow and methodical, cataloging each inch he encountered, each dip and rise. It was torturous, but exquisitely so. Only when his mouth began to follow the same pathways did Jennifer begin to become impatient.

After what seemed like hours of their hands and mouths exploring the other, blurring the line between where one started and the other ended, Arthur carefully and gently joined their bodies. This was by no means Jennifer's first time, but it had been quite a while. She clung to his wide shoulders as he began a slow rhythm, pulling every sound of pleasure from her that he could until they both reached the heights of bliss. The pleasure of it hit Jennifer hard, making her shudder and cry out.

Never had it felt so good. So right.

As Arthur gripped her tightly to his chest, both lying in the silence of the aftermath, a few tears rolled from the corners of her eyes.

This time, Jennifer knew for sure it was a dream.

She stood in the middle of the meeting hall, devoid of people. The fire had gone out, but only recently, as the embers still emitted wisps of smoke. The bright glow of the sun shone down through the smoke hole in the ceiling, raining its rays down on her. Jennifer looked around, trying to find the presence she could feel, watching her from the shadows.

"Who's there?"

Her voice had an odd echo, even in the empty room.

A floorboard creaked to her right, and Jennifer whipped around to try and spot the source of the noise. She couldn't see through the shadows, but did not see a flicker of movement.

Her unease grew, and when she tried to take a step toward where the noise had sounded, she found she couldn't move her feet. They looked perfectly normal, but as if they'd been glued to the floor.

The creak came again, this time closer.

Jennifer still couldn't see anything. Surely something would've stepped into the light by now?

She made to move again, this time with a bit more force.

Her feet still would not budge.

The floorboard creak came again, even closer. Her heart beat so quickly in her chest, she thought it would fly out through her mouth. Surely whatever was there would hear its furious staccato.

Jennifer still could not see, but she could feel it. Whatever the presence was, it was heavy. The closer it got to her, the more oppressive the air around her felt. Whatever the thing was, it was evil. Pure, raw evil. She could feel the hairs on her arm stand on end, and a slinking, icy feeling crawled down her spine. Jennifer had never known real fear, but she sure felt it now. A low breath exhaled at her ear, cold and dank, and for a moment Jennifer felt chilled to the bone, so chilled she thought she may never feel warm again.

A strangled scream ripped past her lips, and the harsh breath came again. The cold seeped into her blood, into her very marrow.

Her feet were rooted to the floor, with no escape, and the ominous presence hovered near her.

It sounded like a horse's pant, like a deep breath through a long snout. The presence was not human at all.

A low hum began, quickly filling the room. Jennifer couldn't identify the source of the sound, but it grew louder and louder. The hum took shape, took form into words. Into a language she'd never heard before, something malevolent and not of this world. Her brain didn't even attempt to try to translate it, and for once, Jennifer was grateful.

Icy tingles curled around her shoulders, one by one as though physical claws, inhumanly long fingers.

A breath came again, as did the urge to turn around.

When she did, what she saw horrified her, nearly making her heart stop.

Her mouth parted, and she screamed.

The light of the early morning sun trickled in through the window openings, falling across Jennifer's face and rousing her from her dream. She hadn't thought she'd actually sleep, but it seemed she was able to doze, however tenuously. Never had her dreams been so vivid, and she couldn't help but feel they were all a warning. She knew she'd seen the face of whatever the presence had been in her dream, but now that she was awake, she couldn't recall what it looked like. Probably for the best.

As her eyes blinked open, focusing on the bedding, she saw Arthur had slipped out at some point. She vaguely recalled him pressing a warm kiss to her forehead, and then shifting their positions. His clothes were gone, along with the leather armor.

Christ, she'd nearly forgotten.

Scrambling up, she grabbed her clothes and shoes,

dressing in record time. After slinging her pack across a shoulder, she burst into the main hall to find it filled mostly with women, children, and the elderly. Frantically, she searched the crowd, but couldn't find Galahad.

Distantly, the steady staccato of drums began to beat.

The battle was starting.

CHAPTER 22

"Jennifer!"

She turned at the sound of her name, and breathed a sigh of relief at the sight of Galahad making his way to her.

"Galahad, thank God. You're alright?"

The boy nodded. "The men left about a half hour ago," Galahad said, looking forlorn.

"Hey, he's going to be fine. They all are," Jennifer reassured him.

Galahad looked as skeptical as Arthur had been at her predictions. She was beginning to doubt them herself.

"I want to watch from the ramparts," Galahad declared.

"We can't. We have to stay in here with everyone else."

Galahad's chin tipped up, defiance in his eyes. "I want to watch."

Jennifer had to admit she too wanted to watch. She glanced around, wondering who would stop them anyway. She sighed.

"Okay, but we have to duck low and keep out of people's way."

Galahad nodded enthusiastically, grabbed her hand, and began tugging her toward the entrance of the hall.

Outside, the sun hung low on the horizon, climbing its way up. A mist had settled over the top of the fort, and with one glance down into the field, Jennifer saw it covered the expanse. As the two scurried over to a section of the stone wall, they could see their men, but they couldn't see the Saxon force clearly. Jennifer hoped the sun rose as quickly as it could and burned off the fog.

It took a moment, but Jennifer finally spotted Arthur down at the front line. She was hurt he hadn't said goodbye, but she wasn't great at them either.

He'd win the day, and she'd see him again.

She just knew it.

Arthur walked along the line, and she could see his lips moving. Perhaps another motivational talk to get the men in the fighting spirit? At one end of the formation stood Kay, and Gawain at the other. They were all so familiar to her, she could pick them out in a crowd easily.

Across the far end of the field, the Saxons began chanting. Based on a rhythmic thumping sound, they'd begun to beat their weapons against their shields. And on top of all this, the war drums still echoed around them.

The Britons did not sway; they did not flinch. From here, Jennifer could see their rigid poses, completely in control of their fear.

For a time, the two sides just stood, neither moving to advance. The sun crept higher and higher, the heat of it finally ridding the field of the fog. The Saxons became more visible, and honestly, Jennifer didn't know why the Britons didn't run terrified. They looked fierce across that field, continuously thumping against their shields, chanting to their gods to keep them safe and to make meat of their enemies. It was a good thing she was most likely the only one that knew what they were saying.

Jennifer kept an arm around Galahad's shoulder, pulling him tightly to her side, as though that alone could protect him.

Finally, the atmosphere shifted, and Arthur raised his arm, ancestral sword aloft.

On the other side of the field, a lone Saxon stepped out. The leader. No doubt Torvulf, Morgan's husband.

The battle was about to begin.

Arthur waited, as did the Saxon.

Finally, the Saxon grew impatient. He raised both of his arms, one empty, the other clutching an axe. He brought them down, chopping through the air violently. The Saxon army roared and began to advance, many of them running at full tilt.

Arthur waited still.

The Saxons didn't falter; they came forward like a wave. Jennifer's heart leapt into her throat, the anticipation of the two sides clashing becoming too much.

Finally, Arthur's arm went down, and he ran ahead with the rest of the front line, while archers unleashed a volley from behind. Some of the Saxons fell to the ground, arrows sticking out from their bodies.

The two lines drew near, and Jennifer held her breath. It was as if all the air and sound in the atmosphere disappeared, becoming a vacuum, just as the two sides collided.

With a sickening thud, the first weapons hit, and the battle roared to life.

For what seemed like ages, all Jennifer could see was pure chaos. But she kept an eye on Arthur who mowed his way through his opponents as gracefully as always. If there weren't men's lives being lost, she would have called his movements majestic, an art form.

She turned to check on Kay first, seeing him also holding his own as the fierce fighter he was. Gawain as well, his more of a brute strength, taking down two and three Saxons at a time.

Despite all of the clamor and activity on the field, Jennifer didn't miss the figure dressed in dark clothing stepping from the far tree line.

Long dark hair gave her away.

Morgan.

Jennifer's instincts had been right. She thought she'd felt Morgan's eyes on her yesterday. With her husband being the leader of this army, where else would she have gone anyway?

Morgan continued forward, casually, as though a whole bloody battle was not happening right in front of her. She picked her way through the fighting crowd, no man getting near her. Jennifer wondered if that was just Morgan's raw power, or if men subconsciously knew she was there and avoided her.

When nothing befell her, Jennifer's worry grew.

Morgan wasn't trying to battle any of the men.

Morgan was coming for her.

For the book.

Jennifer swallowed thickly, and began pulling Galahad away from the battlement.

"You need to get inside the meeting hall," she told him. "Please. Do not argue with me. Get inside the meeting hall. *Go!*"

Galahad must've heard the desperation in her voice. For once, he did as she bade and ran off back into the meeting hall.

Jennifer hiked the pack up higher, feeling the heft of the book as if it weighed tons instead of mere ounces.

Morgan had cleared the fight and calmly began the ascent

up the hillside. Her light gaze leveled on Jennifer. She felt it, as though a living thing crawling across her scalp.

Jennifer's heart rate kicked up, beating so wildly she thought it might just stop.

What could she do to fight Morgan?

The woman had *power*. And with Jennifer's luck, probably knew how to use a physical weapon as well.

Jennifer's gaze started wildly looking around, looking for anything she could improvise with.

Then she remembered the knife. The knife with the strangely familiar symbol.

Quickly, she swung the pack around in front of her and began rooting around until her fingers circled around the hilt of the dagger. She then returned the pack to resting against her back and held up the knife.

Dear God, she hadn't anticipated this.

She could very well die in the next five minutes.

Her stomach roiled and knotted, anxiety scrambling rational thought.

Hesitantly, Jennifer took off the scabbard and held out the knife, pointy side forward. She planted her feet, hip-width apart, and dug in. As she waited for Morgan to appear, an unexpected calm fell over Jennifer. Her breathing slowed, and her heart began to beat at a much more manageable pace.

And then, there she was. Morgan had made her way to the rampart gate a few yards down and had easily picked her way through. She walked with that same displaced calm, as though she already knew she'd won.

"Give me the book and the necklace, and I will let you live."

Perhaps in better circumstances, Jennifer would've admired Morgan's ability to cut right to it.

"You're not getting either," Jennifer told Morgan with

more confidence than she felt. Morgan laughed, but the sound was completely devoid of humor.

"You act as though you have a choice in the matter. Either you give them to me, or you die."

Jennifer shook her head, moving her weight from foot to foot. "And I say again as I said in my dream. You. Are not. Getting. The book. Or necklace."

Morgan frowned.

"You don't need to die because of it," she said. "It's meaningless to you. As are these people. I know you don't belong here. I can help you get home. But I need that book."

Jennifer's palm slipped slightly on the hilt of the knife, sweating from nerves. She didn't know what she'd do, but she knew she had to do something.

"The book and *those people* are not meaningless to me. Your words are what are meaningless to me. *You* are the real enemy here," Jennifer sneered.

Morgan looked taken aback, surprised Jennifer had a spine.

Jennifer was surprised herself.

"So be it." Morgan took a step forward, and Jennifer tensed, then lashed out with the knife. It went nowhere near the dark-haired woman, but it showed Morgan that Jennifer meant business. Morgan jolted back, away from the careless swipe. She smirked, then lifted her hand.

An invisible force clamped around Jennifer's throat, squeezing just enough to disable. Jennifer went ramrod straight, dropping the dagger. She couldn't move one muscle in her body.

And she had really thought she could stand her own against Morgan?

The other woman stepped forward again, circling Jennifer's frozen form. Morgan reached her pack and began to root around. She paused for a moment when she spotted the stack of parchment. Shoving her hand in, Morgan pulled it out.

"I told you it didn't have to be so hard," Morgan purred in Jennifer's ear as she came back around. The only thing Jennifer could move were her eyes, and she saw the dark-haired woman clutching the book to her. "Thank you for retrieving this for me, Jennifer. I truly meant what I said. I do not wish you harm. But them..." Her dark gaze turned toward the rampart, where they couldn't see the battle waging beyond it. "Descendants of Roman scum. They can rot." She spat on the ground.

Morgan began to walk away, but then turned, as though remembering something else.

"I wish you only the best of luck returning home." She smiled, but it was far from genuine. She stepped up, reached down the neck of Jennifer's gown, and yanked the necklace from around her neck. "I have a feeling we may yet see each other again. I long for that day, in fact."

Then, she was gone, back over the rampart.

Jennifer could still not move for a time, and then suddenly the magic lifted, and she collapsed to the ground. Stunned, she lay there for a beat.

The book was gone. And so was the necklace.

Taken.

Her only means of returning to her time, returning home, gone.

She'd failed at the task she'd been given by Emrys and Father Lucas.

As fast as she could, Jennifer scrambled to her feet, rushing forward and grasping the edge of the rampart as she looked over.

The sight she saw startled her to her core.

The Britons had been well on their way to winning the last she'd seen, before her attention had moved solely to Morgan. Something had happened in the short time she'd been occupied.

The cavalry had split, and instead of flanking the Saxon forces, another group had appeared from the trees. The Saxons had split their army as well, anticipating Arthur would do the same. And now, Jennifer watched the bloodbath, as the second wave of Saxons came charging forward into the fray, catching the Britons off guard.

Jennifer watched helplessly as the Saxons began overtaking the Britons. She watched as many fell to brutal swipes of swords or chops of axes. Frantically, she searched for any familiar figure, and saw Kay, relieved to see he still held his own.

Her gaze swept the field and found Gawain.

Just as a Saxon swung high with his axe and brought the blade into Gawain's chest.

Jennifer could almost hear the sickening crack and thud from where she was standing.

A scream rent the air. She didn't realize it was her.

Vibrant, flirty, handsome Gawain fell to his knees. The Saxon wrenched the axe from Gawain's chest and didn't hesitate when he swung again, this time connecting with Gawain's neck.

Jennifer looked away just in time. She couldn't bear to watch.

Everywhere on the field below, Britons began dropping like flies, overwhelmed by the surprise Saxon attack.

How had it come to this?

The Battle of Badon Hill was supposed to have been an overwhelming victory for the Britons.

Morgan.

She must have done something.

Hot tears streamed down Jennifer's face. She panicked further when she couldn't find Arthur. But there he was, fighting like the hounds of hell were on his tail, and he had only moments left to live.

Brave, gallant Arthur.

Jennifer watched in horror as the Saxon from earlier, the one that had signaled the initial attack, Torvulf, fell into step before Arthur. Leader against leader, they circled each other, weapons at the ready. Their swords clanged when they met, and a fierce duel began. Once more, Jennifer held her breath, hoping against hope there was still a way to salvage this.

If only she had the book and the necklace.

If only she had read the book more carefully.

Arthur went in for a decided attack, and the Saxon bent under the force of the blow. He fell to his knee, and Arthur appeared victorious. Only, as Arthur went to deal the death blow, the Saxon reared up, not having been as injured as first thought.

Jennifer could only look on as the Saxon surged forward, ramming the point of his blade into Arthur's gut. Arthur, his arms having been above his head to make the crushing blow, froze. His arms fell to his sides, and his sword, the one that was supposed to lead him to victory, fell to the ground. He went to his knees, the shock of his impending death numbing him.

Jennifer's throat quickly went raw, screaming and screaming as Arthur slumped to the side, motionless. The Saxon raised his arms, eliciting a victorious roar from his men. She felt as though she'd be sick, but she couldn't look away from Arthur, so still, lifeless.

Her heart tore open, and she couldn't think. She couldn't process. She couldn't fathom this was the true outcome of the day.

"No," she said over and over between choked sobs, and

watched as the Saxons began racing up the hill to take the hill fort. It was only a matter of time before she met her end too.

The tears came, in waves it seemed. She couldn't see the battlefield in front of her anymore, as it blurred and shifted. All sound around her stopped. She couldn't even hear her own breathing. The Saxons had been screaming as they began their climb up the hill. Their mouths were still open, as if still screaming, but no sound could be heard. Despite their nearness, they became out of focus, blurring even more.

Where was Emrys?

He could fix this, couldn't he?

After all, the man *had* to be Merlin. And Merlin had all of the power, *right?*

God, Emrys, please.

Jennifer panted, her chest rising and falling as she tried so hard to take in deep breaths. But she couldn't, as though all of the air around her had been sucked away. Everything felt like it was closing in on her. She felt the weight of Gawain and Arthur and probably Kay's death on her shoulders. She felt Galahad's, she felt all of those helpless people's deaths were on her.

Oh God.

Jennifer blinked furiously, trying to rid her eyes of the salty tears that burned, to see how close her death came.

But no matter how much she tried, she could not clear her vision.

Then, she heard it.

The sound began faintly. So low, she couldn't make it out.

It grew louder, now a dull roar.

The roar grew louder and louder until she was sure it would deafen her. She clasped her hands to her ears, as though that would keep out the sound.

But it was coming from *inside* her head.

There was no stopping it.

Just as the thunderous noise reached its crescendo, Jennifer fell back, hitting the ground. If she could breathe, the very wind would've been knocked from her lungs. Stunned, she lay there, letting the noise deafen her.

And then everything went black.

CHAPTER 23

Darkness.
Or perhaps just the back side of her eyelids?
Silence.

The silence jarred her, catching her by surprise purely based on the fact she'd been on a battlefield.

Sound came rushing back, softly at first and then rapidly growing louder until Jennifer's eyes slammed open.

She lay on the ground, looking up into a group of concerned faces gathered around her.

Arthur? But he had...

Gawain?

Kay?

How could this be? She'd watched them all die one by one to a Saxon axe or sword or knife.

All she remembered was this overwhelming feeling, like the air had been stolen from her lungs or had solidified. Her vision had blurred, jarring in and out of focus, until she'd lost consciousness.

At least, it *seemed* like she'd lost consciousness.

"Red, what happened?" Arthur asked, concern in his eyes, making her chest ache more.

"I...what...how are you...?" Jennifer stuttered, looking from face to face.

"How much did you drink last night?" Kay joked, earning a chuckle from Gawain.

With some help from Arthur, Jennifer sat up, taking in her surroundings.

She was still in the hill fort, only in a different location. The battle hadn't yet occurred.

How was that possible?

They had lost not five minutes ago!

At least she'd thought they'd lost?

God, how the terror had ripped her apart. After reassuring Arthur she couldn't imagine anything but a victory over the Saxons. She'd all but guaranteed them the win.

Arthur helped her to her feet and held her steady even as she swayed.

How had this happened?

Arthur was still alive.

The battle hadn't happened yet.

Looking around the landscape with critical eyes, Jennifer realized she'd somehow found herself back in that moment from the previous day, where they had stood on the ramparts of the hill fort, looking down at the field below, planning their strategy.

Somehow, some way, Jennifer had traveled back to before the start of the battle.

There weren't any stones around. She'd lost the book and necklace to Morgan...

But that wasn't true either, because the book was on the ground, in her pack, having dropped it when she collapsed. She'd had it on her shoulder the entire meeting.

Could she have done this on her own? Or had there been

an outside force to help? Had Emrys somehow helped her? Or some other unknown entity that could bend time?

"You alright, love?" Kay's face came swimming into her line of sight, looking genuinely concerned. "You're as white as milk."

Jennifer shook her head. "I'm fine. Promise." A pause. "What happened?"

"Well," Kay began, "we were standing here, discussing strategy, and then all of a sudden you just keeled over. It was odd. You fell back like something had knocked into you."

What the hell?

"Huh," Jennifer mused, trying to play the whole situation off as if nothing had happened. "I felt a little dizzy. But I'm okay now."

Kay accepted the answer, and so did Gawain and Galahad. Arthur didn't look convinced.

The men continued discussing their strategy, in the exact manner and tone in which they had before, right down to the same words.

"Don't split your cavalry," Jennifer blurted, realizing that, regardless of how she'd gotten there, she'd be damned if she didn't ensure the Battle of Badon Hill went off as it should. Arthur was to have a resounding victory, the kind that would make him infamous throughout the whole island.

Rule Number one be damned.

"What do you mean?" Arthur huffed, brow crinkling. "You said—"

"I know what I said," Jennifer snapped, desperation rising in her chest. "Forget that I said it, and don't split your cavalry."

"But—"

"Arthur!" Jennifer growled, reaching out to grasp the sides of his face between her palms. She softened her voice. "Please, just...do this. *Please.*"

He must've seen something in her eyes. His handsome face hardened, a muscle in his jaw tightening ever so slightly. He nodded.

"Thank you," Jennifer breathed. Then she turned without another word, scampering off as fast as her feet would carry her.

The people of the hill fort rushed to and fro, exactly as she had remembered. Preparations were well underway, fortifying weak spots to keep the women and children safe while the men were on the field.

Jennifer hit a patch of mud and slid a couple of feet before catching her balance. She had to hide the book. She had to put it in a safer place.

Dodging around people and between groups, Jennifer pushed, her chest burning from the exertion. When she got home—*if*—she'd take up the gym again.

"Jennifer!"

She stopped dead, clutching the strap of her pack tightly. Glancing over her shoulder, she saw Galahad trying to get around the throng of people bustling about.

"Galahad," she said, turning.

"What're you doing?" Galahad asked. "Can I help?"

Poor kid. She remembered from—well, last time — that he had wanted a task, but no one would give him one, especially not a sword to join in the fray. Arthur had insisted he keep his head down, to stay safe.

"Sure." Jennifer forced a smile. "Come on."

Spinning on her heel, she made for the back of the hill fort, carefully picking her way down the side of the hill. She could hear Galahad huffing and puffing behind her, trying to keep up.

"Where're we going?" he asked between panted breaths.

Jennifer didn't respond.

Mostly because she didn't know.

About halfway down the hill, she stopped and turned back, looking around the side of the hill, then down the rest of the slope. Finally, she spotted an outcropping, some sort of natural rock formation near the base of the hill.

"I need to keep it safe," Jennifer said in response to Galahad's confusion. She made for the rocks, double-timing it.

Skidding to a halt, with one look at the way the rocks sat, she knew this would be the perfect place.

Morgan had expected her to have the book near her at all times. That's what Jennifer had underestimated before.

Not again. Not with this second chance.

Reaching into the hollow space formed by the rocks, Jennifer swept out the leaves and sticks that had blown in over time. Once satisfied, she pulled the bound stack of parchments from the pack, then pulled the necklace over her head. Turning to Galahad, she set the necklace on top of the book and held the objects out to him.

"Try and hide these as best you can. Make it look natural, though. No one but you and I can be able to find this. Do you understand?"

Galahad's eyes widened at the severity of Jennifer's tone. She'd entrusted him with this task, and by the set of his slim, little shoulders he would take the command seriously.

And he did.

As Galahad worked, Jennifer took the opportunity to scan the surrounding area. There was a concerning tree line a handful of yards away, but she didn't see anything that seemed out of place. She didn't feel the spidery crawling of her skin, that feeling of being watched. Her gut told her it would be safe this time.

And Arthur would win, as he was meant to.

Kneeling down, she rummaged around in the pack, adjusting the contents, attempting to give the illusion something important resided in it.

"What do you think?" Galahad asked, prompting Jennifer to turn back to him. She glanced over his handiwork, trusting he would have handled it well enough. And he sure had. The rock formation almost looked as how she'd found it.

"Perfect." She forced a shaky smile she didn't feel, stood while slinging the pack over her shoulder again, and reached out to ruffle his hair. "Come on, we've got to get back before they close off the fort for the night."

The climb back up seemed to take forever, mostly because Jennifer kept looking back, making sure the surrounding area remained empty and no one would follow them or try to claim the book.

It was a risky-ass move. One she wouldn't have taken under normal circumstances. Based on what had happened, though, Jennifer felt—*knew*—this was the right course of action.

The atmosphere was even more tense when Galahad and Jennifer returned to the center of the fort. All of the women and children made their way into the gathering hall, while the men finished their last-minute preparations.

Through the thinning crowd, she found Arthur and practically hurled herself into his arms, clutching tightly.

"Whoa, now, hey...what's this about?" he muttered against the crown of her head as he held her close.

"No reason," she replied damply, the tears welling. "Just wanted to hold you."

The rest of the night played out exactly as it had before, though this time without the disturbing dream. Jennifer stayed up, unable to sleep knowing what would happen if she wasn't vigilant in trying to change it. She watched Arthur sleep. Their lovemaking this time had been a bit more desperate. She'd not wanted to waste a moment.

Eventually, Arthur rose just before the sunrise and began to dress. She watched him, hoping like hell this wouldn't be the last time she saw him. Eventually, she extricated herself from the warmth of the makeshift bed to dress herself.

Outside the main hall, the air possessed a chill she didn't remember before. Jennifer shook off the thought.

Arthur was armed to the teeth with daggers and his sword. He clutched a spear in his non-dominant hand. His thick leather armor conformed to his broad chest.

She wondered if he had left any parts of his family's Roman armor behind in Caerleon. He'd look so handsome in the shining metal.

Arthur continued to give last-minute directions, waving his hand around, pointing here and there. Gawain stood off to his side, his hands folded casually on the hilt of the sword at his side. Kay had much the same stance on Arthur's other side.

It inexplicably made Jennifer's eyes well with tears.

Arthur's knights. Faithful warriors always at his side.

The stuff of legend. Right there. Right in front of her eyes. Galahad just needed to grow a few more years to be at Arthur's side as well.

Knights of the Round Table.

After Arthur felt satisfied all innocents were well cared for within the gathering hall, he turned to Jennifer and Galahad, motioning for them to do the same. Like hell she'd stay there, but for his peace of mind, she'd let him think they were in there. Safe and sound.

"Be safe," Jennifer said.

"I promise," Arthur whispered, brushing his fingers down Jennifer's cheek. "I'll come back."

"You better," Jennifer growled, pressing her forehead to

his. Arthur chuckled, stealing a quick kiss, before forcing himself away and over the edge with his brothers-in-arms in tow.

This time, the battle progressed as originally intended. And this time, Jennifer hunkered down on the back side of the balustrades, watching the single point on the slope where she'd stashed the book. Some of the men had been stationed at the back of the hill fort to be on the lookout for attempts to sneak an attack from this side. Knowing it wouldn't happen, Jennifer had allowed Galahad to stand next to her, with a sword an armorer had assured her was dull. It gave him the illusion of being helpful, but like hell she'd let him actually engage in combat.

When a victorious cry rang from the front side of the hill, Jennifer bade Galahad to remain where he stood and keep an eye on their little secret. He nodded, looking resolute. He'd watch those rocks like a hawk.

Jennifer raced across the hilltop until she reached the edge of the fort and looked down.

The field beyond was reddened with blood, and the air rang with the cries of the wounded and dying. There were pillars of smoke where some clumps of peat had been set ablaze, but the most heartening sight was the dozens and dozens of Saxon warriors fleeing as fast as their legs could carry them.

God, how it had been harrowing to wait through this battle a second time. The first felt as though an eternity had passed, but this one ended as though in the blink of an eye. Jennifer let out a relieved breath. Every fiber of her being tugged to race down the hill as fast as she could to check on Arthur.

Where was Morgan?

The dark-haired woman hadn't appeared from the tree line as before. Had she gone elsewhere?

Turning, Jennifer once again traversed the top of the hill to the other side. She grasped Galahad's shoulder, then looked around the base of the incline. When she felt satisfied there was no danger, she bent to his ear. "Let's go retrieve our secret, eh?"

Galahad nodded enthusiastically, and they clambered over to the break in the fortifications. They began their descent, both keeping a sharp eye on the far tree line and on either edge of the hill.

The book and necklace still remained, tucked beneath Galahad's handiwork.

Another sigh of relief as she clutched it to her chest.

"Our task is complete," Galahad said proudly, and Jennifer chuckled, ruffling his hair affectionately once more.

"That it is. Let's get back up. I am sure there will be a lot of celebrating tonight."

Galahad ran ahead a little, happy at the prospect of a bit of merrymaking. Jennifer followed after him, but had only made a few steps before that smooth, familiar voice called from behind her.

"Thought I wouldn't find you?"

Ice slid down her spine, fear more for Galahad than herself. The boy turned, having heard Morgan. A fierce look overcame him, and he ran back down. Jennifer barely managed to catch her arm around his waist before he could go at Morgan fruitlessly.

"Don't..." Jennifer hissed, lacing her voice with more warning and bravado than she actually felt. "You won't get it. Not this time."

Morgan's eyes widened, and Jennifer knew she'd said the wrong thing.

"*This time?* Have you used it?"

If Jennifer didn't know any better, she'd say Morgan sounded awed and impressed. She had to watch what she said, lest Morgan surmise she hadn't needed the book to travel. She pushed Galahad behind her, ready to tell him to run, as fast as he could.

Galahad's safety was what mattered.

"You *have* used it," Morgan breathed, taking a step forward. Instinctively, Jennifer backed Galahad and herself up a step. The dark-haired beauty couldn't have been more than fifteen feet away, but that was fifteen feet too close for Jennifer's liking. "Tell me, please, what is it like?"

Jennifer scoffed. "Like hell I'd tell you."

Morgan pouted. "Aw, my dear, do not be so rude. I only asked a simple question."

"One I don't have to answer," Jennifer shot back.

Morgan took a few more steps, and this time, Jennifer held her ground but gave Galahad a shove back. He didn't appreciate it, because a second later, he'd settled at her side again, the dull sword clutched in his trembling hands, blade held toward Morgan. The other woman's dark gaze fell to him, to what he held, and she laughed. It was so unlike the laughter she'd shared with Kay and the others during their travels. The sound made the hairs on Jennifer's arms stand on end and goose bumps prickle up. The laugh seemed to echo, and a minute later, Galahad hissed in pain and dropped the sword as if it were on fire.

Jennifer glanced down to see the handle fade from a glowing red back to the normal color. Her jaw clenched.

"Give me the parchments, girl, and I will let your little urchin live," Morgan hissed before raising her hands, palms raised toward the sky, fingers curled as if claws.

"I would not do that if I were you, Bodiclara."

Emrys appeared out of thin air, mere feet behind Morgan

—or Bodiclara? There was no telling where the mage had Traveled from, but the fact he could was a true testament to his power. Jennifer suspected that didn't even scratch the surface. And judging by the barely concealed fright on Morgan's face, the other woman knew Emrys was capable of so much more.

"Do not get in my way, old man," Morgan warned, though Emrys waved the sentiment away as if it were a pesky fly.

"I will let you walk away with your life, Bodiclara. Just for today. Jennifer is under my protection and will remain so. Harm one hair on her head, and it will be your end."

Morgan's hands had fallen to her sides, where they clenched into fists now. She was angry, but wouldn't risk physical harm.

"I swear to Brigantia, Emrys. One day, I will be your end."

Once again, Emrys didn't seem concerned.

Morgan glanced from him to Jennifer. What happened next went so quickly, Jennifer was only left stunned. Morgan whipped to face Jennifer, held out her hand, then balled up her fist. Jennifer felt a sharp tug, as though someone was pulling on the book. She held fast, but did not anticipate Morgan spiriting the necklace into her hands. She clutched the wooden wheel by the leather cording, gave Jennifer the most wicked smile, then disappeared.

Jennifer let out the breath she'd been holding. Galahad, his hands clinging to her arm, softened his death grip.

"What the... Emrys, she took the necklace!" Jennifer cried, feeling her chances of returning home slip away.

"Yes, I can see that," Emrys replied.

"So...I need that to get home, right?" she asked, incredulous.

"Well, yes and no."

"What—?"

"Do not worry about it."

Jennifer sighed, unsure how in the hell she was supposed to *not worry* about this. Especially when her ticket home was just snatched. Instead of arguing with Emrys, which seemed futile, Jennifer asked, "Why did you call her that name?"

"That is her name," Emrys said, matter-of-factly. "The name her parents gave her. Many years ago."

Vague answer, Emrys's specialty. Jennifer knew well enough she wouldn't get much more out of him than that.

"Thank you, Emrys."

The old man nodded. "I had all the faith you would have gotten away."

Jennifer let out a burst of laughter. "Uh-huh. Which is why you intervened?"

Emrys looked offended. "Exactly. All the faith you would've been able to Travel yourself and your lad there back to the top."

"What do you mean by that?"

"I will explain later. But you did well, not allowing her the book. She craves it. Would do anything to get it."

Jennifer swallowed. "She said she wanted to right a wrong. Do you know what she means?"

Emrys nodded. "I do, but it is not my story to tell. We all have mistakes we would fix or wrongs we would make right. It is human nature. And while much that is inhuman pulses through Morgan's veins, at the heart of it, she is still very much a scared little girl." He waved his hand again, dismissing the thought. "But that's enough of that. We must get back up to everyone else. Your other lad will want to celebrate with you, no doubt."

Jennifer's cheeks reddened at the implications of his words and the teasing twinkle in his eyes. She wanted to reach out and swat at the old man, but didn't think she could risk losing a hand. Linking her arm with Galahad's, she turned them around and headed back up the hill.

CHAPTER 24

A steady stream of people had begun to pour from the hill fort and toward the city. In the chaos, Jennifer had yet to find Arthur, or even Kay or Gawain. She clutched Galahad to her side as they made their way into the center of Bath where everyone seemed to have gathered in what used to be the old forum. Emrys had tagged along, relatively silent. There were many cries of joy and tears of relief. Tavern owners had already begun distributing their product, mugs of ale in nearly every hand Jennifer could see. Someone had already produced instruments, and a lively tune had begun drifting across the teeming square.

It was bittersweet to know the truth. This happiness wouldn't last forever, and soon the island would become overrun with the culture of groups from the continent. Jennifer tried her best to tamp down her heartache.

"Kay!" Galahad exclaimed from her side, and ran off into the crowd toward wherever he had seen the lanky man. Jennifer stood on her toes, trying to get a glimpse of him. She turned, expecting to find Emrys next to her, but the little old man had disappeared.

Before she could wheel back around, a familiar scent reached her, of leather and grass and sweat, with a hint of copper this time. She knew it instantly, and then a sensation of warmth and safety washed over her.

"Alright there, Red?" Arthur said, so close his lips grazed the hinge of her jaw. Her eyelids fluttered shut and she shivered. Strong arms wound around her waist, clutching her close to a warm, firm chest. "You gonna thank me now from saving you from bloodthirsty invaders?"

Jennifer couldn't help but laugh, recalling that night in Corinium when they had first officially met, what seemed like so long ago.

"I'd rather thank you for saving me from a drunkard. I had the bloodthirsty invaders handled," she replied.

Arthur chuckled, the sound low and rumbling in his chest. She could feel the sound against her back.

"Of course you did," he whispered, his breath grazing across the skin above her pulse point. His lips soon pressed against that same spot, causing her breath to hitch.

After ensuring that Galahad was safe with Kay and Gawain, Arthur led Jennifer to the outskirts of the city, to where the River Avon rushed along its current. With no one else in sight, they began to remove each other's clothes and waded into the refreshing coolness of the water. Jennifer helped cleanse Arthur of blood and dirt, and they shared intimate kisses and touches well until the sun dipped low in the sky.

Hand in hand, they returned to the city center where the party still carried on.

After Arthur procured them both mugs of ale, they sat and talked and drank, heads tipped toward each other. At one point, Jennifer glimpsed Emrys in the crowd, tapping his wrist as if indicating a watch before disappearing again.

Her heart sank.

The time had come.

Jennifer had known it would, sooner or later.

After all, she had to go home, return to her family, her apartment, her job.

Her *life*.

When she had first found herself in Dark Ages England, Jennifer never imagined she wouldn't want to leave.

After excusing herself from Arthur's side, she headed off to the periphery of the celebrations. And there was Emrys, a sad smile on his face.

"I'm afraid we have to get you back to Avebury now," he said.

Swallowing thickly, Jennifer nodded.

"I will escort you back and help get you home," Emrys continued.

Raucous laughter filled the night air, the epicenter back in the old forum. Arthur was there, as were Kay, Gawain, and Galahad, laughing and reveling in the continued safety of their way of life.

The hot sting of tears pricked at Jennifer's eyes at the acceptance she would never see Arthur again. In such a short time, they had both been through so much together. A bond had been forged, one that couldn't easily be broken. Arthur had helped Jennifer live again, in the roundabout way only he could. Her feelings for him, whatever they were, hadn't been in any of her plans, but then again, being whisked away over a thousand years into the past hadn't been on the itinerary either.

"I'm ready," Jennifer said softly.

"Do you wish to say goodbye?" Emrys asked.

"I don't think that'd be a good idea."

"Fair enough. Shall we go?" he bade, before heading off toward the boundary of the city.

"You can't just magic us there?" Jennifer asked, taking off

after him, the pack he had given her feeling heavy on her back with the added weight of the book.

"I could ask you the same thing!"

Jennifer's brow furrowed. "What do you mean?"

Emrys sighed, shaking his head. "By the gods, I'm going to have to spell it out to you. When we get to Avebury, there are some things I will need to tell you."

Jennifer hated his cryptic replies.

They had nearly reached the gate out of Bath when a shout rang out behind them. Jennifer's heart seized.

"Red!"

It was Arthur.

"Where are you going?" he asked, halting at Jennifer's side. His cheeks were pink from the exertion and the drink he had consumed, but there was no mistaking the hurt just beneath the surface.

It took a lot from her to say the next five words.

"I have to go home."

Emrys backed away and around the wall of the city, giving them some privacy.

"Home." His voice was far away, soft, resigned. He knew exactly what she meant by *home*.

"Yes. I need to get back to my family. My friends." Jennifer reached forward to grasp Arthur's hands. She brought them up to press a soft kiss to the knuckles of each. "I'm sorry. But I don't belong here."

Though he might not fully understand it, and at this point who really did, Arthur knew Jennifer spoke the truth.

Jennifer had done what she needed to do, had learned a lesson in destiny the universe had needed to teach her. And along the way, she'd given this man a piece of her heart, whether he knew it or not, and now she would have to leave him with it.

"Are you...are you sure you cannot stay a while longer? Or...forever?"

Jennifer's heart shattered at Arthur's honesty, and the dam burst. She began to sob, clutching his hands like a lifeline. Arthur instantly wrapped her in his embrace.

He shouldn't be doing that. It would only make it harder to leave him.

"I'm sorry, but I can't..." she choked out past a sob, her chest burning like she couldn't breathe, tears pouring forth with no end in sight.

Arthur pulled back, enough to catch her gaze. "But what of those here that care for you? Galahad looks to you as though you hung the moon. Kay will be lost without you. Gawain will resume being the pain in my ass instead of you. And I—"

Arthur stopped. Jennifer held her breath. No more words came, and the tiny pieces of her shattered heart began to dissolve into nothingness, little by little.

It didn't matter whether he asked her to stay. Jennifer knew she couldn't, for many reasons beside the obvious. She didn't belong here, and the rules in the book said it was too dangerous to remain out of one's own timeline for very long. For the sake of her family, her job, and the safety of life in the universe as they knew it, she had to leave.

"Maybe we'll meet again someday," Jennifer said softly. The words reminded her of that song by Vera Lynn, about smiling through the pain and maybe seeing each other again. Don't know when, don't know where...but someday. She had to believe that.

"But—"

"No, please..." Jennifer interrupted. "Just...there's so much to say, I know. But we don't need to say it. It's better not to."

Arthur grimaced, his mouth pursed, trying to bite back his own tears.

Rocking up on her tiptoes, Jennifer pressed her lips to Arthur's in a soft, lingering kiss. Slowly, she pulled back, holding his watery gaze.

"I'm sorry," she whispered.

She forced herself to take a step back, and with one last longing look, she spun and hurried through the gate as fast as her feet could carry her.

The journey back to Avebury passed in a flash.

It seemed mere seconds in comparison to the arduous trek to St Michael's Mount. They met no one on the road, no remnants of the Saxon army, no Morgan.

They traveled through most of the night, only to stop and nap for a few hours before continuing on. They reached Avebury by midday, to find it was as quiet as when Jennifer had first arrived. The small village with a handful of buildings sat inside the stone circle. The locals were out, herding their livestock and tending to their small farms.

"You will need to be inside the stone circle this time," Emrys informed her as they set foot within the limits of the henge. "At the moment the solstice occurs tomorrow morning."

"That's all well and dandy, Emrys, but you have yet to explain to me how I'm supposed to get home without the talisman you gave me," Jennifer snapped as they made themselves comfortable near one of the standing stones.

"Oh, yes, right..." Emrys grumbled. "I forget sometimes that I have to spell the obvious out."

"Don't give me the condescending bullshit and just tell me."

"Fine. You've read the book, yes?" Emrys asked.

Jennifer shrugged. "Sure, I've read a good chunk of it."

"Then you know the ways a person is able to Travel?"

"Uh...I think something about natural and unnatural portals, and it being an inherent gift?"

Emrys nodded. "Guess how you came to be here, my dear."

"A natural portal here at Avebury?" Jennifer asked, but even before vocalizing her answer, she had the sinking feeling that what she had once believed to be the reason for being here was not the truth.

"I'm afraid not."

Jennifer sighed. "It was me?"

"After a fashion, yes. Your inherent abilities were dormant until you arrived here, where the potency of the henge awakened them."

"I don't understand how it's possible I have this ability."

Emrys sat down in the grass and patted the area beside him. Jennifer plopped down, every muscle in her body tense.

"As the book says, it is very rare for someone to possess the ability to Travel through time and space without the need of a portal. Because of this, the gift is generally confined to a family, because it can only be inherited through blood. There is someone, somewhere within your family tree, that possessed this same ability."

"My Grandmother Cassidy," Jennifer replied immediately. It had to be. It would explain her appearances and attempted warnings in her dreams. "But my father—?"

"It is quite possible, in your family's case, only the women inherit the ability."

"She never said anything..." Jennifer trailed off.

"Who would have believed her? Besides, she never fully understood how. She never had the book. She did have that ring, however."

Jennifer glanced down at her hand where her grandmother's moonstone ring had remained throughout her entire ordeal.

"It helps to steer, so to speak," Emrys explained. "You never needed that talisman I gave you. Just your ring."

"Why the hell did you lie to me?"

"Because I didn't want Morgan to realize the truth. The talisman is useless."

As much as she hated being lied to, Jennifer understood Emrys's reasoning.

"So, there was a moment when Morgan forced one of my companions to attack me, and I somehow got out from under him... That was me?"

Emrys nodded. "Indeed. Not only can you travel through time, you, of course, can travel through space."

"Like teleportation?"

"More or less."

Holy shit.

"Which brings me to why I wanted us to get here before the solstice. We will spend the remainder of the day practicing."

"I wouldn't even know how to make it happen. It just...did."

"In a moment of great need, sure. So let's see if we can get you to do it at will."

For the rest of the afternoon and evening, Emrys and Jennifer pored over the contents of the book, going over the mechanics of movement. It had taken her nearly all that time to move herself a mere five feet.

"Do not be so discouraged," Emrys said in an attempt to soothe her frustration. "It takes a lot of time to perfect these skills. Be proud of the distance you can move. And in time, you'll be able to not only transport yourself, but also others."

It took a lot out of her, attempting to teleport herself. By the time they broke for a late dinner, she was out of breath and drenched in sweat. The energy she had used made her voraciously hungry, and she made quick work of the leftover dried meats and fruits she had in her bag. "You know, I didn't think to ask," she said, after chewing a piece of venison. "Since you can Travel, are you like me?"

Emrys sighed. "That's a complicated question that I can't really answer. It's a yes and a no. But the explanation is for another time."

"Meaning I'll see you again?"

His expression turned grave, before he nodded. "Unfortunately, yes. And it won't be a friendly visit, that much I can say."

Of course not.

"Fantastic," Jennifer said ruefully.

"It seems all I ever give you are warnings, Jennifer," Emrys said. "But know that Morgan exists in your time, wearing a different face. Be careful who you trust, especially knowing what you are now. She will know who you are, and she will try to get the book from you again."

"Lovely."

"She won't be the only one trying to get the book from you either."

Jennifer was silent, her chest tight in panic.

"I'll never be safe again, will I?"

Emrys reached out, pressing a comforting hand to her shoulder. She could tell from the awkwardness in his pose he didn't do this sort of gesture often. "We all have to realize our destiny at some point. Your destiny just happens to be a bit more complicated and...exciting than others."

They remained in the darkened field, facing one of the

standing stones. Emrys dozed at some point in the night, but Jennifer couldn't sleep. So, she practiced. Moving herself a half inch farther every time. At some point, she exhausted herself and finally slept.

It didn't seem long, however, before Emrys was shaking her awake. The sky had begun to lighten, indicating the coming sun.

"Alright, you remember what you need to do?" he asked, positioning her in front of the stone. He double checked that the book was safely lodged in her pack. "Focus as hard as you can on the moment just before you fell asleep in that clearing. The ring and your own power will do the rest."

Jennifer nodded, panic setting in, choking off any reply she might've given. She shook out her arms, trying to loosen her shoulders. She bent her knees in a couple of squats, limbering up. It's not like she had this whole time travel thing down to a science. For all she knew, if she didn't concentrate hard enough, she'd end up in the damn Stone Age.

Shit, no, don't think about the Stone Age!

"Right. Okay. Let's do this."

"I will alert you to the right time," Emrys said. "Hold on to that moment as tightly as you can."

Jennifer nodded and focused on the stone in front of her. Her heart beat almost violently, nerves giving rise to nausea.

The stone didn't have as much lichen growing on its surface as it probably did in the present. To anyone else, it looked like any old stone, but she felt it now. Felt the power emanating from it, that drowsy pull that had driven her into the woods so many days ago.

Just as Jennifer closed her eyes to begin focusing on that day, the sound of hooves reached her ears, pounding on the dirt road leading inside the henge. Her eyes flew open, and as her gaze focused, she saw a flash of brown she'd recognize anywhere.

Llamrei.

On top of her sat Arthur, bent over her neck, pushing the poor horse to her limits. Jennifer gasped and turned to Emrys, who had already spotted the approach. The old man rolled his eyes and looked as though he was about to gag. He glanced at the horizon, judging the encroaching light, before turning back to her and nodding reluctantly.

Jennifer grinned and jetted out from behind the stone, her legs moving as fast as they could toward the approaching rider.

Arthur yanked poor Llamrei's reins back, causing the mare to come to a sliding halt. He was off the horse with one swing of his leg, and he hit the ground running.

As soon as Jennifer drew near, she launched herself into his arms, and Arthur caught her easily. Their lips crashed against each other in a furious kiss, and God, did she hold on. She held on so tightly it was a miracle their bodies didn't fuse.

Arthur lowered her to her toes but didn't break their embrace. His hands fisted in Jennifer's hair, holding her still, ravaging her mouth like she was his last meal. Jennifer clung to him, following the wave as best she could. Arthur was relentless, a man desperate, holding tightly to her as though she would become vapor and slip through his fingers.

After what seemed an eternity, he wrenched his mouth from hers. Gently, Arthur pressed their foreheads together, their pants mingling in the minuscule space between them.

"Please don't go," Arthur begged. "Stay with me."

Tears ran freely. Jennifer hated and loved the fact he'd ridden after her, to see her one last time with one last attempt to get her to stay, as if she had a choice. As if this was some romantic movie where the hero and heroine lived happily ever after together.

This wasn't one of those movies or novels.

This was a tragedy. A gut-wrenching divide Jennifer couldn't fix.

"I can't," Jennifer forced out, watching matching rivulets of tears staining Arthur's cheeks.

"It was worth another try," Arthur huffed, hopeless.

"You are pretty stubborn," Jennifer joked, their noses brushing against each other.

"Oh, *I'm* the stubborn one?"

Jennifer laughed, before pulling back. Her gaze caught his, and something in those crystalline eyes broke her further.

"You lost the battle, Arthur," Jennifer blurted. She had told herself she'd never tell him what had happened, but in that moment, she couldn't bear to have anything hidden between them. "The first time. You lost it because I lost the book to Morgan, which led to the Saxons winning."

Arthur's eyebrows arched. "But we won the battle?" His statement came out as more of a question.

"I fixed it," Jennifer said softly. "By moving through time."

And potentially creating trouble for herself down the line.

"St Michael's Mount? The set of scrolls?" Arthur asked.

Jennifer nodded. "Apparently, I am what you call a Traveler. There aren't many like me. But, with training, I can freely move through space and time. I needed to travel to St Michael's Mount to retrieve the book. I didn't...I didn't know what I was going there for, Arthur. I just knew that when I got there, *someone* would be able to point me the way home. Turns out...I was the key all along. *I'm* the one that can get *me* back home. I'm sorry I couldn't tell you up front. I had no idea. I knew I just really needed to get to the Mount, and without you...I really and truly would have never gotten there."

Arthur was silent for a time. His eyes seemed distant, but she'd been with the man long enough to know he was weighing variables, thinking of possible outcomes and scenarios, like the good war leader he was.

"What is it like? The future? Where you're from?" he finally asked.

She smiled slightly, reaching up to cup his cheek. He leaned into her touch.

"I have a job, I make money. I teach children a bit older than Galahad. About things that have happened. History."

That was all she could say, though Jennifer longed to tell him what his legacy would be. How his stories would pervade through the centuries, inspiring many creatives, and sparking the fascination and imagination of so many.

"And you have your family," he stated.

Jennifer nodded. "I do. My parents, my brother, my niece... I don't belong here, Arthur. As much as I'd like to stay with you, I can't."

"You are not out of place with me," Arthur finally spoke after too long of a silence.

Jennifer couldn't respond, too afraid to open her mouth. Too afraid of what would come out.

"Will you stay with me until I've gone?" she asked instead.

Arthur looked for a moment as though he would refuse, but he reached out his large, calloused hand, nodding. Jennifer took it, and she led him back toward the stones, with Llamrei, ever faithful steed, following after.

Emrys had busied himself with nothing at all, doing his best to afford them as much space as he could. He looked relieved when they entered the circle, and judging by the slight appearance of the sun in the sky, Jennifer knew time was of the essence.

"You best get into position, or your window may close." Emrys gestured for her to stand once more in front of the stone.

Jennifer nodded and looked to Arthur, as though all of the answers she sought lay with him.

He just looked lost, as though everything he'd ever known had been taken away from him. It hurt her to the core, cutting her to the quick, but knowing he had some family remaining comforted her.

Swallowing thickly, Jennifer stepped up to the stone she'd been examining earlier, and remembering the exact way in which she needed to touch the stone, she did so. But not before turning one last time, taking in Arthur's form. He was resolute, like a sentinel.

Jennifer reached out, pressing her palm to the stone, not once looking away from Arthur.

"I will miss you," he breathed, let out on one long, low burst of air.

Jennifer smiled sadly. "I'll miss you too."

With one last longing glance, her eyelids slowly closed, and she pushed her fingers against the stone.

It gave, ever so slightly, and she was gone.

CHAPTER 25

AVEBURY - PRESENT

For the shortest of moments, Jennifer felt weightless, adrift.

Then the ground came rushing up to her.

Eyelids shot open and she immediately spied a forest canopy. Despite her body aching as though she'd run a marathon, Jennifer sprung up.

The clearing.

She'd come back to the same spot she had left.

Everything looked...well, it looked the same. As though the trees had been there for thousands of years. And maybe they had.

Looking around, Jennifer didn't see anyone walking her way or waiting for her or watching.

No Emrys. No Arthur. Just her and the eerie stillness of the forest around her.

Sickness welled within her, and she scrambled to lean over as she emptied her stomach of its contents. There had been commentary in the book about the body not being made for

Travel, and that it would never adjust to movement through time.

Glancing to the right, she saw the backpack she'd come to Europe with.

Miraculously, everything she'd left in it remained, including her phone, passport, and all the essentials.

With the added addition of the book.

She let out a breath, glad she hadn't lost it to the streams of time or something, and rushed to her feet. Slinging the backpack over a shoulder, she scurried from the clearing. It didn't take long for her to find her way out and back on the road into the town. Across the giant, wide open field, Jennifer could see the metallic bulk of the tour bus.

She'd made it back, and it hadn't left without her.

Jennifer had never been much of a runner, but she did it now, rushing to the bus as though fire nipped at her heels.

The other members of her tour group had already begun to form a line outside the door to the bus, slowly boarding and getting settled. One particular person at the back of the line noticed Jennifer's approach. Vicki's face lit up with relief, and she gestured wildly with her arms.

"Oh, my dear, we thought we'd lost you somewhere!" She fretted like a mother hen as Jennifer drew near. "Where have you been?"

Jennifer couldn't help but feel a bit sheepish, as though she'd actually disappointed her mother instead of this veritable stranger. Her backpack weighed heavily on her shoulder, heavy with the knowledge of the book hidden there. She tried to play off her absence, shrugging.

"Went to explore the woods outside town. Got a tad lost, but I found my way." Jennifer forced a smile, selling the lie as best she could.

Vicki didn't seem convinced, but to her credit, she didn't push.

"Ah, there you are!" Grace called out, appearing from around the backside of the bus. "We weren't sure where you'd gotten to, but I'm glad you found your way back in time."

"Yep, sure did." Jennifer pressed her smile wider.

"Time," Vicki sighed, almost wistfully. "Such an equalizer, don't you think?"

"Oh no, I'm not one for philosophical debates. Excuse me, ladies. We should be off within the next five minutes." Grace begged off, stepping around them to climb on the bus. Jennifer couldn't make out the words, but the tour guide began addressing the old folks, reminding them of their next destination.

"Time?" Jennifer asked, gripping her backpack strap tighter. Not out of fear Vicki would make a grab for it. The older woman had no idea it existed, but the poignant thought made Jennifer pause. Consider. And remember Vicki's sixth-century doppelgänger, back in that temple near Axminster.

"Yeah, in the end, time catches up with us all," Vicki said, as though stating the most obvious concept. She turned to make for the open doorway, lifting a foot to put on the bottom step. Before she climbed onto the coach, she turned to Jennifer again. There was an odd twinkle in her blue eyes, something that made Jennifer uneasy, but not uncomfortably so. It was like Vicki knew something. Or it could've just been Jennifer's paranoia. "Too bad we can't bend time to our will, huh?"

Jennifer froze.

Vicki disappeared up into the bus, and Jennifer watched the vague outline of her figure make her way toward the back where they had sat since they left London.

What in the hell had that been about?

The rumbling bus let out a blast of exhaust, shaking Jennifer from her thoughts.

Coincidence. It had to be. It was a perfectly normal thing

for people to say, right? It just seemed more relevant now than ever knowing she was what she was.

Turning, Jennifer stepped toward the doorway, reaching out for the handle. She hauled herself up onto the first step and walked slowly down the aisle.

For the first time since arriving at Heathrow, getting in that van, and realizing she'd signed up for the wrong tour, Jennifer felt...well, *light*.

Her gaze moved from couple to couple, to the few singles, and finally onto Vicki's weirdly knowing smile. Jennifer knew she'd been on this trip for a reason.

To appreciate the time she had?

To know her time on this mortal plane meant something?

And every single person's presence on the bus meant something too.

Life was a precious thing, and you had to make the most of it.

For Lynn. For herself.

Vicki motioned for Jennifer to take her seat. Sliding into it, Jennifer basked in the blessed air conditioning of the bus, and startled just a little when it lurched to life, trundling out of the town square and out of the town. Their next stop was Bath. And after that, she would follow Arthur's steps again—and her own.

"You look like you've been through it," Vicki commented. "You sure you just got lost in the woods?"

Jennifer took a second to think. It felt jarring that she'd been in the past for damn near a month, but not even a few hours had passed here. It was like jet lag, complete with ears popping. Her head ached ever so slightly, probably from having tuned back in to the language she knew, no longer needing translations anymore.

She *had* been through it.

But it'd been worth every damn second.

"Yeah. Yeah, I'm good." Jennifer grinned.

The remainder of her trip passed in a blur.

It almost seemed trivial now, after her experiences. But it also seemed appropriate, because of the places she'd been. To see Tintagel as it was, and as it is now...Jennifer found herself wondering what Arthur would think of his home in this time. What would he think of Bath? Glastonbury? And St Michael's Mount?

That part of the trip had been the hardest.

Jennifer opted to go on ahead with Vicki, walking along the natural shelf that revealed itself once the tide was out. The rest of the group would follow later on a ferry.

A Norman-era castle now sat on St Michael's Mount. Whatever remnants of the church that once stood, guarding the sacred well, had disappeared. In fact, nothing of the Mount looked the same as when she'd seen it.

Vicki decided to take a rest just outside the castle grounds, and Jennifer moved on, wandering. It didn't seem as wide open as it had. Over the years, other buildings had taken the place of the thatched-roof huts and the smithy and the stables. Jennifer wondered what Father Lucas would think.

As she turned the corner of one of the castle's outbuildings, Jennifer caught herself before she collided with a person.

When the shock wore off, and Jennifer's bearings had returned, she glanced up to see Emrys.

"How—"

"What are you still doing here?" he hissed, grabbing her elbow with surprising strength for someone who seemed ancient, and hauling her farther around the side of the building where no one would find them.

"I paid a lot of my hard-earned money on this trip. I wasn't going to just go home," Jennifer argued, attempting to wrench her arm free, but to no avail.

Emrys growled in frustration, smacking his forehead. "Are you daft, girl? What part of 'forces of evil are after that book' did you not understand?"

Jennifer's anger roared to life. She'd always been an even-tempered person, always going with the flow. But not now.

"Whether I'm at home or I'm here, I'm as in danger as I would be anywhere. So why not take advantage of what time I have in this life, and make it count?"

Emrys gaped, aghast Jennifer would have the stones to actually argue with him. Up to that point, she hadn't...much.

"Look, it's never left my person," Jennifer continued, hooking a thumb at the pack slung over her shoulders. "I keep this bag with me at all times. I'm surrounded by old people. If I keep my head low, they won't notice I'm the odd one out. They'd just assume someone as young as I am would be traveling with people similar in age. I'm fine."

Emrys didn't look convinced, but that wasn't Jennifer's problem. She was her own person. She'd never felt more at home in her own skin. More empowered and ready to take on the world. No one would take this book away from her. It was hers to protect. And she would. She knew, on a molecular level, it was her solemn, sacred duty.

The Guardian of Time.

Kind of had a nice ring to it.

"Figures it'd be a willful girl," Emrys muttered under his breath.

"Excuse me?" Jennifer said, ice dripping from her words.

He at least had the decency to look a little ashamed.

"You know, I..." Jennifer sighed, shifting from foot to foot. "Never had the opportunity to ask you—"

"About Arthur?" he interrupted. "About what would become of him?"

Jennifer nodded, feeling her heart race at the mere mention of the name, then blinked back the sting of salty tears threatening to roll down her cheeks.

"Did he... Did he live a decent life...after?"

Emrys stayed silent.

Jennifer wondered if he was trying to come up with a lie that would make her feel good about leaving Arthur behind. His hesitation was enough. Dread spread through her, crashing over her like a wave. She felt sick, and forced her feet away from the old man to gasp in a deep breath. Then another.

"I'm sorry," Emrys said softly. "It...it wasn't all bad. After Badon Hill, the people flocked to him as their leader. He ruled from Cadbury hill fort, in Somerset, for many years. War lords and chieftains from all over the island came to him for guidance. He was just. And fair. And many greatly admired and respected him."

A sob wrenched from Jennifer's mouth. She felt as though she couldn't breathe. Pressing a palm to her sternum, she focused on her heart rate, which had skyrocketed. She forced herself to take deep breaths and willed her heart to slow.

"How long did he live?" she asked, words whispered, barely audible above the crash of the waves against the tidal island's craggy cliffs.

"He was forty-five," Emrys responded, his words grave. "He was killed."

Jennifer's heart lurched, and she felt her breakfast from that morning would make an appearance again. Her mind raced with thoughts of the legends, about how Arthur had met his end.

"Where? How?" she croaked.

"Camlann," Emrys replied. "He fought bravely, but Medraut killed him. In battle, if that is a comfort."

It wasn't, but Jennifer knew that would have been the way Arthur would've wanted to go.

"Who was Medraut?" she asked, having almost called this mysterious man by his more popular name—Mordred.

"A misguided man," Emrys sighed, a heaviness to his shoulders that implied he might have had something to do with that. "He believed what he was doing was right, but...it led to his and Arthur's end. Arthur died childless. And he never married."

It shouldn't be a relief, considering the other bombs Emrys had just dropped on her. But Jennifer didn't pretend to be a perfect person, that was for sure.

"Though there were mentions of a woman. A witch, some said, that had ensnared Arthur's heart so firmly and truly, he would never love another," Emrys continued. Though she knew he meant them as comfort, tears began to fall all the same, until she was openly sobbing.

"The whispers were that her name was...Gwenhwyfar."

Jennifer's eyes widened. Her head shot up to see Emrys's face, to glean whether it was truth or a lie. It appeared he was telling the truth, or he was great at hiding it.

"What?" she breathed, her palm still clutched to her chest. Her heart had slowed a bit, but now it felt larger than life. "That's my name...but how—"

"Funny how time works," Emrys chuckled. "Your name is Jennifer, a derivative of Guinevere. But because of what happened, your travels, your name became Gwenhwyfar, then eventually Guinevere, and thus, the legend of her was named after you. A loop, forever intertwined."

The very idea caused a pulsating ache to form behind her right temple. No matter how long she'd pored over the book, trying to understand the nature of time and how it worked,

Jennifer still couldn't wrap her head around it. The math, the physics, the *philosophy* of it all...

"Gawain?" she pressed on, trying not to dwell on Arthur for longer than she had to. "Kay?"

"Gawain perished at Camlann with Arthur. Kay lived, but only for a few years more."

There was one name she didn't want to ask about, but knew she must. "Galahad?" she whispered.

This time, Emrys smiled. "Galahad lived to a ripe old age. That I promise you. With many children, grandchildren, and even great-grandchildren. He was a loyal soldier to Arthur, and fought at Camlann. He watched Arthur fall, and took his sword."

Jennifer began to sob uncontrollably. She hated to cry. Hated losing control of her emotions. To know Galahad led a good life after she left? It was the deepest kind of relief she'd never felt before.

"What happened to the sword after Galahad?" Jennifer asked.

Emrys looked worried. "I don't know."

"Is that why you're still around? Are you looking for it?"

The old man's lips pursed, as though clamping tightly to not spill the secret. Again, his silence was all Jennifer needed to know.

"You are! Let me help!"

Emrys shook his head furiously, nearly displacing the newsboy cap on his head. "No, gods, no. You need to finish your tour and get back to the States with that book as fast as you can. I will continue to look for the sword."

"What're you going to do with it if you find it?" Jennifer asked. "What's its purpose?"

Even Father Lucas hadn't known the destiny of the sword and of its bearer. He could only make educated guesses.

"I cannot tell you," Emrys declared, straightening his

spine to fight her if she pushed back. Jennifer didn't, knowing full well she wouldn't get the real story from him anyway. Especially not after the stunt he'd pulled about traveling to St Michael's Mount being her only option to get back home.

Glancing around the corner of the building, Jennifer saw the rest of her crowd wandering the grounds, snapping pictures, and making awed noises at the ancient structures.

Funny how she thought of them as *her* crowd now.

Jennifer turned back to Emrys, surprised to find him still there. He loved doing the disappearing act on her.

"Will we ever see each other again?" she asked, wondering if this was the time he had mentioned before or not, not sure if that idea saddened her or relieved her.

Emrys looked thoughtful for a moment, then shrugged. "I know a lot, Jennifer, but I'm not omniscient. Who can really say whether we will see each other ever again? I suspect, however, we will, as I said before." The uncertainty turned into surety, that now familiar little twinkle appearing in his ancient gaze.

"I better get back. Thanks for your help...what little help you've given," Jennifer snorted, only half teasing. The man's help had come in roundabout, very frustrating ways. But eventually, he came through.

"It's been a pleasure, Jennifer Cassidy. May your travels be safe and fulfilling." With a tip of his chin, he turned and disappeared around the far corner of the building. Jennifer rushed over, peering around, only to see that he'd vanished into thin air.

Dramatic.

"There you are!"

Jennifer turned to see Vicki flanked by Grace and a couple of the other members of the tour group. She smiled.

"Just wanted to check out the backside of this building,"

Jennifer said as nonchalantly as she could muster, tapping the old stone for emphasis. "It's a nice...er, backside."

Vicki snorted, shaking her head. "Mm-hmm...well, we're going to take a tour of the castle now, so..."

"Right! Coming!" Jennifer kicked into action. Clutching the straps of her backpack, she motioned her head behind her. "I'll meet you at the entrance."

Wind whipped through the wide alleyway Jennifer trudged through, causing her to shiver. She paused, turning to look out over the whitecapped waves of the bay.

The view hadn't changed much in 1500 years. For a moment, Jennifer felt as though she were back there. A quick glance around confirmed she was still very much in the present, and that her concentration and thoughts hadn't caused an unwanted jump through time. As much as she wanted to return to Arthur, something inside of her knew her moment in his day was over. She had work to do here in her time.

Besides...she wasn't ready for big jumps.

Baby steps. Learn to walk before flying, right?

CHAPTER 26

EASTFALL, MASSACHUSETTS - PRESENT

The quiet of her apartment seemed foreboding after so much time spent outside.

The thud of her backpack broke the silence, the heaviness of it hitting the beat-up linoleum of her tiny foyer. Jennifer locked and bolted her door, leaving her rolling suitcase next to her backpack.

The book, though...that needed to be put somewhere.

Unzipping the backpack, Jennifer carefully removed the collection of bound pieces of parchment. She then went room to room, scouting the best hiding place. It was difficult to do so in such a small space. Eventually, she opted to hide the book in the crawl space in the ceiling of her closet.

Jennifer wandered back, aimlessly going from room to room again as if trying to regain some semblance of normalcy. After what had happened to her in England, the people she had met, the events she helped set into action...there was no going back to normal.

After a phone call to her mother and father, letting them know she'd gotten in and would hit the hay early due to jet lag, Jennifer made another quick phone call for Chinese delivery.

Even watching television seemed so mundane. Jennifer tried her hardest to fall into the hilarity of *Brooklyn Nine-Nine* as she always did, but she just couldn't laugh. She simply ate her beef and broccoli and watched.

Despite the time difference and the exhaustion she felt to her very core, Jennifer could not fall asleep that night. Thoughts whirled, Arthur's face at the forefront of them all. He had died young, at least for her time. He had never married. How lonely he must've been. She had not wanted that for him.

Would she ever find someone else? Arthur had been... someone truly special.

A metallic click and a thud had Jennifer sitting bolt upright in bed. Glancing over at her alarm clock, the digital readout said 2:47 a.m. She sat stock-still, ears straining to hear. The thud and metallic click happened again, and her heart leapt into her throat, thundering in her ears.

As quietly as she could, she leaned over the side of her bed and slid her hand beneath the bedskirt. Her hand grasped wood immediately, and she gingerly slid the hockey stick out. Her brother had gifted her with a hockey stick one Christmas, purely for protection's sake, because she sure as hell didn't know how to play. Jennifer could barely ice skate.

The thudding came again and then a low, slow creak of her front door opening.

Jennifer swallowed thickly, feeling her blood rushing, her heart surely loud enough for the intruder to hear. Armed with the hockey stick, she gripped low, just as Arthur had attempted when trying to teach her how to hold a sword. Taking a few deep, steadying breaths, she focused.

Slowly, she crept across the carpeted floor of her bedroom, thankful for the fibers to muffle her steps. Whoever the intruder was, she could hear them riffling through her stuff in the living room—her backpack, her suitcase. Cabinets squeaked open, then the oven. Whoever they were, they were trying for stealth as well.

What could they possibly want? The apartment complex she lived in was middle-class at best. She was a humble teacher, with no real riches to her name. Yes, she was a woman that lived alone but still... She owned nothing of value, truly.

Her thoughts turned to the book in the crawl space of her closet.

They had to be here for that. It would seem her calling to protect the book was beginning a lot sooner than she had anticipated.

How could someone know about it already?

Jennifer recalled something Emrys had said, about how Morgan knew who she was, though Jennifer wouldn't know her. Had she been waiting for Jennifer to return, knowing she'd have the book?

Footfalls sounded closer.

The intruder headed toward her bathroom. There was the metallic *shing* of the shower curtain being pulled back, then the opening of her cabinets under the sink.

They'd be coming to her room next.

Glancing around, Jennifer tried to figure out her best vantage point for surprise. Quickly, she crossed the minimal distance to the doorway, hiding just to the right of the door. It was cracked open, and when whoever came through the door, she'd be able to swing at them with the hockey stick.

Just as Arthur taught her.

Except with a sword.

God, Jennifer hoped the intruder didn't have a gun.

Footsteps left the bathroom, and her heartbeat ramped up again in her chest.

Now was the time. She raised her arms, poised to strike. Jennifer saw movement in the hallway, a shadow darker than the darkness of the hall. A gloved hand reached out, fingers pushing the door open ever so slowly. Jennifer raised her arms a little higher, waiting for them to step farther into the room.

When the intruder stepped into Jennifer's sweet spot, she swung with all her might, connecting with whatever she could. The stick slammed into the intruder's chest, and Jennifer heard a resounding *oof!* as it did. The intruder recovered quickly though, much to Jennifer's dismay, and stopped another swing of the stick with both gloved hands. She grappled for the stick, trying to yank it from their hands only for the butt of it to slip and collide with her forehead.

For a few essential seconds, she saw stars. And then warm droplets of some liquid, probably her blood, dripping down her nose.

She couldn't allow this to stop her from defending her home.

And the book.

The intruder made a grab for her, but quick thinking and concentration had Jennifer Traveling across the room. That odd sensation of being sucked through a tube overcame her, and then she was out of arm's reach.

Her action caused the intruder to stop dead. She couldn't see much of their face in the dim light of the room, but she did see the surprised whites of their eyes. Jennifer reared back, holding the stick aloft, ready to bring another blow if need be.

But the intruder, it seemed, was sufficiently spooked, and beat feet for the door.

Like someone with a death wish, Jennifer went charging down the hallway after them with a bloodcurdling cry, never once getting a good look at their face. The tall build and wide shoulders would suggest a male; she figured that much. The intruder was fast, as they were already running out into the parking lot by the time Jennifer reached her front door. Quickly, she shut and locked it, then dropped her hockey stick in order to drag the couch over to act as a barricade.

Jennifer leaned down for her stick as she traversed her living room, checking to make sure her sliding glass door was locked. Not that she expected the person to climb to the second floor, but one never knew. She then flicked on every light in her apartment and checked all of her windows.

Once she had finished the sweep of her apartment, only then did she think to reach for her cell phone to call the police.

Two of Eastfall Police Department's finest arrived not long after she placed the call. Once they knocked on her door, she pushed the couch away and opened things up. Jennifer thanked the dispatcher on the line and hung up once instructed. After giving the course of events of what happened, the police officers taking notes the whole time, they asked her if they could take a look around just to be safe.

"I'm impressed..." one of the uniforms, Officer Ramirez, said coming back from her bedroom. "Good stickhandling."

Jennifer snorted, thankful for the officer's attempt at humor.

"And you're sure nothing was actually taken?" the other officer, Officer Hall, asked.

"Not that I could tell, no," Jennifer replied.

"Maybe they thought you were still away on your trip.

They could've been casing your apartment. Is there anything specific you can think of that anyone would want to steal?"

Jennifer shrugged. "I...I bought an antique book when I was in England." The lie spilled out easier than she thought it would. "It might be worth some money, but no one knew I had it, I don't think."

"And do you have this book in a safe place?" Officer Hall continued his questioning.

Jennifer nodded.

"Okay. Good. Are you sure you don't want us to call for an ambulance?"

She shook her head, though the action caused pain to lance across her forehead and temples. "No, thank you."

"You should probably go to the emergency room, though. Let us take you. You may have a concussion."

Sighing, Jennifer knew she should do as they suggested. "Fine, I'll go. But I can drive myself. Really."

Both officers looked skeptical, but they didn't push.

"Do you have anyone you could go stay with for a while? It might be a good idea to at least not stay here for the rest of the night."

"I'll be okay. I just got home from a long trip, and I really just want my bed," Jennifer replied, tired beyond belief.

Both officers nodded.

"Fair enough," Officer Ramirez said. "We're going to file a report, and a detective should be in touch with you later today or tomorrow."

"Thank you so much for coming out. I really appreciate it." Jennifer shook their hands.

"We're going to stay in the parking lot for a while longer, just in case they come back while you're gone to the ER," Officer Ramirez offered, leaving no argument on that count at least. Knowing this did give Jennifer some peace of mind.

"Great. Thank you."

"Of course. If you feel at all unsafe, you know what to do."

Eastfall General Hospital's Emergency Department was quiet, but then, Jennifer would've hoped so for such an early hour. Clutching her bag tighter to her body, she approached the check-in desk. Inside the bag was the book. She hadn't wanted to leave it alone.

Once she had provided health insurance information, as well as a couple of completed forms, Jennifer sat and waited to be called back. She shared the waiting room with only a handful of people. She found a seat that satisfied her, and sat heavily, resting her head back against the wall behind her.

Hockey stick to the head, jet lag, and the attempted burglary had done an interesting number on Jennifer's state of mind. Not to mention the stress, and the anxiety, and—oh yeah—the ancient book that needed her protection.

So this was what her life was now, huh?

Her eyelids grew heavier and heavier with each passing minute. When she finally heard her name, Jennifer had nearly dozed off. Her head jerked around, finding the owner of the voice.

It was an ER nurse, who appeared to be about her age. She wore a set of burgundy scrubs with all-black cross trainer Nikes. The nurse's hair had been pulled back into a neat ponytail, but it didn't hide the long, thick, ebony waves. Her light-brown skin tone highlighted the jet-black of her eyes, the delicate line of her jaw, and her full lips.

Jennifer quickly jolted out of her chair, as though she'd been goosed in the ass, and crossed the wide open space. The nurse had a genuinely kind smile for her.

"Hi, Ms. Cassidy, my name is Dayana. We're gonna get you checked out, okay?"

Jennifer nodded and followed after her.

The emergency room had a number of beds all partitioned with curtains on tracks. Only a couple were closed off, but the rest were open.

Dayana motioned for Jennifer to hop on the foot of a bed, and she complied.

"So...home invasion, huh? That must've been scary?" Dayana said, sliding the curtains around the bed shut. She then pulled up a rolling console, complete with blood pressure cuff and thermometer, to settle in front of Jennifer.

"Um, yeah, pretty damn terrifying," Jennifer admitted, though if she was honest, the home invasion had been the least scary part of her past month.

"I can't imagine." Dayana shook her head, then got to work taking Jennifer's vitals. When she was finished, Dayana pushed away the console and clacked away at a laptop set up on a bedside table. She asked Jennifer a few other questions, taking notes, and then stepped back over to the foot of the bed. Her dark head bent forward to examine the wound on Jennifer's forehead. "Looks like the bleeding has pretty much stopped, but you might need a stitch or two. I'm going to prep the materials for that and get with the doctor to schedule a CT scan to make sure nothing got too knocked around in there. Is there anything I can do for you while you wait?"

"No, thank you," Jennifer murmured, as Dayana ducked out between the openings of the curtains.

It didn't take very long for the nurse to return with a doctor in tow. Or maybe Jennifer had dozed off with her eyes open. At this point, she wouldn't have been surprised.

"Hi, Ms. Cassidy. I'm Doctor Laine. I heard you got into a tussle?" The doctor didn't look much older than Jennifer. He was handsome, with dirty-blond hair and blue eyes. He was tall with a lean body covered in a pair of green scrubs, and had a kind, soft face. Jennifer felt at ease.

Dr. Laine pulled out a pen light to test the response of her pupils. He then took some gloves from a nearby box and slipped on a fresh pair. Gingerly he examined her forehead. "How did this happen?" he asked curiously. Jennifer gave him a quick rundown of events and how the butt of the hockey stick got really familiar with her head. Dr. Laine nodded as he listened. "I think you got lucky. The cut's not too deep, but will definitely need two or three stitches. Dayana's going to prep the wound, and I'll have you sewn up in a jiffy. Then we'll get you up for a CT scan."

Any other time, Jennifer might've laughed at someone her age using the term "jiffy," but the adrenaline that had been keeping her going was beginning to run its course.

In no time, Dr. Laine had her sewn up, bandaged, and sent off to radiology. The CT scan process was painless, and in no time she was back at her previously assigned bed. Dr. Laine didn't take long before he appeared again to give her a clean bill of health as far as brain trauma, and promptly sent her off with a prescription for some painkillers. Dayana provided instructions on how to keep the wound clean, and explained that the stitches would need to be removed in a few days, which could be done at her primary care office, any Urgent Care, or back in the ER.

Jennifer thanked the doctor, and Dayana took her back up front to be checked out. As Jennifer said goodbye to the kind nurse, their gazes held for a moment, and she felt this strange sensation trickle across her scalp, like little painless pin pricks. She might have thought it had to do with her injury, but she knew that wasn't it. She didn't know how, but Jennifer had a feeling she'd see this nurse again, and not in a medical capacity.

CHAPTER 27

"How could you fail so incredibly?"

The useless excuse for a thief cowered from the CEO's outburst, watching as all of the objects on top of his sturdy oaken desk shot across the space, some falling just short of the desk, other objects hitting the wall with a resounding thud. Subconsciously, he took a step back, lest something be hurled at him.

"I am so sorry, sir," the man replied, voice shaking. "She knew I was there. She was... She was armed. And she moved across the room in the blink of—"

"What did you just say?" the CEO interrupted, leaning across the desk, both palms braced on the varnished wood.

The would-be thief stopped short of what he was planning to say next. "Um...well, she was right in front of me and then she wasn't. Like, poof! And then she was across the room."

The CEO was still, his gaze suddenly focused on nothing, giving the thief some relief from the penetrating stare. The man behind the desk stood so still, it was as though he had turned to stone. Emotions played out across the CEO's face, which was rather surprising considering how well he had always been able to mask his thoughts and feelings. Realization soon dawned on the man's face, and he sat back *heavily into his high-backed desk chair. Fingers reached up to pinch the bridge of his nose, leaving the thief confused but still unwilling to say anything yet.*

"Shit," the CEO hissed beneath his breath, massaging his fingertips across his forehead as though a tension headache were forming right in that moment.

After what felt like an eternity, the man finally broke the tense silence.

"Did this woman have red hair?"

The thief shrugged. "I'm not sure, sir. It was rather dark."

"I should've known."

The thief didn't reply, as he felt the comment was not directed at him.

"Cassidy. Of course. Fiona Cassidy's granddaughter." The CEO huffed a humorless laugh. "Even in her twilight years that bitch is still giving me problems."

The thief shuffled awkwardly in place, once more uncertain how to proceed. He would rather get out of this office, but didn't want to risk the further ire of his employer.

"This development complicates things." Then, as if remembering he wasn't alone in the room, the CEO looked up at the thief, waving his hand. "Leave. I have no more use for you."

The thief could not leave that room fast enough.

Behind the CEO, the early rays of the morning sun were trickling in through the tinted windows. He was exhausted, even before learning of this...well, snag.

For the first time, in a very *long time, the CEO felt...scared.*

Terrified, really.

Not because he had failed at acquiring the book, not because Fiona Cassidy's hell spawn could Travel as she had, but because he would have to answer to the benefactors. He would have to explain his epic failures to them. The very thought made his stomach roil and churn, and the CEO leaned sideways over the arm of the desk chair and dry heaved, gagging on nothing but air and a little bit of bile.

He went to reach for his cell phone, which had been among the casualties on his desk, and noticed that his hand shook.

Make that both hands.

The CEO looked around the pile of debris and spotted the familiar rectangle. He grabbed it off the floor with clumsy fingers, nearly dropping it twice before he could get a hold of it.

Gods, what would he do?

CHAPTER 28

There was no sleeping for the rest of the early morning. Jennifer watched the first rays of the sun peek over the horizon, illuminating the tree line outside her apartment building, giving it the appearance of being on fire.

By seven, Jennifer felt it useless to sit around anymore. She showered and dressed, resolved to go to Eastfall Trust the moment it opened. A safety deposit box seemed the safest bet, as she didn't know what else to do with this book.

Emrys had been vague about it all. Simply insisting she needed to bring it back with her, to keep it safe at all costs. Emrys, in the short time she'd known him, had been nothing but enigmatic, always skirting around the full answer, answering questions with more riddles. Must be the nature of such a powerful being.

Jennifer reached for the hook by the front door where she kept her car keys. The shrill sound of her cell phone startled her. She yanked her phone out of her jeans pocket and checked the display. It wasn't a number she recognized, but she answered it anyway, remembering what the officers had said last night about a detective who would call her.

"Hello?"

"Hello, is this Ms. Jennifer Cassidy?" It was a female voice, professional but not robotic.

"Yes, this is she."

"Hi Ms. Cassidy, this is Lieutenant Lara Nadeau with Eastfall Police Department. I'm calling in regard to the break-in that occurred at your apartment last night. We met last fall, after Ms. Rickerson..."

"Yes, thank you for calling, Lieutenant. I remember. How were the cookies?" Jennifer sighed, brushing a few strands of her hair from her face. She retreated back to her living room, sitting heavily on her couch. She did recall the lieutenant, a woman about her age, fierce in her drive to catch Lynn's murderer.

"They were delicious, thank you. I wanted to ask first about how you're doing?" the woman asked.

"I'm...I'm as okay as I'm going to be, I think." Jennifer let out a huff of laughter lacking any humor.

"Understandable. I have numbers for personal security companies if you feel you would like to add an extra layer of safety," the lieutenant offered. "As well as numbers to several professionals in Eastfall that are available should you want to talk to anyone."

Ah yes, a therapist. Jennifer nearly laughed again. There was no therapist in the world that would be able to talk her through what she'd been through...hundreds of years in the past...in another country...involving magic and armies and swords.

The break-in was small peanuts compared to that.

"Thank you, Lieutenant, that is very kind of you," Jennifer replied, touched at the other woman's genuine concern and compassion for her well-being.

"I would like to talk to you, to get your statement again for my investigative purposes. Would you be available to come to police headquarters to talk with me?"

"Yes, actually, I am available."

"Excellent, how is your availability this morning?"

"I can come right now."

Fifteen minutes later, Jennifer shouldered her way into police headquarters. She stopped at the front desk to check in, adjusting the strap of her tote bag higher up her shoulder. After this, she'd head to the bank to get the book safe *and* away from her.

The front desk sergeant and she exchanged a few words before he made a call to inform the lieutenant of her arrival.

"You can have a seat until she gets down here," the sergeant offered, pointing at the chairs behind her. Jennifer thanked him but opted to step away from the desk and stand.

She didn't have to wait long before Lieutenant Nadeau stepped from the elevator. The woman looked exactly as Jennifer remembered. Brown hair pulled back into a haphazard style, and golden-brown eyes that looked shrewdly at anything and everything. The lieutenant was taller than Jennifer, slim but fit. She wore a pair of dark slacks, a cream-colored blouse, and a smart suit jacket with her gun and badge displayed on her hip. A pair of sensibly heeled boots rounded out the professional but stern persona.

"Ms. Cassidy, I'd say it's nice to see you again, but we keep meeting under unpleasant circumstances," the lieutenant greeted, holding her hand out. Jennifer took it, shaking firmly.

"Agreed." Jennifer nodded, a little unnerved at the way the

lieutenant's gaze seemed to bore into her, almost like she could read her thoughts.

"Follow me; we'll go chat in my office." The lieutenant's gaze flicked to the bag at Jennifer's shoulder, giving it a lingering glance before calling back the elevator. Once inside, the other woman swiped an ID badge, granting them access to rise to the second floor.

Jennifer followed Lieutenant Nadeau down a long corridor flanked by office after office. Some of the doors had names on them, along with titles. Captains, lieutenants, and joint offices such as one for major crimes detectives.

The lieutenant came to a halt by an open door, then stepped back to let Jennifer in first. Jennifer settled into one of the visitors' chairs, as the lieutenant shut the door and took up her seat behind her desk.

"I know this might be difficult, but try and tell me every detail you can about what happened," the lieutenant began, plucking up a pen and notepad to take notes. The woman didn't waste time.

Jennifer recounted the events of the early morning, from reaching for her hockey stick to wielding it like a Fury, running the person out of her apartment. The lieutenant smiled slightly.

"Hockey saves lives, am I right?" the lieutenant joked.

"I don't watch it much myself," Jennifer chuckled. "But my brother played. He's the one who got me the stick."

"And you're sure nothing was missing? Did you notice anything between the time the officers left your apartment to when you left to come here?" the lieutenant asked.

Jennifer shook her head. "No. Nothing's missing."

The lieutenant frowned slightly, but looked down to her notepad to jot something down.

"Look, Lieutenant, I know it's probably not feasible at

this point to find the person. It was dark, I didn't see them, and they left quickly after I fought back."

"I won't lie and say there's a guarantee I'll find them," Lieutenant Nadeau admitted. "But I always try."

Jennifer knew that. From what she could tell after Lynn's murder, the lieutenant had worked tirelessly to find the killer. It had been a big splash in Eastfall when the news hit the papers. An assistant district attorney had been responsible for the horrific deaths of three women. As far as Jennifer cared, justice had been served for her friend. The guy could fry.

"In the officer's report, they wrote something about an antique book?" the lieutenant said, consulting a piece of paper resting on her desk.

Jennifer nodded. She didn't want to lie, but she didn't want to divulge too much either. "Yes, it's a book I picked up on my recent trip to England. I imagine it could be worth something."

The lieutenant's expression changed. Something lurked behind the brown gaze, something Jennifer couldn't identify. It prompted her to clutch the tote bag, which she had set on the floor, closer. The other woman's lips parted, on the verge of saying something, but the lieutenant remained quiet.

Something akin to resolve washed over the woman's features. Lieutenant Nadeau sat back in her chair, folding her hands in her lap.

"If it's the kind of book I'm thinking it might be, then we need to have a talk."

"What do you mean?" Jennifer asked, eyebrows furrowed.

"It's old, isn't it? Like, really old? Written in Latin or some other really obscure language you can't recognize. And as a history teacher, I bet you can recognize a fair many languages. It has diagrams and other very carefully hand-drawn pictures.

It probably feels strange when you hold it, like it gives off its own warmth."

"How do you know that?" Jennifer asked, voice barely a whisper.

The lieutenant's eyes closed as she sighed heavily, suspicions apparently confirmed.

"There's something you need to know about the book. There are others like it. Twelve others, to be exact."

"There's thirteen of these?" Jennifer asked, incredulous.

Lieutenant Nadeau nodded. "Look...we don't know each other. I can't ask you to trust me blindly, and you can't ask me to trust you blindly either. But...these books are dangerous. People will *kill* for them. Which is why you need to be very careful who you tell. And you need to be very careful about what you do with it, where you keep it."

No, Jennifer couldn't blindly trust the lieutenant. Not with the grave way in which Emrys had urged her to keep the book safe, nor with his parting warning about Morgan still being around, only with a different face. What had *that* meant?

But, in the two interactions she'd had with the lieutenant, she couldn't help but already feel like she could trust her. Like she knew her already. Besides, the woman knew about the book. She was a sworn member of an organization meant to protect. That had to count in her favor, right?

"Will you take it?" Jennifer asked, regretting the words the moment they left her lips.

The lieutenant seemed shocked by the offer as well.

"It's probably not a good idea to have more than one in the same place."

Which implied the lieutenant had at least one.

Swallowing thickly, Jennifer reached into the tote bag and pulled out the bound manuscript. The lieutenant's eyes widened ever so slightly, and she watched as Jennifer placed the book on the desk.

"I've read some of it. It was written in the sixth century... in perfect modern English," Jennifer said. "The...the man that gave it to me didn't say much other than to keep it safe. That it was very important."

The lieutenant made no move to grab it.

"I can't tell you much about them," the lieutenant replied. "I only know what I've been told. But I trust the person that told me."

"So, what do we do?"

"We keep them safe."

"Do you think...do you think it would be safe to put it in a safety deposit box?" Jennifer asked.

The lieutenant shrugged loosely. "I suppose it wouldn't hurt. If you can be as discreet as you can about it."

Jennifer nodded, thinking that she could definitely try. Anything was better than having it in her apartment and being on constant alert of someone trying to steal it.

"Do you mind if I take a couple of pictures of the interior? So I can send it to my resource for possible identification."

Jennifer shrugged, then nodded.

The lieutenant pulled out her cell phone, carefully opened the wooden cover, and snapped a couple of shots of a few of the brittle pages. Once the lieutenant finished, she closed the book and slid it closer to Jennifer. The suggestion was unspoken but clear.

Put it away. I won't take it from you, but keep it hidden.

Indeed, no sooner had Jennifer slipped it back in her tote than a knock came at the lieutenant's office door. The woman glanced at the time on her phone and mumbled something under her breath.

"I forgot I had a meeting with the new Assistant District

Attorney," the lieutenant explained, standing and rounding the desk. "I have your contact information. I'll be in touch the moment I know more about what this book is."

Jennifer stood, catching the resolve in the lieutenant's eyes. She believed her.

The two women shook hands, and the lieutenant opened the door. From her position to the lieutenant's right, Jennifer couldn't see yet who had come knocking.

"Morning, Lieutenant."

The low, rumbling voice sounded *very* familiar.

"Morning, ADA Penn. I almost forgot you were coming."

"No worries, I've got time. I can wait out here..." said the voice, so damn familiar yet different.

"I was just finishing up with Ms. Cassidy."

The lieutenant turned back to Jennifer, offering the slightest quirk at the corner of her lips.

"I will keep you posted. The number I called you from? It's my cell. Call me any time, okay?"

Jennifer nodded. "Thanks, Lieutenant."

The woman stepped back to give Jennifer room to squeeze around, to get into the hallway.

Jennifer, in her hurry and with her head lowered, misjudged where the lawyer stood and nearly collided with him.

"Oh, Christ, I'm so sorry," Jennifer cried, mortified. She clutched tighter at the tote bag, trying to look anywhere but at the lawyer she'd nearly headbutted into the wall.

"No need to apologize. I was crowding the door," the man said.

In the close proximity, hearing his voice and the way in which he formed words, something clicked.

Her gaze flew up from its rooted spot on the carpeted floor.

The sight that met her nearly had her collapse to the floor from sheer shock.

It was Arthur.

Or rather, someone that alarmingly resembled Arthur.

Jennifer knew she had to be gaping like a fish, mouth opening and closing, trying to form words.

There was no mistaking him.

The same blond hair, even cut similarly, with closely cropped sides and longer on top, carefully styled. The same electric-blue eyes that were capable of piercing one's very soul. The same strong jawline, complete with the same trimmed blond beard. The biggest difference was the modern clothes. Instead of his durable breeches and tunic, he wore a very well-tailored suit, taken in to hug all the right parts of him.

His voice...the same, but unaccented.

"Do I know you?" he asked, blond brows drawn into a V.

"No," Jennifer replied breathlessly, heart breaking. What had she expected? For him to know her? Against all odds, she'd left the man she loved in sixth-century England, and now here he was. But she couldn't know for sure he was the same Arthur. Perhaps it was just genes or coincidence.

But if there was one thing Jennifer had learned, it was that there was no such thing as coincidence.

A smile lit up Arthur's face, the very one he used to charm.

"Well, that's too bad. I'd love to know you."

AUTHOR'S NOTE

Well, I had said I wanted to get this novel out the year after *Cardinal Virtue*, but as you can tell... that didn't happen. While this book's been plotted since the road trip to my cousin Marc's wedding several years ago, I think there's definitely something to be said about the difficulties of the second novel. There were tears, nausea, and a lot of "nutting up" during both the drafting and the editing phases.

Before you start sending me strongly worded emails because this book doesn't pick up exactly where the previous left off, just know that I *swear* to you there is a method to this madness. And by madness, I mean the one meme with Charlie Day standing in front of a wall of pictures/newspaper articles with a web of connected red string looking absolutely crazed.

Just trust me, okay? Would I ever lead you astray?

Anyway, I wanted to take a moment to write up a little something about the history featured in this book.

AUTHOR'S NOTE

First, as stated in the novel, there is zero consensus whether a real "King Arthur" actually existed. There are some scholars firmly on the side of YES, some firmly on the side of NO, and some in the middle at MEH?

Personally, I am on the YES side, but would probably agree with those that say "Arthur" is more of an amalgamation of several historical figures, both named and unnamed in the record.

Regardless, you can't deny that Arthurian legend is some of the most studied, well recognized, and well loved niches of literature in the whole zeitgeist. Quests, chivalry, magic, swords, intrigue, betrayal... the legends have it all! Not to mention, many of the most beloved tropes of today have their origins in the myths.

I am by no means an expert on the myths and legends. I've loved these stories for a long, long time, probably since watching Disney's *The Sword in the Stone*. So, to the best of my ability, this book is my attempt at smashing together the history I know with the bits of Arthurian legend I know, to create a somewhat believable "historical" iteration of who Arthur could've been. Hopefully, I've done a decent job!

My challenge to any Arthur lover out there is to identify all the references to the legends throughout the book, both subtle and obvious. It'd be a fun little scavenger hunt, for sure!

Now, about the general history seen throughout the book.

Disclaimer: While I may be a historian with two master's degrees, this era of English history isn't exactly my area of focus.

All the broad strokes, for the most part, are completely accurate, as far as we can tell. When it came to housing, clothing, the inhabitants of St. Michael's Mount, etcetera, I tried to use the information we do have, along with information from the continent, and what we knew about Roman

AUTHOR'S NOTE

Britain, and made my best hypotheses as to how it might've looked. When I say this part of England's history is often called the Dark Ages, I really mean it. There are few written sources from that time period, and what does exist comes from one or more hundred years after the fact. There is also some archaeological evidence, but without a significant discovery or a time machine, this era of history is lost to the mists of the past.

Which makes it fun for us writers to play in!

-J.R.

ACKNOWLEDGMENTS

I would first like to thank my ever present cheerleader and BFF, Kathryn. None of this would be here without her gentle coaxing to turn this hobby into something more. Oh, did I say gentle? Yeah, I don't mean gentle.

A huge thank you to my mom to whom this book is dedicated. Your love of the *Outlander* series made me hella nervous to write this, but at the same time, determined. This is what I knew I wanted for Book 2, so this is it! Jennifer's no Claire and Arthur's no Jamie, but then not many people could claim that kind of awesomeness.

Thank you, once again, to my family. Every single one of you, in some way, has supported me and encouraged my writing. When you go to a family wedding and three different people ask you the same question — "How's the second book going?" — within the span of thirty minutes, you know you've gotta get rolling. If not for me, then for them. You guys are the best!

My deepest appreciation goes to the Happily Editing Anns for the multiple rounds of editing you went through for this thing. Your comments about already wanting the next book definitely made me feel some type of way. Thank you, thank you!

Huge shoutout to Caroline Teagle Johnson for hitting it out of the park, once again, with the stunning cover. I have zero idea what is going on the cover of Book 3, other than a plumeria on there somewhere.

Thank you to S.E. Davidson, my intrepid mapmaker, for

taking yet another horrible sketch of mine and turning it into a gorgeous map of southwest England. Not sure what's in store for Book 3 yet, but I have an idea or two.

Lastly, I've got to thank my loyal writer fur baby, Juno. She rested in her bed the entire agonizing process of bringing this book to fruition. Thank you for always being my calm little compartment on my crazy train.

ABOUT THE AUTHOR

J.R. Lesperance is an award winning author of paranormal thrillers and romance featuring strong female characters.

To keep up with J.R.'s latest news and releases, check out her website at www.jrlesperance.com and various social media sites below.

ALSO BY J.R. LESPERANCE

Cardinal Virtue

Made in the USA
Middletown, DE
02 March 2025